EMPIRE
OF LUST

EMPIRE

RINA KENT

To my parents
who will never read this book
or any of my books lest they get a stroke
Thank you for creating this oddball of human being
and supporting me when I dropped academics for writing.

AUTHOR NOTE

Hello reader friend,

This book isn't as dark as the rest of my books, but it contains an anti-hero and lots of enemies to lovers goodness.

Empire of Lust is a complete STANDALONE.

Sign up to Rina Kent's Newsletter for news about future releases and an exclusive gift.

My boss. My hell.

When I slept with a faceless jock as a teen, I didn't think I would become pregnant.

I also didn't think I would lose that child.

Several years later, I find out that my daughter is alive and I'm given a second chance.

One problem, though.

The faceless jock isn't so faceless anymore.

He has a name everyone fears; Kingsley Shaw.

A ruthless bastard. A heartless devil. And most importantly, my daughter's father.

Oh, and he hates me as much as I hate him.

We're out to destroy one another with all methods available.

Including a dangerous game of lust that might lead to our downfall.

PLAYLIST

"Gone Are The Days" – Kygo & James Gillespie

"Hurricane" – Halsey

"Nothing's Impossible" – Walking on Cars

"The Enemy" – Andrew Belle

"Animals" – Maroon 5

"Outside" – Hollywood Undead

"Enemy" – Tommee Profitt, Beacon Light & Sam Tinnesz

"Iris" – DIAMANTE & Breaking Benjamin

"Tequila Sunrise" – Maw Barskih

"Rolling Stone" – Hurts

"Blind" – Hurts

"Stay" – Hurts

You can find the complete playlist on Spotify.

PLAYLIST

EMPIRE
OF LUST

PROLOGUE

Aspen

Age fourteen

IT'S THE NIGHT OF MISCHIEF.

Commonly known as Devil's Night.

My mother used to tell me that the gates of hell open tonight and the demons are allowed to roam the earth and spread their evil.

It was one of the few occasions I saw my mother excited, smiling, humming a happy tune.

She made it a habit to hand-sew me a costume and take me trick-or-treating while wearing a huge grin on her face.

That was my mother in a nutshell—innocently childish, irrevocably naïve, and stupidly in love.

And that love? It cost her her life.

And mine, in retrospect.

Because ever since she died four years ago, I've turned into the cynical little monster she tried to save me from becoming.

Maybe she didn't try hard enough.

Maybe she didn't care enough.

Because nothing she could've done would've made a difference. I have my father's genes, after all.

The chilly autumn air penetrates my skin and embraces my bones with ominous persistence. As if that's not enough, it blows my hair and jams it against my eyes.

Thanks to Mom, I was born with naturally bright, excruciatingly attention-grabbing red hair. At times, it resembles the horns of the devil.

Extremely fitting for this night, if you ask me.

"You stand out, and not in a good way, Aspen," the blonde angel to my right says. Clearly fake, unless wearing a costume with wings makes you one.

Caroline is a friend I met in middle school when I first moved to her neighborhood after my mother's death and Dad's disappearance. We've been close ever since because her abusive household mirrors mine. We often find refuge in each other's company, despite having extremely different personalities.

She's the bubbly type who likes being at every party.

For instance, this one.

I didn't really want to come. Not only am I an exemplary student who spends every free moment studying so I can get out of the custom-made hellhole my aunt and uncle have made for me, but I'm also not good with people.

However, after having a pan thrown at my back because I didn't heat dinner to my drunken uncle's liking, I was like "fuck it" and asked Caroline to give me the address to the party.

Obviously, I had to sneak out of the house by climbing down a tree from the attic I use as a bedroom.

My friend jacks up a hand on her tiny waist that serves as the wings' belt holder. "When you said you were coming, I thought you'd be in a costume."

"I don't have one." Nor do I want to hide behind anything. I already have a mask I wear in public; I don't need another one.

"It's Halloween. Everyone has a costume." She throws her hands around, motioning at all the high school kids slipping into the mansion clad in their Halloween outfits. A myriad of colors, clichés, and the ultimate American fairy tale—or in this case, a nightmare.

It's a hilarious parody of vampires, monsters, and the latest popular horror movies.

As for me, I'm wearing a simple black dress, my old sneakers, and a denim jacket my aunt got me from the local church donations.

Definitely not a costume. Unless dressing poor has become a trend, which wouldn't be a surprise in circles like these.

Circles that Caroline does her best to cram herself into. She only befriends those of higher status, class, and definitely have a trust fund. It's how she managed to get herself invited to this party at a preppy boy's house.

Callie and I don't attend the same high school as the owner of this place—no surprise there. He's from the other side of town— the Upper East Side—and goes to a private school whose tuition could send me to college.

I don't know him personally. Being from Harlem's ghetto, we don't usually get to mingle with people like them.

Caroline does, though. People have dreams of becoming doctors, lawyers, and astronauts. She has dreams of dating and marrying rich.

It's a legitimate goal for those of us who've lived on scraps all our lives, go home at night looking over our shoulders, and never *ever* go out without pepper spray.

It's the Cinderella complex of it all that doesn't sit right with me. Why search for a man to give you a glass slipper when you could get it yourself?

Mom was completely and utterly into that fairy tale, and see where that got her.

"Look, Callie. I don't have a costume, so if that's a problem, I can just leave." It's an ego thing. I don't like being belittled or mocked for who I am. That's what's landed me in trouble since I was little and often gets me a beating from my aunt or uncle.

They're Mom's brother and his wife who got custody of me after Dad was sent to prison.

But they might be worse than him.

However, I never lower my head, never let them make me feel small. I stare into their beady, vicious eyes, even as they hit me.

Which naturally makes them angrier and they beat me harder. Often with a belt or the nearest object.

"No, you're my ride or die. You have to stay." Callie rummages in her fur bag. "Besides, you're beautiful as shit. It'll be their loss if they don't have you at their party."

She pulls out a black feather mask, straps it on my head, and fixes my hair so it's framing my face. Then she removes my denim jacket and throws it behind one of the decorated bushes.

"Hey! It's cold." And that's actually the only good jacket I have.

"You can handle some cold for fashion. Also, that thing makes you look like a hillbilly." She fusses in her wonder bag again and brings out some cheap red gloss, then takes extra care to apply it to my lips. After she's done, she studies her creation with the critical eye of an amateur artist. "Perfect. You look like a bad bitch."

"Really, Callie? Red?"

"It goes with the hair. If anyone asks, you're a witch."

Hell no.

But I don't tell her that as she grabs me by the hand and drags me toward the house. She stops before the entrance and stares at me over her shoulder. "Remember, we're sixteen or seventeen. Almost everyone here is a senior and we can't be considered too young. Besides, we look the part anyway."

That, we do. Caroline and I hit puberty two years ago, and ever since, we've been developing breasts and asses that earn us creepy looks from grown men—including our male teachers.

In school, she's the blonde bombshell. I'm the hellion redhead.

She slips the strap of my dress off my shoulder so that it teases more of my cleavage, then interlinks her arm with mine. "Let's snatch some rich boys."

"You do realize they'll throw us out the moment they find out we're from Harlem, right?"

"Shhh." She inspects our surroundings. "There's no reason for them to know."

"They will eventually."

"Maybe by then, it'll be too late." She gives me a sly smirk and flips her hair.

I drop the subject, partly because we arrived at the entrance. But mainly because there's no speaking logic to Caroline when it comes to her boy-hunting endeavors.

A sullen-faced doorman gives us a once-over before allowing us in.

Caroline is like a kid on Christmas morning, running from one place to another—with me in tow. She fawns over the black and orange decorated grand hall, the waiters in every corner, the upbeat music, the high-end costumes.

Everything.

She's practically drugged with all the luxury and is currently reaching cloud nine.

To say I'm not intimidated myself would be a lie. I've always disliked places that make me feel out of my depth. Places where I hold the importance of an insignificant insect that can be crushed at any time and won't be remembered.

That's the prominent emotion coursing through me right now.

I want to go back.

Or disappear somewhere where I'm not under a microscope.

I thought escaping Aunt Sharon and Uncle Bob's house was all I needed, but this scene is probably not what will make me feel better.

So I take a drink—or two. Okay, maybe three.

It's diluted alcohol anyway, but it tastes like rosemary and something exotic. Definitely better than the beer Caroline stole from her alcoholic father so we could try it.

That was no different than unsanitary water mixed with the stench of cigarettes.

Caroline smacks my hand when I reach for another drink. "Don't look so desperate."

"Uh, hello? I only came for the drinks and food, Callie."

"Then do that in a corner, not where everyone can see you acting like a ghetto rat."

I stare her square in the eye. "You're a ghetto rat yourself."

"I don't act like it."

"When was the last time you had a proper meal, Miss I Don't Act Like It?" When she doesn't reply, I scoop up some luxurious-looking snacks and push them against her mouth. "That's what I thought. Now, eat before your stomach starts making embarrassing noises."

She grumbles something, but she does eat, and then accompanies me on the mission to be full for days to come.

After a while, though, her focus returns to her previous mission, and she rakes her gaze all over the crowd.

"Maybe desperate should've been your costume, not an angel."

She smiles at my dry sense of humor. "Don't know about you, bitch, but I'm getting out of that hellhole even if it's the last thing I do."

"I'm getting out, too."

"Wanna bet who's going to do it first?"

"We can do it together."

"Not with your 'I'm gonna do it myself' attitude. Now, help me hunt."

I definitely don't, and keep stealing food and drinks behind her back. What? I'm malnourished at home and started working part-time to pay for my meals. The drinks, however, are an extravagance I'm allowing myself in order to forget and bide my time until I can leave.

My chance comes when Caroline finds her prey for the night—a blond guy in a fallen angel costume.

As soon as she hits it off with him, I slip out of their little group before she shoves me at one of his friends.

I pull the strap of my dress over my shoulder, cradle a plate of pastries and a drink, then disappear out back.

The night's air stabs my bare arms and I consider looking for my jacket.

Stuffing my face with some chocolate cake, I start my way through the vast, dimly lit garden.

My steps are wobbly due to the massive amount of alcohol I've consumed, but that doesn't stop me from taking a sip of my drink anyway.

I feel light and free, and I don't have the brain capacity to think about my life.

Maybe alcohol isn't so bad, after all.

Hushed male voices catch my attention and I freeze when I hear, "…It's Devil's Night. They won't suspect we burned it."

Shit.

I was definitely not supposed to hear that.

I must hiccup, because there's a pause before someone roars, "Who the fuck is there?"

My legs twitch and I don't think about it as I run, causing the drink to spill all over my hand, then I hide behind the bushes.

My breathing shatters when footsteps approach my hideout. If they find me, I'll be in huge trouble.

I'm very familiar with being in the wrong place at the wrong time. I've experienced it first-hand and have the mental and physical scars to prove it.

I also used it to my advantage and made my father disappear from my life.

Some would call me too cunning for my age; but when you come from the wrong side of the tracks, the first thing you learn is to survive.

Even if it means locking away your abusive father.

"I'm sure I heard them go this way," one of the male voices says and I shrink into my hiding place.

My mind crowds with fight-or-flight options and just when I'm considering where to escape to, a leaf crunches right next to me.

I stare up at the larger-than-life shadow hovering not far from me. Even though I'm partially camouflaged by the decorative tree, I'm almost sure he can see me.

"No one's here," he says with a calm that chills me to my rattling bones.

His face is veiled by the darkness, but I'm pretty sure he's wearing a mask. Before I can make him out, he turns around, and the sound of retreating footsteps echoes in my ears like a symphony gone wrong.

My shaky fingers release the plate and cup. They hit the grass with a muted thud, the alcohol slowly soaking into the ground.

Despite my plans to stuff myself full so that I don't feel hunger for a few days, I abandon my haul and inch toward the back door. I have no doubt they'll continue searching for me until they find me.

My hands are clammy as I retrieve my phone. My teeth chatter—not sure if it's due to the cold or the haunting fear—and my vision is blurry, partly because of the alcohol, partly because of the unusual kick of adrenaline surging through me.

Bodies are special like that, they know danger, even if our minds are oblivious to it.

I retrieve my old phone that Uncle Bob got for me. To say that made me suspicious would be an understatement, but he told me they needed to know where I was at all times and that if they called and I didn't pick up, they would kill me.

Sure enough, there are five missed calls from them. I wince at the thought of a beating, but it's better than being in this unfamiliar place.

Ignoring them, I type a text to Caroline. She said she received her phone as a gift from a boy she was talking to, and her father has been trying to sell it ever since.

Aspen: There's been a complication. Let's leave.

No reply.

Aspen: I'll wait at the back door for fifteen minutes, then I'm taking the subway home.

Aspen: *Callie, please. Let's go home. I'm scared—*

I delete the last text before sending it.

So what if I'm trembling all over? If I'm sweating? If I feel like throwing my guts up? I'm not a weakling.

I really shouldn't have had so many drinks and put myself in a vulnerable position, where I can't even defend myself or run properly.

The rustling of leaves reaches me first, followed by thudding footsteps. The next thing I know, two guys are approaching me. I can't see their features, because the one in the purple suit has his face painted as the Joker and the one in all black is wearing an "Anonymous" mask.

Joker approaches me with purpose, but Anonymous stays back, a hand in his pocket and the other toying with an unlit cigarette. For some reason, I think I should be worried about him the most. Not only because he's taller and way buffer, but also because those who wield the actual power often stay in the background.

"Told you I heard someone here," Joker says, his voice resembling a frat boy from an Ivy League college.

My feet automatically falter and I hit 911 on my phone, but before I can call, Joker snatches it and throws it out of my reach. "That's not a wise choice."

"I didn't see anything…" I whisper, fruitlessly trying to control the tremor in my voice.

"Oh, yeah?" He grabs me by the arm, his meaty fingers sinking into my flesh. He smells like foul cologne that should be a crime to wear. "We'll have to take insurance."

"Insurance?"

"You'll let us have our way with you as a show of obedience, won't you?"

"No." It takes everything in me to stare into his glimmering eyes in the darkness instead of hyperventilating. "Let me go."

"Wrong choice." The sadism in his voice freezes me for a second.

Only a second, though.

Adrenaline kicks in my veins, and I can see straight through to where this is headed.

It's my sixth sense. Predicting scenarios before they come along. It's not that I have witch blood, as many of my classmates say. It's that I'm really good with connecting patterns and seeing the bigger picture.

And the picture currently says that I'm the prey in this scenario. And I have to do something about it if I don't want to be eaten.

When I twist my arm in the Joker's hold, he tightens his grip and pulls me down. I try to stay upright, I really do, but he's strong and I'm so drunk that I don't feel the thud until I'm flush with the grass.

The bruise on my back from the pan hitting it earlier throbs, and I open my mouth to scream for help, but he slaps a firm palm over it.

The stench of his cologne and sweaty male musk gags me as he maneuvers himself above me. While he's searching for a comfortable position, I lift my knee and hit him in the balls.

He jerks away with an animalistic wail and I use the chance to crawl from beneath him.

"You fucking bitch!" He grabs his hurt genitals and yanks me back by the hair. The world is ripped from under my feet, but before I can hit the ground, he pushes me forward and I slam against a tree trunk.

"You're going to regret messing with me, bitch." His repulsive voice fills my ears and the putrid smell of alcohol is the only thing I can breathe. At this point, I have no clue if it's coming from him or me.

"Go ahead, you rotten piece of shit," I spit out from between chattering teeth. "You think I'm scared of you or your fragile masculinity that you need to show by assaulting me? Show me your worst, asshole. See if I fucking care!"

"This bitch…"

He pulls my hair until he nearly rips it from its roots, and tears sting my eyes. I bite my lip hard enough that I swallow the pungent metallic taste of blood.

But I don't whimper, don't show him my pain, and I definitely don't beg. Assholes like him, my aunt, my uncle, and my father are all the same.

They want to display their power by latching onto those who are weaker than them, but I'm not my mother.

I won't be a victim or a statistic.

I won't give them the satisfaction of seeing me suffer.

"Enough."

My spine jerks at the single authoritative word from the third, inactive party in the scene.

It's the same voice from earlier. The one who definitely saw me but told his friends there was no one.

Anonymous.

The Joker breathes heavily. "But she—"

"I said. Enough." His tone exudes more command than earlier. I was right to assume he holds the power, because the Joker pulls on my hair harder and with apparent frustration, the way a subordinate would do in front of their boss.

The way Dad's underlings shivered in front of him.

"I have to teach her a lesson," he says low enough that even I'm barely able to hear him.

"When I say enough…" The sound of firm footsteps is accentuated by the violent silence lurking in the air. "I mean fucking enough."

The weight that's been crushing me from the back suddenly disappears.

Thwack.

I gasp as Anonymous drives his fist in the Joker's face and sends him flying.

He doesn't move.

The Joker, I mean. He's inert on the ground and my heart nearly spills onto the grass beside him.

My strap falls off my shoulder again and my face is on fire, but I can't focus on that right now.

"Is he…dead?" I don't know how I speak so calmly when I'm pretty sure I should be panicking.

"Just unconscious," Anonymous says with dismissive neutrality that only psychopaths have.

After I slowly get up, I inch closer to my phone that's lying on the grass, flashing with a text. Probably from Caroline. However, Anonymous reaches it first in a few purposeful strides.

He flips it around, slides it in his pants pocket, then points at his unmoving friend. Though maybe *friend* is an exaggeration, considering he knocked him out with a single punch. "He might be a weakling, but he's right. Calling 911 here is extremely unwise and borders on reckless foolishness."

"I won't then. Can I get my phone back? I want to go home."

"The night is still young." He approaches me with deliberate ease. "What are you supposed to be tonight? A witch?"

"Femme fatale."

I can't see his face that's hidden behind the stupid mask, but there's a pause and I swear his eyes gleam in the dim light. They look dark blue, like the mystical depths of a merciless ocean.

"Here's how it'll go, *femme fatale*. You'll keep me company until Devil's Night is over."

"Why would I?"

"Either that or I'll lock you in some basement where no one can find you until the cleaning staff comes along. Which, if I remember correctly, can take a few days depending on whether or not the homeowners need something from the basement."

My hand balls into a fist, but I slowly release it when his attention slides to it. I see what he's doing, but those intimidation tactics won't work on me. Not when I learned them all from my father.

"Shouldn't there be a third option, where you, I don't know, just let me go?"

"Not when you could land us in trouble."

"I have no interest in what I heard and I value my life enough not to tattle on you. So give me my phone and we can be out of each other's hair."

"I like your hair, so I don't mind staying in it." He's in front of me in a second and I'm slammed face-first with his smell. It's a mixture of cedarwood, smoke, and premium cigarettes. European cigarettes that my father used to get specifically from Italy.

But that's not the only thing I'm crushed with. There's also his presence. I thought he was tall earlier, but now, he's towering over me, easily pinning me in place with his sheer size and those broad shoulders that no teenager should have.

His fingers brush through my hair and I'm pretty sure it's about to catch fire and we'll have an actual witch accident on our hands.

"Is it natural?" he asks whimsically, sounding utterly fascinated with the mere act of having his fingers in my hair.

I jerk back, startled. "Don't touch me."

To my surprise, he drops his hand to his side. He doesn't take it as a challenge to his masculinity like the Joker did.

And that makes my muscles lock together.

I can deal with assholes, but how do I deal with assertive ones who flip between respecting my boundaries and crushing them on a whim?

There's no pattern to his madness and that's the most dangerous thing about this stranger.

"You still need to spend time with me. That, or the basement."

"I want it to be in a public place." If I can't control the situation, then I can at least strive for the next best thing—a place where I can create commotion and escape.

"Afraid I'll pounce on you?"

"It's just insurance."

"You're in no position to ask for any insurance, but I'll be benevolent and grant you that wish if you answer my question."

"What?"

"When he"—Anonymous cocks his head in the Joker's

direction but doesn't look at him—"had the power over you, why did you provoke him? Logically, you should've begged."

"Logically, that wouldn't have gotten me anywhere. How many women do you think begged and cried in situations like that and still got assaulted? Countless is the answer. I refuse to show that scum or any other jerk weakness."

"Even if you get hurt for it?"

"Especially then. I'd rather swallow my poison."

There's a pause, a long one that nearly makes me fidget, before he releases a humming sound. "Interesting. Maybe you really are a femme fatale. You should be careful, though. If you gaze into an abyss for long, the abyss gazes into you."

My lips part. "Nietzsche."

"*Beyond Good and Evil*." He motions at his pocket. "You have the quote on the back of your phone case."

"It's a favorite of mine. How do you know Nietzsche?"

"That should be *my* question. Aren't you too young to read him?"

"Aren't you too quick to assume I'm young?"

"How old are you then? Oh, forgive me. I forgot that it's a blasphemy to ask the age of a woman, not to mention a femme fatale."

I smile despite myself. Then I quickly hide it.

I can't be fooled by his obvious manners or his eloquent way of speaking. It's how the rich get what they want.

Besides, he just knocked someone out, which means he's prone and used to violence.

Definitely not someone I should allow myself to get comfortable in the presence of.

"I'm sixteen," I say, all businesslike, and it's not only because of what Caroline told me. Being young is a vulnerability where I come from. "How about you?"

"Seventeen."

"You don't look seventeen."

He laughs and either the sound has some black magic or I'm

too drunk, or both. Because the tingles it causes escape the confines of my ears and flow in my blood.

"You don't even know what I look like." He taps his mask. "Maybe I'm a scarred monster underneath."

I lift a shoulder. "I wouldn't be surprised."

"Is that so?"

"Yeah. You'd have to be a monster in one way or another to save me, watch as I'm about to get assaulted, then play a knight in black armor right at the end, just to indulge in violence. Oh, and you like Nietzsche. One has to have achieved a certain level of weirdness to be a Nietzsche fan."

"First of all, I didn't save you. I just pretended I didn't see you in order to avoid complications. Joker amateur wasn't about to assault you if you hadn't provoked him. And I'm no knight, sweetheart. I only interfered to learn why you provoked him when you could've used a different approach. As for punching him, that wasn't violence. Violence is being punched back. The act was a mere display of authority as a response to his audacity of questioning my orders. Oh, and I'm not a Nietzsche fan just because I read him."

Damn it.

I'm out of my depth here. For the first time in forever, I feel like I can't handle someone.

Definitely not when I'm drunk and my inhibitions seem to be disappearing to someplace I can't reach.

I try to hide that, though. Playing nonchalance like it's my favorite game. "Then who are you a fan of?"

"Myself."

"Wow. Narcissus called and he wants his arrogance status back."

He laughs, the sound equal measures easy and haunting in the silent darkness. And for some reason, I think I could listen to that tenor of his voice all night long.

"What if I decline to return it?"

I lift a shoulder. "Congratulations for your narcissistic status.

You might need a reality check about how your achievements and talents hold little to no value, and using others doesn't make you grandiose."

"Then what does it make me?"

"Subhuman."

"Subhumans are those who allow themselves to be used."

"Let's blame the victim, shall we? A tale as old as time."

"A victim chooses to be a victim, whether by desperation or other circumstances. A lamb walking into the forest is well-prepared to be eaten."

"No lamb wants to be eaten. They walked into the forest for the food they need in order to survive."

"And the wolf eats the lamb, also to survive."

"Your predator mentality is revolting."

"And your blush is cute." He motions at my neck with a smirk in his voice. "It's visible even in the darkness."

I touch my nape, feeling more heated than when he said the words. "Stop looking."

"On the contrary, now is when I'll keep looking. I'm bored and you're interesting, so this should be a fun night, don't you think?"

Before I can answer, the ground is pulled from beneath my feet for the second time today. But this time, I'm flung over a shoulder.

His shoulder.

Hard, sturdy, and so broad, it actually fits my waist.

And then he's marching with sure, purposeful strides in the direction of the mansion.

"What are you doing?" I ask, mortified, as the blood rushes to my head.

"I told you, sweetheart. You're spending time with me tonight."

ONE

Aspen

Age thirty-five

I've never liked weddings.

But this one is different.

This one is my daughter's.

I'm sitting with a stiff posture in a seat in the back corner so that I don't make her uncomfortable on her big day.

It's a poolside wedding at the house I wish to never enter—her father's.

I honestly thought the slimy man would close the gate in my face, but thankfully, he respected her wishes for once and let me attend. Though I haven't seen him since I arrived, so the chance of him putting on the devil's horns and actually throwing me out is close to one hundred percent.

The land surrounding the pool is bigger than any other potential wedding venue. Not to mention the two-story mansion sitting majestically in the middle of it. Although the property is old, it's worth every inch in gold, considering its close proximity to Manhattan.

Due to the numerous legal battles regarding its ownership, its value has been calculated to be over sixty million. A price tag that's made it a meaty subject for the press and real estate moguls.

It has a history of blood and deceit, and its current owner conveniently holds the title of "Savage Devil."

The air is chilly, but the sun shines between the tree leaves that frame the garden as if the weather itself is celebrating this day. Countless guests occupy the rows of chairs decorated with vanilla orchids—the flowers that produce my daughter's favorite flavor.

Only a few of the people present are her friends; the rest are here to kiss her father's or her husband's ass, either for their wealth, their names, or their positions in the legal circuit.

Nathaniel Weaver—or Nate—stands at the end of the aisle in a dashing black tuxedo with his hands crossed in front of him.

He's the co-owner of Weaver & Shaw's law firm and technically my boss, since I'm a senior partner, my only friend, and the man I trust to make my daughter happy.

He actually legally married her a few months ago for convenience reasons when her father was in a coma. At the time, I didn't know she was my daughter and even suggested he use her for the firm's sake, but he vehemently refused.

Nate is like that. Responsible to a fault. Completely and utterly methodical with no sneaky, backhanded personality.

What started as a marriage of convenience obviously turned into more, and they're now finally having their official wedding ceremony.

The press had a field day when the news first broke. They were utterly nasty about how a thirty-eight-year-old man is marrying his partner and best friend's daughter who's only twenty years old.

They began their disgusting speculations about his predatory tendencies. But I know for a fact that Nate didn't see her as a woman or touch her until they were married. I also know that they love each other in a way I only thought was possible in fiction.

The press has always been hungry for anything "Nathaniel,"

partly because of his position at Weaver & Shaw but mainly because he's the only son of a senator.

Said senator and his wife are in the front row, pretending to show their support for their son, when they're practically estranged.

My heart aches as I stare at them acting like doting parents and smiling. I wish I could sit there, even for a moment, and be recognized as my baby girl's mother, but if I attempt that, I'll probably be chased out by the dogs.

But it's okay. Watching from afar is better than not watching at all.

The orchestra switches to an instrumental of "House of Gold" by Twenty One Pilots—my daughter's favorite band. All eyes turn back to where she walks down the aisle, her arm interlinked with her father's.

Gwyneth Shaw.

That's my baby's name. The baby I couldn't name when I thought I lost her twenty years ago.

Never in my wildest dreams would I have thought she'd grow into such a beautiful, impossibly compassionate, and irrevocably headstrong young lady.

Her long white dress skims the grass and her auburn hair, a shade darker than mine, is pulled into a neat twist. Her makeup is simple, but her smile is contagious, turning her face the most radiant I've ever witnessed.

To see her as a bride squeezes the heart I thought died with her twenty years ago.

The heart that's been gradually reviving ever since I learned she's alive and mine.

I first met Gwyneth seven years ago when I started at Weaver & Shaw. She clung to her father's side like a shadow and looked up at him with the same wonder children hold for their superheroes.

The fact that I never suspected she was my daughter has been killing me slowly. What's worse is that I associated her with her devil of a father and, therefore, kept as much distance from her as possible.

As a result, we already had a strained relationship. We still do.

She barely let me help with the wedding preparations.

The reason that I was able to help at all is the man escorting her down the aisle with a smile that could blind the photographers' lenses and start an unintentional riot among the single ladies.

His name is Kingsley Shaw.

The co-owner of Weaver & Shaw. With Nate married, he's now the most eligible bachelor in the States. The heir of the notorious Benjamin Shaw's countless billion-dollar Wall Street portfolios. And most importantly, a devil who's campaigning for Lucifer's position in hell.

He has the type of beauty that matches his reputation. Savage, cold, with a discreet touch of danger.

There's a mysterious way in which his strong jaw, straight nose, and slightly narrowed eyes harmonize, as if they're an epic symphony brought together by a masterful composer. Each feature on his face is godlike in its perfection. He has a large physique, muscular and tall, which makes him look like a model in suits. Too bad the owner chose the devil's fruit, route, and throne as his asylum.

He walks our daughter—whom he considers only his—down the aisle, snatching everyone's attention on the way.

This is Gwyneth's big day, but people are more mesmerized by her father, who can't just keep a low profile. But then again, he's always attracted everyone's eyes, ears, and total existence like a powerful magnet.

He stops in front of Nate, who's been spellbound the entire time Gwen has been walking toward him. Kingsley kisses her forehead, then leans forward and whispers something in his friend's ear—most likely a threat, because he was against this whole thing not too long ago.

Then both he and Nate share a fake smile before he steps to his side to play the role of best man.

I dig my nails into my palms for the duration of the ceremony, barely holding on to reality by a thread.

If only I could have a drink or something to calm my nerves—obviously the one I had in the car before I walked in here wasn't enough.

By the time Nate kisses Gwen, my state of mind is about to break on the ground like fragile china.

People rise, clapping and throwing out congratulations to the happy couple. I try to join, but my shaking legs fail me.

I massage them once, twice, then suck in a deep breath and stand up right when they reach my row.

Since I'm in the back corner, I don't expect Gwen to see me, but she does. My daughter pauses for a second, and her unique heterochromia eyes, which are a mixture of my hazel irises and her father's blue-gray ones, fill with tears.

My lips tremble and it takes everything in me to smile instead of running to her and holding her in my arms.

Once. Just once.

That's all I pray for and I'm not even the praying type.

Actually acting on my wish would be awkward, embarrassing, and would definitely attract unwanted attention.

She offers me a small, demure smile before Nate whisks her away to the reception area that's set up around the back pool. Because, of course, this place has two pools.

Everyone follows suit, some youngsters dancing to the music and having fun.

A sudden chill grabs hold of me as my legs fail me and I drop back to my chair. After I make sure no one is looking, I retrieve the flask I keep in my handbag and take a sip.

The burning taste of the tequila slowly snaps me to my senses. I inhale a calming breath as I'm about to stand up, congratulate the couple, then leave.

There's no point in staying longer if I'm going to make her uncomfortable.

A shadow falls over me like doom from an apocalyptic movie. I smell him before I see him.

His cologne has strong notes of cedarwood, pepper, and musk. As loud as he is, but not gutting.

It's subtle enough to announce his presence without him having to speak a word.

"You're done here. Get off my property."

I grind my teeth, but I fake a smile when I stare up at him.

Okay, I should've really taken another sip of my drink. I'm never drunk enough to deal with this bastard.

Men don't unnerve me. In fact, I've learned to play their game, to climb in their ranks and snatch their positions until some have argued I have a manly personality myself.

However, Kingsley is on the small list of those who drain me whenever I think of or, worse, deal with them.

Sharing space with him is similar to being thrust underwater for minutes at a time.

We've always clashed. Fucking always. I'm the angel on Nate's shoulder—the one who's as diplomatic as he is when it comes to dealing with the firm's delicate matters and futuristic vision. A fact that pisses this bastard off because he's the offensive type.

The hit first, file charges later type.

The punch them when they're down type.

In short, violence is his middle name and diplomacy has left the building of his egotistical, hellbound brain.

"The wedding isn't over," I say in the sweet tone that gets on his last nerve. "I think that means I'm staying."

His eyes gleam and that highlights the tones of dark blue and stormy gray in them. They share the intensity of a sea hurricane, one that even pirates wouldn't be able to survive. And when he glares down at me with his stupid god complex, it's like he's directing that destructive energy toward me with the sole purpose of destroying me. "Tell you what, witch. How about you leave and save us all the unpleasant sight of you?"

"I decline."

"Either leave or I'll report you for trespassing."

I stand, no longer weak in the knees and definitely charged up for a challenge. "I was invited. I have the invitation to prove it."

"As the owner of the property, I can revoke my hospitality at any time."

"If that word and you met in an alley, they'd shoot themselves and splash your precious Italian shoes with blood."

His face remains the same—timeless, emotionless, and utterly merciless. With the sun at his back, he appears as ominous as an old gothic chapel. "That's two minutes since I rescinded my invitation, which should've been used to walk off my property."

"I'm not leaving until I congratulate my daughter on her wedding."

"You mean *my* daughter."

"I'm the one who gave birth to her."

"I'm the one who raised her during the twenty years you were out of the picture."

"For the thousandth time, I thought she was dead!"

"For the thousandth time, I have zero fucks to give."

We both breathe heavily. Or I do. Kingsley Asshole Shaw has no problem making someone feel smaller than a poor fly on his shoulder before brutally murdering it.

He's the type of lawyer who advises his clients not to compromise, even when the other party abides by their demands.

"You'll get more if you sue" is his famous line, the bane of the opposition's existence, and the reason behind his ruthless devil-may-care reputation.

No wonder he's the ace of criminal defense in the whole country—if not the world.

But if he thinks his assholish methods will work on me, he doesn't really know me.

Or how far I'll go to gain my daughter's trust.

To be part of her life and make up for the twenty years I lost.

He retrieves an old gold Zippo and flicks it open, then closed.

"Either you used your witch blood to summon a clone of yourself or you're still here. Would you rather have the police drag you out?"

"And risk a commotion at your own daughter's wedding?"

"Small sacrifices for the greater good."

"You're unbelievable."

"And you're still here."

"I'll leave," I say with a calm that doesn't betray my need to stab him with the nearest sharp object. Because, unlike him, I don't want any problems at my daughter's wedding.

"You're not walking."

"I'll only leave after I congratulate Gwen and Nate. Not a minute before."

"Allow me to decline the offer. Get the fuck out before I have you arrested."

"Then I'll vandalize something on my way out."

"Then I'll sue you."

"You have no grounds or witnesses, nor a strong case. Besides, it's bad press to sue your own subordinate, not to mention it creates a hostile work environment." I flip my hair. "You're welcome for the reminder."

"Bad press means jack shit to me. And you won't be my subordinate for long." He steps forward until he's towering over me, stealing the air and replacing it with his stupid damn scent. "I'll get you kicked out of my firm if it's the last thing I do."

If his eyes were lasers, I would be incinerated right now.

It's no secret that Kingsley and I never got along before, but ever since he found out I'm Gwen's mother, he's been sprinkling my path with mines, trip wires, and an unhealthy dose of sabotage.

He hates me with a passion that resembles the way he loathes his stepmother. And I don't understand it.

It's not like we had any relationship prior to conceiving Gwen, and we definitely didn't part with bad blood between us.

It was one night. Nothing more, nothing less, unlike what the young version of me tried to think.

The truth remains. Kingsley and I are the personifications

of water and fire. Coexisting is impossible. A healthy relationship is mythical.

Nate told me Kingsley is acting this way because he's overprotective of Gwen and doesn't want me to take her away from him. But if the asshole had any logical brain cells, he'd know I would never attempt that.

He was her only parent for twenty years, and no one could take his place in her life, least of all, the mother who just came into the picture.

"Good luck trying, Kingsley. Curious to see how that works out for you."

"You might want to sharpen that armor of yours, witch. You'll need it when you job hunt at a second-rate law firm."

"What's that?" I cup my ear, pretending to strain. "I can't hear bullshit." I smile again, so sweetly that his eye twitches. It's a cringe reaction, or an anger reaction—I don't know and I don't care as I turn around and leave.

My lungs fill with air after being suffocated by his smell for longer than should be considered healthy.

The asshole really needs to stop talking to me and using up eighty percent of my energy reserves.

And could he look less physically intimidating in the process? Though I think it's about his presence and charisma more than anything else. I've never considered good-looking men intimidating.

Obviously, he's the damn exception.

I'm about to mentally prepare myself for my brief meeting with Gwen when my phone vibrates in my bag.

I retrieve it with the intention of silencing it, but the name flashing on the screen makes me pause.

It's from Attica Correctional Facility.

My pulse skyrockets as I answer, "Leblanc speaking."

A long pause stretches between us and if it weren't for the static, I would think we'd been disconnected.

The old male guard's voice reaches me in a low tone. "I have unfortunate news, Ms. Leblanc. The court has decided to grant Mr. Locatelli a parole hearing. This time, your father will probably win it."

My hand that's grasping my phone drops to my side, and the tears I've been holding in the entire ceremony gather in my lids.

And just like that, the nightmare restarts.

TWO

Kingsley

I'M GOING TO KILL SOMEONE.

Preferably my ex-best friend, who's currently living on borrowed time.

With a sledgehammer.

Or better yet, I could drown him in a pool of acid.

All the guests have slowly left my property after consuming my food and alcohol and nearly throwing a coup d'état to get into my infamous wine cellar.

Try again in a century, cunts.

There's a short list of the people who have gotten to taste my decades-old wine that goes back to the first generation of the Shaws.

Nate, but only when he had the privilege of being my friend. Now, he's just a fucker who stole my daughter.

Said daughter when she celebrated her twentieth birthday.

And me.

Now, the whole list is just down to me.

And the devil currently doing kinky shit to the mute angel on my shoulder.

Some of the staff buzz around, tidying up the reception area with the diligence of worker bees, nonverbally announcing that the dreaded day is over.

Or maybe not really.

I yank my bowtie free, throw it on the nearest chair, and pull out my Zippo from the pocket of my jacket. The urge to have a cigarette is almost stronger than my compulsion to bash Nate's head against the nearest object.

I'm not a quitter.

In fact, quitting and I don't share the same universe. So even though I haven't smoked in twenty years, since a tiny infant with rainbow eyes showed up at my door, smoking still feels like a part of me.

A large body falls on the chair opposite me, looking as silly as a clown with a vanilla orchid in his breast pocket that Gwen most definitely stuck there.

Nate is a tall man and an inch taller than me, as he likes to remind me, but he's leaner. What he lacks in muscle, he makes up for in brains and boring diplomacy.

This motherfucker has never lost a case in his life, holds the un-breakable record of a one hundred percent success rate, and appar-ently, also holds my daughter's heart when he had no business to.

He watches me with that blank stare of his that could com-pete with that of an eighty-year-old monk. Nate smells of spice, woods, and Gwen's fucking vanilla perfume.

And no, I don't like sniffing people for fun, but I've had an overly sensitive nose since I was thirteen and was hit by a rotten stench.

It's how I would know if this bastard needs a new one ripped the moment he starts smelling of anything that's not Gwen.

"Bad mood?"

"Bad timing. Don't speak to me unless you want to suffer enough body harm to cancel your honeymoon."

Nate doesn't even react to my crass tone, remaining as un-movable as a rock. "Charming as usual, King. Better tone down the psychosis a notch or else Gwyneth will suspect something is wrong. You can be crazy anytime you like, except on her big day."

"I am toning it down, considering the fact that you're still breathing…for now."

"I thought you'd already accepted me as a son-in-law."

Because my angel was getting depressed and proved with actions more than words that she can't live without this fucking bastard.

And fine, I know he loves her, too, which would've been blasphemy in his life plans not so long ago.

Still doesn't change the fact that he's a thief who's snatching my little miracle.

For good.

I vehemently refuse to admit that there's any form of codependency between me and Gwen or that losing her is similar to backpedaling into the brooding, lost version of myself that I was before she came into my life.

"You're in a trial period, so you should start counting your days and revising your will—which better have everything in your name left to Gwen."

"Ever thought she doesn't want me for my money? Maybe it's something else she's after—"

"Don't even finish that fucking sentence."

"I meant my affection and company, asshole. As if I would ever discuss with you or anyone else what my wife and I do. Get your mind out of the gutter."

"It wouldn't have been there in the first place if you hadn't put us all in this motherfucking situation. Just why did it have to be her?"

"If I answer that, will you tell me why it had to be Aspen?"

I flip my Zippo open, then shut it and press my thumb against the metal. "Why did she have to be what?"

"The woman who gave birth to your only offspring."

"That was a drunken mistake I made when I was clueless,

debauched, and lacked common sense. As thankful as I am for Gwen, I wouldn't remember that night if it smacked me in the face."

"Allow me to call bullshit on your and her nonsense." A smug smirk covers his awfully symmetrical face that he could've used to become president if he'd chosen his family's political route. "I might have allowed you and Aspen to claim amnesia in front of Gwyneth, but I know for a fact that no amount of alcohol would cause you to forget everything. Besides, if there was fucking involved, neither of you was that hammered."

"Didn't know you were an expert on the resident witch's sexual flavors and drunk attitude. You fucked her, didn't you?"

"And that's any of your concern because…"

"You're Gwen's husband, who, according to a DNA test, happens to be that witch's daughter. I'm under a moral obligation to stop whatever shitty mother-daughter kink you're trying to satisfy."

"The word *moral* has never existed in your vocabulary, so once again, I'm calling bullshit on that and your well-crafted but still flimsy excuses. Why don't you tell me the real reason you're so terribly interested in Aspen when you loathe the ground she walks on?"

"If by interested in her, you mean I'm interested in expelling her from the planet, then sure. I'm searching for methods to summon aliens as we speak. My efforts will remain in full operating mode until she fucking disappears and spares us all her tedious presence."

"If you say so." He smirks again and I'm about to rearrange his features and fuck our "we can punch anywhere but the face and dick" rule.

I seem to have lost my ability to remain in control for extended periods of time ever since I woke up from my coma a couple of months ago. A coma that lasted only a few weeks but still cost me my daughter because she married this bastard during it.

Yes, the main reason behind the marriage was to protect my assets and blah fucking blah, but they ended up falling for each other for real. I attempted multiple strategies to separate them, ranging from manipulation, to divide and conquer, to pure violence.

That obviously didn't work.

And it's all because of the damn coma that I ended up in due to an accident that happened right before I received unsettling news about the identity of Gwen's mother. I'd hired more PIs than I could count to find the woman who abandoned a one-day-old baby at my doorstep when I was seventeen going on eighteen. And while that baby became my world, I needed to corner the woman who thought she could get away with abandoning her.

All the previous PIs who'd handled the job were incompetent, so imagine my fucking surprise when the last one not only found out her identity, but also gave me the witch Aspen Leblanc's name.

The same Aspen who has a habit of antagonizing me for sport.

The same Aspen whom I've known for seven years, since Nate and I first started Weaver & Shaw and he decided she was a good asset to add to our arsenal.

Naturally, I didn't believe the PI, but he had the DNA test to prove that she is indeed my angel's mother. And that knowledge made me lose control of my car and the wreck sent me into a coma.

A coma I physically survived, but its repercussions are still slamming into my face. In retrospect, the witch is the reason behind this marriage and my constant need to sever Nate's dick snuff movie style.

My plan comes to a screeching halt when a cloud of vanilla perfume surrounds us. Gwen appears by Nate's side and has changed into some jean shorts, a loose top, and her signature white sneakers—that she definitely wore with her wedding dress earlier.

Nate stands up and she interlinks her arm in his and looks up at him. When she smiles, her rainbow eyes glimmer with a myriad of colors. "I'm ready, husband."

Kill me, please.

Or him.

Either would do—but preferably him.

When I first met Nate in high school, I didn't think we'd come to this point in our relationship. We used to be rivals and fought a lot in underground rings in order to expel the pressure being put on us by both our families.

Later on, we came to the realization that our destructive methods would be better utilized if we used them to take over the world.

Which is how our partnership began and would've been perfect if not for the small detail that he took away my daughter.

Said daughter pulls out her phone and frowns at it like she used to do whenever she was waiting for her favorite band's updates.

"What's wrong?" Nate asks her before I can and keeps on climbing his way up my shit list.

He's now snuggly sitting at position number three.

Right after my stepmother from hell and the witch whose sole merit is giving birth to my angel.

"Oh, nothing." Gwen does that fake laugh thing that she's absolutely terrible at and tucks her phone in her pocket.

"Is it about Aspen?" he asks, and the moment she flinches, I slowly open my Zippo to stop myself from clenching my fist.

As much as I like to think I'm enough for my little angel, I've learned the hard way that she's been longing for her absent mother since she was eight. It was around that time that she learned by accident that her mother didn't die as I'd lied to her and that she'd actually abandoned her at my door with nothing more than a measly note, a thin blanket, and tears.

Gwen wanted a mother and had the sleep talks to prove it even before she knew it was Aspen. That fact and others, such as how Aspen claims she thought her baby had died, made Gwen slowly get close to her mother.

Despite my not-so-subtle attempts to paint the woman as the devil's favorite spawn.

Gwen stares between us with a wince. "No...yes...I mean, have you run into her? I'm pretty sure I saw her during and after the ceremony, but she wasn't at the reception, right?"

"No, because running away is what that woman does best," I say coolly, flipping my Zippo shut.

"That's not true," Nate counters with calm. "King kicked her out."

That's it. This fucker will die in his sleep tonight.

"Dad…?" Gwen looks at me with that pout that's able to smash through my black stone heart.

"I did not kick her out. I just reminded her that my hospitality isn't infinite and I was approaching my limit. But I didn't think she'd need to snitch to Nate to drive a point home."

So yes, I did kick her out, but I didn't think she'd comply. She never has in the past, and she even walked away with that infuriating snobby confidence, as if the world's her battlefield and I'm a mere vessel in it.

I was so sure she'd do as she promised, but she disappeared without a trace.

Or maybe she did leave a trace since she tattled to Nate, who's watching me with a slow smile.

"She didn't snitch to me. I saw you trying to throw your weight around with her after the ceremony."

"I was only *talking* to her."

"By trying to intimidate her."

"Hey, fucker, whose side are you on?"

"Gwyneth's. She wanted her mother here today and you had no business trying to kick her out."

My daughter gives me that kicked puppy look again that makes me feel lower than fucking dirt.

She's never gone against me, except for when it comes to the bastard standing next to her. And I'm starting to think Aspen will soon belong on the list of "People Gwen stands up to her father for."

Even though she was hurt by her absence, she still watches Aspen from afar and often asks Nate about her.

She never asks me, because she knows there's no love lost between me and the redhead.

Gwen's phone lights up in her hand and she smiles, then clears her throat and answers, "Hello? Aspen?"

Speak of the fucking devil.

I mean witch.

My angel listens for some time, kicking an imaginary rock and tightening her hold on Nate's arm, then says, "It's okay."

She bites her lower lip and whispers a shy, "Thanks."

As soon as she hangs up, she looks at Nate and blurts, "She congratulated us on the wedding and apologized for leaving abruptly. She said something unexpected came up and she had to go."

"Something unexpected?" Nate frowns. "She wouldn't have left your wedding for anything…unless…"

"What?" Gwen asks.

"Nothing." He smiles at her, then stares at me.

He doesn't have to say the words for me to understand the meaning.

Something far more important than Gwen's wedding happened. And considering that woman's infuriating intent to be part of her daughter's life, my guess is it's something dangerous.

Maybe it's my chance to hold something over her head.

⚖

Anyone who's met me knows I am prone to violence, exploit fine things, and have an unending feud with my stepmother.

Our dirty laundry is all over the news, along with her Botoxed face and my immortal *Forbes* status.

Unlike what others think, Susan Shaw's original sin wasn't sucking my father's dick or worshipping it for her Chanel wardrobe. It was her audacity of snatching my mother's place, kicking her out of the house she called home, and eventually driving her to slice her veins open.

Being a gold digger wasn't enough, so she upgraded herself to wife status. That might have given her some of my father's billions, but it also presented her with her own custom-made hell.

Me.

It's said that revenge is a dish best served cold, and I intend to make the blood in that woman's veins freeze until she wishes for death.

I arrive at the charity event one of her friends is throwing—without invitation—in a flash of paparazzi.

The organizer is flustered when I show him my hefty donation check and he has no choice but to let me in.

I could've asked for an invitation beforehand, but that would have killed the element of surprise. Nate says I like doing things the hard way, but that's only because the easy way is more boring than sleep.

Being dashing, rich, and having a "fuck you" attitude has put me on numerous lists, such as "Daddy I want to fuck." Not sure if that applies to my parenthood or means I'm daddy material or both. I don't honor that status or the other ones with a sliver of care.

Fucking is done on my terms, with chosen escorts and only after they sign an NDA that basically sells their soul—or, more accurately, their pussy—to the devil.

Aka me.

I don't return any woman's smile, don't engage in any form of hair-pulling small talk, and I sure as fuck don't give two shits about societal standards unless it plays in my favor.

When I order a whiskey at the bar, a few girls fall over their tits contemplating whether or not to approach me.

Pathetic.

The fact that they hesitate immediately crosses them off my list with a red Sharpie. Not that I would've considered them if they'd actually talked to me, but it would have shown that they at least had courage, a trait I would've admired before crushing it and their advances.

Only one woman is worth my time, smiles, and words. Gwen. And the reason she's an exception is because my blood flows through her veins.

The charity ball is held in an extravagant hall with a faux French socialite atmosphere. The windows are a poor imitation of *Le château de Versailles*. The tall, ornate platforms appear to be expensive but share the dullness of a sewer rat from the Middle Ages.

Even the fact that they put a gold-trimmed bar in the middle of the space has a desperate "I'm rich" vibe that can definitely be used to describe Susan and her vain socialite friends.

I stare at my watch.

Three, two, and…one.

"What are you doing here?"

I lift my head as my nemesis stops a few steps in front of me. Once upon a time, Susan was a beautiful woman with sandy blonde hair and an hourglass shape that she used to seduce any dick available. But the beauty disappeared as she grew older and had unfortunate acquaintances with plastic surgeons' knives.

She's now a silicone monster with puckered lips that are close to hanging to her—no surprise here—fake tits.

Her eyes are beady, too big for her face, too muddy in their color, like an abandoned house in the slums.

Oh, and to make matters worse, she likes to dress in loud shades of pink, as if her sole purpose is to bleed people's eye sockets with the view of her twisted version of Barbie. Her dress for the night is a shiny piece that's paying tribute to the eighties horrible neon pink that should have its own dedicated section in hell.

She taps her toe in an impatient move that makes her look like a petulant child with anger management issues. "I asked you a question, Kingsley."

I take a sip of my Macallan and pretend the ice is an undiscovered world wonder before I finally slide my attention back to her. "Oh, you were talking to me? Not interested. Try in court next time."

The flashes of cameras intensify and I don't have to search for them to know they're focused on us. The battles Susan and I have in court are infamous, ruthless, and downright barbaric.

And since the press's only job is gossip, they're like dogs drooling over the latest bone on the Upper East Side.

She steps closer to me, faking a smile that appears painful

with her latest Botox injection, then speaks in a whisper-yell so that only I can hear, "What the hell do you want?"

"My mother back. But unless you're thinking of picking up necromancy as a side gig, you won't be able to revive the dead, so I'm compromising with watching you suffer until the last breath you spit out of your silicone lungs."

"You're nothing more than a small boy trapped in a man's body." She has the nerve to smirk like a C-list Disney movie villain. "Your mother had the personality of chewing gum—sweet at first but bland as time goes by. Not to mention, she could be thrown away without a hitch. So if you miss that plain thing, how about you do the world a favor and cure your mommy issues by joining her?"

My fingers tighten on my glass, but if this bitch thinks she can get a reaction out of me, she hasn't been dragged through enough courts. "I have a better idea, which includes stripping you of every last dime to your name."

"That money is rightfully mine."

"Rightfully? You never worked a day in your life after you married my father. Unless opening your legs and being a trophy wife counts which, spoiler alert, it does not."

"You're just jealous and bitter that your father chose me over you and your mother."

"My mother, maybe, but never me, Susan. As much as you tried to tamper with the old man's mind, the fact remains that I'm his heir and the one who inherited over eighty percent of his fortune. Life lesson for the day, pussy doesn't compete with blood. Maybe you should've killed me with that pillow, huh?"

She pales, her lips trembling.

When I used to drive Susan insane for damn sport, she nearly lost it. And the fact that I was manipulative enough to never get caught by my father made her even more of a raging bitch.

One night, she walked into my room and placed a pillow to my face, but she gave up at the last second, probably remembering that my father would kill her with his bare hands if she hurt his only heir. And I was the only heir he could ever have since a few months after his marriage to Susan, he had prostate cancer, and while the surgery was a success, they had to remove his prostate and he became permanently infertile.

So I was the only Shaw his dick could bring into the world. And he was the type of closed-minded, old-fashioned man who refused fathering any children that weren't his flesh and blood. He explicitly told Susan there would be no adoption when she suggested it and was completely inflexible about it, no matter how much she sucked his dick.

My father was an indecent man, the worst father to ever exist, but I was his only treasure. The legacy he had great plans for out of pure self-serving intentions.

"Kingsley is my only son and heir" is the line he often repeated and metaphorically slapped Susan's greedy little heart with.

Which is why she thought she could get rid of me that night. But she got cold feet, threw the pillow away, and ran out of the room in hushed, frantic steps.

To this day, I have no fucking clue why I remained still, pretending to be asleep long after she left. I remember the renouncing feelings so well. The "what if this could end?" questions that ran through my head.

That was a few months after my mother's death.

And I was naïve enough to think about letting this woman have it all.

Said woman pats her hair, then clutches her diamond necklace. "I don't know what you're talking about."

"You know exactly what I'm talking about, and believe me, that was your only chance to kill me. Now, you'll reap what you sowed."

"I'm still suing for the community property."

"Is that so?"

"Your father gave me the house and thirty percent of his properties. That includes the shares in Weaver & Shaw since you used his money as a percentage of the capital."

"Susan, Susan," I muse as if I'm speaking to a kid. "If you'd been listening to your idiot attorney for even one minute instead of ordering him to file for meaningless lawsuits, you would already know that I proved my father senile when he wrote his last will a year prior to his death. The probation case on that is over and the judge ruled in favor of executing the most recent will that he notarized five years prior to his death."

Which gives me control over his estate, including the house. Susan only got a percentage of the properties he owned after their marriage, which is less than twenty percent of Benjamin Shaw's overall fortune. A twenty percent that I will strip her of sooner rather than later.

Actually, let it be later. I want her to keep suing, hoping for something more and losing each and every one of those cases.

"Now, as excruciatingly tedious as it is talking to you, your time is up. You might want to pack your medication for the night you'll spend in jail."

"What…?"

I tilt my head to the photographers. "I have at least a hundred witnesses and a thousand pictures to prove that you breached the restraining order. Be on your toes, Susan. The police will drag you out of here like the criminal you are in about five minutes."

Her face pales and she tries harder to keep her plastic smile in place. If there's anything Susan hates more than lack of attention and money, it's putting her fake social façade in jeopardy.

She must've forgotten that, during the few weeks I spent sleeping like a distorted version of a mummy, Gwen asked Nate to file a restraining order against my dear stepmother out of fear that she'd cause me physical harm while I was in the coma.

Which was smart. This woman is not above injecting acid in my veins. She'd even take pictures with my corpse and safeguard them as precious memories.

One of my few regrets about that unfortunate coma, aside from Nate romancing my daughter, is giving this woman a pause.

Susan steals a peek at the horde of crooked journalists watching our every move.

"This isn't over, devil," she hisses under her breath, then leaves in a cloud of pink, revolting rose perfume, and horrible memories.

I empty the contents of my glass in one go, then slide it across the counter toward the bartender who seems to have been waiting for a nuclear war to erupt.

He nods, appearing half-fearful, half-disappointed, before pouring the amber liquid.

I retrieve my Zippo and flip it open, and it's like I can breathe the pungent smell of Dad's cigar. He used to have a peculiar liking for the finer things, including women, wine, and cigars.

Mom ordered this special edition gold Zippo for his birthday when I was about five. I remember his joy and how he only used it to light his cigars.

How my mother smiled with pride and muted happiness.

Until she didn't.

Until he threw the Zippo, along with her clothes out on the lawn, when he kicked her out of the house.

Until she held this damn object in her hand during the last moments of her life.

This Zippo is a reminder of my father's betrayal, my mother's vain hopes, and her short life.

I grab the new glass of whiskey, intent on drinking it and leaving. My mission for the night is done, and I can go back home, hit the bag for an hour or so, and pretend the house doesn't feel like a cemetery without Gwen in it.

It's been two days since her wedding and she's called me only once a day. Apparently, she can't find time for me now that she's on her honeymoon.

I pause with the glass halfway to my mouth when I spot an infuriatingly familiar mane of red hair. It's the color of erupting volcanos, furious embers, and Satan's favorite wallpaper.

Aspen stands in the middle of a group of men, listening in to what I'm sure is nonsense. She's wearing a black dress that molds against her voluptuous curves in a "you can look, but you can't touch" kind of way.

She holds a flute of champagne with the elegance of an ancient goddess and smiles with feigned interest.

Aspen might have inherited her ancestors' wickedness, but she also got their soul-shattering beauty. The type they used to lure men and feast on their livers, hearts, and dicks.

She has the type of presence that steals everyone's attention. And it has little to do with her defined cheekbones that could cut stones, the way her eyes reflect both the earth and the sun, or how her full lips would look perfect with a dick in them.

It's her confidence, her finesse, and her infuriating determination.

She's a hellion and the worst part—she knows it and wears it like a crown.

And while she's not my type now, I can see why young me used his dick-for-brains energy when he hooked up with her.

She's a puzzle any man would want to solve.

A wild horse they'd strive to tame.

That's what the sorry fucks who are eating her with their eyes are currently trying to do. Unfortunately for them, she chews on their testosterone for breakfast.

She nods, excusing herself from their King Arthur-like circle, discreetly checks her surroundings, then makes her way to the stairs.

I don't think about it as I abandon my glass on the counter and follow after her.

Aspen and I aren't close; in fact, we're the opposite of close. But I've known her for enough years to recognize when she's up to something.

And I'll be damned if I miss a chance to drag her down.

Crown and all.

THREE

Aspen

THE HUMAN MIND FORGETS.

It's a defense mechanism, a healing process, and a necessity to push oneself forward.

I'm *not* the type who forgets.

I have archives upon archives of files stored neatly in my brain with name tags and rotten memories.

But even I have fallen prey to the mind's need to move on. Even I have started to blur the stench of my childhood hellhole in the ghetto and everything that transpired within its walls.

I lived the last twenty-five years of my life looking over my shoulder, counting calendar days, and later, getting drunk on a grave I thought was my daughter's.

I lived twenty-five years waiting, surviving, and biding my time for this day.

The day when my monster of a father would be unleashed back into the world, twenty-five years older, wiser, and deadlier.

I have no misconceptions about who his first target will be once he gains his freedom. He told me so the day he was arrested.

"I'll come back for you, my red dahlia. Whether you run or hide will have zero effect on the final result."

That's what he used to call me. A red dahlia, the worst color for that flower, holding the meaning of betrayal and deceit.

Something my father and I share in our DNA.

We also share the belief that hiding is useless. In the past, I used to think running was my best option. That's why I made friends with his guard or, more accurately, bribed him so I'd know when my father was getting out.

In the meantime, I received news about all the people he killed while he was on the inside. Just because a monster is locked up doesn't mean the danger he poses is gone.

I planned to run away as soon as he was out. I had nothing to hold me to the States and I mapped out my fresh start in another country. I would take my experience with me and crush different goals.

But that was before I found out my daughter isn't in the fake grave I've been getting drunk on every year.

That was before I "met" her and was given another chance to make things right.

If I run, I might as well sign an abandonment contract and give that asshole Kingsley the satisfaction of saying "I told you so."

Which isn't an option.

Being accepted as Gwen's mother is my new goal in life and might as well be my calling, meaning, and what gives me the power to wake up every day.

And to achieve that, I need to face the demon that's custom-made with my blood type.

Bruno Locatelli is a made man, a hitman for an influential Italian crime family, and has an assassin's cult that worships at his monstrous altar.

He's been doing business as usual from prison without a hiccup. In fact, he's been staying there under his bosses' order, taking the fall for some of the higher-ups' crimes like a made man should.

Now, he'll be rewarded for his services and given the power he bloodied his hands for during all these years.

But before he asks for my head as a sacrifice, I need protection.

Which is why I'm at this charity ball.

After a round of excruciating small talk, I climb the stairs to where I saw my target heading.

I stop around the corner when I spot two buff men scrutinizing the area with eyes fully devout of humanity.

In my line of work, I see people like them all the time. Men who are so far gone that they deteriorate to the animal category.

And the worst part is, they're fully comfortable that way.

Just like my father.

My target comes out of the restroom, looking refined in his handmade three-piece Italian suit and matching leather shoes.

He moves with the confidence of a man who's well aware that the world is at his fingertips and people are mere vessels at his disposal.

The moment he rounds the corner, I pretend to stumble and spill my half-full champagne flute all over his expensive suit.

A flash of movement is all the warning I get before I'm slammed against the nearest wall, both my hands locked behind my back. The glass of champagne crashes to the floor and my face is smashed against the surface. While I was ready for such a reaction, I didn't sign up to have my cheekbone broken.

"I'm sorry, I didn't mean to," I say in a half-muffled voice, but my words aren't directed at the guard who's jamming my head into the wall.

They're for the man who hasn't even glanced at his wet clothes and is watching me with unnerving attention.

"I'll pay for the dry cleaning," I offer, my voice still calm, considering my situation.

I've been manhandled countless times, but not once have I cowered like a scared kitten. It still gets on my last nerve, though.

I catch my target waving off his guard and he releases me not so gently, leaving what I'm sure are bruises on my wrists.

Small sacrifices.

I turn around and come face to face with none other than Nicolo Luciano.

The underboss of the Luciano crime family.

The tenth generation of a line of underworld lords who've run New York City for almost a century.

He has a terrifying calmness to him, a beauty that's shrouded by the stench of blood and the decadence of rotten money.

He's a shock of darkness—black hair, dark eyes, and a grim expression that could be used as a lethal weapon.

"I'm truly sorry." I guard my light tone, wincing at the sight of his soaked jacket.

"No, you're not." He speaks with a hint of a refined Italian accent, like aristocracy. "You did that to get my attention, and you got it at the expense of my clothes that are worth more than selling you on the black market for body parts. So how about you spare us both the nonsense and tell me why you're interested in my attention? Think carefully, for your livelihood and next shipping address depends on the answer."

I swallow, realizing that I might have bitten off more than I can chew. But I don't consider backing down. My chances of being a mother worthy of Gwen depend on it.

"My name is Aspen Leblanc, and you want me on your legal team."

He raises a brow. "And what makes you think I'm hiring?"

"Nothing, but you should be."

"Elaborate, and make it both quick and convincing. Your zip code is changing as we speak."

I raise my chin, adopting my legal voice. "I noticed you only have criminal attorneys by your side and while those are good for getting an underling out of jail or in case of murder, they're absolutely useless when it comes to earning profit. You need a civil attorney, one specializing in corporate law, to end legal quarrels, strikes, and get you state compensation. I'm also able to find tax loopholes for you."

"I can get those my way."

"That's true, but it's more profitable and less of a hassle if you let an experienced attorney take charge. Since you're legitimizing some of your business, it will look good on paper if an appropriate legal counsel is in charge."

"I see you've done your research."

"I've done more than that and I'd be able to end the week-long workers' strike at your metal factory downtown effective tomorrow if you hire me."

"And?"

"And what?"

"The catch, Ms. Leblanc. What is it?"

"Four times my hourly rate for every shady operation I do for you."

He pauses. "I thought you would use legal methods."

"I might have to use illegal methods to get there, and I want to be fully compensated for it."

"Double."

"Triple."

"Double and permission to stay alive as long as you're useful."

"Double and protection while I'm in your world."

He pauses at that. "Got a target on your back?"

"From your hitman, yes."

He raises a brow. "Elaborate, and don't leave any details out, because one of my men is background checking you as we speak."

"Bruno Locatelli is my father, and he'll be after my neck as soon as he's released."

Nicolo's lips twitch. "You're the red dahlia he's been keeping an eye on."

My throat closes and it takes all my goodwill not to freak out. I thought I'd escaped their world the day I left Aunt Sharon and Uncle Bob's house.

But Nicolo just said that I've been on his radar all this time. I shouldn't be surprised, but my brain must've deleted the detail of how dangerous my father actually is. It must've tried to self-comfort by thinking our lives have been separate up until now.

"See, Bruno has been loyal and lucrative to the family business for decades. Long before you were born. You have to offer way more than he does for me to even consider twisting his arm in his private family matters."

"Give me a chance and you won't be disappointed."

"I better not be or I'll personally sign your death certificate."

"Does that mean you'll give me a chance?"

"I will, after you end that strike by morning."

"Thank you." I approach him to shake hands, but once again, the breath is knocked out of my lungs.

His buff guard plasters me to the wall, spitting, "You have not earned permission to breathe that close to Boss."

Ugh. This jerk really needs to train his dogs better.

"Got it…" I mumble to get out of his hold.

I expect Nicolo to call him off, but the guard's weight disappears from my back in a sudden whoosh of air.

Thwack.

Thud!

I whirl around to find the guard on the floor, clutching his bleeding nose. Over him stands the resident devil of my custom-made hell in his signature black suit, hand-made Italian loafers, and an expression that matches a vampire hungry for blood.

I wonder if this is how he looked under that Anonymous mask twenty-one years ago.

A dark lord with a thirst for violence.

The irony of him punching someone in my presence again doesn't escape me. Unlike the Joker from back then, the guard stands, raising his fist. The other guard cocks a gun and puts it to the back of Kingsley's head.

Either this man has no regard whatsoever for his life or he's much crazier than I thought, because he simply smiles at Nicolo with the air of a rebellious underworld boss.

"Now, I'm not chauvinistic myself and I won't honor the dated thing with any form of defense, but shouldn't the use of violence against a defenseless woman be frowned upon in your proud culture?"

That's it.

This man is batshit crazy with suicidal tendencies.

"Shaw," Nicolo greets with a nod to his guards.

"Luciano."

The men swiftly retreat to their boss's side, and a breath rushes out of my lungs. I thought I was seconds away from witnessing Kingsley's head being blown to pieces, but it turns out, they're acquaintances.

Wait…

I stare between them. "You…know each other?"

"Our fathers were friends who had the habit of comparing us." Kingsley smirks. "Nicolo here likes guns because he sucked with all other toys—women included."

"And yet, your woman came to me for help."

"I'm not his woman."

"She's not my woman," he says at the same time and we glare at each other.

Head-on.

Damn this asshole and whatever voodoo he possesses to strip my energy.

Whenever I'm in his orbit, it takes everything in me to hold on to the control I've cultivated for decades.

He's unnerving and destabilizing, and there's no cure in sight.

Nicolo's lips lift at the corners like a cat who's found a mouse. "I'll leave you to it, then. See you tomorrow, Ms. Leblanc."

"You'll see my assault charge tomorrow, motherfucker," Kingsley informs him.

Nicolo merely smiles as he turns around and leaves with the company of his guards.

As soon as they disappear, I storm to Kingsley until I'm toe to toe with him. "What the hell was that all about?"

He stares down at me with an arched brow, channeling a gorgeous villain with black morals. "Is that your way of saying thank you for saving me, what can I do to show my gratitude?'"

"Gratitude, my ass. Who told you I was in trouble? I was doing just fine."

"Clearly, judging by your earlier pained expression that resembled a whore faking an orgasm."

"You're one to know, considering all the whores who had to fake an orgasm to stroke your earth-sized ego."

"I don't fuck whores; they're called escorts. And believe me, not one of them has had to fake an orgasm."

"I'd be shocked if that were the case, seeing your selfish, narcissistic tendencies."

"Are we going to pretend I didn't give you more orgasms than you could've counted the night we conceived Gwen?"

My body heat turns up a notch despite myself, and I speak in a snotty way to camouflage my reaction. "The only thing I remember about that night is leaving. Guess your orgasm-giving abilities are *that* forgettable."

"Liar." His voice drops to a deeper tenor and I swear I can feel its vibration on my skin before it settles at the base of my stomach. "You can make everyone believe you've forgotten about it, but here's the thing. I don't belong on the effortlessly fooled list, sweetheart."

"Don't call me that. I am *not* your sweetheart." And I hate that my heart is beating so loud, I can hear the thumps in my ear.

"You prefer being labeled a witch?"

"I prefer my given name."

"It's too bland for me to remember."

"Has anyone told you that you're a dick?"

"In the last hour? Twice. And before you ask, no. As much as I appreciate your special attention to my dick, I'm afraid it's closed for business when it comes to you."

"Funny. I recall it being so open for business that you slept with it inside me."

He grins and I internally curse myself.

"I thought you didn't remember."

"I only remembered after I woke up. Not during."

"Don't be cute. It got you knocked up when you were jailbait."

My stomach cramps in painful intervals with intense consistency. His words, the meaning behind them, the emotions associated with them are slowly but surely chipping away at my control. Kingsley, however, looks as vicious as a demon lord with a beef against everyone—hell included. I wish I could peel off his aloof mask and see what type of mess is exactly going on in his dysfunctional brain.

But since I can't do that, and I don't want to let the conversation steer down that old and minefield-like lane, I clear my throat. "How close are you with Nicolo? I didn't think you'd be friends with a mafia boss."

"Nicolo and I share the same amount of friendship between a scorpion and a frog."

"But you just said your fathers were friends."

"Doesn't mean we've kept the legacy going. Marco Luciano worshipped the billion-dollar road Benjamin Shaw walked on and my father admired his boundless power. A connection Nicolo and I abhorred until it eventually broke apart. He stayed in his shadow-shrouded world and I kept my billions, blinding looks, and eternal *Forbes* status."

"And arrogance, apparently."

"Arrogance is flashing my status in front of the world until they gag on it. I'm not arrogant, sweetheart. I'm merely assertive about who I am and what I have."

I pause, staring at him.

Like really stare at the man behind the Apollo-like appearance and fashion god style. And it hits me then.

Kingsley might be a loud mofo who likes throwing his weight around with the infuriating confidence of a deity, but he's not a fan of the media.

Or attention.

Or press conferences.

In fact, he's made it his mission to live his life as far away from their watchful eyes as possible. Never engaged in their petty questioning or given them the time of day.

In fact, he's as private as me and Nate. Just not quiet, and he definitely lacks the rationality that would've kept him out of the spotlight if he'd practiced it.

But then again, he breathes for the antagonistic forces conflict brings him.

His attention remains firmly on me, and even though his stance is relaxed, it doesn't fool me. Kingsley will always be a predator, ready to pounce.

"Now, are you going to tell me why you went to Nicolo for 'help,' as he so eloquently put it?"

"I don't see how that's any of your business."

"It abso-fucking-lutely is if you're a senior partner at, and I can't stress this enough, *my* firm."

"Your and Nate's firm."

"That's fifty percent my business. It'll be one hundred percent our business if I tell your dear bestie you're asking the mafia for help."

I grit my teeth. This asshole really knows how to get on my last nerve. "Nate has nothing to do with this."

"I'll be the one to decide whether or not to call him in the next five minutes, depending on your answer."

"You're not possibly thinking of disturbing him on his honeymoon, are you?"

"Not if you start talking in…" He looks at his watch. "The next four and a half minutes."

"First of all, fuck you."

"Your less than subtle advances are bordering on obsessive, but I digress. Second of all?"

"I just need Nicolo for something."

"Such as?"

"You don't have to know."

"On the contrary, I most definitely do. The whole truth and nothing but the truth."

"Since when are you a fan of the truth?"

"Since I learned that the strength of a man's spirit is measured by how much 'truth' he can tolerate, or more precisely, to what extent he needs to have it diluted, disguised, sweetened, muted, or falsified."

My mouth falls open. "Did you just quote Nietzsche?"

"Did you just prove you're still a nerd?"

"And you still refuse to admit you're a fan."

"I'm not a fan. I'm an observer." He steps toward me and the air automatically vanishes. The space is stilled, intensified, and has enough tension to slaughter someone. I'm so in the habit of bickering and fighting with this man that I tend to be taken off guard when he invades my space.

When I'm the only presence in his eyes that shares the lethality of a storm and the intensity of an earthquake. He should give his name to one of them.

And why the hell does he still smell like back then? The cedarwood and male musk submerges me with memories I thought I'd murdered with my naïve little heart.

What type of person doesn't change his cologne for twenty-one years? Shouldn't that be frowned upon in some manual?

I wish he wasn't so close that all I can breathe is his presence. I wish he wasn't so close that I can see the flecks of gray in the ocean of his eyes or see myself drowning in that bottomless ocean.

If I said he had no effect on me, it'd be the lie of the century, what people in the Middle Ages got flogged and stoned for.

"Now, what is it? The undiluted harsh, naked version of the truth?"

"What makes you think I'd offer you that?" I say in a voice lower than my speaking one.

"Then I'll find out on my own." His fingers reach for my hair and he grabs a strand, then brings it to his nose.

I'm shocked, spellbound, and all other synonyms that imply frozen in place.

My attention is stolen by the way the red contrasts against his tan, lean fingers. How it touches the veins on the back of his masculine hand.

The moment he inhales deeply, it's like he's sniffing my most intimate part.

"Don't blame me for how I use such truth, sweetheart."

I slap a palm on his chest and shove him away with a harshness that matches my breathing. "Why…the hell are you touching me?"

He never does that. Not even when he's bringing the whole office down by telling me to disappear. Not even when we both found out that Gwen was my daughter.

We might have been enemies, rivals, and the villain in each other's stories, but we kept the fight verbal, legal, and sometimes with petty moves.

But never with touching.

And the change is throwing me off more than it should.

Apparently, though, it pleases Kingsley, because he smirks, lifts a shoulder, and whispers, "And why shouldn't I touch you?"

"Because there was an unspoken rule about that, asshole."

"I'm removing it then. You're like a painting of a battle, but whoever said war and art should be watched from afar didn't have the audacity to come close, touch, breathe, and taste."

My lips tremble, but I manage to say in a warning tone, "Stay the hell away from me, Kingsley."

"Again, that depends on whether or not I get what I want." He slips a strand of my hair behind my ear and his fingers leave a trail of burning acid on my skin as he steps back.

"And what is that?"

His eyes glimmer with sadism as he says, "The naked truth, sweetheart."

FOUR

Kingsley

"To what do I owe this unpleasant visit?"

I slide onto Nicolo Luciano's hard leather sofa that has an exterior that matches its owner—uncomfortable.

He remains seated behind his old desk in the run-down office he's been trying to keep in shape for the past two decades with no results in sight.

The man has countless companies, both legal and illegal, under his thumb, but he's holding on to this rotten legacy with the stubbornness of a petulant child.

"Not your grim face, naturally." I flip through a half-torn Italian magazine from the nineties, pretending the affair is more boring than missionary sex. "Might consider putting on a different expression than 'Hello, awful to meet you. I'm a killer.' if you don't want to get locked up for it."

He leans his elbows on the desk, steepling his fingers at his chin and showing off the fine lines of his handmade Sicilian jacket. "Didn't realize you had the time of the day to care about my freedom status, King. Either you're more bored than an old hooker or you're less subtle than a rookie detective with a badge hanging out of his ass."

I throw the magazine back on the sturdy wooden table and stare at him. "What's your relationship with Aspen Leblanc?"

I want to jam my fist into my mouth for uttering those words, but then again, I'm direct to a fault.

Always go in headfirst.

Never sideways, never backward, and definitely never stagnant.

I've been thinking about Aspen and her crimson hair and fuckable lips all night in my empty mansion. Mind you, the whole process was against my will and I fought it with the determination of a gladiator.

Yes, I'm after the woman's demise, but she should, under no circumstances, occupy my thoughts.

Or worse, stroke my libido that she had no business coming close to.

Punching the bag didn't help, working out for hours was a laughable distraction, and my escort contacts appeared as enticing as expired milk.

Despite my best efforts, I couldn't come up with a reason for what the fuck changed last night.

It's like a foreign demon took over my body the moment I saw her being manhandled by Nicolo's thug. I don't hit for women—except for beating Nate the fuck up when I found him making out with my daughter under my roof, because fuck that guy.

Point is, I'm the furthest thing possible from Prince Charming and his friend Knight in Shining Armor.

I have the assertiveness to admit I'm violent—prone to it, breathe it in the air, and dream about it. However, the reason is not, and I mean absolutely *never*, a woman.

Or a man, for that matter.

But last night, the demon who possessed my fist and flowed in my blood was definitely driven by a woman. And it wasn't just any woman.

Fucking Aspen.

I'm going to bet my nut that her stubborn mouth had little to do with it. The truth remains, I'm used to verbally sparring with that witch as our favorite sport. But last night was the first time I've treaded into dangerous territory.

One filled with distant memories and clichéd nerd moments about Nietzsche.

Unable to find a logical reason that would satisfy both my brain and my dick, I graced myself with the repulsive presence of the asshole Nicolo first thing this morning.

Said asshole retrieves a cigar from the box on his vintage desk and slides it to the corner of his lips. He takes his sweet fucking time lighting it, inhaling and blowing a cloud of hashish-like smoke into the air. "And I should tell you because…?"

"She's a senior partner in my firm." That I've been plotting to kick her out of for as long as I can remember. But he doesn't need to be privy to that small detail.

"Do you often play a knight in a black suit for all your senior partners?"

"Only when the necessity arises."

"Didn't think you'd let your demon peek through for a woman."

"Might want to check your eyesight, Nic. Must be blurry from all the blood that's gotten in it."

"I'm twenty out of twenty. But are you, King? The way I see it, either she'll shatter against your hard edges or you'll get yourself a cut from her sharp cheekbones."

"Are you sure your ophthalmologist isn't blind? Someone needs to look into that license and give you a second opinion before you start seeing aliens."

"Hmm. Interesting." His lips pull in a disgusting smirk that should be at the same museum as ugly impressionist paintings. "Unfortunately, though, I don't discuss my business with outsiders, which you made sure to become as soon as your father died."

"Oh, I'm sorry. Did I take away your toys again, Nic?"

"Yes, and you won't get a word out of me unless you give them back."

"No, thanks. I'm not investing legitimately earned money in a blood pit."

He leans forward, blowing smoke with the sole intent of turning the office into a life-hazard location. "Riddle me this, King. Is it still considered legitimate if the root is bloodied?"

"Yes. Nothing a little laundering can't fix. I don't give a fuck what type of deal my old man had with your family. I made it clear early on that I wouldn't hold to the same bargain, and your brother, the actual Don, agreed."

Though the janitor and his grandmother know that the actual leader of the Luciano family isn't the eldest brother, Lazlo Luciano.

Nicolo has been pulling the strings, playing his demonic games in the background, and being a surrogate leader.

Lazlo is the accepted façade by the family and the world. Nicolo is too nihilist, eccentric, and barbaric for anyone's liking. Stories of his secret torture chambers are enough to propel fear in anyone's soul.

"My brother doesn't control bookkeeping, I do. And I'm telling you that the only means to protect your woman is to pay up for it, rich boy."

"Might want to visit your ENT and get those ears checked as well, because I told you she's not my fucking woman."

The idea itself leaves me with irritation deeply rooted in years of visiting the same memories about a certain femme fatale.

Fucking years of wondering if she was alive or if her last stamp on the world was Gwen.

"Sounds convenient then. Don't let the door hit you on the way out, but do leave it open for when Ms. Leblanc shows up for our meeting in a bit."

This motherfucker's head will be hanging on his office door by the time she shows up.

Instead of acting on what I'm thinking and inevitably getting myself killed by his guards, I retrieve my Zippo and flip it open.

"I'll call my broker and invest in one of your legitimate businesses, *and* I get to choose which."

"Three. One illegitimate."

"Two. Legitimate."

"Done."

I flip my Zippo shut. "Now, speak."

He offers me his box of cigars. "You might need one."

Fuck no. This shit reminds me of my father's adultery and the surrogate killer role he played in my mother's death. It's why I've had a queasy feeling in my stomach since Nic started smoking it. Which I'm sure is on purpose because the bastard has more of a penchant for moral torture than physical.

I wave him off with the cool expression of an unperturbed monk. "Speak."

He traps the cigar between his lips, blowing out polluted air. "She's one of us."

"One of who?"

He points a thumb at himself. "Us. Bloodbaths, laundering, and battery included."

"What the fuck is that supposed to mean?"

"Did you know Leblanc was her mother's last name?"

No, I didn't fucking know, because everything Aspen was so witch-like in nature, I avoided it while wearing fake charms.

"And that detail is important why?"

"She was born Aspen Locatelli."

"Locatelli…" I rack my brain for the familiar last name, then stop. "You don't mean the man who killed for your father like it was an Olympic sport?"

"That's the one. Bruno Locatelli, an extravagant killer with a taste for fine torture devices. He's the family's favorite Grim Reaper and Lazlo's best dog, but he's old, so there's no harm in expanding my options with his daughter." He checks his phone. "After all, she ended a strike even my boys had trouble taking care of."

I stare at him as if the load of information will materialize into a being beside him. "Aspen is Locatelli's daughter?"

"Yes. But here's the most interesting part." He slides his elbows on the table. "She was the bird who sang to the FBI about one of his murders and landed him in prison. And in our world, snitches not only get stitches, but they also get thrown in ditches."

⚖️

Half an hour later, I've contemplated whether or not my earlier plan of putting Nicolo's head on display would still work, then promptly decided I need to live for my angel's sake.

There are a lot of things I gave up for Gwen. Including almost getting myself killed in a variety of dangerous activities or fully embedding myself into Nicolo's blood-flavored world.

But the questionable truce I've formed with the man, as well as the deal we've made, is worth it. If not for anything else, for the expression on Aspen's face the moment she walks into the grandpa-themed office.

If a mood can be measured by temperature, she's definitely at the boiling point.

I take a sip of my coffee, pretending her presence bores me to death when all I want to do is trap her against the nearest wall and make her spit out the naked truth.

Or, actually, get her naked.

Wait. Hold on. What—and I mean this—*the fuck* was that thought all about?

I don't want to get Aspen naked.

My type is mute, only screams when I'm pounding them, and doesn't ever, and I mean, *ever*, talk back to me. In short, everything Aspen Leblanc—or Locatelli or whatever the last name the witch coven chose for her—fucking isn't.

Soft and angelic wouldn't touch this woman with a ten-foot pole. Even her younger self was a hellion through and through.

But then again, what do you expect from a kid from the ghetto who offered her father to the FBI on a platter?

No wonder she's a hard nut to crack—or a nut that's not to be cracked. She's been in constant survival mode since she was a kid.

Not sure what that load of information adds to my agenda, but it's nowhere near good.

"And what are you doing here?" she asks with the exasperation of a fed-up, stern teacher.

"He's my chief legal counsel until further notice," Nicolo answers, still sucking on a damn cigar like it's a Popsicle.

"Guess that means we'll be working together." I tilt the coffee cup in her direction like a mock salute. "Again."

"I came first," she's addressing both of us, but the glare is only for me.

"This isn't a marathon. First or last doesn't matter." I cock my head at Nicolo. "Toys and connections do."

"You gave me your word." She jerks her attention to Nicolo now.

The asshole smiles at her, taking my advice about his grim expression seriously for the first time, and I want to reach out to the me from half an hour ago and kick him in the balls. "And I'm keeping my word, Ms. Leblanc. I never said you'd be appointed as my chief legal advisor. I just said you'd be on my legal team. The chief position never concerned you."

"Because I'm a woman?"

"Because I don't trust you…yet."

"And you trust *him*?" She enunciates the "him" with a jerky finger in my direction.

"I trust his money, his profit-oriented mind, and his character that I've known for decades. You, however, are still on trial."

She taps her toe on the floor, which is both a sign of distress and haughty behavior. Having survived and thrived in a male-dominated world, Aspen, like many of us, doesn't take defeat so well.

I'm ready to bet half my fortune that she's concocting a plan to bounce back up. This time, she'll aim for the top.

She's not a sore loser, she's just not a loser. Period.

The word has never been in her vocabulary. Probably long before I first met her in the form of a seductress femme fatale.

"Will working with Kingsley cause any issues?" Nicolo asks on a puff of putrid smoke.

"Not at all." She smiles at him, then glares at me. "We work *so* well together, he and I."

"Is that so?" He stares between us like a dog with a bone. "From my extensive background check, I gathered you two are rivals who, by a stroke of fate, happen to share a daughter."

More like a stroke of the devil while high on his lush desires.

And alcohol.

There was definitely an excessive amount of alcohol in both our systems that night.

"You heard the lady." I offer her a smile that screams fake. "We can find a compromise."

In hell.

While she's riding my face under a volcano waterfall.

I pause again, my fingers tightening on the cup. That's the second erotic thought I've had about the witch in the span of an hour.

What the fuck am I? An animal in heat?

She smiles back, mirroring my dishonest one, and I can almost see the venom spilling on the ground in a splash of black. "Of course we can."

It's on.

Looks like I'm in for a fucking ride.

FIVE

Aspen

SWING MY CAR DOOR OPEN, THEN SLAM IT SHUT UNTIL THE loud sound ricochets through the silence of the parking lot.

It's old, grim, and has potholes the size of Central Park in the asphalt. But the most unfortunate thing about this place is the man who stands in the middle of it in his signature dashing black suit.

I'm starting to think he never looks less than perfect, as if he were born with the sole purpose of intimidating humans.

Kingsley strokes the handle of the door of his car—a special edition Audi—like it's an old lover.

At the sound of the slamming, a small translation of my temper, his lips tilt in that infuriatingly gorgeous smile. "Any objections, witch?"

Disregarding my constant need to remain calm, I fully face him with a hand hiked on my hip. "I get you've been interfering in my business and actively trying to kick me out of W&S in order to get me out of Gwen's life, which will not be happening, by the way. And while you're a goddamn asshole, you're not an idiot. So why the hell would you get your prim and proper hands dirty with the freaking mafia?"

"Is that worry I hear in your venomous tone? I'd be touched if I had any fucks to give."

"You could be hanging from a frozen mountain by your dick and the only thing I'd do is bring out the popcorn while I watch. So no, worry is the last emotion I'd feel for you."

He dips his brows in mock reaction. "Sounds painful."

"It looks painful, too, in my head."

"Didn't know my dick had a personalized section in your head."

"All dedicated to torture. The extreme type."

"Seems kinky."

"Guess you'll never know." I flip my hair to suppress a smile. I'm supposed to be mad at this jerk, and I am, but at the same time, I can't resist gravitating toward bantering whenever I'm with him.

He brings out the worst, the twisted, and the fucked up in me.

All at the same time.

Which means I should stay away from him. Especially after his audacious move last night, a touch that I couldn't banish from my head even as I plotted and pinned names and pictures on my whiteboard à la serial killers.

But then he had to show up out of nowhere right by Nicolo's side with the nonchalance of a psychopath.

As if he has nothing to lose, which I'm well aware is far from the truth.

"Have you thought about Gwen in your little plan to become besties with the mafia?" It's that tone again, harsh but with a hidden softness that pisses me off.

He raises a brow. "Have you? I thought you intended to conquer the title of her mother, but that won't be happening if you end up in a body bag, whether by pissing off Nicolo or by your father's gun when he gets out of jail."

I jolt, my eyes growing in size.

This…he didn't just say what I think he did, did he?

"What?" He steps closer in that charged way that leaves me

on my toes. "You thought I wouldn't find out the truth if you hid it well enough?"

"My truth or the lack thereof has nothing to do with you."

"On the contrary, it has everything to do with me, considering you intend to bring your messy past and bloodied family ties into my daughter's life."

"I would never do that. I'd protect her with my own life."

"That won't be possible if your father kills you and moves on to your next of kin." He steps toward me, his height and personality metaphorically expanding to fill the horizon. "Listen here, witch. I'll personally put you in a body bag before your chaos affects Gwen. I didn't raise her all these years so you could fuck it all up with your past mistakes."

"I've only made two mistakes in my life. The first was meeting you and the second was not suspecting my daughter was alive. Putting away a murderer doesn't belong on that list and I won't let you or anyone else make me feel otherwise."

He pauses, narrowing his eyes in pure contemplation. Kingsley has an unnerving way of looking at people as if he's able to read the deepest minds and the darkest desires.

I've always prided myself on being above his stupid games, but something is different now.

His hands are metaphorically around my throat due to the piece of information about my father.

In the past, his disdain toward me was illogical, but he's now found all the logical reasons to separate me from Gwen.

And that scares the shit out of me.

"You do realize that Nicolo's protection is neither absolute nor infinite, right? The moment you're no longer a useful dog, he'll euthanize you."

"Worry about yourself."

"I hold toys over his greedy head. You hold fucking zilch."

"I'll find a way to stay in his good graces. Just do me a favor and stay out of my business this time."

"I'll only consider that if you pay for such a favor."

I release an exasperated sigh. "You're richer than oil princes and just as hedonistic. Why the hell would you need more money?"

"Money is not the currency I was envisioning." His gaze drops to my Louboutins, then slides up my blue slacks, to my beige button-down, and stops at where the first button is undone.

I'm surprised I don't catch fire from the charged way he looks at me.

It's intense and absolutely disarming in its novelty.

He just looked at me as if he wants to devour me for lunch, dinner, and tomorrow's breakfast.

The image sends my heat up a notch and I regret not having more coffee-tequila this morning.

What. The. Hell?

The need to run out of his watchful gaze and asphyxiating atmosphere hits me like a need.

And that in itself is also a what-the-hell moment. I don't run from men, situations, or my fears. I'm the type who stands right in the middle of a storm with the determination of a buffalo. Either I survive or I die. No in-between.

But this isn't just any man or any situation. It's *the* man who messed up my whole life twenty-one years ago and continues the legacy of destruction in the present.

He's my worst enemy and most villainous rival.

He's the devil who'd crush me without a second thought.

"Don't even think about it," I warn, my voice as rigid as my posture.

"I haven't said anything." He feigns innocence, but his voice has lowered to a rumble.

"You're looking at me weird. Stop it."

"Weird how?"

"Like a man looks at a woman. I'm not one of your playthings, Kingsley. I'll cut your dick off in your sleep before you put it anywhere near me."

"Is that a challenge, sweetheart?" His voice drops to a chilling range at that damn endearment and so does my stomach.

But that's not the worst of my illogical reaction. Bats explode in sickeningly loud squeaks in the black cave of my chest and the running away option becomes mandatory instead of optional.

However, I attempt to hold on to my fast-withering calm. "It's a warning."

"I don't do well with those." He steps forward and it takes all my tenacious control to keep from backing up. "In fact, I most definitely take it as a challenge, so keep an eye open in the dark. You never know what will be lurking in the shadows."

He remains there, making me breathe the notes of cedarwood and fine cigar off him, as if daring me to make a move.

I glare up at him, but no witty comeback comes to mind. If I speak right now, all I'll spout is nonsense.

"I don't usually wish people good luck when I intend on breaking them, but you need lots of it, sweetheart."

With one last provoking smile, he turns around and heads to his car.

⚖️

Before my meeting with Nicolo's sister-in-law, I practice three breathing exercises and count to one thousand.

My cool is nowhere to be found, though, and neither is my usual meticulous way of organizing emotions. Which is basically shoving them to the basement of my psyche where no one notices them, let alone sees them.

Ever since the showdown with Kingsley in the parking lot this morning, they've been viciously attempting to break the surface and turn me into a blasphemous version of an emotional mess.

I contemplated calling Nate, but what the hell would I tell him?

Why is your asshole friend bringing up the crazy a notch?

Or maybe I should ask him why the fuck I'm honoring his crazy with a response other than pure disdain.

Either way, the calling Nate option was aborted soon after it formed. Unlike the jerk Kingsley, I won't bother him or my daughter on their honeymoon.

Which is why I'm sitting at my desk, posture rigid, fingers tapping away at my keyboard with practiced efficiency. Now, if I could focus, that would be perfect.

The phone call from my assistant announcing that Mrs. Luciano has arrived saves me from the mess going on in my head.

I'm good with work, and despite Kingsley's sexist, dick-shaped ego, I'm considered one of the best in the law circuit with a win rate of ninety-five percent. Only a point lower than his ninety-six percent and not far from Nate's one hundred percent.

And no, I don't closely follow the percentage of wins.

Okay, maybe I do. But deep down, I've always considered the asshole a rival. Logically, it should've been Nate since he's a civil lawyer like me.

Kingsley is the most notorious criminal defense attorney in recent history, so our scope of expertise differs vastly. But I've often followed how he wins his cases—from the background, of course.

He's a natural at dealing with monsters and making them obey his every command. I guess it all boils down to the fact that he's a monster himself, but watching him in action is annoyingly fascinating.

He's assertive to a fault, has the confidence of an arrogant god, and is so unpredictable, everyone in the courtroom leaves extremely entertained by his witty speeches.

The jerk will never know those facts obviously.

He'll also never know that I'm sure he'll get what Nicolo asked of him done in no time, which is getting his brother out of a battery and assault charge.

As for myself, I'm stuck with a divorce case.

It's not even my scope of expertise, but what Nicolo wants, Nicolo gets. Besides, he said my job is to convince his brother's wife to accept his conditions and leave.

The same brother with the assault charge, Mateo Luciano, is going through a divorce. Nicolo wants me to convince Mateo's wife to take $300K, sign away all her rights to the Luciano fortune, and disappear from his brother's state.

Due to my pending cases, I haven't had the chance to do an appropriate background check on her, but I will later tonight.

It could be my negligence or the load of emotions running through me, but I'm not ready when she walks in through my office door. And it's not only because she showed up alone instead of being accompanied by her lawyer.

It's the woman herself.

The girl I thought I'd never meet again in this lifetime after we parted ways in a less than glamorous manner. Her fair hair falls to her shoulders and it's way less shiny than when we were teenagers.

"Let's get this over with. I want nothing of his money, so we're done here…" She freezes mid-sentence when her eyes meet mine. "Aspen…?"

The rotten taste of memories bubbles in my throat and I clear it. "Caroline."

She kicks the door shut with her foot, completely disregarding her "public" code of conduct. Caroline used to have two personalities—one for the people, one for me and herself.

I liked the crass, misbehaving Caroline who got me addicted to beer way better than the plastic version she showed everyone else.

Her designer dress sways with her movements as she storms toward me and plants her hands on the desk. She dresses like a Stepford wife and her makeup isn't as loud anymore. But her face is the same, older, but still striking in its beauty.

"It's really you," she lets the words out on a small breath. "Wow. You actually look the femme fatale role now. How have you been?"

"Fine." I stand up and motion at the sitting area in my office.

She complies, flopping onto the dark red sofa and crossing her legs. "I'm speechless. You've done so well by becoming an attorney in this big firm and all. You really are getting that glass slipper for yourself as you said back then. Too bad you're still a dog for men like my soon-to-be ex-husband."

"I'm no one's dog. I'm merely doing my job."

She snorts, running her gaze over my office without saying a word.

"Will your lawyer be joining us soon?" I ask, trying as hard as possible to sound professional.

"I fired that tool. Too much money for nothing."

"Will you not be getting a replacement?"

"No…unless you're thinking about switching to my side."

"I'm afraid I can't do that."

She clicks her tongue. "Shame, though I really don't need your services."

"Not mine, no, but you need a lawyer to negotiate what you can get out of this divorce."

"I want nothing but the piece of paper to prove I'm no longer the piece of shit's wife."

"Still, you can and should get compensation out of this. He's offering three hundred grand."

I planned to start with $150K and go from there until I reach Nicolo's final offer, but seeing as she's not interested, and the fact that she's Caroline, of all people, changed my course of action.

After all, this is the "I'm going to marry rich" Caroline, the "I'll take you on a states tour in my Porsche one day" Caroline.

"He can keep his blood-stained money."

"Since when do you care what money is coated with? This is your livelihood, Caroline, so take it and you can even demand more, depending on how much damage he inflicted on you."

She smiles a little. "I thought you were his attorney, but here you are offering me advice. Sure you don't want to change sides?"

"Quit joking." I pinch the bridge of my nose. "Take the money."

"No."

"Since when is that word in your vocabulary when it comes to money?"

"Since I grew a backbone." She stares in the direction of my floor-to-ceiling window that overlooks the skyline.

As tiny droplets of rain hit the glass and countless others follow, Caroline's low voice carries with the sound like a haunting melody. "I was married when I first met Mateo. My first husband was everything I'd ever wished for. A frat boy with Mommy and Daddy's oil fortune. He gave me my fairy-tale dream. A big house, luxurious cars, and trips to exotic places. Oh, and a few black eyes. But hey, some fairy tales need to have an abusive Prince Uncharming with fertility issues, right? He crushed my dream to conceive children of our own, and I still stayed. But then he cheated on me. I grew a backbone between that and hearing that he'd been telling people I was the infertile one.

"Mateo came into the picture when my loser of an ex-husband chose his girlfriend as his next affair. In pure mafia fashion, Mateo kidnapped them, strapped both her and Steven to chairs with duct tape, brought me over, and told me, 'Want some old-fashioned revenge?' And then we fucked in front of them. It was the best sex of my life, which is probably a poor reason to stay with Mateo now that I think about it. We got married soon after I divorced Steven and I thought I was turning over a new leaf."

"But?" I ask in a soft voice.

Her eyes fill with tears and she blinks them away. "But he's no different than Steven and all the other men. He got bored, and bored men cheat. I walked in on him wrapped up with his side piece in a hotel room."

"Did you sign a prenup?"

"No. Nicolo threatened me to do it, but Mateo was vehemently against it."

"Did Mateo own things after the marriage?"

"Yeah. A resort and some real estate."

"You can own some of that if you can prove emotional and maybe physical distress. If you were trying for a baby, that can be added to play on the judge's favor. You have to emphasize that you stayed with your infertile, abusive and cheating ex-husband and thought you'd get a new chance with Mateo, but he didn't keep his part of the bargain. There's an eighty percent chance you'll win half of his assets owned after the marriage."

She snorts out laughing and I pause.

"What?"

"You really haven't changed. People usually try to comfort me and offer fake apologies in these situations, not suggest I sue for a mafia boss's assets."

"Only half, not all, and it's not all of his assets. You have no right to his inheritance. Besides, I'm not good at comforting. It'll just come off as uncoordinated and awkward and will serve no purpose. My advice, however, can be useful."

"Are you sure you should be offering me that advice? Nicolo will off you if he finds out."

"He doesn't need to find out. Any lawyer, including the one you fired, would give this advice. Besides, how did you know Nicolo hired me and not Mateo?"

"Nicolo calls all the shots in that godforsaken family. The only reason he's allowing the divorce and not sending one of his goons to off me is because he doesn't want to lose Mateo."

"Why?"

"Mateo is the rook in his chessboard, and apparently, that's important according to my soon-to-be ex-husband."

"I meant, why would he need to allow the divorce? Isn't this yours and Mateo's idea?"

"Mateo doesn't want a divorce, which is why he's in jail after beating the hell out of my date last night. I hope he stays there for a few days."

"I wouldn't hold out much hope. He's probably out as we speak." Especially if Kingsley is his attorney. He'd get him out on bail in no time.

"Oh, well. Doesn't hurt to wish."

"You really want nothing of his?"

She shakes her head with a whimsical expression on her face. "When I first divorced Steven, Mateo made sure my ex-husband signed the house, the cars, and two yachts over to my name. I felt so triumphant, because I hated the slimy asshole and was happy I could get some monetary compensation for the physical and mental abuse I went through. But it's different now. I don't want anything that reminds me of Mateo. So tell Nicolo you convinced me to walk away with nothing. He'll be pleased with you for driving the gold digger, aka me, away."

She retrieves a card from her small bag and slides it across the table. "Now that the crap is over, let's meet for mimosas sometime under less stressful conditions."

I grab her wrist as she's about to retreat and my eyes widen at the violet fingerprints on her arm. I pull her down and stare closely at her face. Sure enough, there are bluish marks beneath her heavy foundation and concealer.

My blood boils as I say in a guttural voice, "Did Mateo hit you?"

She swiftly jerks from my hold and plasters on a fake smile. "It's nothing you should worry about."

"Caroline, either tell me or I'm taking your ass to report this to the police, even while you're kicking and screaming. Actually, I'm taking you anyway, so speak while I'm still being nice."

"Bitch, please. This is nice?" She laughs.

"Caroline," I warn.

"It wasn't Mateo. That date I mentioned earlier? He's from a rival crime family and, shocker, he doesn't like being told no. So he decorated my face with his own lash of violence." She clears her throat. "Mateo doesn't know about this. Don't tell him or he'll be sent back to jail for a lifetime subscription. This time for murder. I mean, yes, he's a prick and a damn cheater, but I don't want him to spend his life behind bars because of me."

"Jesus." I sigh, joining her side.

"Not sure he can do anything. Some people are just off his mercy radar."

"Stop joking."

She gives a bitter smile. "Would you rather I throw a pity party and wallow in misery?"

"At least take this seriously. Why did you even go to another mafia man?"

"Why do you think? For old-fashioned revenge the Mateo way. Karma and I are cut from the same bitch cloth and have a similar dark sense of humor."

"You should get a restraining order against both men and hire some bodyguards."

"Stop acting like my nonexistent mother, Aspen. I'm an adult."

"Who still can't sense danger even after it hits her in the face. Literally."

"Ouch. *Touché.*" She smiles, then hugs me out of nowhere. I freeze as her frail arms wrap around me. "I missed you, bitch. I'm glad we met again."

I slowly lift my hand and pat her back, and I can feel her sniffling against my chest, but I don't say anything out of fear of dropping the most awkward bomb of the century.

After a few moments, she pulls back and wipes her eyes. "Enough about me, tell me about you."

"I'm as you see."

"Don't give me that. Wait, are you still mad because you think I told your aunt and uncle about that night?"

"No. I kind of forgot about that."

"It wasn't me, Aspen. I swear."

"What do you mean it wasn't you? Aunt Sharon said you told her. Forget it, anyway. It's all in the past."

"I can't just forget it. That hooker lied to make you feel alone. You were my ride or die, and I wouldn't have sold you out. I tried talking to you, but they had you under house arrest during the period of your pregnancy and had thugs watch over your house. I came to the hospital after you had the baby, though, but you were too dazed to even know I was there. After that, you were gone."

My throat dries as I whisper, "I ran away."

"I know. I searched for you and left corny phrases with my lipstick on bathroom mirrors, hoping you'd see them."

"You did?"

"Why do you look so surprised? Of course I did. I said, 'You're my best friend ever, call me.' 'I'm sorry you lost your baby, no one deserves that. I'm here for you.' 'Please don't leave. You're my ride or die.' You ghosted me anyway."

My lips part and those stupid emotions are now banging on the surface of my heart. I clear my throat. "I didn't see them. I left the state."

"I figured you did." She lifts a shoulder. "I'm sorry."

"About what?"

"Your baby being stillborn. I know you wanted the child, even though you were a kid yourself."

"She wasn't stillborn."

"W-what?"

"They lied—the hooker and the alcoholic, as you called them. They shoved a stillborn in my arms and made me think it was my daughter while they sent my real daughter to her dad."

"Oh my God, they found him?"

I nod.

"Even though we searched for him for weeks and couldn't?"

"Yeah. They could've gotten outside help. I thought it was yours."

"Of course not. I'd rather drown in shit than snitch to that hooker."

I frown. I was sure it was Caroline who hid Kingsley's identity from me yet told my aunt and uncle. But if it wasn't her, then who?

"Does that mean you found your daughter now?" she asks hopefully, scooting closer.

"I did. She still doesn't consider me a mother, though."

"Oh, she will once she gets an earful from Auntie Caroline."

"No, Callie. We're fragile as it is. Don't meddle."

"You're fragile because you're being stupidly careful as usual." She grins.

"Careful is intelligence, not stupidity. And stop smiling like an idiot."

"What? You called me Callie again."

"Whatever," I say with nonchalance, but I can't resist the smile.

Caroline smiles, too, and we keep talking for an hour, then grab lunch together before we finally part ways because I have to meet a client.

She texts me immediately when she gets home as I asked her to. She even sends me a picture of her giant huskies and proof that she activated the alarm.

Caroline continues to text me throughout the day until night-time when I get home. Her updates include a burned lasagna, a millionth rewatch of *Friends*, and bad dad jokes.

She makes me smile anyway and feel lighthearted at how fate has thrown her in my path again.

When I reach my building, I step out of my Range Rover and pause. I swear I just saw a shadow in my peripheral vision.

Pulling out my phone, I dial 911 and head to the elevator with my finger hovering over the call button.

I expect someone to jump inside the elevator or jam his hand against the door as it closes, but nothing appears.

Still, an ominous feeling accompanies me even as I enter my apartment.

The feeling of being watched.

SIX

Kingsley

"Forget whatever my brother told you. I won't agree to the divorce." Mateo chugs a shot of triple vodka like a Russian mobster on his initiation day.

He's disheveled curly hair sticks to his forehead like broken leaves, and his crumpled suit resembles a hand-me-down. He's all dark—eyes, hair, expression, and personality.

Not as demonic as Nicolo, per se, but close enough. He also happens to be one of the most feared members of the Luciano family due to his no-nonsense personality.

He slides the glass across the counter in the bartender's direction, wordlessly asking for a refill.

He, Aspen, and I are having a daytime meeting in his empty club downtown. An obscure though elegant place that only allows the rich and their kinky grandmothers within its walls.

Nicolo was supposed to join us in the unholy union, but some other business came up. Probably torturing a poor soul until they wish for death.

Aspen, who's sitting on my right at the bar because I

unintentionally—or intentionally—made sure I was between her and Mateo, listens carefully to his statement.

She has already consumed her tequila and also asked for a refill. She releases a breath, exasperated at that as if she's a teacher and Mateo is a naughty boy in her class, then hikes her sleeves up her arms.

The woman is dressed in black pants and a white button-down, but she looks sexier than a naked pole dancer.

And I obviously need to stop thinking about ramming my cock into her cunt if I don't want to end up with a missing ball complication sponsored by the witch coven.

"Ms. Blunt asked for a divorce. She doesn't even want alimony or compensation."

Mateo, who's been watching his shots like a hooker obsesses over money, whirls around in his chair to stare at Aspen. Maniacally. Like she's next on his shit list.

"What did you just call her?" There's no slur in his Italian-accented voice. The man spent two nights in jail, partly because he used his fists to draw a map on the other man's face, and partly because that man is a Della Roma. Aka, one of the Lucianos' rivals, and there was more work than I signed up for to get him his 'get out of jail free' card.

"Ms. Blunt," Aspen repeats, obviously not reading the atmosphere. Or maybe she read it loud and clear and is provoking him anyway because she's sadistic.

"Her last name is fucking Luciano." Mateo points a finger at her.

"She prefers her maiden name."

"I don't give a fuck what she prefers. In front of me, you call her Mrs. Luciano."

She nods, though not meekly, and definitely with her spunky defiance that I want to sink my fucking teeth into.

I hate this woman with more passion than should be allowed, but I still want to fuck her anyway.

Hate-fuck her, to be more specific.

The logic my dick goes by is that I'll finally be able to control her and show her the actual brand of my crazy. Even if only in sex.

And no, this new logic didn't start after I learned she's the femme fatale from twenty-one years ago.

Absolutely not.

Mateo chugs half of his glass. "Go to Caroline and tell her the fun is over. She better come home today or I'll be the one to drag her back."

"She might file a restraining order in case of any threatening behavior."

"Then make fucking sure she doesn't." He staggers to his feet, resembling a soldier in a defeated battalion.

Just when I think the unpleasant meeting is over, Aspen has to open her mouth. "I'm afraid I'll have to decline. She has the right to protect herself from you and I won't be the one to take that privilege away."

The little fucking shit.

Mateo spins around in a flash of movement and lunges at her. I step between them at the last second and he slams into my chest.

I grab him by the shoulders. "Let's calm down, Mateo."

"Repeat that," he speaks to Aspen who didn't even stand up. "The part about how she's protecting herself from me. I dare you to fucking repeat it."

She finally slides from her seat and moves beside me, her expression as cool as Siberia's ice. "You cheated on her and have shown you'll be violent when it comes to her, so she wishes protection from you."

"I did not fucking cheat on her." He grunts, sounding out of breath.

"I'll take care of it," I tell him. "Go home, Mateo."

Aspen opens her mouth to say something, probably foolish and unnecessary, again. But I elbow her and she steps on my foot with the pointy part of her heel.

Mateo staggers out of the club, shoulders drooped and definitely not walking the line.

"For the record, I don't need you to defend me. I could've done that myself just fine."

"And when would you do that? When your blood is the club's new wallpaper?" I face her, my jaw locked as tightly as her crossed arms. "Mind your words before you speak them. I thought I was the one lacking diplomacy, but apparently, you lack common sense. Besides, if you still want Nicolo's protection, you won't get it by pissing off his brother."

She pales and it cements the idea I had from earlier. Aspen was speaking from her emotions, being illogically angry at Mateo and lashing out with her icy attitude as a response.

I doubt she thought about the deal she made with Nicolo concerning this whole charade.

"Is there something I should know about?"

She lifts her chin with defiance that hardens my dick. Her eyes shine in a mixture of forbidden earth and mysterious forest. "Why? So you can sabotage me with it?"

"If that was my intention, it would've happened with or without your cooperation."

"Excuse my stoicism and inability to believe you have any noble motives."

"Nobility and I don't share the same universe, beliefs, or social standing. Also, your idol, Nietzsche, was a self-professed nihilist who was highly critical of stoics, so to adopt their philosophical term should be presumptuous to your little Nietzsche heart."

"Being stoic and actually adopting the philosophy are entirely different."

"That's like the chicken and egg conundrum. Being a stoic is to adopt the philosophy that, unlike what your darling Nietzsche wants you and his vintage fan club to believe, actually share common ground with nihilism. Neither thought an individual has free will and, therefore, cannot actively play a role in their own fate. But at least stoics give people the room to find ways to exist within nature. Nihilists do not."

"So now you're a stoic?"

"I'm neither of those fools. I decide my own fate in spite of what those bands of textbook nerds say."

"That's not how it works."

"That's exactly how it works." I pause, running my gaze over her face that has no business being so fucking attractive. "For instance, if I want those pretty lips wrapped around my finger or another part of me, all I have to do is take action."

She remains unaffected, short of the splash of red that explodes on her neck, which completely gives her away.

That, and she swallows, twice, before speaking in her usual haughty tone. "The only action you'll be taking is defending yourself when I sue for sexual harassment, dick."

"You're the one who just mentioned my dick, so the suit could go both ways. Though a lawsuit would be the last thing on your mind once I have you writhing underneath me."

"Your arrogance should get you banned from breathing."

"Again, it's assertiveness, not arrogance, sweetheart. Want to test it?"

"Test what?"

I step forward, murdering whatever space that separates us. Instead of moving backward like any woman in this position would, she stands her ground. So I slowly push her back until I trap her between my chest and the bar counter. My hands rest on the dark wooden surface on either side of her, and for a moment, the noises surrounding us vanish.

All that remains is a faint buzzing in my ears and the controlled sound of our mingled breathing.

Her eyes never leave mine, too bright with challenge and unsaid words and killer tension that should only belong in wars.

She'd be a hellion general with the mere purpose of beheading the king.

Too bad for her, this particular king has a different approach to headstrong warlords.

My face lowers and I relish in how she watches me carefully, albeit with heat. "I will kiss you and if you show no reaction, I'll back off, return your boring space, and even get out of your hair about Gwen."

Her lips part before she seals them shut. "What if…I do show a reaction?"

"The ball will be in my court and I'll use it to strip that bitch persona away, then eventually fuck you." I remove a hand from the counter and slide it from the slender curve of her waist to her hip.

Despite her big personality, she's so small in my hold, so fragile and breakable, and that shouldn't give my dick more ideas to get harder.

My fingers dig into her flesh, and although a piece of clothing separates us, her heat collides with mine as if we're dancing around a fire. One that's wild as fuck with the mere purpose of burning the earth and touching the sky.

And then something happens.

She squirms—or trembles—I have no clue which. And it's a sight to behold because Aspen isn't usually the type who shakes.

She's the type who shakes others.

I lower my head farther with the intention of feasting on her lips and biting them until either I make her bleed or she does. The thought of her fight gets my dick in "I want to fuck" mode and that's a fucking first.

But I don't think about that as her reaction escalates from surprise to feral desire that collides with mine. Blotches of red appear on her face, bleeding from her neck like lava.

Her lips purse and she bunches her fingers in my dress shirt. "Don't."

"Afraid of a little challenge, sweetheart? Didn't take you for a quitter." My voice is so low and close to her cheek that she blinks slowly, her nostrils flaring.

My lips nearly skim the dusting of freckles underneath her eyes. They're like stars in an island's night sky, so small and bright, and give her an edge sharper than her high cheekbones.

I don't deny myself a taste and dart my tongue, licking them as if they're dessert.

She tastes like exotic fruit and the purest patchouli. Not exactly sweet, but it's as intoxicating, earthy, and spicy as the woman herself.

She smells of that, too. Patchouli. A scent that's as rare as she is and just as strong.

Aspen shudders, her brown nails digging in my chest. "Kingsley…"

She stills and I pause, but I don't take my tongue off her cheek.

And the reason is that she just moaned my name, like a chant, a prayer, or something in between. I don't give a fuck, because she just gave me the "all-access" card, and I intend to make use of it.

My lips slide down, leaving a wet trail on her face. I nibble on her cheek, then lick the assaulted place as I continue my way to her mouth.

And just when I'm about to devour her lips for lunch, my phone vibrates between us.

She startles, and I curse under my breath.

Even though I intend to ignore the call and go back to eating Aspen, she's the one who pushes me away, both of her elegant palms flattening on my pectoral muscles.

I retrieve my phone fully intent on ignoring the call. When Aspen tries to pull away, I keep one of her hands hostage on my chest.

Her wrist is thin, frail, and I'm starting to notice how slim she is. Has she lost weight?

Or maybe she's been this size all along and I'm only just now paying attention to it. Granted, before, I didn't see her as a woman, but more of a constant headache and a pesky complication.

Correction, I didn't see her as a woman I want to ram my dick inside.

She was always a woman to me. Infuriating as fuck, but a woman nevertheless.

Admittedly, ever since I found out she's Gwen's mother, as in the same femme fatale who played the main role in the unforgettable erotic/thriller night of my life, things have changed. Not only do I want to hate-fuck her until we're both spent, but I also need to control her in some way.

In any way.

I refuse to believe this unwanted tension and destructive energy has anything to do with some unresolved issues from the past. I simply don't allow my brain such disgraceful behavior.

The name flashing on the screen murders my thoughts and almost kills my hard-on.

Almost.

Aspen sees "ANGEL" written in capital letters and she quits her attempts to escape me.

I clear my throat, think of elderly women, bestiality, necrophilia, and Susan.

The last one is enough to put the boy down.

"Daddy!" Gwen squeals from the other end of the line with contagious excitement.

"Who is this?"

"What…? It's me, Dad."

"I thought the police were calling to inform me of your disappearance since you seem to have forgotten my existence."

Aspen rolls her eyes. Gwen bursts out laughing.

"Oh, don't be silly, Dad. I only skipped last night's call because I was…busy."

Two thoughts stab my brain. The first is that I didn't need that image of my angel, and the second is an honest question of why I didn't kill that bastard Nate again?

"Anyway, we're having loads of fun, but I miss you so much.

I'm going to hug the hell out of you when I get back, so you better be ready for the attack."

"Always ready for your hugs, Angel." And I hate the things with an undying passion.

Aspen's long lashes fan her face, but she's focused on the conversation. Judging by her expression, she can probably hear Gwen's voice on the other end.

My fingers splay over hers when they clench until they're flattened on my chest again.

Gwen continues speaking about her adventures with Nate, the nonsexual ones, because even I have limits. She chatters happily, saying she bought me things, plural.

"…we had local wine last night and it was strong! I got so drunk after one glass and couldn't even walk."

"Gwyneth Catherine Shaw, what did I say about drinking before you're twenty-one? Where's Nate? Let me talk to the bastard."

"Oh…uh…the reception…is getting bad… Gotta go, Dad. Say hi to Aspen for me…"

Beep.

The little shit can't lie to save her ass, and that bad reception lie was the worst performance in years.

I slide the phone back into my pocket, contemplating whether or not I should relay the last piece of dialogue.

Aspen watches me expectantly, like a kid who's waiting to find out if she's on Santa's naughty or nice list.

"Is she okay?" she murmurs.

I'm starting to realize the witch only becomes soft when it comes to Gwen.

"Judging by her still horrible lying skills, she's doing great."

"I'm glad she didn't take after you in that department."

"Or you."

"Or me." She smiles a little and fuck it.

Fuck this.

I grind my back teeth. "She says hi."

Aspen's eyes widen. "W-what?"

"Do you have hearing problems?"

"No, but…I'm thinking this is a dream."

I pinch her cheek and she swats my hand away with her free arm. "Ouch! What was that for?"

"Proof that it isn't a dream."

"Jerk," she spits out, but she doesn't remove her hand from beneath mine.

And she's still smiling, brighter now, like a much younger version of herself.

A version that's engraved deep inside me.

A version that I intend to bring out.

SEVEN

Aspen

"EARTH TO ASPEN, HELLO?"

I stare up from sipping my coffee that's spiked with tequila at Caroline's expectant face.

We're sitting in my apartment with her two huskies on either side of her like guardian angels—or devils, considering their names—Lucifer and Cain.

The excuse Caroline came up with is that her giant house is too cold and lonely and she needs a warm body to hug.

The victim has been me for a week now. I tried kicking her out the first few days, but I eventually gave up.

Caroline is way softer than me, like *too* soft, so she's been squashed more times than either of us can count, but she also happens to be a stubborn little thing when it comes to those she cares about.

Part of her freeloading bribe is bringing alcohol and putting on a rerun of *Friends* every night. There's barely any watching involved, though, since she uses the time to talk about the past, her train wreck of a life, and attempts to milk me for information.

"I was listening, Callie."

She throws down a plush pillow—that she brought with her because God forbid I have those fluffy things around—and attacks another slice of chocolate cake. In her rabbit pajamas and with her hair pulled into a bun, she looks creepily young. Especially when she scowls at me. "Oh, yeah? What was I talking about?"

"How good Mateo is in bed." I roll my eyes. "For the millionth time. Are you sure divorce is what you're after at this point?"

"Just because he's a good fuck doesn't mean I'll step on my pride for him. I don't go catching feelings for dicks, Aspen. Come on, that's like the first rule in the girl honor book."

I swirl my coffee and pull up the strap of my cotton dress that's fallen off my shoulder. "That's good and all, but my neck is still on the line."

"Don't worry. I told Mateo you're like my sister from another mister. He's an asshole, but he's honorable enough and has stupid codes he abides by—that don't include cheating *obviously*. He won't touch you."

"Nicolo would."

"Not if we get divorced. That's been the snake's aim since the beginning."

I slide to the edge of the chair. "Listen. Are you sure he cheated? He denied it in front of me and again in front of you the other day when you had an epic fight. In my apartment, mind you."

Her cheeks flush a deep shape of red. "I saw him sleeping with a woman sprawled all over his chest in a hotel. What more proof do I need?"

"And how did you happen to go to that hotel? To that specific room?"

She stares at the loud characters on TV, tears shining in her eyes. "I found the hotel's business card and the reservation receipt in his jacket pocket. The hotel manager let me into his room with the master keycard once I told him I'm a Luciano, and then I found Mateo with a side piece. A *young* side piece, who looked barely in her twenties. I know we've been having issues trying for a baby and shit, and he's not exactly the affectionate type, but he's also well aware that putting his dick in New York's available holes is a hard limit for me. Sometimes, I can't believe he'd do that to me. Other times, I remember the hard evidence."

I tap my bottom lip. "That hard evidence is suspicious."

Caroline looks at me from beneath her wet lashes. "Suspicious how?"

"The day you had a fight, Mateo said his memories are hazy about that night. He went to see a business associate and had a drink, yet he's well aware he slept alone and didn't touch another woman."

"Mateo would say anything to deceive me."

"He doesn't seem like the type who sugarcoats anything, Callie. If he'd cheated, he would've flat out said it and used force to make you go back to him. But he's been visiting like a reserved Victorian era duke who's courting a lady. Not to mention his goons' black cars that keep following you everywhere so that no scum like Della Roma can put his hands on you."

She purses her lips. "Bitch. Are you on my side or his?"

"Yours. It's clear you're suffering, considering all the sugary things you keep consuming to an unhealthy level and how you get emotional out of nowhere."

She winces, licking the cake that's stuck to her fingers. "You noticed that?"

"Of course I did. So how about you see to the end of this instead of torturing yourself and him?"

"I thought your boss Nicolo ordered you to get us divorced. He'd be after your head if he finds out you're playing marriage counselor."

"Nicolo doesn't matter."

She grins girlishly, like when we used to exchange Christmas presents, because the only gifts our families gave us were traumas. "And I do?"

I clear my throat and continue drinking from my coffee.

"Oh my God, look at our little hellion catching feelings for me."

"Don't push it, Callie."

She laughs and jumps up from the sofa to snuggle into my side, on a freaking chair. It barely fits us, but she wraps herself around me like a koala. As if that isn't enough, her dogs also join in the sappy family hug. We had a rocky start, but Cain and Lucifer have taken a liking to me.

Caroline hugs my waist like a needy toddler and I sigh. "I'm trying to drink my coffee."

"Just call it tequila already. Also, it's not good to drink coffee in the evening. You'll have trouble sleeping."

I have trouble sleeping anyway, but instead of admitting that, I say, "I have to review some drafts before going to sleep."

"Did anyone ever tell you that you're a workaholic?"

"You. Every day."

"Someone else needs to say it. Is your baby daddy exploiting you? Want me to unleash Mateo on him?"

I pause with the cup at my lips, then take a long sip that clogs my throat.

In her attempts to rekindle our relationship, Caroline got me drunk one night and I ended up telling her everything about the Kingsley mess.

How I hadn't realized he was the one who took my virginity, innocence and knocked me up on the first try. How he raised our daughter on his own. And how irrevocably out of depth he makes me feel.

Especially lately.

A shudder goes through me in mere remembrance of how he licked my cheeks and almost kissed me that day at the bar.

And the worst part is that I gave him the reaction he bargained for before his lips even met mine. Embarrassment is just the beginning of what I felt and still feel for that lapse in judgment. I lost control with an ease that scares the shit out of me. Which is why I've been avoiding him with a passion that rivals my need to escape my filthy origins.

"We don't really work together," I tell Caroline with a dismissive tone that should propel her to drop the subject.

But then again, she's worse than her own dogs with a bone. "Yeah, but you're always in each other's vicinity doing Nicolo's legal work and even having *meetings*."

I narrow my eyes at her. "Why the hell did you emphasize meetings?"

"Because that's where all the action happens. Duh."

"N-no action happened."

"Oh my God." She finally releases me, her lips opening like a fish. "It did!"

"No, it didn't."

"You stuttered like a high school girl with a crush on the quarterback, and you never even had crushes."

"Shut up." I slam a hand to her face to block her gleeful expression, but she just pokes my side and continues grinning as if she's high on weed.

She escapes my clutches and adopts a narrative tone, pretending to hold an imaginary mic. "Dear diary, I found the man who flipped my world upside down on Devil's Night twenty-one years ago, and I want a redo on Satan's lair. Please and thank you."

"Callie, I swear to fuck, either you shut up or I'm throwing you out the window."

"Sounds kinky and would be more action than I've had in weeks. The other day, I *accidentally* set the shower spray too high and came immediately."

"And you're telling me because…"

"Uh…I don't know, you might need the tip, considering your own lack of action. That, coupled with tension, can be a hassle to deal with."

"Thanks for the concern."

"Anytime!"

"Can we please change the subject?"

"No way in hell. I'm not getting off your case unless you tell me what happened today between the two of you."

I take another sip of my coffee. "And what makes you think something happened?"

"Because you've been sighing like an old woman who has the world sitting on her shoulders."

"I'm just thinking about cases."

"You're too much of a boss bitch to worry about work. You can do that shit with your eyes closed. Besides, I heard you muttering 'that motherfucker' under your breath while you were making your tequila. Sorry, I mean *coffee*. And there's only one motherfucker who gets you angry to the point of cursing him out of the blue."

I groan. "Is there any way I can convince you to drop this?"

"Yes." She smiles sweetly. "By giving me deets."

"It's nothing important."

"You tell me and I'll decide."

"He was just being a jerk, as usual." I release a frustrated breath. "I mean, I get it. He kicks it up a notch whenever he has a hearing with his stepmother, but he had no damn business taking it out on me. I was only five minutes late to the partners' meeting because of a client, and he asked me, in front of all the partners, if I respected them. When I said, of course, he was like 'Apparently not enough or you would've shown up on time, Ms. Leblanc.'"

"No, he didn't."

"Yes, he did. That's the closest I've been to murder. He is such an asshole with Machiavellianism running in his veins instead of blood."

"Yeah, off with his head in the guillotine. The jerk."

"Asshole."

"Dickhead with fragile masculinity."

"Motherfucking bastard." I huff. "I can't believe he won two cases in one damn day. I swear he gets his energy from sacrificing poor souls at the devil's altar."

"Aspen, honey, you're not supposed to admire him when we're planning to cut off his dick and feed it to my dogs. What do you guys call it? Right, conflict of interest."

"I don't admire him. I just…"

"Consider him a rival?"

I sigh. "The worst kind. Sometimes, I wish I was as assertive as he is, but I guess that means discarding my newly found heart, and I kind of need that."

"Yeah, no discarding hearts. That shit will leave you empty. Besides, maybe the fact that he's rich, hot as sin, and successful is all a façade to hide his hollow insides."

"There's nothing hollow about Kingsley, Callie. He's bigger than the world and could be seen from space."

"Or maybe that's what he likes you and the world to think." She raises a brow. "I've been married to a mafia boss for, like, three years and I've breathed the air of dangerous men every day, so I know when they bubble wrap their exterior with dazzling shit that's meant to blind anyone who attempts to look closer. Your Kingsley ranks high on the bullshit scale."

"He is not my Kingsley."

"Oh, I'm sorry. Your baby daddy and the man who stole your fourteen-year-old heart. Maybe we should add villain of your soul to the list?"

Before I can smack her and risk being bitten by her dogs, the doorbell rings. Caroline pales and it's my turn to grin. "Your own villain is finally here, so you can stop obsessing over staring at the clock."

"Don't open the door," she says, but I'm already up. "I swear to God I'll send Kingsley your actual diaries from back then, bitch."

"Joke's on you, already burned them, *bitch*, so unless you're up for a vacation in hell, that won't be happening. Oh, also, you have mascara on your cheek, might want to remove that." I'm smiling as she curses and runs to the bedroom to make herself look presentable. She says she hates the man, but she still wants to look her best in front of him.

I grab a sweater from the dining area and put it on before I open the door. Caroline can be a bit naïve sometimes or else she wouldn't think I'd be able to keep this door shut when Mateo is right outside. It's not like he'll dutifully stay put.

He might be acting patient with her, but he'll bring the thing down if she refuses to see him, and I kind of need my door.

"Aspen," he greets as soon as I open it, looking way better than his haggard state that day he nearly slashed my face.

"Mateo. Do come in, though I don't think you need the invitation."

"I actually do."

"Are you a vampire, after all?"

"No, just a well-mannered Italian around my wife's friends." He narrows his eyes and I narrow mine back before stepping aside.

"I'll get out of your hair for about thirty minutes. And, Mateo?"

"Yes?"

"Do us all a favor and either convince her you're innocent or just let her go. Either way, please stop using my space for your courting sessions."

"Noted." He nods once and enters as if he has every right to.

Shaking my head, I shove my feet into my nearest comfy shoes, grab my wallet, and step out.

I regret not wearing a thicker sweater or a coat as soon as the cold air licks my skin. But freezing is a better poison than witnessing Mateo and Callie's repetitive fights.

There's the option of asking his goons parked outside to get me the coat, but Mateo will probably throw them over the balcony if they interrupt his sacred wife time.

So I opt to walk at a brisk pace to generate more body heat. I pass by a boutique that's showcasing a beautiful dress with vanilla orchid motif and don't think twice before I go inside and buy it.

Then I ask the lady to wrap it and send it to Gwen's new address.

She'll be coming home soon, and while I want to give her the gift personally, I'd make it awkward and she'd be turned off by me. So a contactless gift is the best option I have while hoping she'll like it.

My lips pull in a smile at the remembrance of how she said hi.

My daughter told her asshole father to tell me hi. Not to exaggerate, but I didn't sleep at all that night. And fine, maybe some of that had to do with how I kept tingling due to a certain man's touch.

As much as I like to think I'm unaffected, my heart picks up speed whenever I recall the sensual way his lean fingers held my face or how his lips and tongue feasted on my cheeks. Why does he affect me so? Just...why?

I walk faster in a fruitless attempt to chase away thoughts of him and even try to focus on my surroundings. It's the best method to keep from getting stuck in my busy head.

That's when I notice I've stepped into a not-so-good neighborhood. Having lived in the ghetto my entire childhood, I recognize the stench of piss and vomit as a sign of poverty, drug overdoses, and bodies sold in the dark.

Oh, and a woman sleeping on stinking sheets with pills all around her.

Bad neighborhoods taste of bitter tears, expired food, and human waste.

Bad neighborhoods have a dangerous soul, a black heart, and the mercy of a tyrant god.

And even though I've done whatever it took to escape, I find myself back in this hellhole again. I wonder if I'll always gravitate toward the danger from my childhood the same way Caroline did.

Maybe, like her, I'll only find solace in a ruler of the underground who wouldn't be scared of bad neighborhoods.

I slowly remove that thought from my head and whirl around to leave.

A rustle sounds from behind me and before I can investigate it, a thud pierces the air. My eyes burn, and the next time I blink them open, I'm on my knees, head lolling to the side.

I don't try to look at my assailant or make sense of this situation. My shaky fingers find my wallet and I manage to grab my small pepper spray that's attached to my keychain and press it aimlessly behind me.

The moment I realize I've made a mistake, it's too late. I thought there was only one attacker, but a heavy boot slams into my chest, knocking me back with frightening ease.

My head hits a disgustingly warm surface—another person's

body—and stars form behind my eyes when a man punches me in the face.

His friend steps on my shoulder with his boot and I bite my tongue to keep from screaming.

The second punch comes, then the third, and by the time they finish, my mouth is flooding with a pungent metallic taste.

I don't realize they've disappeared until I hear heavy retreating footsteps. Still, I lie there, my head as heavy as a brick, and my limbs sprawled out in an unnatural position.

The need to dissolve into the ground is far greater than my will to live, but the thought that they could come back and rape me, or leave the job to someone else from the slums, gives me the energy I wouldn't have thought was possible.

I don't know how I manage to use the wall for balance, pull my sweater around me, and walk, but I do.

Pain explodes in my every joint, one of my eyes is too swollen to see with and my lips feel too big for my face.

I think something is fractured or bruised in my chest, too, because breathing is similar to hiking Everest with a broken leg.

Logically, I know I need to see a doctor, but I'd rather die than go to the hospital.

Yes, Gwen is alive, but I've been traumatized by hospitals ever since they placed a stillborn baby in my arms, and I haven't dealt with that trauma or any of the other traumas in my life.

I don't know how long I walk, but it's long enough that I lose feeling in my legs, get weird looks from dispassionate New Yorkers, and collapse against a wall a time or two—or a dozen.

Finally, I manage to catch a taxi and throw myself inside. The driver stares at me through the rearview mirror, his brown eyes appearing hazy and demon-like in the mirror. "Are you okay, miss? Should I take you to the hospital?"

"No...not the hospital..." I blurt my address incoherently, my lips barely moving, then I collapse against the faux leather seat.

I shake my head every now and again, fighting the black dots that spread across my vision and the lull of unconsciousness.

I just need to go home and pull myself together and then report this—

My chest clenches when the car stops and I lift my head but don't find the building I live in.

Instead, I'm staring into a toothy demon at the top of a large black metal gate that's fresh out of a gothic film.

Kingsley's mansion.

Damn it. What am I doing here?

"We're here, miss," the driver says, his voice sounding far away.

"This isn't my apartment…"

"This is the address you gave me. Do you want me to take you someplace else?" His eyes flicker in the rearview mirror, blurry and fresh out of a thriller movie.

"No, thank…you…" I shove a few bills in his hand and practically wrench myself out of the car.

He remains there, for a while, probably thinking I'm crazy. Or maybe he's one of them and they sent him to finish the job.

It takes all the strength I have to approach the gate, dragging my feet and gasping for air.

The taxi finally leaves, and I release a breath. Then my legs decide it's as good a time as any to abandon me.

I'm ready to slam against the ground, but I fall straight into warm arms.

"Aspen?"

His hard face stares down at me with a frown that's as dark as a demon lord.

And it shouldn't make me feel safe.

Or peaceful.

Or fucking right.

But it does.

My fingers dig into his arms and I swallow my own blood as I croak, "I…had nowhere else to go…"

I don't realize the gravity of my confession when the darkness finally whisks me away.

EIGHT

Kingsley

MY ATTEMPTS TO PREVENT MYSELF FROM BREACHING THE rage category are proving to be an astounding failure.

I pace the length of the room where Aspen lies on the bed like a broken beauty.

I've opened and closed my Zippo so many times and with zero gentleness that I'm surprised the thing doesn't break.

The light coming from the window forces me to stop and stare out at the garden and the multicolored leaves falling to their death.

Fuck. I've been at this the entire night.

Pacing, punching a wall—or two—and contemplating the best way to commit murder.

I shouldn't.

Because as my week-old thoughts stated, I don't fucking commit violence for women. There's only one reason for violence—release. For me, myself, and my dick.

And yet, there's always that error in the matrix. The exception to the rules. The fish in the Dead Sea.

It all happened when I came back from my evening jog, suppressing the need to commit arson on Susan's house, and saw Aspen hobbling by the front gate in a state that would give zombies a run for their money.

Since then, I haven't thought about my stepmother's ruin or her provocations in court yesterday about how weak my mother was.

She likes to remind me why I rejected the very idea of growing up into a replica of my mother.

Liliana Shaw was as delicate as her name, and while I was human enough to love my mother, I knew early on that she was the type to be protected, never the type to protect others.

She was the type to be treated with kid gloves, flower-scented like her favorite perfume.

And because fucking Susan's words ring a bell every damn time I see her, I usually put myself on self-exhaustion mode until I collapse by the end of the day.

It's not a secret that I become neurotic, high-functioning, and a special flavor of dick whenever I meet the plastic monster in court.

Couple that with a teenage-level sexual frustration, and by the time I got home, I wasn't to be approached by any human who valued their life, property, and dignity.

So imagine my surprise when the woman behind said frustration was playing an apocalypse survivor by my front gate.

The doctor, a family one who's always just a call away, showed up to examine her last night and said she was physically assaulted.

"No shit, Sherlock. I can see that," I told Dr. Werner, running a hand through my hair and being colossally irritable due to two facts.

One. Aspen was beaten.

Two. The doctor was touching her.

Maybe the family doctor needs to be a woman.

But even that option didn't sit very comfortably at the base of my revolted stomach.

"Was she sexually assaulted?" I asked, my chest squeezing for the first time since...Gwen fell from her bike and hit her knee when she was fucking ten.

"Nothing indicates that from the outside, but I can't tell for certain until she wakes up and gives me permission to examine her."

"At least take care of her injuries."

"Can you step out?"

"Why do you need me to step out for that? You'll do that while I'm here."

"Mr. Shaw, I understand your distress, but from what I've gathered, you're not next of kin to Ms. Leblanc and, therefore, shouldn't be present during any medical examinations."

"I've decided that I *will* be here. Now, do your job or I'll get you blacklisted from the city."

The threat was enough to propel him to action, which in turn made me burn hotter than the room's temperature. And while he confirmed the absence of serious injuries, I was still two seconds away from bashing his head against the nearest object and cutting off the gloved fingers he clinically examined her with.

There's no rhyme or reason to the raging possessiveness I feel toward this woman. A possessiveness that up to now, I've only held toward the wellbeing of my legacy, Gwen, and the need for Susan's inevitable destruction.

And the worst part? This feeling is completely different from all of the above, irrevocably illogical, and it burns like acid.

Dr. Werner left after I opted to dress her wounds myself and kicked him out. If he'd touched her one more time, he'd be floating in the pool as we speak. Besides, I've been constantly getting cut, bruised, and bloodied in one way or another since I was a teenager, so the task wasn't foreign.

I put ointment on Aspen's skin, covering the galaxy of bruises on her face and shoulder and a slight red mark on her upper chest. Not to mention the black eye that was the size of City Hall and just as grim.

That was ten hours ago.

Ten hours of pacing, then watching surveillance camera footage of her movements after I called in favors with detectives to track her from when she left her apartment.

I didn't miss that Mateo entered her building minutes before she went out dressed in casual clothes. Then she went into a boutique and came out empty-handed but with a girlish smile. The assault happened after she wandered into a non-surveilled alley, because five minutes later, she limped out, hugging a wall, and sporting a map of bruises.

The only suspicious thing I noticed was a black van with tinted windows that was caught by a ring door camera near that location. It kept away from the surveillance cameras like a pro, so it captured no license plate and definitely no faces.

It could have been Mateo's men, for all I know, but I already made sure they were still acting as their boss's watchdogs during the time that she was being beaten.

My gaze fixates on her form—sleeping, her brows knit, her skin marked in a grotesque way.

I know how her fair flesh looks when bitten, sucked on, and pleasurably sated. I remember putting all those marks and more on her twenty-one years ago and leaving a path with my teeth, tongue, and lips.

And although she kept that damn mask on, I recall the feeling, the possessiveness, and the illogical urge to do it all over again.

But that image and this one are as opposite as day and night. While Dr. Werner assured me the injuries are superficial and will heal, it still sits fucking wrong with me.

From the part of her being followed, to how she was beaten, and eventually, to how she ended up here.

That last tidbit fills me with an emotion that I vehemently refuse to put a name to.

A moan rips from her lips and it resembles a dying person's last plea for mercy.

This woman is stronger than the universe and its aliens, a fact that has always infuriated me yet fascinated me in equal measure, so to see her battered is weird.

Forget weird.

It's rage-inducing in a way that I've never experienced before.

She shifts in her sleep, blinks her non-swollen eye once…twice, and then she springs up into a sitting position, immediately staring down at her flimsy cotton dress.

I threw away the sweater—it was dirty, bloody and had a hole the shape of my fist in it.

The dress is bloody, too, but the chances of removing it and remaining sane were below zero. So I left it intact.

"Kingsley," she whispers, then winces, probably due to the double size of her lips and the cut.

"Morning, sunshine," I say with no warmth whatsoever, flipping my Zippo open. "Now that you're out of your Sleeping Beauty phase, mind telling me what, and I can't stress this enough, the *fuck* happened?"

"I…" She blinks the mucus that's gathered in her eyes, despite my attention to cleaning the shit out of those fuckers, then inspects her surroundings. "Wait…where am I?"

"In my house, previously known as Black Valley Manor before I sued the state to have the liberty of stripping the pretentious name and won, obviously. You showed up here with bruises the size of Texas, remember?"

She opens her swollen lips, closes them, and opens them again in a poor imitation of a goldfish. "I…didn't mean to come here."

With crab-like movements, she attempts to stand, winces, then falls back with the grace of a broken feather. But since she's more stubborn than an Italian-made leather shoe, she attempts to stand again.

This time, I push her back down with a firm yet gentle hand. "You're not in a position to sit, let alone stand, so unless you plan to bleed on my floor and personally scrub it, stay the fuck down."

"What a charmer." She sucks in a pained breath.

"Charming you is the last thing that I'm after, and I don't give jack shit whether you meant to come here or not. You did anyway, and you still didn't answer my question."

She looks at my hand that's casually resting on her shoulder. Again, not hard, so as not to hurt her, but it's firm enough to let her know there will be no escaping my hold.

"Do you mind?" she croaks.

"Not at all." I sit beside her without removing my hand and she releases a sound that resembles an injured animal's growl.

She doesn't put up a fight, though, probably in too much pain to care. She stares at the opposite wall, at paintings done by breaking black glass, because chaos is the only form of beauty I approve of. "I was attacked."

"I have enough deduction skills to figure that out on my own. Who, where, why, and how are the questions I'd like the answers to."

"I don't know." She swallows and winces.

"Where you sexually assaulted?"

"No."

"Are you sure?"

She glares at me with her one good eye. "What do you mean am I sure?"

"No need to get defensive. I'm only looking at it from all angles here to form a mental picture."

"What's there to form about no, I wasn't sexually assaulted?"

"The fact that you could've lost consciousness."

"I didn't. Drop it."

"Fine. Did you recognize who did it?"

"No. Could have been anyone."

"You have that many enemies, huh?"

She glares at me with her one good eye and it holds more punch than the seven billion pairs of them scattered around the earth. "You're one to know, considering your track record."

"Let's not go down the throwing jabs route, because I'll crush you easily and you're in no state to verbally spar with me until you lose your breath. Now, let's make our time useful and narrow it down to the known suspects. Who might have a beef with you lately, aside from me and your psycho father?"

Her eye widens and her lips tremble.

Fuck.

"It's your father?" I ask, adding a needless question mark.

"I...don't know."

"Oh, but you do know. It's obvious."

She avoids my gaze again, this time pulling the sheet over her face and knocking away my hand in the process. "Maybe it's you, asshole."

I slide the sheet down, resisting the urge to yank it and possibly hurt her in the process. If softness and I had a one-on-one meeting, I would drive her to wrap a rope around her fragile neck. But I still find myself trying not to cause Aspen more discomfort.

"I'm many things, but a woman-beater is not on the list. My battles with you are exclusively mental with no physical violence involved—unless they're sexual in nature, of course. Besides, if you really believed I hurt you, would you have come to me, of all people?"

"I meant to go to Nate," she mumbles under her breath and I nearly forget why I shouldn't be wrapping my fingers around her throat and choking the shit out of her.

"And yet, you're here because you had nowhere else to go, as you so eloquently told me, remember? Such a lonely little thing."

Her lips part, then close before she hisses, "Fuck you."

"Gladly. But we need to wait for the bruises to heal because this scene is oddly similar to a snuff movie and I'm not a fan."

"You'll be a fan of my tongue when it's healed enough to chew you out. Or my teeth when I bite your dick off, asshole."

I chuckle and that takes her aback since she stares at me as if I've grown a third red horn.

Fuck me.

Or her.

I don't care which at this point.

Well, at least she's back.

I reach to the bedside table and point at a bowl of oatmeal that's been kept in a heated container. I had my housekeeper, Martha, make it and three flavors of herbal tea for her.

"Eat this, then take the painkillers and rest. If you need anything, ask Martha and she'll get it for you."

"I don't eat breakfast. Besides, why are you talking as if I'm staying here? I'm going to work."

"You'll eat breakfast today, and there's no way in fuck you're going to the firm looking like a poor imitation of a zombie."

"But I have meetings!"

"That your assistant will reschedule."

"But…"

"That's final, Aspen. No work in your state. Don't be a baby."

"I'm not a baby."

"You're throwing a tantrum like one."

"I just want to do my job!"

"And as your boss, I'm putting you on a vacation. Mandatory, not optional."

And with that, I leave the room, her frustrated groan the last thing I hear before I close the door. I remain there for a few minutes, then I steal a peek inside. The stubborn little shit loses the battle and falls back to sleep.

Martha, a kind middle-aged woman with a plump figure, who helped me raise Gwen, hands me my briefcase. "Any special instructions?"

"Give her food, some of Gwen's clothes, and assist her in showering if she needs to. She's prideful and won't ask for help, so offer it instead. Don't let her out under any circumstances. You're allowed to use any methods necessary to ensure that—locking her inside is one of them."

She nods and points at a phone that's dancing on the table. "That one has been vibrating for a few hours."

Aspen's.

I tossed it and her wallet somewhere in the entrance when I carried her inside and haven't checked it since. Correction. I haven't left her side since, except when Martha came along and I took a quick shower and changed my clothes.

Grabbing the surprisingly intact phone, I find the name "My Ride or Die" surrounded by ten hearts, flashing on the screen.

No kidding. Fucking ten sparkly red hearts.

Logically, I know Aspen isn't the heart type of person and

would rather be eaten by a shark than be affectionate. It's one of the few traits we have in common.

Illogically, however, the thought that she has a man in her life who's the exception to her no-emotions rule burns in my veins like cheap whiskey.

I answer it, fully intending to wield my dick card in a glamorous swing.

The shrill voice that greets me from the other end puts a not-so-glamorous halt to my plan. "Aspennnn! Where have you been? I've been calling you for hours and seriously contemplated going to the police and shit. And that would be for two different reasons. Your disappearance and Mateo's one thousand percent chances of committing mass murder. He knows about the jerk Della Roma hitting me, and his battery charges will look like a joke in front of his 'I'll murder him and his entire family' charges. I tried stopping him and keeping him with me, but he left first thing this morning while I was asleep."

"You should've tried harder then. Now, I have to clean up your mess."

There's a long pause on the other end before who I'm sure is Caroline Luciano whispers, "Kingsley?"

"The one and only."

"Hi! I'm Caroline."

"No shit. I assume you're the one with enough audacity to save her name as My Ride or Die with a disgusting amount of hearts."

"Shhh. Don't tell Aspen." Her humor disappears. "Wait, she didn't change it back? Where is she and what have you done to her?"

"She's hurt and asleep. Don't bother her until tomorrow."

"What—"

I hang up before she can finish her sentence and head out with plans for my favorite dish.

Revenge.

NINE

Aspen

Age fourteen

"AND NOW WHAT?" I CROSS MY ARMS OVER MY CHEST, pretending I'm not in fact barely trying to toe the line. At this point, there's no doubt that alcohol is probably flowing in my system instead of blood.

The cold air bites my skin with the consistency of a venomous snake, but I keep my lips shut to prevent my teeth from chattering.

Any semblance of warmth is provided by a hand that's crushing mine. Anonymous's strong fingers have been holding my own hostage for the past half an hour after he led me out of the house.

When I tried to protest, he said either I go along with this holding-hand thing or I could resume my previous position on his shoulder.

This asshole has an infuriating way of giving stupid choices that aren't really choices in the first place.

We're now walking down the streets that are filled with blinding lights and a horde of people.

I've never liked the nice side of town. So even when Callie comes here any chance she gets, I avoid it with everything in me.

The nice side of town smells of dollar bills, expensive perfumes, and a luxury we're not allowed to breathe near. So until I make my own way to this place, I'd rather not be here.

Anonymous stares ahead, but he doesn't seem absorbed in the festivities, the joy, or the endless people in costumes of different colors and shapes. If anything, he appears bored by it all. However, he still stands out in the middle of it, and that has little to do with his mask and more to do with his whole aura.

His black slacks and T-shirt stretch across his muscles, hinting at some sort of physical discipline. Which makes sense, considering the way he knocked someone out earlier. But there's more perfection than his physical superiority. It's his presence, his edge, and his well-spoken manner.

He'll probably grow up to be a man of power, like the people my father works for.

Maybe he'll be so much worse.

And yet, I can't help being trapped in his orbit with no chances of ever wrenching myself out of this trance.

I've never felt so drawn to a person before, so caught up in someone that I want to hear their voice and stay in their presence for as long as possible.

"And now what?" I ask.

"Now, we walk, femme fatale."

"Can't we do that without holding hands?"

"No, because you'll run away."

"This is called kidnapping."

He tilts his head in my direction and for the dozenth time tonight, I wish I could take that mask off and see what's truly beneath it. Is he really a monster?

"With all these people around?"

"The presence of people or the lack thereof doesn't deny the kidnapping."

He lifts a shoulder, his voice completely neutral. "I'm kidnapping you, then."

My heart squeezes and my lips fall open. Is he for real? I mentioned kidnapping so it'd rattle him a little and he'd think that the hassle this situation presents isn't worth it. I thought there was at least an eighty percent chance he'd let me go, but he completely ignored that risk factor.

"You really don't care that I would report you to the police?"

"You have no evidence or facial description. Your report will sit on the incompetent police's desk for days, months, and then will be thrown into the archives."

I dig my nails into his hand and attempt to scratch the skin.

He *tsks*, voice dripping with amusement. "Do you watch CSI a lot?"

"What? Why?"

"I assume the show is behind your attempts to get some DNA off me. I advise you to drop it, though. Not only will you complicate things for yourself, but your parents might pay the price for dragging me through the mud. See, my father takes offense when the family name is touched, and he has dangerous friends."

I don't release my hold on his hand. In fact it, I dig my nails in deeper. "I don't have parents."

His pace slows and I suddenly become the sole subject of his previously scattered attention. The shift is subtle, but it's so intense that I swallow.

"My, my. You keep getting more interesting. Why do you not have parents, femme fatale?"

"That's none of your business."

"Maybe I want it to become my business."

"Why?" I meet the gleaming color of his eyes. They're definitely light gray or dark blue—or a mixture of both. "Why would you want to know about me?"

"Because you interest me. Which, by the way, is an emotion hardly stirred within me."

"Should I be honored?"

"Yes. You should also answer my question."

"If I do, will you let me go?"

"I would say yes, but that would be a lie and I'm sure you don't prefer that option. We should adopt an honesty policy."

"Honesty is just an illusion invented by people to allow them to manipulate others."

"You're too smart."

"For a girl or for my own good?"

"You're too smart for your age. But that's a good thing. If you use your brain the right way, you'll go places."

I pause, my nails subconsciously easing off his hand. That's the first time someone has praised my brain without sounding condescending or full of pity. Even my teacher said being too smart is not a good thing for a woman on our side of the ghetto.

Aunt Sharon said it'll get me killed.

And yet, this stranger, a boy in nothing more than a mask, said the words I've been longing to hear from someone.

Anyone.

As long as they believe in me. As long as someone out there wants to see past my origins and into my actual soul.

But then again, he doesn't know where I come from, so maybe he'll change his mind once he figures out my zip code.

"And how do you know that?" I ask, feeling a bit sober all of a sudden.

"I just do. Now, for that honesty policy. Care to take part in it?"

"Offer me something first."

"Like?"

"Why did you take me—or, more accurately, *kidnap* me?"

"You heard a detail you shouldn't have been privy to."

"If you were so concerned about the arson or whatever your friends were plotting, you would've ratted me out or stayed to take part in the action. You definitely wouldn't have chosen to promenade me like in some medieval time."

His chuckle echoes in the air like the most haunting piece

of music. And the worst part is that I can't stop being drawn to it. I can't stop staring at him and his height and broad shoulders.

"True on all accounts. The reason I took you, or *kidnapped* you as you prefer to label it, is as I previously mentioned, I'm bored and you're interesting. In a nerdy kind of way, which is unusual for me. I only like girls' bodies and have zero interest in their minds."

"You're a misogynistic pig."

"And you're a fan of labels. But I like your sense of intuition. It's a fucking turn-on."

My stomach cramps and I don't understand the emotions that slash through it at the same time or how my temperature rises despite the cold.

He stops and my eyes widen when I expect him to do something. Instead, he picks a wide wool scarf from a vendor on the street, throws the man who sells them a one-hundred-dollar bill, then releases my hand to wrap the scarf around my neck and arms.

I stare up at him, dumbfounded.

"You might want to stop looking at me as if I'm the holy messiah. There's nothing remotely sin-free about me."

"Why did you buy me this?"

"Because judging by your chattering teeth and trembling limbs, you're cold. This happens to be an easy fix."

"I don't want to owe you."

"You don't. Consider it compensation for kidnapping you." His voice becomes amused at the last part.

And I can't help the feeling of internal and external warmth that floods me.

He interlinks our fingers again and continues walking. We remain silent for a while, and I find myself too focused on his touch, his warmth, his fingers that stroke mine, then stop and start again in a chaotic yet soothing rhythm.

I pull the scarf tighter around me to hide my creepy attempt to breathe more of him in. It's the first time I've found male cologne so…enticing.

"Aren't you forgetting something?" he asks after a while, his head tilting to the side.

"Forgetting what?"

"I offered you a truth. Now, it's your turn. Care to share?"

"There's nothing to share. My mother died and my father is as good as dead."

"As good as dead," he repeats slowly. "I imagined that type would be common, but not this common."

"You're familiar with the experience?"

"If you mean having a useless father who would've been better off dead, then yes, I'm extremely familiar." He strokes the back of my hand, but the gesture isn't affectionate; however, it's not threatening either.

It's a mixture of both. The gray that slashes through the black and white.

The calm that precedes and comes after a storm.

Said storm manifests in his eyes as they pin me down through the mask. "Seems you and I have more in common than I initially thought. Maybe that's why you stood out to me in the first place."

"Is that a good thing or a bad thing?"

"If you're lucky, neither. If not, both."

"And how do I know whether or not I'm lucky?"

"You'll know when it's time."

"Why can't it be now?"

"There's no excitement in knowing when the goal is going to score. Predictability is boring."

"Not always." I stare at him, once again trapped in the way his height and build nearly fill out the horizon. "And don't tell me you're a jock?"

"What makes you think that?"

"Your analogy about goals."

"Anyone could use that analogy. It's not a privilege that's exclusive to jocks."

"Well, are you?"

"What if I am?"

"I would be surprised. You…seem well-read."

"And all jocks are supposed to be fucking idiots? You know, those same stereotypes paint redheads as witches that should be burned at the stake."

"I…didn't mean it that way. It's just that all the jocks I know are arrogant assholes."

"And I'm the exception?"

"No, you're the king of the crowd. Why did you become a jock when you seem well off?" The jocks from our school are chasing the NFL dream to switch social classes.

"To control the bursts of adrenaline."

My steps falter, partly because of his answer. Partly due to his tightening hold on my hand. "Why do you need to control it?"

"Some of us are wired differently and have an abundance of that stuff, so we search for coping mechanisms to control it." He motions ahead. "We're here."

I lift my head and realize that we've not only strayed away from the main street, but there are also no people, bright lights, or indistinct chatter.

In short, all the elements I used for some fake sense of protection.

The only thing that exists in front of me is a dark dirt road surrounded by tall bushes with no end in sight.

"What is this place?" I try and fail to prevent my voice from shaking.

"Privacy."

"And who told you I want privacy?"

"You might not, but I do."

"You promised we'd stay in a public place."

"Never promised anything, I said I would grant you that option, and I did for the past hour or so."

"Is that your way of making me lower my guard?"

"Could be. Is it working?"

My lips purse and moisture stings my eyes, and I hate this feeling of utter helplessness. I can't believe I was lured by him. Not that I had any chance of pushing away his advances, but at some point, I thought maybe he cared.

Turns out, I'm the only one in that boat. Everything that led to this moment was probably calculated to have me fall for his charms.

And I did. With embarrassing ease.

"What will happen now?" I spit out to hide the pain. "If I say no, will you finish your friend's job and force me?"

"Force you? No. Force you to admit you want this as much as I do? Yes."

"And how will you do that?"

"I'm going to do something, and depending on your reaction, I'll either keep you or let you go."

I don't get a chance to say anything, because he tugs on my hand that's in his and brings me flush against his chest.

My heartbeat roars and I'm sure he can hear the frantic thumps against his rib cage. But any attempts to regulate it vanish in the cold air when he slowly lifts his mask.

I can't breathe.

And it has everything to do with what I'm seeing.

He only revealed his square jaw and sensual lips, but it's enough to make me yearn for more.

More of him.

Of this.

His eyes shine in the darkness from behind the mask as he dives straight to my lips, capturing them with a harshness that knocks the living breath out of my lungs.

My chest and stomach explode in a myriad of emotions as he thrusts his tongue inside and unapologetically feasts on mine.

Then two of his fingers clutch my chin, tilting it up to get more access. To devour me like an animal would.

Until I have no choice but to melt against him.

Logically, I should fight.

Logically, I should try to run.

But logic doesn't exist on Devil's Night.

Logic is the last thing on my mind as I let him ravage me with an intensity I've never experienced before.

Maybe I'll never experience it again.

And I know, I just know that he probably won't let me go.

And maybe I don't want him to let me go either.

My thoughts are reinforced when he releases my lips, and whispers against them, "I decided to keep you, after all."

TEN

Kingsley

I ROLL MY SLEEVES UP TO MY ELBOWS WHILE I APPROACH THE two unconscious scums hanging from the ceiling by their wrists.

"Are you sure you want your hands dirtied, rich boy?" Nicolo taunts from his position in the corner, lighting a cigar and crossing his legs at the ankles.

"Fuck off, Nic. This has nothing to do with you." I reach for the water hose and spin the handle to the highest pressure.

"On the contrary, this has everything to do with me, considering my boys were able to find you these two."

"Which you've already been compensated for with money your companies don't deserve." I tilt my head to the side. "You're not doing me a favor. This is a business transaction."

"Shouldn't you be a bit more grateful? Not only am I letting you use my basement for your small fetish, but I'm also going against Bruno by catching these two in the span of..." He stares at his Rolex. "Twenty hours."

Right after I watched that footage at the end of which Aspen came out with a bloodied face, I forwarded it to Nicolo and told him to find them. Of course, he's a cat who never hunts without a purpose, so his condition was obviously more money for his company.

I didn't even pretend to manipulate him into reducing the amount. Any negotiation on my part would've propelled him to perform a sloppy job. A slow job.

So I gave him the exact amount he asked for. Thus, the quick result.

I spent the whole day in court, defending a mentally ill man who murdered his own parents in cold blood twenty years after they physically and emotionally abused him.

And I enjoyed every second of getting him the 'not guilty' verdict and rubbing it in the prosecutor's face. That tool stood no chance, because I take abuse by parents seriously, personally, and handle it mercilessly. The media can call me a savage devil all they like, but just because these people gave someone life, I don't consider them above reproach. Many of them are flawed humans who should have been made infertile, and if they need to die for their sins, so be it.

That's why I barely felt any sense of loss when Benjamin Shaw passed away. That old man finally met his end with a heart attack while he was in his extravagant Jacuzzi. He drowned just like my mother did. Irony is the pettiest bitch that way.

But even with the endorphins I got in court, I couldn't chase away the needle-like sensation that pricked at the back of my head or the tightening in my chest at the thought of who I left back in my house.

I called Martha twice during the only recesses I got, and apparently, Aspen spent most of the day sleeping. I contemplated sending Dr. Werner to check on her again, but the thought of him touching her while I wasn't there quickly erased the blasphemous thought.

She's probably recuperating all the lost hours of sleep deprivation. It's no secret that she spends all-nighters at the office more often than not and has an incurable workaholic soul.

The only reason I haven't gone back home to check on her

myself is the phone call I got from Nicolo announcing that he'd found the owners of that unidentified car. He could have been lying, of course, and picked up two random men, but the quick background check he did on them indicated they were thugs who'd spent time in the same prison as Bruno.

Ignoring Nicolo's presence and words, I direct the hose at one of the men, who has a blond beard and the build of a wrestler, and turn it to wide open. He gasps awake, his eyes unfocused, and guttural breaths leave his parted mouth. I give him a break to wake his leaner friend with a nose and lips that are too big for his bland face.

He rouses with a start, jolting in his binds like an animal taken for slaughter.

"What the...what the fuck?" blond beard drawls, still dazed.

"You put your filthy hands on someone you're not supposed to touch, that's what the fuck." I raise my fist and punch him so hard, the crunching of bones echoes in the air as he reels back in his bindings.

I do it again and again until the sound of breaking bones is the only thing I hear and the metallic stench of blood lingers in the air. The red splatters on my shirt, arms, and face, but I don't stop.

Don't take a break.

And I definitely show no mercy.

I've always loved violence, but this is the first time I've revered it.

Fuck the law. Sometimes justice can only be achieved with old-fashioned eye for an eye.

Specifically his eye that I punch over and over until capillaries explode in it, but no matter how much I hit it, there's no erasing the image of Aspen's swollen eye or how she could barely open it this morning.

The fucker faints on me somewhere in the middle of my adrenaline-induced fun. So I turn to his friend who's been watching the show while trembling.

"Hey...hey...we can talk about this." His friend swallows,

smelling of revolting sweat mixed with cheap cologne and pure fear.

I drive my fist into his face, making him choke on his own spit. "That's the thing. I have nothing to talk about."

"Please." He coughs. "Surely you got us here for information, right? I can tell you anything you want if you spare me."

My breathing is harsh but collected, like a predator in the middle of a hunt. I don't need information from this fucker since I know Bruno sent him. I already asked Nicolo to get to Bruno while he's still in jail, but apparently, the bastard is more untouchable than a god within Attica's walls.

"How much did Bruno pay you to follow and assault his daughter?" I ask the scum.

He pales under the fluorescent light, his thin lips shaking. "I don't...that's not..."

I deliver an uppercut that makes blood explode in his nose. "I thought you'd tell me anything. But if you're ready for your death, never mind."

"No...wait... Bruno doesn't pay. He...gave us protection when we served time and demanded compensation when we got out. That's all, I swear. We didn't even know she was his daughter. He only gave us a picture and a name and told us to teach her a lesson."

A lesson.

My blood roars in my ears.

Their lesson could've been rape, and yet, the old man didn't even care to prevent that.

I slam my fist against his jaw and the fucker wails like a baby.

"You said you'd spare me," he cries.

"No, I didn't." I pull him by his shirt and breathe against his blood-and-sweat-stained face. "Here's how it will go, motherfucker. I'll punch you until you lose consciousness like your friend here, then I'll waterboard you to consciousness and do it all over again. I'll torture you for every mark you left on her skin. By the time I'm done with your sorry excuse of an existence, you'll wish for death."

And then I do as I promised until my knuckles, hands, and arms are bloodied and the lowlifes hanging on to life by a thread.

The problem is, it still doesn't feel like enough.

"You know, I have tools that can be used instead of your fists. What are you, a caveman?" Nicolo, who's been watching from the corner with a gleam in his sadistic eyes, joins me. His expensive woodsy cologne stands out amidst the piss, blood, and sweat.

Even I have started to smell like the scums. If Aspen were here, she'd tell me her favorite quote.

If you gaze long into the abyss, the abyss also gazes into you.

Maybe my rich boy status, as Nicolo likes to point out, is a mere camouflage of the monster I was always meant to be.

Normal people would feel a smidgen of remorse or a pang of guilt for not feeling guilty. Me, on the other hand?

The only thing I feel as I stare at their unconscious, barely breathing forms is the need for more.

I watch the blood dripping from their faces and my fists like a serial killer would. "Tools don't give the same satisfaction as my bare hands."

Nicolo's laughter echoes in the space with the evilness of a super villain. "Are you sure she's still not your woman? Because at this point, you're doing more for her than a man would do for his wife, honor, and power."

I don't like the sound of that.

In fact, I don't like it at all, to the point that I decide to call it quits.

Leaving Nicolo behind, I grab my briefcase and jacket from a nearby chair and don't feel anything as I smudge the tailored cloth with blood. But I make a note to buy a change of clothes on my way home.

"What do you want me to do with these two?"

I look at him over my shoulder. "What you do best, Nicolo."

He doesn't need me to elaborate. His sadistic smirk is the last thing I see as I close the door behind me.

ELEVEN

Aspen

WE'LL MEET AGAIN, MY RED DAHLIA.

I wake up with a gasp for nonexistent air. Moisture gathers in my eyes and my heart nearly spills out on the ground.

For a second, I'm disoriented as to where I am. But the memories soon trickle back in, steady and horrendous in their accuracy. I can almost hear the *thwack* and the sound of my suppressed screams of pain.

My head whips around and I wince at the sudden movement.

I slowly slide out of bed, expecting Kingsley's shadow to appear out of nowhere and dunk me back onto the mattress.

I release a broken breath when that doesn't happen.

Only that asshole would take care of a hurt person while flashing his dick diploma from "Bastard School."

And yet…I stare down at my dirty dress and the bruises on my arm and shoulder, at the map of destruction all over my body. And the most prominent feeling that overwhelms me is gratefulness.

If it weren't for him, I would've passed out in some unknown corner and had a worse fate than being beaten to a pulp.

I carefully get out of the room, trying and failing not to be impressed by the mansion.

This place has a soul that can be felt from a mile away. Like an old gothic cathedral that was used to hide skeletons.

It's the first time I've been within its walls. During Gwen's wedding, the garden was all I saw of this imposing building.

Previously known as Black Valley Manor, this place has a presence as grim as its current owner, but it has its charms, too.

The ornate antique pillars belong to some architectural museum and the marble flooring mirrors a sophisticated taste. There's so much space, hallways, and intricately decorated sitting areas that it's easy to get lost within its walls.

There's an air of sinister intent in the house's soul. Again, a replica of its owner.

According to his very public trials about the mansion's ownership, Kingsley has a sentimental attachment to this place. So when his father died and his wife, Susan, inherited it, Kingsley went berserk. The fact that he inherited almost everything else—billions worth of portfolios and a higher tax bracket included—meant zilch to him.

He's the type of crazy to prove his father was senile in his last years, render his will null and void, and then revert to the most recent will before that, in which he has ownership of this mansion. After all, he was born here and should inherit it as the tenth generation of the Shaw clan.

The press painted him as a "Savage Devil" and threw in standard sexist misogynistic traits because he evicted a woman from the house she'd lived in for most of her life.

And while all those adjectives apply to the asshole for other reasons, it's not the case when it comes to Susan.

I met her a few times when she showed up to flex her nonexistent muscles at the firm, and they were unfortunate events that I would rather never witness again.

If Kingsley hadn't graduated from jerk school, I would've felt sorry for him. But then again, birds of a feather flock together. So maybe he and his stepmother share a fitting fate.

Nate never saw the charm in this house, but I do. Part of it has to do with the fact that my daughter has lived here for so many years.

My feet come to halt in front of a huge painting of demons eating angels. The details are so striking, it's hauntingly intimidating.

All the demons have repulsive faces, horns, and blood on their hands, and all the angels scream in agony as they're devoured alive.

I'm pretty sure there's a version of this where the angels slay the demons, but why am I not surprised that Kingsley would prefer this scene instead?

Hell, even the outside gate has a demon sitting on top.

"This was the last painting Mrs. Shaw purchased."

I startle but hide my reaction when a short woman with generous curves stops beside me. Her brown hair is pulled into a conservative bun and she's wearing a classic maid outfit that makes her appear refined.

"Hello. My name is Martha and I'm the only housekeeper Mr. Shaw keeps around."

"I'm…Aspen." I pause when pain bursts in my shoulder, reminding me of the assault.

"I know," she says with a warm smile.

"You said Mrs. Shaw—as in, which one?" I motion at the painting, reverting the conversation back to it.

"Mrs. Liliana Shaw. The only one to be called Mrs. Shaw in this place. The other one is just Susan." She pauses. "Or any other colorful names Mr. Shaw calls her."

I snort. Of course, he has colorful names for everyone.

Martha, however, seems oblivious to my reaction as she continues staring at the demons. "As soon as she moved here, Susan attempted to vandalize the painting. So Mr. Kingsley Shaw hid it in Mr. Nathaniel Weaver's house, then took it with him when he moved out of here at eighteen. He brought it back with him when he returned five years ago."

"It must hold a lot of value for him if he went to those lengths for it." But then again, it makes sense for a demon to protect those of his own kind. For hell's greater good and all that.

"While that might be true, it's a message more than anything else. The painting and Mrs. Liliana's memory are here to stay. Susan is merely an unfortunate stop in Black Valley Manor's history." Martha smiles. "Or so Mr. Shaw says."

She appears too happy about it. Something tells me Martha is the type of maid who has a fierce loyalty to Liliana and, therefore, to Kingsley as an extension. I wouldn't be surprised if she spied for him when Susan was the lady of the house. Which would make sense that he would approve of her when he approves of no one.

Martha faces me. "Would you like to have a shower? I've prepared a change of clothes in the guest bathroom."

"Uh, no. I better go home and get to work."

Because fuck Kingsley. He doesn't want me to show my face at the firm, fine, but I can at least work from home.

"It's the afternoon, miss." Martha motions at the glass doors, and sure enough, the sun is about to make its descent.

Holy shit.

Did I sleep a whole night and a day? That hasn't happened in…forever. I'm the five hours of sleep type of person. Anything more and it should be reported to the weird police.

"It'd be better to take that shower." Martha gently pushes me toward the bathroom, not taking my reluctance into account. "I'll help you."

"No, I can do it myself."

She shakes her head, lips curving in a smile. "He mentioned you'd say that."

I narrow my eyes. "Say what?"

"That you won't accept help. I'll be right outside if you need anything." With a nod, she steps out and closes the door behind her, leaving me with cloudy thoughts that I refuse to put a name to.

Like how the hell does he know me so well when he's detached from everything and everyone?

Taking a shower proves to be harder than pulling teeth. But I go through it, hissing and whimpering every time a cut burns. No matter how hard it gets, I don't call for Martha.

I refuse to be babied or treated like a delicate flower.

As a result, I finish about forty minutes later, feeling less refreshed and more like a soldier out of war.

I'm glad the clothes she gave me are a dress and some cotton undies. Surprisingly, they fit. The dress is white and loose with a fashionable cut in the collar and barely reaches the middle of my thighs. Definitely too short for my preferred length.

The scent of vanilla envelops me as soon as I put them on, and I step out of the bathroom without bothering to dry my hair.

Martha stands there with her hands clasped above each other.

"Are these...Gwen's?"

"Yes. I'm sure she wouldn't mind."

My heart squeezes, and even though I have to tug on the dress to make it cover more than my butt, I don't consider removing it.

It might sound creepy, but I want to smell her close, even if it's like this.

All of a sudden, I miss her so much.

Or maybe it's not sudden at all. Even when I thought she'd died, I still missed her with every fiber of my being.

In the nightmare I had a while ago, my father was coming to kill me and all I could think about was that I'd abandon her again.

I mean, yes, she's older now, married, and probably doesn't need a mother, but I need her.

I always have.

The memory of her is what's kept me going for decades. Ever since I ran away from home and carved my own path like a rolling stone.

"Would you like to see her room?" Martha asks.

"You mean Gwen's?"

"Yes. She took almost everything she considers valuable, but there are a few of her belongings around if you want to look around."

"I would love that."

Though I hate to have Kingsley fire the woman for it, I wouldn't miss the chance to take a tour in the place my daughter called home.

Martha delivers a speech that's worthy of a real estate mogul as she shows me around first. She breezes past Kingsley's room and office, though. Not even bothering to open their doors.

Then she motions at Gwen's room. "You can stay here as long as you like. I have to prepare dinner."

I thank her and she nods, going about her chores.

My greedy eyes take in the princess-like decor. The lace comforter on the bed, the muslin curtain that surrounds it. The wallpaper with vanilla orchids, no surprise there.

In fact, her entire room is vanilla-themed, from the carpet to the doors of her walk-in closet, even the desk and the multi-colored pens.

She's definitely more girly than I've ever been—not sure who she takes after. Not me or her father, that's for sure.

Probably Caroline. She rubbed her stupid fluffy energy on me before I even found out I was pregnant.

I sit on the bed, running my hand over the sheet, then I spot a framed picture on her bedside table.

It was taken on her high school graduation day, judging by the clothes and the hat.

Kingsley is holding her up by the waist in the air as if she's flying and Gwen is laughing uncontrollably.

They look at each other with so much love that it cuts me in two. At that point, I'd already met her and categorized her as the asshole's daughter.

It never occurred to me that she was my daughter, too, and that I was missing a moment of her life that I'd never get back.

I run my fingers over her face, feeling the bitter emotions gathering in my eyes.

Accidentally, I touch Kingsley's face and it startles me. Not the contact itself, or how illegally attractive he is, but the fact that right now, I can't hate him.

If it weren't for him, Gwen wouldn't have grown into the fine young lady she is. It takes a man of stone to raise a baby all on his own from the time he was seventeen.

You're not supposed to idolize someone you hate, bitch. I hear Caroline's voice in my head and put the frame back where I found it.

I can't resist opening the drawer. Inside it, there are sleeping buds, a collection of them, more vanilla-colored things, and an album.

Excitement courses through me as I pull it out. From the moment I open it, it feels as if I'm transported down memory lane.

It's filled with pictures of toddler Gwen, her birthdays, her first tooth. Her first steps. First day at school. All of them are documented with Post-it Notes at the top in Kingsley's surprisingly neat handwriting.

He's in almost all the pictures, either carrying her, cheering her on, or laughing with her at the camera. It hits me then that he's only ever carefree when around his daughter. It's like she's the only person allowed within his walls.

Hell, I didn't even know this side of him existed until I saw him laughing out loud when she brought lunch to his office a few years back.

I remember being struck by the view, his laughter, his joy, and how the rareness rivaled an eclipse.

Through the album, I can clearly see that he has a version he shows the world and a version that's exclusively for her.

And I don't know why bitter emotions keep mounting in me. Probably because I missed the most important parts of Gwen's life while he's been there during all of them.

I continue flipping, going through the phases of her life like it's a movie.

Even Nate is present in some of the pictures, mostly her birthdays, as solemn-faced as ever.

The green-eyed monster rears his head inside me and I couldn't chase away the pain even if I wanted to.

But I go through the whole album. Twice. On the third run-through, I find myself pausing on certain pictures.

Like Gwen's fifteenth birthday. She's smiling, but it appears more forced than the government's wars. Her eyes appear a bit puffy, her expression mechanical.

I cried on my birthdays because they reminded me of my mother who abandoned me on them.

Her words from when she first found out I was her mother, which coincidentally happened to be the same day I found out, rush back to me.

"I'm so sorry, baby," I whisper to her picture.

"Shouldn't you be more sorry for breaching someone's privacy?"

My head snaps up and I grunt when pain explodes in my shoulder. Then I wipe the moisture that's gathered in my eyes because showing even a hint of weakness in front of a predator is a sure way to have them attack. Ruthlessly.

And Kingsley is the worst predator I've come across. Right up there with my father.

The fact that he took care of me doesn't fool me. It could be a mere sham to hurt me later.

He stands in the entryway, clad in his usual black suit that shouldn't look this good on him.

Kingsley has always been physical perfection and it's not only because of his face, piercing eyes, or well-honed body.

It's the charisma that comes with it. The silence that harbors storms as deep as the color in his eyes.

A few cuts decorate the backs of his hands, and my curiosity gets the better of me. I know he fights with Nate as a hobby, but he's not around, so how did he get those?

Don't they bandage their hands before any fight? Also, I'm pretty sure that isn't the same suit he was wearing this morning.

It's still black, but the cut is different. Not that I'm focused on his clothes or anything.

I still can't help the nagging feeling of wondering where he could've been that he had to change suits.

He's casually leaning against the frame with his legs crossed at the ankle as if he's been there for a while, watching, biding his time as all predators do.

Unlucky for him, I'm no prey.

"I breached no one's privacy." I'm surprised at my cool tone as I calmly place the album back in the drawer. "You willingly brought me inside your house and forgot to post rules about freedom of movement where I can see them."

"You must be better if your tongue is back to its favorite hobby of talking back."

Actually, my tongue is sore and hurts like a mother, but that doesn't mean I'll go down without a fight.

I stand up, holding my head up with effort. "Sorry to ruin your twisted fantasies of seeing me on my knees. Better luck next time."

He pushes off the door frame and reaches me in a few determined strides. The force behind them knocks the living breath out of my lungs, but not more than when his chest nearly grazes mine.

The distance that separates us is merely a hair's breadth, and even that is crowded with the smell of cedarwood mixed with the potent scent of his masculinity.

All my attempts to breathe properly splash on the floor and shrivel to a slow death when he grabs my chin with his thumb and forefinger, slowly tilting it up until he has my full attention and then some.

His other hand lands on my waist, controlling and so possessive that I can barely feel the fabric separating us.

"As I insinuated this morning and you refused to accept in your pretty head, seeing you physically beaten brings me no sense of victory whatsoever. The only position where you'd look good on your knees is when you're choking on my cock, sweetheart."

My lips part and it has nothing to do with how swollen they

feel. I scramble for a scathing reply and come up embarrassingly empty-handed.

"If your tongue is healed, we can start right away."

"In your dreams, asshole."

"In my dreams, you're taking my cock up your ass like a pro."

"Good thing it's a dream, because it won't be happening in this lifetime. And for the record, you're a damn pervert."

"The number of fucks I have to give about your opinion of me is in the negative."

"And yet, you still want a piece of me."

"Not a piece. *Pieces.*" His voice drops and so does his hand—from my waist to my hip and then to my ass.

I yelp when he squeezes the flesh, pulling me straight into his chest. The pain that explodes in my body has no bearing whatsoever on my reaction.

Logically, I should be appalled to my bones, but that's shamelessly absent. Instead, my heart starts a war as if intending to jump straight between us.

My thighs shake against his and I'm sure he feels how much of an effect he has on me.

Something I don't like.

The weakness. The being at someone else's mercy.

The only sex I take part in is when I'm riding. Never when I'm dominated.

Not after that first time, at least.

It scared the shit of me, the power he had and continued to have on me when he was nothing more than an Anonymous mask. Now that he has a face, an illegally gorgeous one at that, it's even more dangerous.

So I slam a palm on his shoulder, trying, and failing, to push him away.

"Kingsley," I attempt to warn, but my voice is too soft, even to my own ears.

"The way you say my name is nothing short of a 'come and fuck me' invitation."

"Fuck you."

"I'll get to that in a bit, but first…" He kneads the flesh of my ass and audaciously rubs his massive erection against my lower stomach.

I want to remain unaffected, to curse him to a special nook in hell, but I'm crumbling.

My core is clenching, and even the pain in my face and shoulder pales in comparison to the wild desire spreading through me.

But why?

Just why am I inexplicably turned on by his touch?

Please let this be a twisted case of gratitude and not something entirely different and disastrous.

As if sensing my inner turbulence, Kingsley tilts my head further back to stare into my eyes with his savage ones. "Remember that challenge?"

"What challenge?" I'm thankful that I'm able to regain some of my composure, considering the circumstances.

"The one where you avoided me after for a week because you were scared to give in to what we both want."

"I don't want you."

"Are you telling me that if I reach under this dress, I won't find your cunt swollen and wet and ready to be pounded into?"

"No." The word is so quiet, I'm surprised he hears it.

A devilish grin splits his face. "Let's test that then."

Before I can object, the world is pulled from beneath my feet.

TWELVE

Aspen

THIS IS THE SECOND TIME IN MY LIFE THAT I'VE BEEN carried. Or more accurately, the third, since he probably carried me into the house last night.

Ironically, the first time was also by him.

Kingsley.

Aka the most infuriating man to have ever walked the earth. The most attractive, too.

Only, I'm not over his shoulder like all those years ago. Now, he's carrying me bridal style like in some cheesy movie. For a second, I'm too disoriented to decipher the change of events. It isn't until we're out of Gwen's room and down the hall that I snap out of it.

I slam my fist against his chest and I swear the hard thing makes a sound under my hand. Maybe he's not human, after all, and I'm trapped with a soulless machine.

But would I be this out of my depth if he weren't flesh and bones?

"What the hell are you doing, Kingsley?"

"Taking you to a more fitting setting. I don't know about you, but sex in my daughter's room is a turn-off."

"Let me down!" I grind out, kicking my legs in the air to make him loosen his hold.

He digs his fingers into my waist and I wince. "Unless you want to worsen your injuries, stay fucking still."

I'm about to bite his ear off when he shoves a door open to... his room.

I merely passed it earlier in the midst of Martha's obvious attempts to keep me as far away from it as possible.

White light fills the space, highlighting the clean, minimalistic, and almost clinical appearance of the room. The colors are just as basic—gray, black, and white.

My heart skips a beat when I realize those are the exact colors in my own bedroom. Jeez. Talk about some twisted coincidences.

Kingsley drops me on the bed, gently but also with the type of firmness that displays his need for dominance.

I lift myself on my elbows just in time to witness him remove his jacket. His movements drip with control, ease, and the confidence of a man who knows what he's doing and where he's going.

His white shirt stretches across his muscular chest as he throws the jacket somewhere I can't see. Then, without breaking eye contact with me, he unbuttons his cufflinks and rolls the sleeves of his shirt over his powerful forearms.

I couldn't look away even if I tried. Because the thing is, Kingsley is veiny. He has big hands with long fingers and visible veins that stretch from the backs of them to his arms.

And even though I somehow forgot the details from back then, the memory of what those hands did to me is starting to hit me. Right between my legs.

Not to mention that the cuts on the back of his hands and knuckles add a barbaric edge to his already callous appearance.

At this moment, he could be classified as a merciless monarch with a penchant for conquering.

"Here's the thing, sweetheart," he speaks in a voice full of lust that drags out my own. "Your lips are injured and your tongue is chewed on, probably because you refused to give the fuckers the satisfaction of seeing you weak. As a result, you bit on it, constantly, until you nearly bit it off."

My mouth falls open. "How…"

"You said it back then, right? You'd rather swallow your poison. I know Nietzsche is your idol and the holy messiah of your brain, but he's a fucking moron who couldn't make up his mind, so the next time you're in a life-threatening situation…" His knee drops between my legs, effortlessly prying them open as he slams a hand on the mattress by my head. The other cups my jaw again. His thumb glides over my lips, and they tingle with both pleasure and pain. "You'll open these fucking lips and scream for help. Am I clear?"

"I told you I don't believe in that." I try to push his hand away, but he leaves me no room to fight. He has the type of infuriating authority that's impossible to budge, and while I rebelled against it before, I can feel myself losing that warrior spirit now.

"You'll start to…eventually. Now…" He slides his thumb back and forth over my lips again, not sparing the swollen or cut or broken parts. "Seeing as you're in pain, I'm upgrading the earlier challenge from a kiss to something else."

"Something else…?"

My low-spoken question remains hanging in the air as he tactfully drops his hand between my breasts and fingers them through the material until both my nipples protrude. The friction against the dress is so painful that I gasp.

"You're so sensitive here, aren't you?" he says with dark sadism, then closes his lips around the nipple through the cloth and sucks. The fact that he didn't even bother to remove the dress and is doing it through it is dirtier than anything I could've imagined.

He licks and probes and bites my nipple so hard, I think I'll come from the friction alone. The bursts of pain from my shoulder and upper chest blend with the pleasure and spreads to my aching core.

It's too much.

Him.

This.

Everything about this moment is too surreal in nature that I can't wrap my mind around it. All I can do is fall into its trap with the helplessness of a prey.

My hair forms a halo over my head from how much I'm writhing. The discomfort from my bruises and his unapologetic claiming makes the atmosphere animalistic in nature.

And just when I think I might orgasm from the sensation alone, Kingsley releases the tortured nipple, leaving a wet, transparent blotch on the white dress and licks his lips as if proud of his handiwork.

I'm ready to call him a hundred colorful names, but that thought vanishes because his head lowers to my other nipple, gracing it with the same attention he gave the previous one.

My hands ball into painful fists, strangling the sheet, and I wish it was in disgust. In denial. Anything but what I'm feeling right now.

Excitement and a scary sensation of letting go.

My nipples throb, sending a straight zap between my legs with each of his brutal bites.

"Oh, God…"

"Bit unfair that he gets the praise for something I'm doing," he says, flicking his tongue on my nipple, then he bites down until I gasp. "Now, say my name."

"Fuck you, Kingsley."

He chuckles, the sound dark and demented as he bites my nipple one final time and slides between my legs. "I'm going to fuck that attitude out of you, sweetheart."

I'm disoriented when he lowers himself to the foot of the bed. I don't understand what's going on until he kneels there and flings my legs over his hard shoulders and dives between my thighs.

The delicious feeling of being stretched to my limit barely registers because he's yanking the dress up to my waist.

His lips find my inner thigh and I shudder when he breathes me in slowly, as if savoring a chef's main course.

Then he bites the inner flesh. Hard.

"Ugh. That hurts, asshole." I grab both his shoulders trying to push him away, but he bites again, this time, ripping a whimper out of me.

"Stay still or it will hurt more," he speaks against my skin, then sucks on it, flicking his tongue back and forth until I'm a wiggling mess.

I fall back on the mattress, my hands, just like my resolve, barely holding on.

My skin is lit on fire with his bites, nibbles, and eventual soothing sucks. It's like he takes pleasure in how I jump, then fail at suppressing my moans.

By the time he reaches my underwear, I'm panting and struggling to breathe.

"You're the only woman who looks sexy as fuck in cotton panties, witch." He proceeds to prove his words by biting my folds through the material.

A spark of fire spreads through my core and damn near jolts me upright. Kingsley shreds the underwear with his bare teeth, creating unbearable friction against my most intimate part.

"You're so wet for someone who claimed not to want me."

"S-shut up, jerk…"

"Is it a wise idea to call me names when your pussy is soaking my mouth like a little whore?"

My thighs physically tremble and I hate my illogical reaction. "Don't…call me that."

"Call you what?" He does a long lick from the bottom to the top of my slit, stealing my breath in the process.

"W-hore. I'm no one's whore."

"No one's but mine, because I'll eat your pussy like you are one." He jams his tongue against my clit with a force that sends me over the edge.

The climax is so strong that my mouth remains open in a

wordless cry. And then I'm screaming so loud, I'm surprised I don't bring the whole place down.

Kingsley, however, doesn't seem to be done. He thrusts his tongue inside my opening, slamming the earlier wave into a more powerful one. He tongue-fucks me hard, fast, and with so much control that I'm gasping for air.

My fingers mindlessly sink into his hair and I pull on the silky strands, practically grinding against his mouth.

I'm desperate for something that I can't pinpoint.

Something that's building inside me with the power of the storm that's glinting in his eyes whenever he stares at me.

Or glares.

I don't even know anymore.

Sometimes, he looks at me as if I'm the conquest he intends to wreck into irreparable pieces.

And maybe I look at him like the challenge he'll never win. The black horse that's never going to be tamed.

It's push and pull. Give and take. Even right now when he thinks I'm completely at his mercy, though I'm absolutely not.

Kingsley tightens his hold on my thighs, putting a halt to my frantic movements. But he continues to suck, nibble and fuck my folds until I'm delirious.

Jesus. He's driving me insane.

Just when I think I'm going to become one with the bed, the sound of something vibrating echoes like doom in the air.

Kingsley emerges from between my legs and licks his lips. "You taste as wild as you look."

I expect him to come back for that taste, but he retrieves his phone from his pocket, stares at the screen, then tells me, "I have to take this. Be quiet for me, sweetheart."

I start to pull back, but Kingsley releases my thigh and thrusts two fingers inside me at the same time as he answers, "Shaw speaking… Yes, I'm free to talk."

Holy shit. Is this crazy asshole for real?

Apparently, he is, because he curls his fingers inside me and

I have to slam a hand on my mouth to silence any embarrassing sounds.

"Yes, I understand," he says with the calmness of a sinning priest.

How the hell can he stay in his element while he's rearranging my insides?

I don't get an answer to that, but I get another finger, and this time, the three of them are so deep inside me that they hit my G-spot. Once, twice…

My head rolls back and a lusty noise slips from me.

Kingsley smirks with the cunningness and dripping charm of Lucifer himself as he shakes his head, then proceeds to finger-fuck me. In and out with a frantic rhythm that robs my sanity.

Goddamn it.

God. Fucking. Damn. It.

The fact that someone else could hear my cries of pleasure doesn't seem to stop me from releasing them. If anything, all I hear is the sloshing sound of his fingers sinking in and out of my arousal and the pure filthiness of it tugs me to the edge.

An edge so steep, I'm both exhilarated and terrified to take the leap.

"I'll make a final offer after I review last year's statistics. If they're below my standards, I'll drop them before they take their next dose of oxygen." He pulls the phone away and mouths, "There. Good girl."

I come then. From the combination of the situation, his words, and how his fingers pound into me fast and hard.

My noises are uncontrollable and I turn my head to the side and stuff my face into the mattress to muffle them.

Kingsley continues lazily thrusting his fingers inside me until he finishes the call.

I stay hidden in the mattress, both shame and thrill coursing through me with equal intensity.

Just what the hell happened to me just now? Do I need to start seeing some therapist to understand myself better? Because my body, soul, and heart seem to have given my brain the time out of his life.

Two powerful hands cup my cheeks forcing me to face him, and that's when I find him standing above me, looking at me with an expression he has no business directing at me.

The same way he looked at me all those years ago. When he said he decided to keep me after all.

His fingers slide all over my face and hair with a gentle yet possessive touch. "So beautifully broken, my little whore."

I snap out of it and push him away, scooting backward on the mattress. "I'm not your whore."

Light shines in his usually dim eyes. "Would you rather be called a good girl then?"

"N-no."

"You just came for it. But then again, you got wetter when I called you a little whore, so that means you have both a degradation and a praise kink. Interesting."

"Your death will also be interesting if you don't stop this. And can you tell me what the hell that was all about just now?"

"You'll have to be more specific than that. Just now, a lot of things happened and all of them ended with filthy orgasms and your pussy falling in love with my fingers and tongue. Next up will be my dick's turn."

I can't help the heat that covers my neck at his crass, dirty words. Just why does he say them with such ease? Still, I force myself to respond, "The talking on the phone while touching me part. What the hell is wrong with you?"

"The same variation of what's wrong with you, because you came like a *very* good girl."

I jolt at that word again and the bastard doesn't miss it, because he smirks. "Needless to say, I win. Better wear your best armor, sweetheart, because shit is about to get real when I seriously pursue you."

⚖

EMPIRE OF LUST | 139

After I freshen up, I put on the nearest sweater over my dress to hide the embarrassing wet spots. Then I'm ready to bolt out of Kingsley's house and get my brain checked by a doctor.

Maybe the thugs hit my head hard enough to knock some screws loose. That's the only way I can make sense of the fiasco that just happened.

The whole situation doesn't make sense and it's making me suspicious. Just why would he want me? He never did before—at least, not as Kingsley Shaw.

Is it only because he recalled that night from twenty-one years ago? But that's still ambiguous. He has some sort of antisocial and narcissistic tendencies, and the amount of people he genuinely cares about amounts to Gwen and Nate. So he couldn't have been pining for me all this time.

In fact, he made it clear that he'd get rid of me. Is that what this is all about? He couldn't find a method to take me to the board so he's playing a seduction game? But he's not the type to stoop to that level, not to mention, he's direct to a fault.

Goddamn it.

All this thinking about his motives is driving me insane and his closeness makes matters worse. I need to get out of here to clear my head.

But Kingsley has other plans. Of fucking course.

He basically drags me to the dining room which is big, cold, and dispassionate just like him.

The table is set for two and Kingsley sits at the head of it like a dark lord in hell. It's stupidly unfair that he still looks as elegant as ever in his white shirt, black slacks, and perfectly styled hair while I'm struggling to remain standing.

Grabbing a napkin, he motions at the chair to his right. "Sit down and eat."

"Can you stop acting like you're my boss outside of the firm?"

"That would be a no. And it's not like you allow me to act like your boss at the firm."

I flip my hair. "That's because I happen to be as good as you at what I do."

"Arrogant much?"

"You're arrogant, too, but since you have a dick between your legs, it's called charisma. Yet when a woman has confidence in herself and her work, she's labeled an egotistical bitch. If we're going to be fair, you should be called an egotistical dick."

"Then I guess we're fair, because you call me that all the time. But you might want to stop giving attention to my dick or he'll take it as an invitation."

"On another planet, asshole."

"You speak as if I can't arrange it. Also, don't pretend you don't want me. Not only is that a blatant lie, but I also have the evidence to prove the opposite."

"What evidence?"

"Your body shattered for me, even when you were in pain."

"That's called a physical reaction."

"Physical reaction. Sexual Desire. Lust. The label holds no meaning, sweetheart. The actual effect does. So deny it all you like, but the fact remains, you want me."

"You want me, too."

"Did I say otherwise?"

"Why do you want me?"

"Spur of the moment."

"Not only do you not act on impulse, but you're also putting too much time and effort into something that's supposedly on the spur of the moment. So allow me to call bullshit."

His lips tug in a wolfish smirk. "Your attention to detail about me is touching."

"I have attention to detail about everything. It's not exclusive to you."

"Oh?"

"*Oh*," I mimic his provocative tone. "Now, tell me why you want me?"

"It's just a physical reaction, as you mentioned. A lust for an intense hate-fuck."

"That's it?"

"That's it."

My chest squeezes, and I have no clue why the urge to bolt out of here is stronger than the need for my next breath. Still, I force myself to appear unaffected and remain in place. I force myself to stop thinking about the door he just slammed in my face.

Kingsley lazily drags his gaze over me and I squirm. Jeez. After he so brutally ripped my panties, I'm not wearing any, so no accidents should be allowed. I wrap the sweater tighter around me, and he smiles. "Take the clothes with you."

"Of course I will, genius. You expect me to walk outside naked?"

"No, or I'll have to deal with all the fuckers who witness the strip show in a not-so-nice way," he says casually, as if he's not delivering a threat. "I meant that you don't need to return the clothes."

"They're Gwen's."

"They're yours now. My daughter won't be wearing that after you came in it."

I can't see it, but I feel my neck turning red. The bastard. I definitely and totally and without a doubt hate the shit out of him.

If I could actually not want him, it'd be great.

"Now, sit down and eat. There won't be a third time I tell you that."

"I'm not hungry."

"You haven't eaten a thing since this morning."

"Still not hungry. Have a good night." I take a step toward the exit, but the moment I brush past him, he grabs me by the waist.

I yelp as he pulls me back and shoves me down on his lap. Or more accurately, I'm sitting on one hard thigh, my legs spread open and my bare pussy brushing against his pants.

The temperature escalates from two digits to three of them superfast. I attempt to elbow him, but the hot breaths at my ear freeze me in place.

"If you're still horny and would like to ride my leg, go for it, but I can't promise I won't fuck you right afterward. Hurt or not."

I squirm, my fists clenching on either side of me. "Let me go, Kingsley."

"Not until you eat." He jerks his chin at the bowl of soup and the plate of shrimp in front of me. "All of that."

"And if I refuse?"

"Then your stubbornness and I can stay here all night. You'll eventually either eat, hump my leg, or both."

"You…"

"Bastard, jerk, asshole, dick. I know the tune, and it won't serve any purpose aside from pissing me off, so unless you want to witness a hideous manifestation of those emotions, save it."

I cross my arms over my chest, staring at him behind me. "Let's stay like this then and see how you'll function tomorrow at work when you're sleep-deprived."

"That mouth of yours is begging to be fucked, sweetheart."

I purse my lips so that I don't speak. Anything I have to say under the circumstances will just backfire.

While I don't back down from anything, the sexual department with Kingsley is not my forte. He's the only man I can't even think about snatching power from and while it's infuriating, it's oddly thrilling, too.

And I hate that.

And him.

He cages me between his arms and reaches for the soup and proceeds to eat without any problem.

I stare at the hanging chandeliers and the wall, the door, the windows. Anywhere but at him, but that still doesn't dissipate the tension. If anything, it heightens with each passing second until I can hear my pulse pounding in my ears. His heat beneath me and behind me makes it hard to think, breathe, or focus.

Something warm is placed at my lips. A spoon filled with shrimp and rice. "Stop being fucking stubborn and open up."

I huff but don't follow his command.

"You're an infuriating woman. Did you know that?"

"Funny coming from an infuriating man—" He shoves the spoon inside and I have no choice but to swallow or choke.

"That's not fair!" I speak, covering my mouth with the back of my hand so he doesn't make me eat another spoonful.

"Tough shit, sweetheart. Fair and I have nothing in common. Now, open that mouth and eat."

I shake my head.

He narrows his eyes. "Do you have some sort of an eating disorder? Now that I think about it, I only see you drinking things—coffee, alcohol. *Lots* of alcohol. Wait a fucking second, are you an alcoholic?"

"Shut up. And seriously, why the hell are you so focused on me lately? I liked it better when you didn't give a fuck about me."

He remains silent, and I curse myself.

I didn't exactly mean to ask the question, but now that it's out in the open, I want an answer. But at the same time, a part of me is terrified of the answer.

"I still give zero fucks about you aside from the fact that I want in your pants, and for that, you need to be healthy enough to handle me."

My ears catch fire and I don't know if it's anger or something entirely different. "I'm not one of your whores, Kingsley. You don't get to tell me what to do with my body. If you want that, go to them."

"They're escorts, not whores. And I'll go to them once I'm done with you."

I can feel the volcano rising in my throat and I seriously imagine chewing his head off slasher movie style.

But then he says, "How about a trade?"

"If it's not your life for humanity's peace, I'm not interested."

He chuckles and I hate how the sound vibrates against my neck and penetrates my skin.

"I'm too precious to sacrifice myself for something as dull as humanity. So how about I answer any question you have about Gwen, and in exchange, you'll finish this plate?"

I was so ready to tell him to go fuck a pole. But the bastard went straight for the jugular. He knows how desperate I am for some semblance of a relationship with Gwen, even if I have to sell my soul to the devil—him—for it.

"Not one question. I want an infinite number."

"That's not how it works. One question for one meal."

"Three."

"One."

"Two."

"*One*. If you want more, then you need to join me for dinner some other time."

"You're a cunning asshole." I sigh.

"Thanks for the compliment, witch. Now, open your mouth."

I try to take the spoon. "I can eat on my own."

He keeps it out of reach and tuts. "My table. My rules."

I release a breath and open my mouth, feeling weird. Like a child, but also so utterly turned on, it should be illegal. Part of the desire has to do with the fact that someone is taking care of me, enveloping me, and providing a protection I haven't dreamt of. And somehow, that spurs a strange type of lust I haven't experienced before.

Briefly closing my eyes, I think of Gwen and that makes the sensation slowly wither away.

"Does she ever ask about me?" My voice is low in the silence of the dining room.

Kingsley keeps feeding me steadily, his expression blank, but it's not the anger blank he uses to camouflage his demons. This one is more neutral like when he's in a static state—which is rare as hell.

"She did a few days ago. Said hi again and asked me if I'm giving you a hard time."

"You…never told me that."

"You were undergoing 'Operation Avoid Kingsley,' so I didn't think you cared enough about whatever Gwen had to tell me about you."

I hang my head. "You could've still told me."

"The keyword being *could've*. Besides, what would that change? Unless you go on the offensive with her, Gwen will never consider you a mother."

"*Offensive?*"

"It means to go for it. Be proactive. Don't wait for her to eventually come to you. That might've been possible a few years—hell, even a few months ago—but she's more emotionally stable now, thanks to a certain fucker that shall not be named and, therefore, she probably doesn't feel the need for a mother like she did before."

My lips part. "Did you just give me advice about Gwen? I thought you wanted me out of her life."

"I still would kick you out if that were an option, but then again, I care about her more than anything else in the world, so if she wants you, I can't simply erase you or Nate. Though my murderous plans for the bastard are still alive and functioning."

I laugh.

He narrows his eyes. "What are you laughing about?"

"Nothing. You just sounded like a very strict parent."

"I am a very strict parent, which is why I can't believe I let her marry Nate. Think an annulment would be possible now?"

"I'm afraid not, unless you want to be Nate's subject of how to get away with murder. Seriously, I don't understand why you approach him so much about it. They're both adults in love."

"He's the more adult one and shouldn't have looked in my fucking daughter's direction. You haven't been there, so you don't know the feeling of finding out your 'brother' who was supposed to have your back was fucking your daughter under your damn roof."

"Touché, asshole." I push him away and stand up, surprised to see that I ate almost everything in the bowl. "But for the thousandth time, I didn't know she existed. Stop blaming me for the lost twenty years."

I'm blaming myself enough as it is.

"I'd have to give a fuck to blame you, and as I mentioned, I don't have any."

"Fuck you, Kingsley."

"Very soon. And I'll start with that mouth."

"Better revise your will, because I'll bite your dick off." I flip him the middle finger and walk out, resisting the urge to run as if my ass is on fire.

His evil laughter stays with me long after I'm out of his house.

It isn't until the cold air licks my skin that I realize I left my wallet and phone inside—or I'm hoping I did because I haven't seen them this entire night. I'm sure I picked them up from the alley and paid the taxi driver, though.

"Want a ride?"

I release a resigned sigh as I turn around and find Kingsley toying with his car keys and clutching my phone and wallet. "I can take a taxi."

"None comes out this far, so you'll have to walk for a long time."

"I'll call one."

"Or you can quit the war for the sake of war and let me give you a fucking ride."

He doesn't allow me to protest as he grabs my arm and drags me to his car.

I try not to feel grateful, I really do.

But I fail miserably anyway.

THIRTEEN

Kingsley

"I MISSED YOU SO MUCH, DAD!"

Gwen squeezes me in a hug that could be mistaken for a murder attempt.

I smile anyway and wrap my arms around her. This little girl—not so little anymore—is the reason I was saved from my own mind a long time ago.

If it weren't for her existence, I would've been fucked up to my bones with no light at the end of the tunnel.

Well, I'm not next in line to be Mother Teresa's replacement, but still. Small changes.

My angel added something important to my life, something that due to its absence, I spiraled down a violent, bloody path.

Purpose.

So the fact that she's no longer under my protection—not fully, at least—has been slowly but surely chipping away at that purpose.

"You clearly missed me, judging by how you added three whole days to your trip." I glare at Nate who's sitting in my living room, legs wide apart, position relaxed, and making himself entirely at home.

Fucker looks too pleased with himself. He's even wearing casual pants, a button-down, and a creepy smile.

A whole look that didn't exist in his wardrobe before.

"We just wanted to stay a little longer." Gwen pulls back, looking as radiant as the summer sun. Apparently, getting married didn't change her style, considering the jean shorts, loose tank top, and casual sneakers she's sporting like a second skin.

She tries—and fails—to force her wild ginger hair into submission. "Besides, you know that Nate would go straight back to work as soon as we returned."

"Which he should've done three days ago instead of having me carry all the weight. And stop smiling, motherfucker. It's disgusting."

"Dad!" Gwen gasps, then flops beside her husband. "Don't listen to him, Nate. I like it when you smile."

I take my own seat, narrowing my eyes. "Already taking sides, Gwen?"

"You're unreasonable, Dad."

"Not to mention a jerk," Nate says with his usual blank expression. At least the creepiness is gone.

"Nate," she whisper-yells. "Don't call Dad a jerk."

At least the little shit still has some loyalty toward me.

"Unfortunately, your denial won't negate the fact that he is one." He raises his brows at me in pure challenge. "The worst kind. If only you knew what type of things he does behind your back."

"I'll kill you," I mouth so Gwen doesn't hear and he just smiles again, summoning the version from creepy hell.

My daughter frowns at him. "What do you mean?"

"Nothing you should worry about…yet." He kisses the top of her head and she just lets it go.

Gwen talks about all the fun she had and tells me about the gifts she bought for me, all seven of them, because wherever she went, she thought of me and wanted to get me something.

Then she says she misses Martha and goes to catch up with her.

As soon as Nate and I are alone, I contemplate whether or not he'll die from a single shot from my grandfather's shotgun that's displayed right behind his head.

He flings a hand on the back of the sofa. "You do realize that you're fully transparent when that head of yours is bubbling with violence, don't you?"

"Better run then, motherfucker."

"That word and I are not friends. Speaking of friends, I heard unsettling rumors about you rekindling your withering relationship with Nicolo Luciano."

"Not rumors. News."

He stands up, all nonchalance gone as he reaches me in a few strides and speaks in a low tone. "Did you lose your fucking mind in that damn coma? Why the hell would you willingly go back to the mafia's dirty circle after putting so much effort into cutting ties with them?"

"Nothing personal. Just business."

"Fuck that. You loathed your father's involvement with them and made sure to end it as soon as he was six feet under. So either spill the actual reason or Gwyneth will have to be the one to get the answers out of you."

I jerk up and grab him by the collar of his shirt in one swift movement. "Don't bring her into this."

He clutches me by my jacket. "*You're* the one who did that. She's your daughter, King. If anything goes sideways, which, spoiler alert, always does with the mob, she'll have a target on her fucking back."

She'll have a target on her back either way because of her damn mother. But I don't say that, because it will show that I care, and that's blasphemy in my dictionary.

"She won't." I push him away. "And tell your bird who dares to fucking spy on me that I'll blacklist them from this planet the moment I find them."

He scratches his chin. "Huh."

"What?"

"You said 'your bird.'"

"So fucking what?" I might have the patience of a toddler lately.

Specifically, since four days ago, after I dropped Aspen off at her apartment and she ghosted me.

"You didn't say 'the witch.' As in, you didn't assume it's her, even knowing full well she's my right-hand. What gives?"

It can't be her, because she'd be serving herself on a platter to Nate, and while they're close, she's not close enough to anyone to let them see her weak.

Or disclose her past to them.

Or put herself in an unfavorable position in front of her daughter's husband.

But what she doesn't know is that the more she escapes into her cave, the harder I'll chase her.

So what if she doesn't answer my calls or my texts? I'll eventually catch her.

The only reason I haven't banged her door off its hinges and barged into her apartment is to give her that misconception of being safe.

Or that I've given up.

The surest way to get a guarded, careful person to open up is to delude them into believing they're off the hook.

But if she thinks I would retreat now that I've had a taste of her, she has no idea what she's in for. Because one time isn't enough. I need to see her writhing again, moaning in that throaty voice, and shattering in front of me like an erotic art piece.

That scene from four days ago was so rare in its beauty and surprisingly breakable. It's the only time I've ever seen her so vulnerable with hints of a submissive that I'll bring out if it's the last thing I do.

Aspen Leblanc is the war I'm going to conquer and bring to her knees.

Literally. Figuratively.

I focus back on Nate, who's been watching me expectantly. "Aspen is on vacation."

He rakes his gaze all over the room, then gives me the same attention before he circles me like a poor imitation of a caged lion.

"Did you get high on your way here, Nate? Either that or I need to check you into a mental institute."

"I'm just making sure I didn't somehow land in a parallel universe since Aspen is apparently on her first vacation in a decade and you actually know her given name. I thought she only held the title of a witch in your repertoire of limited names."

After doing two whole tours around me, he stops in front of me and narrows his eyes. "What the fuck is going on?"

I might've underestimated Nate's deduction abilities and his dog-like nose, because he's watching me with zero chances of him dropping this.

So instead of offering the truth that I don't even like to admit to myself, I go with a tamer version of it. "She was assaulted."

He pauses, his face hardening. "When? Where? How? Who?"

All the same questions I asked. And yet, I want to bash his head in for an illogical reason. Like why the fuck does he have that level of concern about her?

"Five days ago. In an alley. Physically. As for who, it's still under investigation. She filed a report, but the incompetent police are coming up with nothing."

And won't. Because I already took care of it.

"Does the physical assault extend to a sexual one—"

"No." I cut him off harshly, realizing I don't want to discuss that particular topic with him, of all fucking people.

"Good." He releases a breath. "Well, not good, but still. How bad is she?"

"Bad enough to be put on mandatory vacation. She was beaten to within an inch of her life but still wants to work as if nothing happened."

"Aspen is a workaholic to a fault."

The sound of a crash reaches us. Both Nate and I stare at the source to find Gwen blinking rapidly, a massacre of a dish and cupcakes lying by her feet.

Her chin trembles like when she was a little girl and reined in her tears. "Aspen...is hurt?"

Nate strides to her side, wraps an arm around her shoulder, and tactfully pulls her from the mess. Because knowing her poor relationship with the outside world, she'll probably step on the glass or gather the pieces and cut herself.

"Not badly," Nate assures her. "She'll be fine."

"But Dad said it's bad enough that she had to go on a mandatory vacation." She releases herself from his hold and storms toward me. The anger and disappointment on her face cuts through my steel chest. "Did you do it?"

"*What?*"

"You always hated her and promised to make her disappear. Did you hit her or pay someone to hit her to scare her away?"

My jaw tightens so hard, I'm surprised it doesn't snap. "Watch your mouth, Gwen. I'm your father, not your friend, and you have zero right to accuse me."

"Why not? You threatened to kill her once. I heard you! You're my dad and I love you, but you're a merciless man to anyone who goes against you. I learned that the hard way when you nearly killed Nate, your damn best friend, because he disobeyed you, so excuse me if I think you're capable of doing more than that to Aspen."

I can feel the volcano rising from deep within me and I clench my fists.

Gwen doesn't notice, because she's too caught up in her emotions to realize it.

Nate, however, senses the change in the atmosphere and wraps an arm around her waist protectively.

He knows I'd never hurt her, but he also knows she's pushing me to my very last nonexistent limit.

"Gwyneth, it might not be what you think," he says gently.

"Why not?" she speaks to him but continues staring at me with that same sense of betrayal. "I've wanted a mother since I knew what a mother meant, Dad. Her absence made me feel empty, like less than a whole person and not worthy of love. I finally found her after twenty damn years, and you had to be selfish about it. You can be so selfish, Dad. You made me celebrate all my birthdays, even though I hated them for reminding me that I was abandoned that day. But you don't care about that, do you? You don't care that all I think about is getting close to the mother I finally found and being constantly scared that she won't like me. She's so smart and successful and I don't think I can measure up to her and it scares me, but those facts mean nothing to you. You hate her and want me to hate her, too, but I'm telling you now that it's not possible. So stop making everything about you, Dad. It's about me this time!"

Silence stakes claim to the room. Aside from the sound of me grinding my back teeth together to keep from fucking snapping.

"Nate, get her the hell out of here." I'm surprised I sound calm, even though it's the "I'll break all hell loose in a sec" type of calm.

He clenches his jaw but starts to pull her away, because even he wouldn't want her to see me in my non-human state.

"No, I want to stay!" She tries to wiggle free. "Tell me it's not you who hurt her, Dad."

"Get the fuck out, Gwyneth," I roar, and she flinches before the most loathsome things I've ever seen on my daughter stream down her cheeks.

Tears.

She sniffles, her face becoming red, then she turns around and runs.

Nate gives me a dirty look, mutters a "fuck you," then follows her.

Me? I want to punch a wall.

So I do just that and drive my fist through the nearest wall.

My knuckles explode in pain, but it's not enough to dilute the image of Gwen crying or the sound of her accusing me.

I don't care if the whole world paints me as the worst villain; she should never belong to the herd.

She's my miracle.

But then again, maybe I don't deserve one.

I retrieve my Zippo and flip it open, then closed in a manic rhythm, contemplating my next course of action.

Obviously, it starts and ends with the woman who gave me that miracle.

FOURTEEN

Aspen

THE DOOR TO MY HOME OFFICE OPENS AND I SIGH FOR THE hundredth time in the span of ten minutes.

Caroline appears at the doorway carrying a plate and wearing her fuzzy pajamas and an expression that's not apologetic in the least.

Lucifer and Cain peek from the door, following her around like clingy children.

I raise my eyes from my computer screen and stare at her, blank-faced. "Now what?"

She strolls inside as if she's not interrupting me for the dozenth time—on purpose. "I just thought you'd want a cup of tea and some cake."

"I don't drink tea or eat cake."

"You should." She slides the cup in front of me. "It's good for your health."

"Thanks, doctor. Now, would you please let me work without finding an excuse to interrupt me?"

She hikes up a hand on her hip. "You know, the whole point behind being on a vacation is to actually relax."

"Relaxing is for the dead."

She gives me an "are you shitting me?" look, then leans on my desk right in the middle of my space and crosses her arms. "I can't believe you're working as usual after what happened to you."

Caroline had lost her shit by the time I got home that night. Apparently, she'd been calling me all day long and couldn't reach me. Kingsley answered her that morning, but he only confused her more and offered no explanations. Considering everything that had happened, I didn't even think about checking my phone until after Kingsley dropped me off.

Anyway, when I came back into the apartment, Caroline was crying while fussing over me left and right. She was always the sensible one out of the two of us and often cried on behalf of both of us.

Ever since that moment, she's been a pain in the ass, trying to stop me from doing my job, even from home—courtesy of my boss from hell.

On one hand, I don't know how to feel about this. On the other, I'm glad I don't have to cross paths with him at the firm. I really have no clue how I'll ever be able to face him and not think about his tongue and fingers inside me.

Any semblance of the professional relationship we had is out the window—not that it was the best, since I secretly considered him a rival. But even that sense of work-related boundaries has vanished now. All I have left are chaotic emotions and hickeys.

Lots of them. Around my breasts, nipples, stomach, and thighs.

They've been healing with my bruises and I don't know why the hell I touch them every night. Look at them in the mirror every morning.

It's not to get the same adrenaline burst from when he left them on my skin.

Absolutely *not*.

"I'm alive and functioning, Callie. Stop turning this into a tragedy."

"It is a tragedy, and why the hell did you use the word *functioning* about yourself? You're not a machine, bitch."

"Are you done?" I glare at her.

"No." She glares right back. "We should do something to make whoever hurt you pay."

"I already reported it to the police."

"The police are useless." She sucks on the insides of her cheeks. "I can ask Mateo to investigate this and provide you protection."

"You would ask Mateo?"

She clears her throat and pulls on her pajamas in an adorable way. "I would for you."

"Thanks, but there's no need to, Callie. I'm already under Nicolo's protection."

She pokes me with the sternness of an angry grandmother. "Nicolo is a damn opportunist who wouldn't hesitate to chew you up and spit you out the moment he's done with you."

"And Mateo won't?"

"No." She lifts her chin. "He's loyal."

"I thought he cheated."

"Well…aside from that." She winces and doesn't even seem to believe her earlier convictions anymore.

At this point, she's either playing an epic hard-to-get role or she really is too far into her head to see what Mateo is doing for her.

He's a man with nothing in his sights but Caroline. The world seems to be a vessel to her existence.

And she's blind to all of that.

The mob is for life and the only way out is death, which means no divorces are allowed. It's the reason my mother killed herself to be able to leave. So at this point, Mateo is only humoring Callie. When push comes to shove, he'll never allow the divorce. Not even if Nicolo gives him the green light to go against their customs for it.

"Anyway." She starts to close my laptop. "Stop working or

I'll call Kingsley and report that you're not taking your vacation seriously."

My fingers twitch and I miss the chance to keep my laptop open. I can't believe that the mere mention of the bastard's name is enough to tilt my psyche off its axis.

This isn't normal, ordinary, or acceptable, and yet, I can't for the life of me control my reaction when it comes to that man.

It's like he muddied my soul and has made a cozy place for himself in my chest.

Even now, images of him unapologetically owning me, taking whatever he wanted without an ounce of hesitation or questions, play in my head like a haunting movie.

I should be revolted by the idea of anyone controlling me, and part of me is, but that's not the most prominent part.

That one is currently making my core throb in remembrance as I struggle to stay in the moment.

"Don't you dare, Callie."

The sweet smile that curves her lips nearly gives me diabetes. "I most definitely will if you keep being a stubborn hellion. The nickname isn't so cute now that it's in real life."

"Cute is the last thing I want to be."

"But you looked hella cute in that little white dress you wore that night. Bet you drove the poor man crazy."

"Callie…for the thousandth time, nothing happened."

"Uh-huh. Sure. I totally believe you."

"Callie!"

"What? You smelled like cologne and had flushed cheeks and glittery eyes."

"I was in pain."

"Pain of desire, sure. But hey, you go for it, girl. At least one of us is getting some action."

"Get out of here before I smack you."

She blows me a kiss. "You know you love me and that I'm right."

I physically have to chase her out of my office, to which she laughs and hugs her dogs, using them as armor.

Once I'm finally back at my desk, I release a harsh sigh, but I don't open my laptop. Instead, I pull out my phone and stare at the text messages I received from Kingsley over the past few days.

We've had each other's numbers for years, but we only contact each other on the rare occasion that we work on a case together. Which mainly happens when a client is both charged criminally and sued civilly.

All our exchanges have been dry, professional, with his usual dash of scathing sarcasm.

However, the texts he's sent over the last few days were drastically different.

You seem to have the self-care mentality of a toddler, so this is your reminder to clean your wounds and take painkillers.

A few minutes later.

Another reminder to do as I just told you. This isn't about you, sweetheart. I don't want Gwen upset when she finds out you're hurt.

Also, I still have your sweet taste on my tongue. Five-star meal. Highly recommend.

The following morning.

If you show your face at the firm, I'm going to have security throw you right out. Eat your breakfast.

Oh, and morning. Are you healed enough to take my dick between your lips? Or legs? Or ass cheeks? I'll take what I can get.

During the day.

I'm in the middle of a meeting, but all I think about is how your greedy little cunt shattered around my fingers.

Do you still have my marks on that bruisable skin, sweetheart? Do you feel me on you with every move you make?

By the way, before those marks disappear, I'll give you new ones.

Did you have lunch?

Dinner?

Are you touching yourself tonight or do you have a toy that does the job?

Just for the record, my dick is certified to give a much better performance. All you have to do is ask.

His texts continued to shift between mundane things to lust-filled ones in the span of seconds. To say I was getting whiplash would be an understatement.

But more than that, my thighs clenched when reading them. Even now, I can feel the heat rising up my neck and cheeks, then spreading over my body with the disturbing persistence of a hurricane.

The reason I haven't replied to any of them isn't bashfulness or lack of words. It's the pure terror of my reaction to him. To this side of him that I didn't know existed but am slowly but surely getting used to.

I don't want to be used to Kingsley. Or his care. Or his dirty words.

As he so eloquently put it, he'll go back to his escorts eventually.

That's what men do when they're bored. They leave.

And I refuse to be another stop on his route.

That doesn't mean I didn't get drunk reading and rereading his texts. I should've thought about the threat my father possibly poses on me more, but no.

Damn Kingsley has the destructive effect of a plane crash. A mass shooting. And a destructive war.

The door to my office opens, and even though working wasn't part of my preoccupation, I sigh. "I swear to God, Callie. I'm going to throw you out the window."

"Might have to wait until you meet your visitor." There's a rare sound of glee in Caroline's voice and when I look up, I cease breathing.

The last person I expected to find standing in my apartment stares at me with puffy eyes, a downward expression, and silent awkwardness.

"Gwyneth," I whisper, still not believing my eyes.

She tugs on her sweater, shifts her feet, and murmurs back, "Hi."

Her voice is so much softer than mine, too feminine and small. She even looks like it now, broken, distressed, and the urge to destroy whoever caused her that boils in my blood with the harshness of a volcano.

"I'm going to bring some tea and cake," Caroline announces with delight, shoving Gwen inside with a less than subtle push.

My phone nearly falls to the floor and I realize that I still have Kingsley's dirty texts up. I quickly throw it in the drawer and stand, my spine straight. "What are you doing here? I mean, no, it's not that I don't want you here, but the fact that you came to my apartment brings up questions. Of course, I don't mean to question you, but…"

Jesus. I trail off when her chin trembles. *Damn it, me.* I finally have my daughter visiting me and I go blurting like a flustered five-year-old.

Gwen fingers her sweater, staring at me from under her lashes. "Are you badly hurt?"

Oh, that's why she came. She must've heard from Kingsley. It's then I realize she must have noticed my bruises, too, and this isn't a state I want to her to see me in.

"No, I'm fine."

"You don't look fine."

"They're just bruises. They'll heal."

Her chin trembles again and she hangs her head. "I'm so sorry."

I slowly approach her, my heart beating louder with each step. I speak low, afraid a higher range will have her bolting. "What for?"

"For what Dad did. I dislike that side of him."

"Wait…what?"

She lifts her head, a tear clinging to her lashes. "Dad hurt you because you didn't leave like he told you to. He also did that to Nate, when he refused to let me go."

"Gwen, no. Kingsley didn't do this to me. In fact, he was the one who helped me and nursed me back to health. If he hadn't,

God knows what hole I'd be in right now." I'm prideful, but that doesn't mean I'd deny what he did for me. A part of me holds so much gratitude to him, I have no idea how to express it.

My daughter's face gets frozen in an odd mixture of relief and horror, then she gasps. "He really did nothing?"

I shake my head, believing it myself. Kingsley is a lot of things, but subhuman is not one of them.

"Oh my God." She starts shaking like a leaf, the tear finally sliding down her cheek. "I called him a monster and other names and lashed out at him for hurting my mother after I finally found her."

My heart literally skips a beat. It doesn't matter if she's talking about me in the third person, but she indirectly admitted that I'm her mother.

Her. Mother.

"He was so mad, like worse than when he deals with Susan mad," she whispers more to herself than to me. "What if he never forgives me?"

The obvious distress chatters her teeth and puts a halt to my celebratory dance.

She's in pain, and while I'm immune to my own pain, hers hits differently.

Hers protrudes through my bones and nearly rips my heart open. It's been the same since Aunt Sharon hit my belly. It wasn't my pain that mattered, it was fear that Gwen would be hurt.

In a poor attempt to soften my voice, I say, "I'm sure if you apologize, he'll forgive you."

She stares up at me with colorful, hope-filled eyes. "What if he doesn't?"

"He cares about you more than anything in the world, Gwen. He will definitely forgive you."

She releases a shaky breath, then whispers, "Thank you for saying that and...and I'm still sorry about what happened to you. Do you know who did it?"

Your grandfather, who will be a threat to your life if I don't do something about it.

However, I settle with a "No."

"I'm sure the police will find them," she says with pure determination, not trying to wipe her tears.

She's the type who wears her emotions like a badge. Definitely unlike me and her father.

"I brought you something." Gwen digs into the pocket of her sweater and produces a small keychain in the shape of a scale. "It's nothing much. I just noticed you don't have one and stumbled upon this and thought it looked cool and would suit you… and, yeah, I got it."

My chest nearly bursts from the emotions coursing through it. I don't think I was built to handle so many feelings at the same time.

When I don't reach for the keychain, Gwen pales. "It's fine if you don't like it, I can—"

"No, I do." I grab at it with both hands. "It's beautiful. Thank you."

She smiles, childlike, and finally wipes her eyes with the back of her sleeve. "You're…welcome."

"I'm all tears." Caroline appears from behind the corner, dabbing at her eyes, probably having listened to the whole exchange, then smiles at Gwen. "I'm Auntie Caroline and I've known your mother since before we both got our periods."

Gwen's mismatched eyes glint. "Really?"

"Totally." Caroline grins. "Wanna have a cup of tea with me, eat some cake, and let me tell you stories about a younger, less stony version of her?"

"Callie, stop it," I hiss, my neck heating.

"What? She wouldn't mind. Right, Gwen?"

My daughter doesn't look at me, but her face turns a deep shade of red as she murmurs, "I would love tea. Do you have vanilla-flavored cake?"

"Of course! I have all sorts of cake." Caroline says, all too joyful, and drags Gwen with her to the living room.

I follow them, feeling lightheaded and partially not believing what's happening.

Caroline tells Gwen one embarrassing story from our youth after the other, interrupted by my protests and my kicking her whenever I get the chance.

My daughter, however, doesn't seem the least bit bored or embarrassed. She listens carefully, laughs, and even asks questions, fully invested in a part of me I have long since forgotten.

A part of me who wrote in journals, gazed at the stars, and made stupid wishes that would never come true.

A part of me who was so naïve that I had to murder it in order to survive.

By the time Gwen leaves, she has a smile on her face, has exchanged numbers with Caroline, and wishes me well.

I feel so high on cloud nine that even Caroline's hyper energy doesn't bother me anymore.

However, later as I lie in bed, a stupid nagging remains at the back of my mind. In fact, it's been there since Gwen was here.

He was so mad.

Her words play in my head on a loop. I've seen Kingsley on the scale of anger a few times, and it was always bad.

The type of bad people stay away from.

And while I was one of those people in the past. It sits wrong with me now.

Inexplicably wrong.

I scan the texts he sent me over the past few days and decide to reply to the last one.

Kingsley: Breakfast?

Aspen: I've skipped most of my meals except for a slice of apple pie, because that's the only thing Callie does right.

He doesn't see the text. So I call him, my heartbeat picking up with every ring until it goes to voicemail.

I hang up and stare at the screen, then call him again.

Still no answer.

I'm about to go to sleep—or try to—when I recall something Nate told me once.

"Stay away from Kingsley when he's angry. He becomes volatile, unpredictable, and has a thirst for blood. I'm surprised he hasn't accidentally lost his life due to those factors."

My fingers shake as a crazy idea forms in mind.

The worst part of all is that the crazy idea is slowly but surely turning into action.

FIFTEEN

Aspen

I F CRAZY IS A TERRITORY, I'VE ALREADY CUT THROUGH ITS wires and breached it with bloodied hands.

The cold air forms icicles in my veins and no amount of pulling my coat over myself is cutting it.

My smartwatch lights up in the darkness to tell me it's late o'clock. As in, super late. After one in the morning late.

And an abandoned cabin in the middle of nowhere is the last place I should've driven to.

Hell, I shouldn't even remember the exact way to it, but I do.

After leaving my car at the end of the road, I trek the rest of the way, watching my surroundings every step of the way. My feet falter in front of the tree that he kissed me under that night. When he lifted his Anonymous mask, devoured my lips, then said he'd keep me, after all.

He basically carried me the rest of the way until we reached the small cabin. We found a bottle of tequila and shared it while we talked. Now that I think about it, that was the first time I tasted tequila and it became my poison of choice. I don't remember much of our conversation, but I remember that it went on for long. Long enough that I forgot that he could be a threat. Long enough that it felt right for him to kiss me again, strip my clothes and touch me like no one did. I might not recall everything that happened prior to the sex, but I remember that he said he came here whenever he felt a need to be alone.

I'm grasping at straws here. It's been twenty-one years, so maybe his methods of venting and places of choice have changed.

The property is as eerie as in the past, dark with shadows that resemble folklore monsters. Back then, I was so trapped by the heated conversation and tension we shared that I didn't focus much while we walked here.

Didn't even think that he could call his friends to gang-rape me as a Devil's Night prank. I trusted him in a way that infuriated me.

I don't trust people easily. If ever.

Young me's logic was that he'd already showed his ugly side early on. And if he wanted to actually hurt me, he would've done it after he punched his Joker friend.

A distant thumping sound flicks my ears and I pause, my feet shifty in the tall grass.

Maybe it's because it's a cold night, a natural event that always reminds me of the past, but the darkness feels like it's an existence with an ominous soul that's hovering over my shoulder.

The thump comes again, and I don't allow myself to think as I head straight toward it. Ignoring an owl's cries and other night animals' haunting sounds proves to be harder than I imagined. I like to think that I have a strong spirit, but this is too eerie even for me.

The path that leads to the cabin is so entirely black that I can't even see my own hands. The shabby building that must be in a ferocious battle with nature to remain standing looks like nothing more than a crooked shadow with horns.

I follow the direction of the thumps seamlessly, almost too naturally.

When I reach the cabin's huge, unruly backyard, I freeze. A large shadow stands in front of a massive oak tree that nearly swallows the house from above. Its roots resemble giant snakes in the darkness.

Only the moon, constantly shadowed by clouds, offers any semblance of light.

It's a night in which monsters would plan chaos, throw their parties, and harvest some poor lives.

The thumps I heard earlier are in fact thwacks as he punches the tree's trunk over and over again.

Since I first met Kingsley—officially as himself and not in an Anonymous mask—he's been the most infuriatingly confident person I've ever seen.

He walks, talks, and breathes with purpose. He owns whatever room he enters and it isn't because he has money.

Kingsley Shaw is the kind of man who not only steals attention but does it so seamlessly that no one notices when they stop to listen to him.

I've always envied his type of confidence that seems as if he was born with it.

So to see him unruly, savage, and like a demon finding refuge in the darkness brings about a whole different emotion.

One that's terrifyingly similar to the past, where the naïve me ruled my life.

"Kingsley." My voice is low but has the weight of a bomb in the silence—or semi-silence.

He shows no signs of hearing me and continues punching the tree. Something dark streams down the trunk, glistening in the night.

Please don't tell me that's blood.

I call him again, and when there's no response, I slowly approach him. To say I'm not afraid would be a lie. In fact, every self-preserving fiber in my being is telling me to go back to my car and drive the hell away from here.

But I don't.

I'm doing this because he helped me once—or twice—and I don't like owing people.

Or that's what I tell myself as I carefully put a hand on his shoulder.

One moment, I'm standing by his side, the next, I'm flung around and pain explodes in my back when I'm slammed against the tree.

With a steel-like hand around my throat.

Eyes that have no glint in them stare down at me. They're dim, blank.

Dead.

And even though I can't see his face in the darkness, I'm almost sure there's no expression there either.

He squeezes my throat enough to make me lightheaded. The lack of oxygen robs me of breath and any thoughts.

My knee-jerk reaction is to claw, kick, hit.

Survive.

That's the only drug I've been on since I was a toddler.

But I don't do that.

I reach my hand to his face, feeling the tension in his jaw, in his demeanor, and in his deep, controlled breaths. "It's…me…"

Though that probably holds the importance of a rock in his shoe to him, I continue stroking his face, desperate to chase away his demons.

I've never seen him without them, even when he's in his element, but I've also never seen them take over him either.

And I hate that.

This isn't the Kingsley I know.

And he's definitely not the Kingsley who raised our daughter for both of us during those long twenty years.

"King…" I croak, my voice breaking due to pressure and the way blood nearly explodes in my face.

I think he'll finish me now and there will be a sad tombstone on my grave that probably doesn't say "Mother."

And that is just not how I'll go.

"King!" I screech with all my power in a last-ditch attempt.

His fingers halt the massacring mission, slowly loosening, but he doesn't remove them.

I suck in greedy intakes of air through the small opening, nearly choking on my own breaths.

"What the fuck are you doing here, Aspen?" His voice is deeper, almost guttural, and draws shivers over my spine.

"Gwen…Gwen said you were mad and I thought…well, you mentioned that this place offers the yang to your yin."

"Fuck," he releases the word in a long breath. "God-fucking-dammit."

His fingers tighten around my throat again and I yelp, bracing myself for the squeeze. But he doesn't do that. At least, not all the way.

Instead, he puts pressure on the sides, turning me dizzy but not in a threatening way. It's a show of who holds the power and almost…seductive in nature.

"Why do you even remember that?" His voice is still rough, full of tension, but it's also not as scary as a minute ago.

"I have a strong memory." *Of you.*

"You're not supposed to be here. Leave."

"I can't do that when you have your hand around my throat, genius."

He uses his hold to pull me forward, then slams me back against the tree, not violently like earlier, more like to drive a point home. "That mouth of yours will get you in a lot of trouble."

"Already done."

"You're a fucking nuisance."

"And you're a damn asshole."

"You might want to shut your mouth, witch. Provoking me is the last thing you want to do under the current circumstances."

My thighs clench and the tingles I've been feeling since he cornered me pool between them.

Sanity must've definitely left the building of my skull because I glare up at him. "You don't tell me what to do—"

My words end in a gasp when he crashes his lips to mine.

It's a violent kiss, as savage as he is and just as destructive. My teeth clank with his and my body comes completely undone.

Any hint of control I used to yield shatters and withers at his feet. I'm lost in the intensity of his lips on mine, of how his tongue conquers my own, leaving me no choice but to kiss him back with a wild energy that matches his.

Still choking me, his thumb grazes my chin, tilting it up so he can deepen the kiss while his other hand slides from my waist to the hem of my dress.

His movements drip with utter discipline, but there's zero patience behind them. He has no interest in seducing me, talking dirty to me, or being somewhat charming like the last time.

Now, he's a man who's set on taking and conquering.

Like he did a long time ago.

He yanks up my dress and pulls on my panties, lace this time, that he doesn't see for obvious reasons. The material stretches against my soaking folds and rips, causing a haunting sound.

I pause when I realize the sound, the guttural moan, is actually coming from me.

Kingsley hikes my thigh up his leg and speaks in hot, dark words against my mouth. "You should've never remembered this place, let alone come here, sweetheart. You, really, *really* shouldn't have shown me how much I can exploit you like a dirty little whore."

Arousal coats the insides of my thighs and I squirm, refusing to believe I got turned on by those words. "I'm not…a whore."

"Not any whore, no. *My* whore, however? Definitely." He thrusts four fingers inside me at the same time with intrusiveness that should be painful, but it's far from it. I get on my tiptoes, breathing harshly against his jaw. "Your pussy knows it's my whore, sweetheart. It's nearly swallowing my whole fist."

"Fuck…you…" I pant, trying and failing to resist the powerful wave that's building inside me.

"You're the one who will be fucked." He removes his fingers just when I'm about to reach the peak. My frustrated sound gets caught in the middle of nowhere when he hitches my leg up and thrusts inside me.

I didn't even focus on him lowering his pants or releasing his cock prior to that.

But all of those details don't matter, because he's so far inside me, I feel like throwing up.

The good kind. The kind after which I'll come.

And it hurts.

It hurts so much that the pain from my bruised shoulder feels like a stroll in the park.

I almost forgot how big, thick, and wide his cock is. It should be anywhere but inside another human.

"Oh…God."

"Stop praising him when I'm doing all the work," he speaks against my jaw, then flexes his fingers around my neck to nibble on the skin between them.

"You're ridiculously huge," I mutter. "Couldn't have a minuscule penis that fits your personality, huh?"

"This. Fucking. Mouth." He accentuates every word with a bite to my lip. Once he's done, I can taste the metallic tang of blood.

Not sure if it's his or mine.

I don't have the capacity to care either, because he lifts my other leg so I'm suspended between him and the tree's harsh surface, then drives into me so violently, I groan in both pleasure and pain.

They go hand in hand with this man. And so does ecstasy and madness.

His fingers knead my ass as he pounds into me deep, then pulls out almost completely before he thrusts back in. I can hear the sound of my arousal and feel myself clenching around him. He slams back in and hits so deep that I groan like an animal.

We're both pure animals right now.

He does it again, then pounds into me with a frightening intensity. My lungs are starved for air, but my body begs for more.

So much more.

He alternates between the two rhythms, driving me absolutely insane. When my legs start to droop, he smacks my ass, and I yelp, my eyes becoming big in the dark.

"What the hell was that about?"

"You stay with me when I'm fucking you. Am I clear?"

I don't get the chance to reply, because he removes his hand from my throat to bite it. Hard.

Then he's ripping off the straps of my dress. They tear at the front causing my breasts to spill out and he nearly sucks a whole one into his mouth.

He bites and fucks and spanks me every now and then, not leaving me room to catch my breath, let alone think.

My whole body comes alive, and simmering energy explodes at the surface.

He fucks me with fast, deep, and violent strokes that forbid me from keeping up. "Slow down."

"Add a please and I might consider it."

"Damn you."

"That's my cue to go harder then."

I didn't think it possible, but he actually does pick up his pace. Despite my coat, the tree scrapes my back from the intensity of his pounding, and I can feel new bruises forming all over my skin.

"Where's that mouth now that you're being pounded within an inch of your life?" he speaks against my nipple, then bites down on it.

"Screw...you..." I breathe, voice cracking as I come in a turbulence of harsh emotions that I can't find an explanation for.

"Gladly."

He fucks me harder through my orgasm. The movements are unapologetic, peppered with smacks against my ass, and bites anywhere his mouth can reach.

I'm in such a state of hypersensitivity that all I can focus on is the in and out of his cock inside me.

"Do you feel your pussy strangling me, sweetheart? Does getting fucked in the dark like an animal turn you on?"

"Shut…up…" I'm mortified that I forgot about that detail. The fact that we're outside, that anyone could wander here and witness this scene.

I'm not a virgin or inexperienced, or a prude, but I've always been vanilla. The "wham, bam, thank you, ma'am" kind. The "I get to run this show" type.

The "I fuck only behind closed doors and on a bed" kind.

And yet, all of my rules seem to be null and void when it comes to this man.

He pushes me far beyond my limits and to a dimension I didn't think existed.

"You're such a filthy little thing, but you're also a good girl." He slaps my ass and angles my thigh up to ram inside me. And it's a flat out ramming that hits my G-spot over and over and fucking over again. "Now, come with me."

I do. My head falls back on a loud scream as he empties himself inside me.

Inside. Me.

Not again.

I don't get the chance to protest, because his lips claim mine. I'm too dizzy, lightheaded, and definitely unable to stand on my feet, so I don't struggle as he pulls me closer.

Still buried deep inside me, he walks with purpose to God knows where.

While kissing me.

And all I can think about is that maybe he's the yin to my yang.

SIXTEEN

Kingsley

THERE ARE SIDES TO US THAT OTHER PEOPLE ARE NOT supposed to witness under any circumstances.

There are dark shadows, jaded edges, and the whole package of untouched corners.

But most of all, there are parts that we don't even like to look at in the mirror.

Everyone has a fraction that they dislike. Mine is everything.

When I was a teen with troubled emotions and a thirst for violence, I thought it was because my father betrayed my mother, who proceeded to hate herself and made me witness her drowning in her own blood.

Then as I grew older, I realized my need for a darker substance of life had nothing to do with my parents and more to do with my head that was apparently wired differently.

So differently that when Nicolo broke every other kid's toy, I just watched without being bothered or excited.

So differently that I used dark emotions, such as hatred, revenge, and violence, to fill the gaping hole I discovered inside me.

And I've been doing so well, wearing the diamond-studded

mask that's made of my billions and being the king my name refers to.

I hide my hungry demons, twisted emotions, and special brand of emptiness so well that even my daughter doesn't see it.

Nate does, but just a portion of it and only when I lose control.

So why in the fucking fuck does this woman who feels so small in my arms see that gaping hole?

More importantly, why did she seek me out when she was fully aware I would be at my fucking worst?

Partially, that doesn't matter, because I've been buried in her tight cunt for the past hour.

After I carried her inside the cottage, I fucked her on the carpet while on all fours as I pulled on her bright red hair that, under the dim light, looks like blood.

My demons' favorite color.

Then I threw her on the worn-out sofa, ripped off whatever was left of our clothes, and fucked her with her legs on my shoulders.

We somehow ended up on the floor again, on which I smacked her ass red, then, not being able to resist, I flipped her around and thrust into her again. I fucked her with renewed, unhinged energy until her moans turned to cries and small whimpers.

That's where we are right now, on the thirty-year-old carpet that only sees the cleaning lady every Sunday, like a church.

I'm on top of her, one of her long legs on my shoulder and the other on the floor.

Her body is a map of bite marks, sucking marks, finger marks, spanking marks. All the marks.

I've taken my time, stamping every inch of her skin with my mouth, dick, and hands.

My cock slowly thickens as I think of all the other places I can mark her in. Places no one but me will ever look at.

Aspen lies on her back, her hair like flames around her face, and she smells like the strongest patchouli and me.

Only me.

Perspiration clings to her skin and streaks of my cum decorate her stomach from earlier. Biting wasn't enough, so I came all over her pink tits and pale stomach.

Caveman much? Probably. But I'm starting to think I have no limits whatsoever with this woman.

If it were anyone else, she would've been on her way an hour ago, a few thousand dollars richer and with a copy of her NDA.

I never wanted to have a woman as soon as I've finished with increasing intensity. But Aspen is an infuriating exception to my habit.

Her eyes widen as she stares at me and then to where we're joined. "You're...getting hard again."

"No shit, Sherlock."

"Get off me, you monster." She slaps both her small hands on my chest and pushes, but the gesture lacks the strength to actually move me.

"The only monstrous thing about me is between my legs, sweetheart."

"You need a doctor for your sex addiction issues." She pushes me again, and this time, I pull out of her.

While I'm ready for round twenty, she is not. Purple bruises cover her shoulder and some parts of her face that aren't concealed by makeup.

I must've been blind to those when I took her like a Neanderthal against the tree—or the million times after.

And yet, I find myself forgetting about it again as I watch my cum dripping out of her pussy and messing up her fair thighs.

A strange feeling of possessiveness grabs hold of me by the balls. The need to own her, again and again, grows inside me with the persistence of a natural disaster.

Releasing a quaking breath, of relief or discomfort, I don't know, Aspen tries to slide back on her ass and winces. "Damn you. My ass feels like it's on fire."

"Don't even pretend you don't like it. The moment I spanked you, you came all over my dick."

Her lips tremble before she clamps down on them. "Shut up."

"Afraid to admit to your kinky tendencies?"

"I'm not kinky. I'm vanilla."

I laugh. "Vanilla is what Gwen eats and breathes instead of air. You, sweetheart, are the definition of a submissive."

"I'm not submissive."

"Yes, you are. You just didn't know it before. If you want proof…" I lean over and whisper in her ear in a low, deep tone, "How does it feel to be called a *good girl*?"

A full-body shudder overtakes her, her lips part, and that dash of red returns to her neck.

By the time she comes back to her senses and shoves me away, it's already too late.

"See?"

"Stop smiling or I'll smack you."

"Your crass mouth turns me the fuck on, sweetheart." I motion at my dick that's definitely running a campaign for another round.

"Don't even think about it." She slides a few inches back, completely ignoring the sting of my handprints.

"I wasn't going to do anything."

"And you expect me to believe you? You have the sex drive of a bull."

"My dick is honored."

"That wasn't a compliment," she grumbles. "Also, you didn't use a condom."

"Should've pointed that out the first time around." I can't resist gathering my cum with my fingers, then slowly smear it on her folds.

She shudders, her toes curling. "I didn't get the chance… Aren't you going to ask whether or not I'm on birth control?"

"Does it matter?"

"What?" she snaps.

"If you are, and there's a ninety-nine point ninety-nine percent probability of that, considering how much of a responsible adult you are, then that's that. If it's the remaining zero point zero one percent and you aren't on birth control, then we'll deal with it when it becomes an issue."

"How the hell can you say that after everything that happened in the past?"

"The past is in the past. I fail to see the reason why this should be made into an argument."

"Gee, I don't know. Maybe the tiny fact that the last time you put your dick in me, Gwen came out of it."

"She must've been a fast sperm."

"You're disgusting." She hits my shoulder. "What happened isn't a joke."

"Never thought of it as one, considering my single parent status. The fact remains, we were kids back then, but we aren't anymore, so quit the dramatics. They don't suit you." I start to fuck her with my cum, but she crawls back like an injured animal.

Her glare could cut stones as she folds into herself. "I said. Don't even think about it, Kingsley."

"You have to elaborate because, unlike the press's claims, I'm unable to read minds."

"Your eyes are shining with that light that means you'll take me again."

"I won't take you, I'll *fuck* you." I smile, falling onto my back to physically subdue my libido. "But I'll give you some time to recuperate."

She remains in a sitting position, facing me, but pulls her knees to her chest and hides most of her nakedness. "Thanks, Your Majesty."

"Most welcome, my good girl."

Her lips part and I grin. To say I like taking her off guard would be an understatement. She becomes docile in a way, and so fucking adorable.

An adjective that I shouldn't even have the capacity to use on this woman.

She has this side of her that's hidden from everyone.

Everyone except me.

"You're in an awfully good mood for someone who was punching a tree in the middle of the night like the main character from a slasher movie."

"An intense fuck does that. You were a good sport." I reach for my pants that are lying nearby and pull out my Zippo.

"I'm not a damn sport."

"You can be the whole fucking Olympics." I grab her coat and throw it on her.

While I'm as hot as a sauna, she was shivering just now. It's a shame to sacrifice the view of her pink tits and pussy, but priorities and all that.

"You can be such an asshole."

"Can be? I thought I was an asshole for certain." I tuck the coat under her chin, then I tilt her head so I can get a better view of her eyes.

They're as deep as the earth but are still reaching for the sky with the stubbornness of tall trees.

She pulls away, then pauses, grabbing my hand between hers and examining it. "You've busted your knuckles."

I tactfully retrieve it, lie back down, and flip the Zippo open with my hand that's resting on my chest. "They'll heal."

"You're not some thug or in high school anymore."

"Thanks for the unnecessary reminder about my existential status. I'll add it as a note in my schedule."

"You know, emphasis on reason and systematic thinking is a synonym to retreating from living."

"Spare me the Nietzsche bullshit." I angle my head to face her. "Besides, ever heard of practicing what you preach?"

"Me?"

"When was the last time you lived in the moment? Aside from when I was fucking your brains out just now, of course."

"The arrogance police are taking you into custody."

I grin. "You're not avoiding the living in the moment subject. Do you do that or are you as theoretical as your mentally unstable idol?"

"I..."

"What?"

"I watched *Friends* with Caroline the other night." She winces as soon as she says the sentence.

"Wow. That's as badass as bungee jumping."

"You don't get to lecture me when all you do is destruction, revenge, and more destruction."

"Either that or dabbling in some disgusting territory like peace, love, and curing world hunger."

She chuckles and the sound is light and air-like in quality. "What blasphemy."

"I know. The worst."

We stare at each other for a beat, the only sound echoing in the air my Zippo's opening and closing motion.

Aspen swiftly slides her attention to the uneventful ceiling and its wooden pillars. "We should probably go before someone reports us for trespassing on their property."

"Unless I can report myself, that's highly unlikely."

Her head whips in my direction. "You own this?"

"And a hundred other properties. Admittedly, it's the most Halloween-themed of the bunch and could be used for some satanic rituals."

She runs her gaze over the older than dirt window frames, the shabby decor that belongs in a low-budget motel set for a cowboy movie, and the faint light from the fixture that's threatening to fall beside us.

"You never said you owned this place."

"Never said I didn't. Technically, it was my father's at the time." My lips twist. "A birthday present to my mother, a vacation cottage where we could come for the weekends."

"It must've been nice."

"Fucking *horrible* is the word you're looking for. There was nothing nice about Benjamin and Liliana Shaw's marriage. All they did was pretend they were the next American king and queen while simultaneously drowning in other things besides each other.

He, in pussy. She, in any pills she could get her hands on—pain-killers, sedatives, antidepressants." I pause, not knowing what the hell came over me to talk about my parents. "But hey, a genius child with godlike looks came out of their unfortunate union, so it wasn't a useless pairing, after all."

She doesn't buy my attempt to lighten the mood and frowns. "Have you abandoned this place because it reminds you of your parents? Or maybe because it reminds you of the child you were with your parents? You called it the yang to your yin, not yin to your yang as it's commonly known. Because you're the yin, the black side of the sphere, so is the child version of you perhaps that yang?"

"You have so many questions for someone who was begging me to stop or they would faint not ten minutes ago. I liked you better when you were mute."

"Your attempts at being an asshole to make me drop the subject are the definition of a failure."

"You're fucking infuriating."

"I know, you tell me that every chance you get. For the record, you're way past the infuriating stage and well into the obnoxious one. Now, answer my question."

"Add a please and I might consider it."

She purses her lips. "No."

"Good talk."

"Joke's on you. I'll just draw my own conclusions. When they're so deeply engraved in my head, no amount of truth you offer will be able to replace them."

"Didn't think you liked to engrave details about me in that busy brain of yours."

"Shut up," she says, her signature "I'm embarrassed" line, her neck reddening. Then she clears her throat. "Anyway, Gwen visited me and I told her you had nothing to do with my attack."

My jaw clenches at the reminder of my clusterfuck of a relationship with my daughter that's been going downhill since she chose my best friend as the love of her life. "Doesn't matter."

"Of course it does." She springs up, letting the coat fall to her midsection. Her tits gently bounce as she leans over. "She was so hurt at the prospect of hurting you. You're a jerk, but you're a good father type of jerk, so don't let this unnecessary rift tear you apart… Kingsley!"

"What?" I don't stop staring at the marked flesh of her breasts.

"Have you heard a word I was saying?"

"Yes and no. It's kind of distracting, not to mention creepy, to talk about Gwen when your tits are on full display."

She covers them with an arm, turning all red. "You damn pervert."

I grab her arm and pull it down, exposing her pink-dusted nipples. "Do you want to see what a real pervert looks like?"

She must catch a glimpse of the lust and the million positions I have planned for her shining in my eyes, because hers widen, flicking between green and brown.

"No, Kingsley."

"Call me King like you did earlier."

"I…did not."

"Yes, you did, in that throaty sexy little voice of yours." I pull her close, throwing the coat to the side.

"Don't you dare or I'll bite your dick off."

"Kinky. You know I love it." I grab a handful of her red ass and she moans.

"Goddamn it…you asshole."

"I know, sweetheart. You have the green light to call me as many colorful names as you can think of while I fuck you." And then I spread her legs and proceed to eat her sweet cunt as if I'm a starving animal.

It's my twisted form of a thank-you for saving me from my own head.

Or at least, distracting me from it.

SEVENTEEN

Aspen

"Is someone going to tell me what's going on?"

I groan around the rim of my cup of tequila—it's useless to call it coffee anymore—and turn around to face Nate.

We're in the conference room at Weaver & Shaw. Massive, sterile, and soulless. Its main use, aside from the partners' meetings, is for strategizing how to extract more money from the rich and influential.

Only minutes ago, we concluded a meeting with a large corporation that's trying to get out of the IRS's clutches. The CEO left with a promise of a seamless process and a wide grin on his face.

The associate lawyers left with tasks to perform and I was hoping to do the same before Nate closed the door and blocked my way.

He leans against the large desk, arms crossed with apparent nonchalance, but his dark eyes pin me down with a demand of an answer to his question.

An answer I don't have unless I blurt out that I fucked his best friend, partner, and father-in-law.

That was yesterday—or early this morning. Since then, I'm

surprised I can walk—albeit slowly, so as not to trigger the feeling of Kingsley inside me. I've been sorer than a warrior out of the battlefield, with bites, hickeys and handprints that should be enough to press charges for assault.

Though an assault is the last thing it felt like. That was pure claiming, intense and unbearably ruthless.

I had no chance to walk away unscathed, and it's not only because of what he did. It's the fact that I lost myself and took pleasure in every moment of it.

And I know that if I don't stay away, there's more of that to come. Next time, I probably won't even be able to walk.

Next time? Why the hell are you thinking about the next time? That won't be happening.

I massage my temple, trying to force myself back into the moment. "What do you mean?"

Nate raises a brow, which translates to, "I'm not the person you can bullshit," then starts counting on one hand. "First, I find out you were assaulted, then I learn King is back to being Nicolo Luciano's side bitch, and as if that's not enough, you coincidentally are getting into bed with the mafia, too. I leave for one second and you switch sides to the underground world? I expected this from King, but not from you, Aspen."

I sip a long drag of my coffee-tequila because I'm apparently too sober for this conversation. "It's just business."

"And life is just a simulation." He stares, utterly unamused. "What's going on?"

"I needed a favor, okay?"

"What type of favor?"

"The type you shouldn't worry about."

"If it concerns you, then it has all the conditions to make me worry. You're my friend and my wife's mother, Aspen. So if there's anything I need to know, now is the time to say it."

"It's really nothing, Nate. I'll take care of it and I promise that the firm will stay out of this."

"How about Gwyneth? Will she be out of your business with

the mafia, too? I thought you wanted a chance with her. Spoiler alert, this isn't how to go about it."

I fill my stomach with more alcohol. "I'd never hurt her."

"Not you, but your new best friends might."

"It won't happen." I sigh, massaging my other temple. "Just drop it, Nate. Some skeletons are better left in the closet."

Nate knows I come from a rough childhood and lost my parents as a kid. He's also aware that I was abused by my foster parents and eventually ran away. However, he doesn't know the details and he certainly has no clue about who my father is.

I might've considered telling him under different circumstances, but now that he's my daughter's husband, it's out of the question.

He's protective to a fault when it comes to Gwyneth and this would just create unnecessary problems. He might become the one who actively distances me from her to shield her from my mess.

"Then riddle me this, Aspen. What does King have to do with your skeletons? Aside from the fact that you once conceived Gwyneth together, the only thing you share is a passionate mutual disregard."

My chest clenches and I have to pause before I speak. What the hell? It's only his name, why am I feeling like a preteen with a hormone-infused crush?

"He has nothing to do with me." I sound so convincing that even I would believe myself if I were less sober.

"Let's see." He counts on his hand again. "He so coincidentally got back by Nicolo's side at the same time you went to him. He now calls you by your given name that I genuinely thought he didn't know. Oh, and he's been so out of control that he fucked it all up with Gwyneth by showing his ugly side. So excuse me if I think there's something more to this tale."

Shit.

My hand starts to become unsteady, so I clutch the mug tighter.

Nate finding out about our sex session—or sessions—is nothing more than an unneeded complication.

Not if it's over.

Keep telling yourself that.

"You, of all people, are well aware of how unpredictably volatile Kingsley is. So I should be the one to ask you what's wrong with him after his coma. Maybe he hit his head too hard?"

"Yeah, no. You're not using a reverse questioning tactic on me, Aspen. You're hiding something, I can feel it, taste it, and smell it in the air."

I wave him off, opting to disappear in my office for the rest of the day and potentially indefinitely.

Before I can take a step, the door flings open without so much as a knock.

Only one person in this building would dare to barge in on the managing partner of the firm.

And the strangest part is that I feel him before I even see him. As if there's a stupid connection between us or something.

When I lift my head and my eyes clash with Kingsley's stormy ones, I'm struck by that scary feeling I had when he actually paused the sex marathon and we talked.

A feeling that goes beyond the physical and dabbles in much more obscure territory.

He slams the door shut, proving to lack a gentle bone in his body, and marches toward us with sure determination and knitted brows.

If he could be less dashing in his black suit and groomed appearance, it would be much better.

Though the last time I saw him, he was out of the suit and looked a great deal more lethal with that weapon between his legs.

My thighs shake in remembrance and the ache I took a bath to erase springs back to life.

I internally curse myself for thinking about him naked and reacting violently to it.

Nate is here, for God's sake.

Stay calm.

Stay calm…

Kingsley stops a hair's breadth away from me, but not before he douses me with his all-male cedarwood scent. "What the fuck are you doing here?"

My mouth opens, then closes before I snap back, "What the hell is wrong with you first thing in the morning? Didn't get a coffee?"

"You didn't answer my question. Why are you here when your vacation isn't over?"

"Because I actually have work to do, and oh, check the calendar. It's an age where women don't get told what to do."

"Check your contract. It's a piece of paper that says I'm your boss and, therefore, will tell you what to do, how to do it, and when. Which is right now. Get the fuck out of here before I call security to throw you out."

"I'll record the whole thing and report you to the board for abuse of power and if I'm in the mood, I might sue you for compensation, too."

"Tough shit, witch. Suits that are based on pure spite are my specialty. Good fucking luck winning against me in court."

"This is popcorn-worthy and all, but why do you look like you're on the verge of kissing or tearing each other's clothes off? Maybe both and not in that particular order?" Nate speaks from my right.

Kingsley and I jerk backward. Or I do, anyway, heat rising to my neck. The fucking asshole who's able to provoke me with his mere presence simply steps back. His expression doesn't even change, still pissed and closed off and all other negative emotions that he excels at displaying.

"Not in this lifetime," I say in answer to Nate's question.

Kingsley narrows his eyes on me in pure disapproval before his rigid façade returns. I know I won't like what he'll say before he opens his mouth. "Then you would be a liar."

I pause, Nate pauses, and the whole world seems to tilt into silence.

What the…

The fucking—

"We made Gwen, remember? There was a lot of fucking involved," he says with collected cool and I nearly don't hear him over the pounding in my ears.

"Huh." Nate scratches his chin. "For the record, if one of you kills the other, whether it's first-degree or manslaughter, I won't represent the other party." He gives us a suspicious look and mutters, "You're parents and are old enough to rise above bickering like children. Pull it together."

Then he's out the door, leaving me with the nightmare in the form of a man.

I jam a finger against his chest. "What the hell is wrong with you? Nate's already suspecting something and you nearly revealed everything."

"Aside from your horror movie-worthy expression, I don't see why Nate shouldn't know. Afraid your ex-fuck buddy will be jealous?"

"More like I don't want complications. And for the last damn time, Nate and I were never fuck buddies, not that it concerns you."

He grabs me by the waist and I shiver when he traps me between his chest and the conference table. My ass burns when it hits the edge, courtesy of the man who squashes all distance between us until only my cup of coffee separates us.

His voice drops to a sexy ramble when he says, "The taste of your cunt is still on my lips, so I say it very much concerns me."

"We're at work," I whisper-yell, surveying our surroundings.

"So? I own the work."

"Well, I don't. So excuse me so I can go make a living, Your Royal Highness."

"Stop provoking me for sport unless you fancy a fuck on the top of this very table."

My hold falters on the cup due to two facts. One, I know this crazy man will go through with his promise. Two, I'm inexplicably buzzing with nauseating excitement at the possibility.

When I say nothing, he takes it as a sign that his threat went through. "Now, are you or are you not going to stop being stubborn and resume your vacation?"

"I'm perfectly fine."

"Hiding the bruises with makeup doesn't make you fine. It makes you a con artist."

"Oh, I'm sorry. Which bruises are we talking about? The ones from the thugs or the ones you savagely gave me like some barbarian? I can't even move without feeling them."

A wide, impossibly proud grin curves his lips. "Mission accomplished. Brace yourself, sweetheart, there will be more marks before those disappear."

"You…"

"Pervert? You're starting to sound like a broken record."

"And you're starting to get too comfortable touching me." I swat his hand away. "I'm not your toy for the week, Kingsley."

"It can be a month or two. I don't mind."

"Well, I do."

He frowns. "What's the duration you're thinking of?"

"None. It was a one-time thing. We fucked each other out of our systems and it's over."

"That might be true for you, but I haven't even started yet, sweetheart." He grabs my chin, spreads his fingers on my skin with domineering command, and tilts my head back. "My place tonight?"

"No."

"Your place then? Though you'll have to kick Caroline Luciano back to her mansion. I don't appreciate an audience."

"No."

"My, witch. I didn't know you were into exhibitionism."

"No, as in, it won't be happening, asshole. Besides, I have to attend an event with one of my overseas clients tonight."

"I'll take a rain check then."

EMPIRE OF LUST | 191

"Take no for an answer instead."

"Allow me to decline." He snatches my cup of coffee. "And quit drinking while on the clock, or outside of it, for that matter."

Then he goes out, carrying my drink and leaving me with mountain-sized frustrations.

EIGHTEEN

Kingsley

A T THE EXPENSE OF BEING CALLED A STALKER WITH SERIAL creeper tendencies, I find out where exactly Aspen is tonight.

Thanks to Caroline's zero sense of hiding information. She was so easy to manipulate into telling me where Aspen is that it's a little suspicious.

Especially with her devil-may-care chuckle at the end and the ambiguous, "You really should've seen those diaries."

At any rate, I acquired the information I needed and got rid of Nate on the pretense that it's an important business call.

He's been spending the entire day either trying to kidnap me or force me to call my daughter. According to him, I should apologize. According to me, he's a daughter-stealer and should go fuck himself.

Besides, she's the one who crossed the line this time. To think I'm a woman-beater is the worst misjudgment anyone, let alone my own flesh and blood, has inflicted on me.

In view of the fact that I lived my whole life watching my mother being emotionally abused—abuse is abuse—any variation of that poison is beneath me.

Unless it's bashing someone's head in.

Conclusion of the story is, Gwen has to be the one who apologizes. And as much as putting a rift between us is no different than discarding a part of me, she needs this lesson.

And I need her mother to stop being fucking difficult.

For that, I have to find her.

It proves to be harder than I thought, considering I've been roaming the Carsons' residence for half an hour and have caught no sight of her.

It's large, ancient, and lacks a soul, like all rich people mansions. The old dog's daughter-in-law is throwing some sort of a charity ball to help orphaned children. She looked serious about it, too, when I barged in here earlier without an invitation, as usual, but with a hefty check for the cause.

I doubt the Barbie-like blondie shares her father-in-law's view that a charity's only purpose is to serve as a tax haven for the rich.

The house has been decorated with soft lights and extravagant tables covered in red velvet. Screens upon screens show a carefully made video of children's testimonials that no one pays attention to.

The guests mingle in closed circles, either gossiping or rekindling relationships. The actual topic of this night, children, is somewhere below nonexistent.

I stroll into the ball and eventually find myself in a group of old buffalos who were friends with my father.

I'm only half listening and definitely not entertaining them. Many of these fools thought that, as my father's heir, I'd continue to invest in their businesses for the sake of our interpersonal relationships.

They soon found out that I don't attend their birthday parties, have no interest in their backyard koi ponds, and I'm heartless enough to watch them go bankrupt instead of being pulled down into a hole with them.

My father was an investor, yes, but too attached for Wall Street's liking. Which is why my fortune is way greater than his ever was.

I'm practical, logical, and absolutely don't go around following people.

Except for a certain redheaded femme fatale, obviously.

I even had to take drastic measures by coming here.

Because, of fucking course, Aspen's event had to happen in our competitor's compound.

Carson & Carson is one of the few rival law firms that I have any semblance of respect toward. Despite the fact that the managing partner, Alexander Carson, used to be my father's friend and attorney.

He's old-fashioned, likes shady businesses because they pay well, and isn't afraid to dirty his hands.

In short, everything Benjamin Shaw was.

Nate and I became his competitors when we started Weaver & Shaw, and we would've crushed him if it hadn't been for his son. New, young blood, and with revolutionary ideas that changed his father's old ways.

That's where I spot Aspen—while half listening to the old men's yapping about taxes. With the younger Carson. Asher.

I have to take a sip of my Macallan to keep from foaming at the mouth.

Aspen has always been a beautiful woman, even when she was an infuriating creature who loved to be a thorn in my side for sport.

There's a sharp edge to her beauty and it has less to do with her red hair and high cheekbones and more to do with her cutting gaze and erect posture.

If confidence could be put in categories, hers is the quiet one. It's bold but not enough to have her screaming or letting irrationality take over. She's determined to a fault, too, which is why I know that when she decides something, there's no deterring her from it.

Not tonight, though.

I rake my gaze over her simple long-sleeved black dress that reaches the floor. She even has a fashionable scarf covering her neck, for obvious reasons.

The thought of her staring at the angry hickeys I left on her in the mirror makes my cock rock-hard.

He's been in a constant wake-up mode since last night and I refuse to be a pubescent and jack off.

The blinding desire to grab her from between those men and ram my dick inside her cunt is so overwhelming that I'm surprised my cock doesn't explode from my dress pants.

She smiles at the two men standing with her. One is Carson junior and the other is a man who appears to be in his mid-forties. Strongly built, blank-faced, and with an erect posture that resembles mine.

I recognize a man of power when I see one and he's definitely on the spectrum.

I contemplate how to send him to the next planet without drawing anyone's attention. Or maybe I *should* draw attention to the fact that he's married—judging by the ring on his finger—and is still standing too close to Aspen.

Just when I'm entertaining the idea of committing arson in Alexander Carson's mansion, Aspen's chameleon eyes meet mine.

They widen, her smile falters, and she clutches her flute of champagne tighter.

I grin, loving the feeling of catching her off guard a bit too much. Probably because she's not the type of person to be caught off guard.

"Surprise," I mouth from across the room.

She purses her lips in a clear indication of "stay away."

Not even offering an "excuse me," I leave the old farts and march toward her. If she was the only one in the circle, she'd remove her shoe and hit me upside the head with it.

But since there's company and societal standards to uphold, she lets the emotions fester inside her to the point of near explosion.

And I know that, because redness spills from her neck to her chin, and the flames ignite in her eyes.

I make it worse by smiling when I barge uninvited into their small circle. "Carson, how have you been?"

Asher shakes my hand. He's in his late twenties, the same age as Sebastian, Nate's nephew, whom he practically raised, so he's, therefore, been around us all our lives.

"Kingsley." He raises a brow, looking more and more like a younger, solemn version of his father. "I heard you were in a coma, but you look as good as the devil."

"And just as manipulative, so you better protect your clients before I steal them."

"Noted," he says with a slight narrow of his eyes. "Aspen is a lot more approachable than you in business matters. At least she doesn't threaten me in my own house."

"Property is proportional," *says me, who's been fighting tooth and nail for my family home.* I finally give the other man my attention. "Where are my manners? Introduce us, Ms. Leblanc."

She gives me a glare that could cut through my nonexistent heart. "Jonathan, this is Kingsley Shaw. The co-owner of the firm where I work. Kingsley, this is Jonathan King. An English businessman who's investing in the States."

We shake hands, firmly, harshly even, and he barely escapes not having his fingers crushed. But the more I tighten my hold, the harder he does it as well, until we let go at the same time. What type of message is the fucker trying to send?

It's with effort that I guard my nonchalant stance. "I didn't know Ms. Leblanc's interests reached the other side of the pond."

He offers a reserved smile and speaks in a posh British accent that's straight out of some historical show. "She's resourceful that way, Ms. Leblanc. One of the best overseas solicitors I've worked with."

I grind my molars and I'm not sure if it's because of his words or how she glows with a prideful smile at said words.

"You're one of my most valuable clients, Mr. King."

He raises his glass. "To more fruitful partnerships."

Asher and Aspen raise their glasses. I don't.

"Glad to know Weaver & Shaw is of value to you," I say instead. "Will your wife be joining us, Mr. King?"

"Unfortunately, no. I spare her the dullness of these events whenever possible."

"She's lucky to have you," Aspen offers, and although it's a statement that could be said out of courtesy, it ticks the last box of my patience.

"Indeed," I say with masked anger, then swiftly but firmly grab Aspen by the arm. "If you'll excuse us, gentleman. Ms. Leblanc and I have matters to attend to."

I don't even wait for their response as I drag her by my side and down the hall.

"What the hell are you doing?" she hisses under her breath, practically jogging to keep up with my long strides. "Kingsley! Let me go."

Her nails dig into my hand, but no matter how much she scratches and claws, I don't release her.

The audience that watches our movements might as well be invisible. All I can see are shades of black, red, and an undeniable urge.

I push her inside one of the rooms and slam her against the door.

She gasps, her lips falling open. "What the—"

Her words end in a gasp when I crash my lips against hers.

She's stunned for a second before she tries to bite me, mumbling and clashing her mouth with mine.

Aspen and I don't just kiss, we war.

We go to lengths that no one else would approach.

I grab a fistful of her fiery hair, biting her lip as hard as she bites mine. A metallic taste explodes in my mouth, staining my lips, and I'm not sure if it's hers or my own.

I don't care either.

Sinking my fingers into her dress, I bunch it up until it reaches her waist.

When my fingers meet her bare pussy, I groan, pulling away from her lips. "You're not only soaking wet, but you came prepared to be fucked."

"Screw you, asshole. How dare you interfere with my work—"

I thrust two fingers inside her cunt and that's enough to cut off her words.

Her eyes droop and her breathing hardens, but she mutters, "I'm going to k-kill you…if you get in my business again…oh fuck."

"Right, fuck, and it's not recommended to threaten me with murder when your cunt is clenching around my fingers."

"You…have…no…right…*shit*."

I shut her up with my lips on hers as she shakes around my fingers. I love how a few rough thrusts and some clitoral stimulation are able to throw this woman over the edge.

She's a fucking sex goddess.

Still gripping her by the hair, I pull out of her and drag her to the tall window that overlooks the back garden.

Her reaction is delayed due to the orgasm, considering that I have to practically carry her. I slam her front against the glass and she gasps, but I don't give her time to process what's happening as I free my cock and thrust into her from behind.

Fuck condoms.

Nothing will be a barrier between me and the warmth of this infuriating woman.

My hand rests on her hip and my other clutches her jaw with non-negotiable command. "Did you like being praised by that motherfucker, huh?"

Her legs shake and her pussy swallows me whole, but she has the audacity to glare back at me. "I did. Not everyone is a jerk like you are."

"And yet, I'm the one who has my cock up your tight little cunt, sweetheart." I accentuate my words with a few harsh and fast pounds that shatter her breaths. "From now on, you'll erase any other man from your life, got it?"

"Screw you."

I release her waist and slap her ass cheek. "That's not the right answer. Now, say it."

She yelps, her moans echoing in the darkness. "N-no."

My palm meets her flesh, but it's so much stronger this time that she screams. "Try again, sweetheart."

"Stop it...damn it..."

Slap.

"Not until you give the right answer."

"You don't get to tell me what to do."

"Watch me." I give her ass three consecutive slaps that leave her gasping and clenching around me. "You're such a little whore, sweetheart. Just a few smacks and you're swallowing my dick."

"Asshole..."

I release her chin and slide my thumb along the crack until I find her back hole. "You mean this one? Mmm, it feels virgin and ready to be fucked."

Aspen goes still. "Kingsley...don't..."

"Not today." I thrust my thumb into her ass. "But one day, you'll take my cock up this ass like a good girl, then you'll scream so loud that the world will know you're being fucked by me." She trembles and I use the chance to smack it. "You still didn't answer me."

Her surprised noise of pleasure pierces the air, but she mutters, "No."

"If you want to be able to sit at all, give me the right answer."

She glares at me over her shoulder and dares to smile. "Still...a no. Show me your worst."

I turn into a pure fucking animal then. My rhythm is frantic, deep, and I feel like I'll never be finished with her. I thrust a finger into her back hole, too, fingering her while fucking her and slapping her ass until small whimpers escape her.

"I'm going to break the goddamn stubbornness out of you, Aspen, and when I'm done, I'll do it all over again." I grab her by the hair so her lips are mere inches away from my own. "Say yes."

She shakes her head in my hold, even as tears gather in the corners of her eyes. Whether they're pleasure or pain tears, I don't know.

"Look at your expression." I direct her face to our reflection in the glass. "You see the ecstasy in it? That's what any guest can see if he walks outside and looks up. He'll see you taking my dick like the filthy little whore you are. Will you give them a show of how thoroughly you're being fucked by me? Or will you be a good girl and only show your pleasure to me?"

Her lips part. "King…stop saying things like that…"

"Say the magic word."

"No—" Her moaned word ends on a gasp when I slap her already red ass cheek.

She comes then, hard, and with a throaty sound that triggers my own orgasm. My balls tighten and my back jerks in a straight line as I drive into her with wild, deep thrusts.

"Fuck, fuck, fuck." I empty inside her for so long that I think it won't end. When I pull out, my cum slides down her legs and onto her shoes and I can't help following the path with greedy eyes.

She slumps against the glass, the hickeys I left on her neck visible from underneath the crumpled scarf that's as disheveled as she is.

I wrap a fistful of her bright hair around my hand and pull her to me until her back is flush against my chest.

"Let go of me," she whines in a vulnerable voice. "I'm sensitive."

I find the fair skin of her neck, right between two fading hickeys, and bite. Harshly.

"Ow, that hurts! Why do you keep biting me like an animal in heat?"

"I'm better than an animal. I'm always in heat." I roll my hips to prove a point.

"Holy shit." She gives me the stink eye. "How can you still be hard?"

"My dick and I agree that we won't stop." I bite her neck again, this time sucking on her flesh. "Not until you give us the right answer, sweetheart."

And then I'm claiming her again.

And again.

And fucking again.

NINETEEN

Aspen

"I HAVE MY OWN PLACE, YOU KNOW." I CROSS MY ARMS OVER my bathrobe, standing near the bathroom door and shooting daggers at the sex addict in front of me.

This is beyond anything I could've thought or imagined.

I didn't sign up for this.

I really didn't sign up to be ravaged multiple times at a party full of people until I could barely move. The only reason I was able to get back to socializing is because I nearly kicked him in the nuts so he'd let me go.

But, of course, Kingsley doesn't let go. At least, not for long. He's like a giant black cat who gives his prey a break just so he can pounce on them afterward.

And that's exactly what he did. At first, he let me socialize on my own while watching from afar, but then he glued himself to my side and introduced me to some of his father's friends.

I couldn't exactly be mad about that, because making connections is vital in the legal field, and many of those businessmen are potential clients.

Not sure why he was doing me the favor, and even introducing me as a senior partner at his firm, which he never does. I would swear that he erased my position from his head a long time ago.

At any rate, he was in a suspiciously good mood and proved it by whispering filthy words in my ear as if throwing me off-balance was his favorite sport.

When we left the event—or I was leaving because his mere presence caused me sexual frustration—he suggested taking me home.

Or rather, he shoved me into his car.

And all that effort was so he could fuck me in his house all over again. Against the door, the wall, and just now, in the shower.

Thanks to his insatiable libido, I'm unable to move. Again. And I'm sore and achy all over.

Jesus. I'm not so young anymore.

And neither is he. So where the hell does he get this energy? He even looks ready to have a redo.

Maybe I need to make friends with Martha and ask her to smuggle me out of this place after I put sleeping powder in his drink.

His dark hair falls over his eyes as he uses a towel to dry it, sending the wet strands flying everywhere.

I try to glance away from his sculpted torso and fail. It doesn't help that droplets of water slide down his abs and to the V-line that disappears beneath his boxer briefs. He has the type of perfect physique that belongs on the cover of a magazine.

"Your place is occupied by a certain mobster wife and her dogs," he says in answer to my earlier statement. "As I mentioned, having an audience is not my thing."

"How did you know Caroline has dogs?"

"When I talked to her on the phone earlier, she said Cain and Lucifer say hi. I honest to fuck hope those are only some edgy dog names and that you didn't invite actual demons to your apartment."

"Why did you even call Caroline… Let me guess, she told you where I was?"

"You guessed correctly."

I'm going to kill Callie.

"Don't be a stranger." He motions at my proximity with a crooked smile. "I won't bite you."

"Won't bite me, my ass. I have the marks to prove you wrong."

"Allow me to correct my statement. I won't bite you *now*." He starts toward me with long, determined strides, draping a clean towel over his shoulder.

I grab the nearest object, a gold candelabra, and hold it protectively in front of me. "I swear to God, Kingsley. If you take a step further, I'm going to bash your head in."

If I thought that would deter him, I'm proven utterly wrong when he keeps approaching with a wicked grin. "You have it in you to knock out my genius-level neurons?"

"Just like you have it in you to drain me."

"Your pussy and your mouth don't sing the same tune, sweetheart." He stops a hair's breadth away. "I bet if I put my fingers inside, that cunt will swallow them and keep them there."

"Stop it…" I jam the candelabra against his chest, but something blinds my eyes.

A towel.

He removes the candelabra from my fingers with embarrassing ease. Then my sight is back when he starts to towel-dry my hair with both hands.

I tense, but he just continues his task. "Relax. I won't fuck you again…for now. You need to eat and drink more water first or you'll be dehydrated."

My lips part as I stare up at him, honestly looking for a sign that this is a joke. When I find nothing, my throat dries.

Since when is he a caring person? Yes, I know that he dedicated his life to Gwen and is a loving father, but other than that, he's been crowned a jerk.

I had assumed that he'd be the same toward his sexual partners, too.

A queasy feeling spreads through my stomach at that thought.

No, nope. I'm not going to think about his fuck buddies, army of escorts, and the fact that I'm one of them.

I am not.

I just let him fuck me to get all the tension between us sorted out. That's it.

That's *all*.

I try to grab the towel. "I can do it myself."

"Stay still." He gives every red strand individual care as if he's on a mission.

"I'm not a baby," I grumble.

"No, but you're careless about your body's needs."

"I can towel-dry my own hair."

"Which you didn't. Stop making this into a fucking event and finding an issue with everything."

I open my mouth to give a scathing reply but choose to close it. I'm being defensive, completely and utterly so, and if I say anything, it'll only serve as proof against me.

"I gather you're not used to people taking care of you," he speaks softly in the silence of the room—or as softly as Kingsley can.

"I'm independent."

"Is that another word for I'm scared to open up?"

"Only a sexist asshole would assume an independent woman is that way because she's scared of something."

"I'm not assuming, sweetheart. I know it for a fact, and if sexist is the label you want to slap on me, by all means. Whatever helps you sleep at night. The fucks I have to give are 404 not found. Just know that no amount of resistance on your part will change my mind about what I'll do to you."

"What is that supposed to mean?"

"Exactly what you heard. I've decided you're mine for the time being, and that means no other man will touch you aside from me. Oh, and you'll come here every other night and spend it in my bed."

I hate that something squeezes in my heart and my stomach tightens. What the hell? "Spend it in your bed?"

"Or shower or counter or wall. Basically, any surface that can be used to fuck you senseless."

"And you just decided that all on your own without, I don't know, talking to me about it or anything?"

"The part about you being mine is absolute. The second part, which concerns you showing up here, is negotiable, but if you want me to go to your apartment, kick the audience out first."

"Wow. You sound so confident about the fact that I would agree to be yours."

"I'm rich, handsome, and illegally smart, not to mention I have a dick you can't keep up with. I'm a catch. Highly recommended. So why wouldn't you agree?"

"I don't know, due to the fact that I don't even like you, maybe?"

"You don't have to like me to fuck me, sweetheart. Your pussy would gladly back my claim."

I slap a hand on his chest and push him away—or try to, anyway. "Allow me to use your favorite line and decline."

He removes the towel from my head but doesn't give me back my space. The color of his eyes darkens like a storm brewing in the distance with pure intention of mass destruction. "Your stubbornness isn't so cute anymore."

"It was never supposed to be." I glare and his jaw clenches.

We remain like that for several long beats. Like a tug of war between two powerful generals. It's almost impossible to maintain eye contact with him for an extended time, but I'm ready to be drained to zero if it means holding my own.

"Let's hear it," he finally says.

"Hear what?"

"Your counterargument."

"This isn't a relationship. Only fucking, that either of us can walk away from at any second. And I'm not yours or anyone else's. I belong to myself."

His eye twitches, but other than that, no reaction shows on his face. "So you want us to be friends with benefits, minus the friends part. So should it be called enemies with benefits? A hate-fucking relationship?"

Now that he puts it that way, it sounds more fucked up than it did in my brain. But it does sound plausible enough and I can stand my ground, so I give a sharp nod.

"How much control do you have, Aspen? A mountain's worth? Two? I want you to remember this moment when I force every inch of it to crumble to the ground."

"Does that mean you agree?"

"To what, exactly? An open relationship where you act as if you're not mine and I get to jam my dick into the city's available holes?"

A bitter taste explodes at the back of my throat at the image he's painted, and a weird negative energy perches on my chest.

It takes me a few moments to find my voice. "If you fuck another woman, I'll fuck a man and make you watch."

"Oh, I won't be watching, sweetheart. *He* will, as I make you scream my name while you bounce on my cock like a filthy little whore, and just when he gets a hard-on, I will slice his throat and fuck you on all fours in his blood."

My stomach tightens, and for a moment, I wish he's joking or that this is a twisted hallucination, but the dark gleam shining in his eyes is nothing short of a lust for violence. A twisted possessiveness that I'm the subject of.

"You're sick, Kingsley."

"And you're blushing."

"I'm *fuming*."

"Semantics."

I release a long puff of air. "I mean it. No other women."

"Sure thing. The price is admitting that you're mine."

"No."

"We're doing it my way then, and believe me, you'll regret this decision." He tosses the towel on the floor and turns around, his shoulders crowding with tension. "Come down when you're ready."

The room gains an unusual coldness once he leaves and I have no clue why I shiver like a stray kitten caught in the rain.

It's not dread.

I refuse to believe it's dread.

After throwing on one of Kingsley's shirts, which swallows me whole and reaches my mid-thigh, I pad down the stairs.

I'm thankful he doesn't have any live-in staff, which should be expected in mansions like his. They seem to come during the day and then leave before he gets home.

I pause in front of the demon painting. Now that I know its meaning and the story behind it, it's gained a different, more sinister light. I can't help thinking about a younger Kingsley staring at demons that might or might not reflect the ones inside him.

He's had them for a long time. Since he was in his teens.

And they might have been what attracted me to him in the first place.

Shooing that uncomfortable epiphany away, I follow the sound of clinking dishes that's coming from the kitchen.

It's spacious, has a built-in marble counter, and contains steel equipment that's fit for a chef's kitchen.

Kingsley's back seems to have lost the tension from earlier as he stands over the stove.

But I know not to be relieved, because if there's anything I've learned about this man, it's that he has a PhD in hiding emotions. What he shows is almost never what he harbors.

I trudge to his side and take a moment to focus on all the ingredients and dishes in the making.

Some lentil soup, I assume. Mushroom sauce and something with lamb.

When did he even get groceries? More importantly, why does he look like he's in his element chopping vegetables into minuscule, perfectly symmetrical pieces?

"I didn't know you could cook."

"There are a lot of things you don't know about me," he says without looking at me.

"When did you learn?"

"Early in my childhood. My grandfather used to say that the secret recipe to being a powerful leader is to know when, how, and for how long one should mix the people at their disposal. Cooking a meal is the same. Every ingredient has a pattern and a purpose—to make a perfect meal."

"Did you just compare people to meals?"

"Ingredients. The meal is the result, as in the money they bring to the table whether by working or indulging in consumer culture."

"You're a capitalist pig with a Machiavellian state of mind."

"Sue my bank account."

"Just because you're rich and attractive doesn't give you the right to exploit people or treat them as if they're cattle."

"I only heard the rich and attractive part." He pauses when he finally lifts his head and focuses on me.

The fire-like storm that ignites in his eyes leaves me breathless. He has a way of looking at me as if I'm his favorite meal. Not a mere ingredient.

It takes everything I have not to squirm or give away what I'm thinking.

"You look hot as fuck in my shirt."

I clear my throat, completely unaware of how to accept compliments. "I thought this was better than traumatizing both of us by borrowing Gwen's clothes again."

"We agree on something." He retrieves a plate, still appearing completely in his element.

He must've cooked for Gwen all the time. Nate mentioned she's a good cook and an even better baker.

Two qualities I definitely don't have.

I live on canned food and takeout, and recently, Callie's burned dishes.

"Were you close to your grandfather?" I ask, then pause at the nagging sensation in my head.

Why do I want to know more about him when I just drew a firm line upstairs?

"Not really, since he died when I was young. I do consider this house his legacy and not my father's, though. Because my father used it as collateral, lost it, then rebought it. So this is definitely not something he valued."

"Because he gave it to Susan?"

"That and the fact that he put it up for collateral several times even after he lost it."

"Susan could've manipulated him into it."

"Unless Susan has black magic talents, she didn't force him to do anything. He was pussy-whipped but not enough to lose his mind. Still pussy-whipped, though."

"Is that why you went out of your way to prove that he was senile in the months before his death? A last 'fuck you' of sorts?"

He grins. "With a rest in pieces sign for his death. I even had a plate made specifically for the occasion that said 'unbeloved father and married to a plastic gold digger.' Susan had it destroyed, for obvious reasons."

"You do realize all these shenanigans with Susan are useless, right? You have the house, the upper hand, and more money to crush her. Wouldn't it be better to let her and, therefore, your grudge go?"

"Not until she becomes a beggar on the side of the street. Just like the day she came into this family. In fact, I'll take this a step further and make her kneel on my mother's grave and beg for her forgiveness. Maybe then I'll let her go."

I see it then. Hatred, anger, and all the negative emotions that shouldn't exist within one person. "Oh my God. Is this your way of doing something for your mother now because you had no power when you were young?" He remains silent, but I know I hit the nail on the head. "It is, isn't it? It's why you refuse to let the Susan thing go. You're stuck in the past."

"That makes two of us, because the mere mention of your father turns you into a trembling leaf."

"My father is alive and a very serious threat."

"So what? Unless you want to go down that road, I suggest

you don't go sniffing near my closet. My skeletons don't concern you."

I purse my lips and he takes it as a hint that I've dropped it.

Damn the asshole. He tells me I'm stubborn, but he's as head-strong as a bull.

When I say nothing, he motions at the counter. "Sit down. The food will be ready in a bit."

"I'm not really hungry...I wouldn't say no to a drink, though."

"You will be eating, and there will be no drinking alcohol under my roof."

"Why the hell not? You have a wine cellar the size of Texas and with as much precious liquor as its oil wells."

"Didn't know you read articles about me."

"It's...a known fact."

"The better known fact is that you're bordering the line of being an alcoholic with your daily drinking habits and even going to the lengths of disguising a drink as coffee. You'll quit that habit."

"Too bad you don't get to tell me what to do."

"In my house, I do. Besides, your drinking while on the clock is enough reason to take your ass to the board and report you to the bar. Maybe you'll have a wake-up call when your license is in jeopardy."

"So this is what you've been doing all this time? Finding out my weakness so you can boot me from W&S and even from prac-ticing law?" I knew I shouldn't have let the bastard see the secret parts of me. He's no different than a snake who slithers to its vic-tim, and when it comes in for the kill, it's already too late.

"If I wanted to boot you, I would've started the process."

"But you're threatening me."

"I'm not threatening you, I'm pointing out your unhealthy drinking habits that you need to get rid of. And don't give me that victim speech. I don't give a fuck about your success rate or how many clients you have under your belt. If you're drinking on the clock, it affects your productivity and could cost your clients more than they've bargained for."

"It's not like I get drunk or that I don't have access to my brain. I just do it to numb unwanted thoughts that I can't escape when I'm sober."

"Still a no. Find a healthier coping mechanism."

"Says the man who punches trees at night."

"That doesn't go against my codes of conduct as an attorney. Your drinking habits do. End of fucking story. Now, sit down."

I glare at him. "And if I refuse, which, for the record, is a one hundred percent chance?"

"Then there's a thousand percent chance that I'll haul you onto my lap, further bruise that sore ass of yours, and eventually shove the food down your throat."

I hate how my thighs clench at the image he paints in my head, and it takes all my self-control to hold on to my cool façade.

"Brute," I mutter.

"Never claimed to be otherwise. Now, are we going to do this the nice way or the brute way?"

My glare is all the answer he needs to practically throw me over his shoulder.

I can't control the excited yelp that leaves my lips or the moans and whimpers that follow when he proceeds to do what he promised.

By the time I come all over his hand, a gloomy feeling hovers over my head.

Is this what he meant by coming after my control? Or is it so much worse?

TWENTY

Kingsley

I'M HAVING DRINKS WITH NICOLO IN THE LUCIANOS' downtown club when he drops the bomb.

"Rumor has it, Bruno will be a free man before his daughter's next birthday. And by rumor, I mean my intel."

I pause opening my Zippo to stare at him. "What?"

He leans back against the leather of the VIP booth we're occupying, a cigarette dangling from the side of his mouth. "He might be thinking about turning her birthday into a date of death. It's a poetic thing some fathers do by taking back the life they gave."

My pulse starts ticking in my ears at the speed of a lethal bomb. But I force a steady pace in opening and closing my Zippo, zeroing my attention in on Nicolo, who looks a bit too relaxed about the facts he just shared. Seeming not to notice my reaction, or noticing and ignoring it anyway, he makes eye contact with one of his staff and they scurry over with a bottle of Macallan.

The chaos in the club fails to penetrate the confinements of my skull. The loud music filters to the background, holding the importance of a used condom. The stench of strong perfume, sweat, sex, and alcohol hangs in the air like a gloomy cloud.

But I don't pay attention to all of those details. I don't even focus on the bottle he offers me. "You can stop it."

"No can do. Bruno is one of our loyal soldiers and Lazlo's trusted man. I might have given the redhead protection, but not at the expense of ending Bruno. My idea of protection is to not let him kill her, and it does not, under any circumstances, entail ending Bruno's life. Besides, she's not keeping her side of the deal. Mateo is still married to the gold-digging blondie and he's been acting like her rejected puppy." He jerks his chin in the direction of his brother, who's refusing two leggy brunettes' advances and looking a second away from having them thrown out of the club.

"Your brother's objections to divorce are on him and you, not on Aspen. And that's her fucking name, by the way. Use it."

He raises a brow. "Are you defending her, King?"

"I'm stating facts. She brought you more money in the past two weeks than all your soldiers combined. I don't fucking care whether you roll it around your dick, shove it up your ass, or soak it in blood. As long as you keep your part of the deal and provide her the protection she asked for."

"I will, but only under my terms." He blows a cloud of smoke in my direction. "But if things go south, and they always do, I hold no responsibility for collateral damage."

"Meaning?"

"I already passed a message to Bruno that the redhead is under my protection now. Even though he's under Lazlo's direct order, he accepted that and promised not to go against me. So unless he breaks that promise, I won't actively plot his demise."

I slam my lighter shut, narrowing my eyes. "He doesn't have to get out to hurt her. He's doing the job from behind bars."

"No evidence."

"Fuck that. You heard those scums mention his name in your basement."

"That was before I passed Bruno a message."

"Oh, I see where this going."

"Care to elaborate?"

"Back in school, you used to surround yourself with as many people as possible—students, teachers, staff, principals. All of them. It wasn't some popularity contest but more of an elaborate divide and conquer strategy. They were all a part of your chessboard that could and would be used down the line. The situation is similar now. You don't want to lose Bruno's services, but you also like the money Aspen brings to the table, so you're keeping both. But you're forgetting something, Nic."

He slides one leg over the other and lights a cigar, then blows the smoke in my direction with the nonchalance of a hedonist lord. "And what is that?"

"I was never part of your pathetic crowd, strategies, or fucked-up god complex. It'll be a cold day in hell before you use me or anyone close to me."

"So the redhead is close to you?"

"*Aspen* is the fucking name. And she is the mother of my daughter."

"Is that what you feed your brain to sleep better at night?"

"No, Nic. You're not using a reversal tactic and switching the subject to focus on me. It's about you, so why don't you tell me what the fuck your game is this time?"

"Not a game. It's…an observation. My old man used to say that there are two types of monsters. Those who roam free, like you and me, only hold the sky as the limit and even consider conquering it. The other type are those like Bruno, who've been locked away most of their lives. Their goal is neither the world nor the sky. They have one purpose—destroying the person who shoved them into that cell."

"In that case, he should take it up with the warden."

He smiles with a coldness that freezes the air. "Do you know the number of guards Bruno has killed or caused their death?"

"No, but I'm sure you'll enlighten me."

"Twenty-five. A life for each year he's spent behind bars. And every time, one of his underlings or prison buddies took the fall for it. So even if you or anyone else sends someone to get rid of him while behind bars, it won't fly. He has a lawless kingdom there that no one is allowed inside of, least of all, your beloved law."

"So you're telling me we should brace ourselves and wait?"

"You have no choice but to wait. The bracing yourselves part is redundant."

I finally reach for the drink and take a long chug, but not even the burn is able to chase away the number of scenarios invading my head.

Nicolo talks business and I'm only half listening to him. The number of his men I saved from jail is becoming countless and while I consider myself the best criminal defense attorney around, this is turning into overwork. His goons are like untrained dogs. Or maybe they're well-trained by Nicolo to be on a constant mission to throw their weight around—and therefore, showcase his power.

He always liked to scare people by his ruthless reputation alone, so they didn't dare to go against him. A tactic that both of us have been using since our childhood.

I never attempted to soften my image or cater to the public's fragile mentalities and emotional hearts. When they fear me, they stay away. When they fear me, they don't have the audacity to look at my throne or touch my power.

Mateo joins us soon after and so do some escorts that are courtesy of the club.

Their attempts to get my attention match the desperation of a dying fish. One of them is chattering about the history of Macallan like she's an automated robot, and I tell her to drink until she no longer pollutes the air with her voice.

I fail to wrap my mind around the fact that I used to fuck her type not too long ago. Granted, I didn't pick them for their communication skills or lack of character.

I picked them because they weren't a fucking headache.

Unlike a certain witch that the mere thought of turns me hard with an urgent need to fuck. Her, specifically.

It's been a week since the day she refused to be mine, both in the middle of fucking and outside of it.

The fact that I spanked her ass to the point that she couldn't sit properly for days held no importance. At least, not enough to make her change her mind.

Ever since then, however, she's been coming to my house daily. Or I've been dragging her with me. Semantics.

Due to her witch blood and alleged relations to Satan himself, she's a hard one to win over. Always putting up a fight in fucking everything.

Except for when my dick plows inside her cunt, of course. And even then, she never fails to sing the tune of how much of an asshole I am.

But that's what makes it all fun. Her resistance, fight, and inability to bow turn me into an animal every goddamn time.

No clue how the hell I was fine with the likes of robot-what's-her-face before.

They're not the flavor of fire that I prefer, and they definitely have the effect of minus degrees frostbite on my dick's state of arousal.

Despite the fact that I didn't fuck Aspen last night, because she chose not to come over. When I bombarded her phone with texts, creeper style, she told me she was going out with Caroline, Mateo, and his friend.

Emphasis on the *friend* part.

I told her not to go or I would show up and fuck up her evening and destroy Caroline and Mateo's chances of ever reuniting. That couple has the combined emotional intelligence of a fat cat and the same philosophy of freeloading.

Aspen hung up the phone in my face after repeating her favorite words of "You don't get to tell me what to do."

The only reason she wasn't buried six feet under my cock was because Nate and Gwen visited me for dinner. I could tell he made her do it. She looked miserable, pouted for most of the night, and had dark circles under her eyes.

The traitor has met with her mother two times within a week. Which is a record, but she probably only came to dinner with me because Nate had had enough of her deteriorating state and took things into his own hands.

Needless to say, the dinner was strained. She didn't apologize and I didn't shower her with love and spoiled princess behavior.

To make matters worse, I was irritable about the whole Aspen fiasco and her double date with the fucker in front of me and his wife.

Since Aspen is actually smart, she avoided the firm the entire day today, working off-site and even asking her assistant to bring her whatever she needed.

You can run, but you can't hide, witch.

Swirling the glass of whiskey in hand, I focus my attention on Mateo. "What's it going to be, Romeo? Will there be a divorce or not?"

He glares at me, then at Nicolo. "The word *divorce* needs to be wiped from your extended vocabulary. I swear to fuck, Nicolo, if you mention it to Caroline again, you won't like what I do."

"That sounds like a threat," I egg on Nicolo, who, despite looking relaxed with a girl hanging on his arm and a cigar dangling from his lips, obviously doesn't like the sound of what his brother has said.

"Mateo knows better than to threaten me. Isn't that right, Teo?"

"It is what it is. Caroline is the one person you're not allowed near."

"Heard you're patching things up with her," I say.

His expression lights up at that. "We're dating."

"Considering you're married, I think you've hit a home run with her enough times to go without the dating part."

"We've been hitting home runs since we met. Never dated. It's different this way. Better."

"Who's this imposter?" Nicolo says with disgust. "Give me my brother back."

"Where do you go on dates?" I ask, ignoring Nicolo's grouchy presence. "Namely, yesterday, and while you're at it, with whom?"

"A restaurant downtown that's owned by my college friend. He later joined me, Caroline, and Aspen." Mateo pauses. "She loved the food and the company."

"Caroline?"

"No." He smirks. "Aspen."

My hand flexes so hard, I'm surprised the glass doesn't break beneath it.

That's it. The witch will have to ask her ancestors for some spell to restrain me once I get my hands on her tonight.

"Speak of the she-devil."

I raise my head at Mateo's voice to find Aspen being directed in our direction by a bouncer.

She's in a pantsuit, which still looks sexy as fuck wrapped around her tall, slim body. Since she has her briefcase, she must be here for work.

A fact that both Nicolo and Mateo forgot to mention.

Doesn't matter, though, because this might as well be my chance to keep my promise to her from a week ago.

"Get on my lap, Julie," I tell the girl who's been fighting with a single drink for the past hour.

"It's Judith." She frowns but does as she's told, her legs stretching out on either side of my thighs.

I whisper so only she can hear, "Put on your best show and you'll be compensated with a better profession than the one you obviously hate and are terrible at, judging by your subpar bar conversation and drinking skills."

Julie Robot Judith shows the first real smile in the entirety of her clusterfuck career and nods.

She fingers my tie just in time for Aspen to see us. I pretend that I haven't noticed her as I smile at some nonsense Julie is saying.

But in my peripheral vision, I spot the slight pause in Aspen's movements. It's a mere fraction of a second that doesn't even translate on her face. Not a moment later, she strides toward us with sure determination, her bright hair swishing over her shoulders.

She clears her throat loud enough to compete with the half-muffled music from the club.

"Aspen," Mateo greets her. "To what do we owe this visit?"

"I need Nicolo's signature for an acquisition." I can feel her attention on me even before I lift my head.

And when I do, she glares at me so hard, it's a miracle that no lasers come out of her eyes.

"Aspen," I say as if I just detected her existence. "Do join us."

"No, thanks. You seem to have your fair share of company." She sounds like she's in her element, which means she still has that infuriating control.

My hand slides up Julie's waist while the other grabs her brown hair in a fist.

Despite the dim light, the blotch of red that explodes on Aspen's throat would be visible from Mars.

Even her lips press harder against one another.

Just for knockout's sake, I let my mouth hover an inch away from Julie's neck as she moans like a porn star.

Even while she turns a curious shade of red, Aspen keeps her composure. I'll give her that.

So I say, "You can still join us. Julie wouldn't mind."

"The only thing I'll join is your funeral," she spits out and throws open her briefcase nearly spilling all the papers inside, then pulls out a file and thrusts it in Nicolo's face. "Sign."

He appears half-amused, half-bored as he takes his time scribbling on the document.

She taps her toe on the floor, completely ignoring me and Julie, who's humping herself on my thigh for an orgasm.

As soon as Nicolo is finished, Aspen practically snatches the file from his fingers and shoves it back in her briefcase. I expect her to turn and leave, but she marches toward us.

I grin. "Changed your mind about joining?"

She stares me straight in the eye as she snatches Mateo's drink and pours it over my head with a sweet smile on her face.

"Have a shitty evening, prick." Still smiling, she nods at everyone. "Gentlemen."

Then she turns and leaves with the grace of royalty.

But not before I get what I want.

My lips twitch and I push Julie and her annoying gasps away from me.

Nicolo, who's been smirking like an idiot on crack, looks at me. "Care to elaborate about why you're smiling?"

"None of your business."

"I disagree." He fingers an unlit cigar like it's a woman's body. "Remember when we were young and our fathers taught us the importance of aiming for someone's center of power? The one thing without which they'll crumble and won't be able to pick up their pieces again? I think I might have just found yours."

"You're too arrogant to think you can hurt me without being crippled in return, Nic. Remember, I dish out toys, but I'm not one of them." I wipe the liquid from my face, not even caring about my ruined tailored suit.

Without bothering to excuse myself, I stand up and trail after Aspen.

She might not have been as forthcoming about it as I'd hoped she'd be, but she gave me the opening I was looking for.

The opening that means she not only cares, but her control might as well be hanging by a thread.

Because no matter how much she tried to hide it, I saw it just now.

Tears shone in her eyes.

Might have been out of frustration or anger, but it's enough ammo for me to use.

This time, she'll learn the hard way that she's fucking mine and there's no fighting it.

TWENTY-ONE

Aspen

I'M SURPRISED I MAKE IT OUT OF THE CLUB AND INTO THE parking lot without bombing the whole place terrorist-style just to broadcast the chaos that's snapping its fingers against my throat.

My heels make a screeching sound on the asphalt and I turn around. You know what? I should go back in there and crush a whole bottle against Kingsley's thick skull. A mere glass of alcohol is nothing in the grand scheme of things.

Releasing a long breath, I half abandon the idea and storm to my car. It's only a half abandon because fuck it. The urge to break something—preferably Kingsley's head and dick—is too much of a temptation to completely let go.

But on the other gloomy end, I refuse to be perceived as emotional, messy.

Weak.

My fingers shake around the car key and I wipe the angry tears that have gathered in my eyes. I'm not going to cry because of that bastard.

Not in this lifetime, Satan.

Dumping my weight against the car, I inhale deep breaths, summoning every inch of the self-control I gained through surviving in the streets, studying my ass off, and working doubly as hard as my male counterparts in order to be recognized in their midst.

Images of Kingsley's hands around that girl's waist assault my head and I close my eyes.

Stop thinking about jerks. Stop making it personal. It's nothing. We're nothing.

Moisture gathers in my lids and no amount of critical, methodical thinking is able to stop the tear that slides down my cheek and into my mouth.

Something shakes me and I startle when I realize it's my phone.

Releasing a breath, I yank it out, slightly thankful for the distraction.

The text that lights up the screen puts my world on pause for a second.

Gwyneth: I just made these. Do you want some?

Attached is an Instagram-like picture of colorful cupcakes with beautiful rainbow toppings.

Gwyneth: Oh, Nate just said you don't really like sweet things. That's okay, I guess. I just made too many, so I thought I'd share. I'd take them to Dad, but he's not really talking to me.

My fingers practically fly on the screen.

Me: I would love to have some. If you don't mind.

Gwyneth: Of course I don't mind! Should I come to your apartment? Will Caroline be there? She likes cake, so I'll bring her some, too.

I smile, about to reply with a capital "YES" when a rustle sounds from behind me.

My mini happy mood disappears. The asshole has the audacity to come for me after what he made me watch. Although this is a good opportunity to bash his head in with my heels.

I suck in a sharp breath as I whirl around. "I'm going to kill you—"

My words end on a muffled gasp when someone jams a cloth against my mouth and nose.

The stench of antiseptic and gut-wrenching chloroform fills my nostrils and lodges in my head with the lethality of a bullet.

A dark figure hovers over me, grabbing me by the shoulders, nearly snapping them from their sockets. I dig my nails into their arm, scratching and clawing with all the survival energy in me.

It obviously isn't much, because he continues crushing the cloth against my face, forcing me to breathe in the chloroform.

Shit…shit…

I can feel my hold weakening and my muscles going limp. The haunting screeching sound of my heels dragging against the ground slowly withers in the background and my eyes droop.

No…

A shock of colors and sounds explodes in front of me all at once.

The cloth is removed from my nose and I slump against my car, sliding to the ground due to the force of my coughs. My gasps for clean air make my eyes water and I shake my head a few times to bring back my focus.

At first, I have no clue what just happened, or if this is maybe a scare or a distasteful prank. But even deep down, I realize that this is much more serious than that.

The scene that materializes in front of me might as well be out of a horror movie.

Kingsley holds the dark figure who nearly blacked me out by the collar and drives his fist into his masked face.

The other man tackles him and they roll on the ground in a blur of punches, kicks, and guttural sounds.

Even in my dazed state, I can see that whoever my attacker is, he's a professional. Despite Kingsley's knack for violence, he won't have the upper hand.

Crawling on all fours, I reach for my briefcase that's fallen on the ground and rummage through it for my pepper spray.

Before I can pull it out, the attacker kicks Kingsley in the ribs and sprints into the night.

Kingsley springs to his feet, probably to go in pursuit, but I whisper, "Don't…don't…go…"

My words are desperate, pained, and raw. So raw that it hurts the shit out of me. Or maybe what really hurts is knowing that if Kingsley follows him, he'll be kidnapped instead of me just to drive a message home.

Or worse, he'll be shot dead.

"Fuck." He reaches me in two long strides and gathers me in his arms. The act is so effortless that I want to disappear in it for a while. And it seems to come naturally, as if he's been doing this—holding me, cocooning me—for decades.

He wraps a strong arm around my waist, letting my body crash into the nook of his. "Are you okay? I'll take you to the hospital."

I frantically shake my head, gasping for air and words. "I'm fine. I just need a moment."

"You can't even fucking stand, Aspen."

"I can." I try to push away from him and promptly fall back into his embrace.

"Stay still and quit the stubbornness."

"No hospital…" I mumble, feeling my eyes drooping. "Please, King…no hospital…"

My fingers go lax against his chest and I hate how safe it feels with him.

How, instead of trying to find my own way and lick my wounds solo, I prefer the warmth of this place.

Where his heart beats against mine.

⚖

When I open my eyes, the sight of white walls damn near sends me into hyperventilation mode.

Not the hospital.

No.

Before I can trip on my own feet, scream bloody murder, and throw myself out the nearest window, I spring up in bed and freeze.

The rest of the room slowly comes into focus and its familiar neutral tones instantly calm me down.

Weird.

I stare down at myself and find I'm only wearing a T-shirt. Kingsley's.

It smells like fresh laundry, cedarwood, and him. I resist the urge to sniff it like a drug addict and, instead, choose to focus on my surroundings.

It's the first time I've slept on Kingsley's bed, though. Yes, we fuck a lot, but that's usually on any surface aside from an actual bed. Besides, I always leave soon after, refusing to spend the night, despite his continuous invitations.

A fact that Caroline has been giving me shit about, calling me a heartless seductress.

But what Caroline doesn't know is that giving more of myself to this man scares the hell out of me. I already lose so much control around him, the least I can do is try to protect whatever's left of my heart.

The door opens and Kingsley comes inside, carrying a plate of food. He's in gray sweatpants and a dark T-shirt, his hair tousled in a perfectly imperfect mess.

I swallow the saliva gathered in my throat, because no matter how much I attempt to be, I'm not desensitized to this man's physical beauty or imposing presence.

Even if a part of my brain will always consider him a rival I want to eliminate and a jerk I need to bring down for humanity's sake.

"You're awake," he says with a hardness that doesn't appear on his face as he places the tray of shrimp, and what looks like chicken broth on the side table.

"How long have I been out?"

"About three hours. The doctor said the chloroform didn't completely take effect."

"You didn't take me to the hospital."

"You begged me not to. Why?"

"They're a hostile environment and I don't feel safe in them."

"Because you thought you lost your daughter in one."

It's not a question, because, of course, he'd put the pieces together and figure it all out. I hang my head, staring at my hands. I have no control over the words that tumble out of my mouth. "Hospitals remind me of the helplessness I felt back then. Of my inability to protect my flesh and blood. I didn't only think I'd lost my daughter. Something inside me died on that hospital bed, so I try my hardest to never relive those moments by avoiding hospitals as much as possible."

"You won't have to go to one. I have a family doctor." He drops onto the mattress beside me. "Though I did change him to a woman."

"Why?"

"What do you mean by why? Shouldn't you be celebrating this as a feminist who has a favorite thing called defending women and career equality?"

"But you're the furthest thing from a feminist, so why would you willingly change the gender of your family doctor?"

"Because you're constantly getting hurt and no man will develop the habit of touching you. If it were up to me, no woman would get that privilege either, but necessity and all that."

"You're crazy."

"Is that a way to thank me, witch?"

I stare at my brown nails, two of which are broken. Probably because of my struggle earlier. The shadow of what could've happened to me if Kingsley hadn't shown up in that exact moment covers me in gloom.

My fingers curl around the sheet. "Thank you."

"I didn't hear that. Can you repeat it?"

"No."

"Where are your manners, sweetheart? Do you find it hard to thank people?"

"Not all people. *You*. Your dickhead behavior makes it impossible to show gratitude. I'd rather gag on my own saliva."

"That's too many words for a simple thank you, but fine, I won't come after your stone heart…yet." He pauses, searching my face. "Did you recognize the man who tried to drug you?"

I slowly shake my head. "He was masked the entire time."

"At this point, it's safe to deduce that your father is pulling strings from behind bars."

I dig my fingers into my palms until I almost break more nails. "He's never done this to me before."

"He wasn't close to getting out before. We should have a code for when you're in danger."

"What type of code?"

"A word in a text with which you'll alert me when you need help."

"Why would I call you for help?"

"The fact that I saved your ass the last couple of times. What do you want the word to be?"

"I don't know…Nietzsche."

"Fuck that asshole."

I smile. "It is what it is. Deal with it."

He narrows his eyes. "You also need bodyguards or Nicolo's men."

"I'll talk to Mateo. I like him better."

A muscle clenches in his jaw as he regards me silently. "Isn't he married to your friend?"

"One more reason I trust him more than that snake Nicolo."

"You trust him enough to have double dates with him, apparently."

"And what's it to you?" My voice gains a cutting, venomous edge as memories from tonight rush back with the bitterness of a pill and the lethality of a gun. "I can choose to go on dates, dinners, or orgies, and you have no damn say in it."

His expression closes down and his eyes darken with the malice of an ocean in the middle of winter. When his hand reaches out for me, I'm not sure if he'll strangle me to death or use the pillow to do it.

I don't wait for it, though, and instead, slap it away. "Don't touch me with the same hand that was all over another woman."

A dark smirk tilts his lips. "Your jealousy is cute."

"It's not jealousy. It's self-respect."

"Bullshit. You made your emotional performance of the century in there and even had the tears to go with it. So how about you admit this open arrangement isn't for you."

"Fuck you, Kingsley."

"I'm going to pass on the offer. Instead, you might see me fucking that girl next time in full HD."

I can feel the hotness rising from my chest to my neck and ears, and I refuse to give in to the volcano.

I refuse to let him win.

"Then you'll be invited to the front-row seat of my next hookup."

One second I'm sitting, the next I'm on my back. Kingsley's fingers wrap around my throat, squeezing the sides until all I can focus on is his weight on top of me. He could crush me in a minute—no, a second would be enough. And the worst part is that my core is throbbing with want.

What the hell is wrong with me? He's choking me and I'm throbbing?

"The only way another man will touch you is if he has a fucking death wish. So unless you want some bastard's death on your conscience out of pure spite, then go ahead and provoke that lawless side of me, sweetheart. I fucking dare you."

"You did it *first*." I can feel the raw words coming out from the depths of my soul and bruised heart. "You touched someone else first, asshole. And I believe in karma. It's my favorite type of bitch."

"You're the one who went on a date and refused to be mine. Touching another woman was your lesson, because both of us know open anything isn't how this works. Next time I say you're mine, you scream it back, am I clear?"

I angle my knee to kick him in the crotch, but he lifts himself at the last second, escaping my assault.

"Try fucking again."

"Fuck. You."

"Not the right word." He has the audacity to *tsk*. "Say you're mine."

I purse my lips.

Still grabbing me by the throat, he reaches for my shirt and bunches it up to my waist, lifts my leg, then slaps my ass cheek.

I gasp, still sore and bearing a map of his handprints from the last time he did this.

Two days ago. It's been only two days, but it feels as if he hasn't touched me for a decade. It's terrifying how my body and other parts of me I don't want to put a name to have gotten used to him.

Kingsley releases his hard cock that's purple and dripping with precum. Seems like I'm not the only one depraved enough to be turned on by this hate-fest.

We're both insatiable animals with a thirst for more.

He digs his fingers into my folds. "Look how soaked you are for me, sweetheart. Your cunt is begging to be fucked."

I shudder when he does that thing with his fingers thrusting inside me and his palm slapping my clit.

"So inviting, tight and ready," he muses in dark words that arouse me more than should be allowed.

Then he pulls out and I bite my lip to keep from protesting. His fingers move through my wetness to my back hole, smearing the arousal all over it before driving inside.

I gather my fists into the sheets and squeeze.

It's a depravity that he's been engaging in lately, taking pleasure in fingering my ass while he's fucking my pussy.

It's always felt arousing in a strange type of way, but one thing is missing—his cock isn't inside me. It's sliding against my folds, up and down in a torturous rhythm.

"Ah, fuck..." I raise my hips, needing to alleviate the pressure building in my core.

"Fuck, indeed, sweetheart." He thrusts another finger in my ass, stretching me to the point of pain.

But what hurts the most is how charged up I am for something.

Anything.

This is why I hate relinquishing control. The unknown and relying on someone else are some of my worst nightmares.

"God-damn-it." I bite my lip. "Do something."

He slowly shakes his head. "Say you're mine first."

"No."

"Then we'll stay like this all night."

"You'll have blue balls."

"And you'll have a blue pussy, but no fucking orgasm."

"Goddamn you, Kingsley."

"God-fucking-damn *you*, Aspen. Just say the words."

"I'm not your plaything, asshole."

"No, you're not. You're the whole fucking game."

My lips part, and a queasy sensation drops to my stomach. Just…why does he have to say things that throw me completely off?

"Would you rather imagine me with other playthings or give us what we both want?"

I wiggle, feeling my heart being chipped away hard and fast. "I don't want you."

"Sure, let's say I don't want you either, while my dick is hard and your pussy is soaked."

"Ugh…"

"Say it, Aspen."

"Fuck me," I whisper, my heart lunging to my throat.

"And?"

"I'm…yours." I glare at him. "Temporarily."

I can tell he doesn't like that last addition, considering the squeezing of his fingers on my throat, but he finally drives into me.

The thrust is so powerful and violent that I slide off the bed and gasp from the intensity of it.

My core is stimulated and wet and I come immediately with his hand on my neck and his fingers in my ass.

"Tell me you're mine, too," I moan in my lusty haze, my eyes half-opened and my heart nearly reaching the sky.

When he says nothing, I reach for his face. "Say it or I'll really kill you the next time you touch another woman."

"I'm yours." He grins. "Temporarily."

The jab of that word creates a hole inside me, but I forget all about it when he fucks me to within an inch of my life and then paints my pussy, ass, and breasts with his cum.

Something has changed between us, and I have no idea what it is.

All I know is that I don't think about leaving when he gathers me in his arms and sleeps wrapped all around me.

TWENTY-TWO

Aspen

"**I**'M GOING TO MISS YOU SO DAMN MUCH."

I can hardly breathe as Caroline squeezes me in a hug that could be mistaken for a bear's.

Reluctantly and with enough awkwardness to spring second-hand embarrassment, I pat her back. "You're not leaving the planet."

She pulls back, sulking. "Well, I'm leaving you after I got used to you."

"We'll meet again, Callie."

"You bet your sweet ass we will." She kisses my cheek. "I'm so, so glad I reunited with you again, you beautiful bitch. Take care of yourself, okay? If anything happens, don't hide and deal with it on your own. I'm only a call away."

I slowly nod and she hugs me again before she ushers her dogs out the door. The two animals release disheartened huffs as they stare at me one final time before they join her and Mateo, who's been waiting for her outside.

After weeks of dating and courting nineteen-century style,

they finally reconciled. Caroline knows he didn't cheat on her, after all, and that the whole scene was a setup, probably by Nicolo.

A gloomy emptiness fills my apartment as soon as the door closes.

I'm finally getting my peace and space back without anyone interrupting me whenever I'm trying to work.

And yet, it feels as if I've been thrust back into that black hole I called my life not too long ago. A life that was filled with checking with the prison guard and holding my breath whenever he talks to me about my father.

I called him after the two attacks, and he said nothing has changed about my father's state. He appeared to be in his element while he sent people to get rid of me—or teach me a lesson.

And the fact that he can hurt me even from behind bars sends trepidation through my soul. What will happen if he actually gets out?

Even with the guards and Nicolo's promises of protection, I can hardly sleep at night anymore, and I always, without doubt, look over my shoulder whenever I'm outside.

It's like I'm back to being the younger, paranoid Aspen.

Wrapping my robe around my chest, I sit on the couch and pull open my laptop, opting to work.

Despite my best efforts, concentration doesn't come.

So I go to the kitchen and open the bottle of tequila I hid out of Caroline's sight. She and Kingsley need to stop trying to deprive me of alcohol when it's the only thing that keeps me functioning properly. Besides, I'm never hammered, just tipsy enough to escape the chaos in my head and the feelings in my newly revived heart.

I pour a glass and then retrieve my phone, glaring at it.

The asshole didn't call me or text me today.

I refuse to think that's one of the reasons why the hollowness is having a party in my heart today.

It's been two weeks since he made me agree to exclusivity and we started our unorthodox arrangement. Unorthodox, because it feels forbidden as hell whenever I face Gwen. It's like I'm doing something wrong and thrilling at the same time.

During those weeks, I've gone to his house or he's come here—but only when Caroline is romancing Mateo. He fucks me until I can't move and then force-feeds me. It's a thing since, apparently, it's a problem that I barely eat any real food during the day.

Sometimes, we spend the night together just so he can wake me up with his dick inside me or his lips on my pussy.

It's scary how sexually compatible we are. I've never had a lover who knows my body better than I do like freaking Kingsley Shaw. The worst part is that he takes pleasure in tormenting me with the knowledge.

And don't get me started on his stamina, because it's as crazy as he is. I just don't understand how he fucks as if he's still in his damn prime.

From my memories of him as a teen, he was fast and determined. Now, he's intense, animalistic in his violent fucking that almost always is coupled with some sort of pain.

The type of pain that adds an edge to each release he rips out of me. At first, I tried to resist the pull, to not fall into his carefully crafted web, but I soon realized it was useless.

Not when I can't get enough of him.

Not when I crave more of his firm hand and unapologetic touch.

Sometimes, soon after we're done. It's an unfortunate addiction at this point.

It's why I'm staring at the silent phone.

It's definitely not because I miss his company or need it now more than any other time or something.

We usually bicker like the worst of enemies. Our philosophies, perspectives, and view of the world are as different as night and day.

He's a manipulator. I'm a rationalist.

He's violent in both thinking and action. I'm more diplomatic.

He's the storm. I'm the sea that refuses to be flipped upside down.

And yet, we have the deepest conversations. He's one of the few men who isn't intimidated by my mind, and the only man who wants more of it.

However, our conversations usually end up in a verbal fight and then a hate-fuck to sort it all out.

It's unhealthy, bordering on toxic, and should've ended a long time ago.

And yet, any moments spent with him are the only time I've ever felt so undeniably alive. The only time I don't think about the threat my father poses or the fast-ticking bomb that is my life.

Besides, it's not like we have nothing in common. Okay, just a little, like how much we both love and care about Gwen or how we both have no tolerance for bullshit.

Especially each other's.

Point is, we can agree.

Who am I kidding? It'll be a cold day in hell before we ever do that.

Still, what we have—whatever it's called—works in a strange way.

Taking a sip of my drink, I open the texts and take another swig. Then I finish the whole glass.

Not that I need liquid courage.

Just to make sure, I pour another glass, finish it, and then quit the bullshit and drink straight from the bottle.

Only when my nerves loosen a little do I type the text.

Aspen: Caroline left with Mateo. I'm alone.

He sees it but doesn't reply immediately. I drum my fingers against the counter and take a few more sips.

Kingsley is usually the one who texts first, picks me up first, barges into my space, mind, and body without apologies first. And as soon as I take the initiative and text him, he ignores me?

I shake the phone, then narrow my eyes on it, then contemplate throwing it in the sink.

Just when I seriously consider the last option, his reply comes.

Kingsley: Congratulations on losing the freeloader and her demon dogs.

Aspen: She's not a freeloader. Callie is my friend.

My lips shake as soon as I send the message. She *is* my friend. One of the few people I can call a friend, actually.

Wow. Look at me having a friend. Or reuniting with an old one or whatever.

There's Nate, but our relationship has always been more of professional camaraderie. I did have a small friendship with a previous assistant in the firm named Nicole Adler and helped her with her custody case, but then she relocated with her boss to England and we don't keep in touch often. At first, I helped her because I understood what it's like to lose one's child, but now I realize it was because she resembled Callie with her blonde hair and fair complexion.

Kingsley: Didn't know that term was part of your life plan.

I basically punch back the reply.

Aspen: Are you going to piss me off for a few more minutes or will you tell me your reply?

Kingsley: My reply for what? Did you ask a question?

I didn't, but I can almost hear the mockery in his voice. One of these days, I'm going to accidentally kill this bastard in pure voluntary manslaughter fashion.

Aspen: I said I'm alone.

Kingsley: I don't see a question mark there. Do you?

Aspen: Stop being a dick.

Kingsley: What? I'm just asking an innocent question.

Aspen: Just come over before I reach into the phone and punch your balls.

Kingsley: *laughing out loud emoji* Your tough love is adorable.

Aspen: You won't be thinking I'm adorable when you come here, asshole.

Kingsley: Who said I'm coming? Maybe I'll channel the Aspen Leblanc in me and play hard to get today.

Is he for real?

I read and reread the text, and sure enough, the words are there.

Aspen: I don't play hard to get.

Kingsley: Is that why you start bantering whenever you don't want to say thank you out of concern of sounding emotional? Or the fact that you go out of your way to look aggressive in front of Nate and everyone else because God forbid they find out about us?

Aspen: You're aggressive as well.

Kingsley: As a response to your behavior. Karma might be your beloved bitch, but pure spite happens to be mine, sweetheart.

Aspen: Does that mean you won't be coming?

Kingsley: Add a please and I'll consider it.

I'm foaming at the mouth as I stare at his words. I'm about to call him a thousand names, but I'm drunk—or getting there—and surrounded by a lonely halo that I need to vanish.

But I'm definitely not going to beg.

So I let my robe fall open and shiver at the gust of air that hardens my bare nipples. I pull one of them and snap a faceless picture that only shows me biting my lip, tugging on a pink nipple, and a hint of my lace panties.

My finger shakes as I hit Send, then type.

Aspen: Your loss.

I've never done this before, because I haven't trusted anyone not to use this against me in the future. I've also never felt like showing this part of me to anyone.

A scary thought spreads through the confines of my brain. Does that mean I trust Kingsley?

Before I can find an answer to that question, my doorbell rings.

I jump, pulling my attention from the text that Kingsley read but didn't answer.

Goddamn him. If he didn't fall for that, then I'll really have to beg. Maybe I should ask one of the guards Mateo provided for me to drive me to Kingsley's house so I can smack him upside the head.

Closing my robe, I sigh, fighting the bitter taste of humiliation, and practically drag my feet to open the door. It's probably the guard who's at the door. They usually get me my packages after they check them.

When I swing the door open, however, it's not a solemn-faced guard that appears on my doorstep.

It's Kingsley himself, dressed in a black suit—the only color he wears—and exhibiting the expression of a dark underworld lord.

My heart flutters with the ferocity of a trapped bird that's escaping its cage.

Goddamn it. I shouldn't be this happy to see him.

And yet, I can't help the surprised joy in my voice. "What are you doing here?"

He grabs me by the chin and basically shoves me backward, barging into my apartment as if he owns the place.

"You didn't expect me to stay away after sending me that picture, did you?" He kicks the door shut behind him, his eyes shining with dark desire.

"I don't know, maybe I did." My mouth is dry with how much I need his lips on mine.

So when he lifts my leg up his thigh, I climb up his body, wrapping my arms around his neck and my thighs trap his lean waist in a stronghold.

"What else did you expect, my little whore?" He kneads my ass and I moan as his handprints and bite marks throb in remembrance of last night.

"Don't call me a whore if you're just going to tease me."

"You're the only cocktease in this equation, sweetheart." He slams my back against the wall, holds me with one hand under my ass, and opens my robe with the other.

I've always loved the way Kingsley handles me with pure command and no chances of me fighting his dominant control. I feel like I can finally let go and not be scared that he'll drop me to the ground.

"This is the culprit you chose for the night." He bites almost the entirety of my breast into his mouth and I moan, pulling at his hair with the same violence.

Then I rid him of his jacket, throwing it somewhere beside us as he devours my nipples.

I try to unbutton his shirt, because he's way too overdressed, but the fact that I'm hanging on the edge of an orgasm doesn't help.

"I thought you weren't coming," I say, fingers scratching on his skin.

"Maybe I wasn't."

"And yet, you were around here even before I texted you."

"I planned to drop off food or you would've gone to sleep without a proper meal in your stomach." His lips trail from my bitten breasts to my neck and then to my mouth.

He thrusts his tongue inside, kissing me open-mouthed as he fusses with his belt.

"You taste like an alcoholic," he whispers near my lips.

"Then stop kissing me," I shoot back, feeling heat rising to my cheeks and shame trickling to my chest.

"Alcohol isn't good for your health. Your liver will bail on you soon."

"Are you really going to talk about my liver right now?" I grind myself against his erection that he's freed from his boxer briefs.

"It's part of you, too."

"Not the most important part." I align my pussy with his erection and just when I'm about to go down, the doorbell rings.

"Ignore it," he says, and I'm fully prepared to.

There's no way in hell I'm going to stop this now.

The doorbell sounds again, this time followed by a murmur of voices. One of my guards says, "She's in."

"Are you sure?"

At Gwen's voice, Kingsley and I stare at each other, stunned, then we stumble in an awkward chaos of limbs.

"Fuck, fuck, fuck!" he curses low, pulling the robe around my waist.

I smooth my hair that he loves to mess up for sport, then point in the direction of the bedroom. "Go there and don't make a sound."

"Get rid of that little cock-blocker. You have five minutes."

"Like hell I will. You had a lifetime with her, but I'm lucky to have as much time as she's willing to give me." I push him. "Go."

He wipes the corner of my lips and that makes me aware of the unsatisfied ache between my legs.

Then he goes to the bedroom and I take a deep breath before I open the door with a smile. "Gwen."

She smiles back, pushing a basket into my hand. "I brought cupcakes."

"Thank you." I move to the side, allowing her in, and she watches me intently as she passes me by.

Shit. Don't tell me my hair is telling the tale of what just happened?

"Why do you look so red?" she asks. "Have you been working out?"

"Uh, yeah, working out. I just finished."

"In a robe?"

"Just a spur-of-the-moment abs workout."

I place the basket on the kitchen counter and offer her some green tea with vanilla. I've been stocking up on everything vanilla since Gwen started to come over.

"That must be why you missed my call."

"You called me?" I check my phone that I abandoned here earlier and sure enough, there's a missed call from her.

I can't believe I was too caught up to notice. Thanks to her damn father.

Sometimes, I look at Gwen and wonder how the hell two unlikely people made her.

It seems surreal.

The fact that she's her own person, completely different from me and Kingsley, is even more surreal.

I'm just glad she didn't experience our traumas. Even if she grew up without a mother.

"How's Nate?" I ask, pouring the hot water into a cup.

"He's coming home late today. Don't you work with him at the same office?"

"Yeah...I was just trying to start a conversation."

She grins. "You're bad at the social game, huh?"

I hang my head. "I'm sorry."

"Don't be. You understood the assignment."

"What assignment?"

She grabs a cupcake that she brought and laughs. "It's just a saying, Aspen. Like when someone does something right or in a way that everyone likes, we say they understood the assignment. So you, like, understood the assignment, because society isn't really that useful. Dad says it's only to be used, which is wrong, by the way, because Dad is evil sometimes."

"Only sometimes?"

"Yeah, only sometimes. Don't believe everything the media says about him. They're assholes and like to paint him as the devil."

"Does that mean you're back on good terms with him?"

"Well, he still wants me to apologize and I refuse." She pouts, looking absolutely adorable.

"Why do you refuse? I thought you wanted him to forgive you."

"He...he doesn't spoil me anymore and...well, I guess he's still mad at me, and I'm scared he'll hurt me again if I do apologize."

"He won't."

"How can you be so sure?"

"He just won't. Next time you see him, apologize. Okay?"

She gives a small nod. "I hate not being his angel, but it's okay. He'll always be my dad. Savage Devil, slightly evil, and everything in between."

The lucky bastard.

Instead of acting bitter and showing my reaction, I ask Gwen about school. She tells me all about the exams and her friends, then joins me in the living room.

She says she misses Caroline and that she wants to go out with her because she's like the fun auntie.

And I'm equally jealous and glad that I can even share these conversations with her.

We put on a movie—horror, per Gwen's choice—and she tells me how she had problems falling asleep and usually watched horror movies to be able to do that.

I have a long way to go to learn all about her, but we'll take it one day at a time.

As long as she lets me, I'm willing to do anything.

Soon after, her head falls on my shoulder with her eyes closed.

I hesitate before I glide my fingers through her ginger hair. I've wanted to do this ever since I found out she was alive and not actually buried in a nameless grave.

Gwen sighs in the middle of the horrified screams coming from the movie.

But then they disappear.

I lift my head to find Kingsley standing there, holding the remote.

He's all dressed up, his expression closed off as he watches us.

Despite his objections to me forming a relationship with Gwen at the beginning, he hasn't commented on it lately.

But I'm not sure if that means he's come to terms with it or not.

"Let her stay the night," he whispers in a low, deep voice. "If Nate comes to pick her up, she won't be able to go back to sleep."

"Are you leaving?" Despite my joy at having Gwen by my side, I can't help the pang of disappointment of losing him.

"Either that or the cock-blocker will find out." He raises a brow. "Besides, didn't you say I'm so evil?"

"You know you are."

He smiles and bends down to kiss Gwen's forehead. "Sweet dreams, Angel."

"Mmm, night, Daddy," she mumbles in her sleep, and I swear my chest is about to rip open from how full it feels.

She told me about her sleep talking, but to actually witness it is a completely different experience.

The fact that even though Kingsley is a bit mad at her but still treats her like his precious princess is also another heart-warming experience.

He has a firm, protective side that I've never seen on any other man. I wonder what I would've become if I'd had a loving father figure like him.

I expect him to pull away, but he captures my lips in a slow, passionate kiss that rattles me to the bones.

"Dream of me, sweetheart."

And then he's out the door, carrying a piece of my heart.

TWENTY-THREE

Kingsley

MY FINGERS TIGHTEN ON MY BRIEFCASE AS I STARE AT THE
unflattering version of my stepmother's face.

But it's not the plastic view that I want to smash to pieces.
It's the feelings behind it. The malice that glitters in her beady eyes.
The smirk that tugs on her lips.

We're standing in front of the courthouse, but with many people as witnesses, murder would certainly not fly under their radar.

This bitch just had the audacity to make her lawyer argue
that my recent investments, my implication with Nicolo's legitimate fronts, are dangerous for my father's legacy. She's going for
incompetence, poor judgment, and therefore, by her flawed logic,
the shares my father used to own in W&S should revert back to
her. They wouldn't. They're rightfully mine, and even if I'm proven
to be incompetent, they would go to my executor, not her. But she
thinks if she files enough lawsuits and throws her weight around,
she'll get something.

Other than my undying desire to finish her, she'll get zilch.
Susan strokes the pink fur that's resting on her shoulder like

it's a pet. "I've got to show proper gratitude and thank you for giving me this opening. Better prepare the keys to the kingdom."

"The only keys you're getting is for a staycation clinic to fix whatever your plastic surgeons ruined." I glare down my nose at her. "Your lawyer is a bit of an incompetent fool and probably forgot to mention that the money I invested was originally mine, not my father's, so suing for it is similar to fishing in the Dead Sea. And no one probably told you this, but here's a small piece of advice—just because you can file a lawsuit doesn't mean you should."

"That's not the money I'm after, dear *son*." I don't miss the mockery in her voice when she says "son." "It's the rest of it that was originally your father's and is, therefore, rightfully mine that I want. I'll continue arguing in court until I have the slice of pie I deserved all along. How does it feel to be beaten at your own game?"

"You haven't even started to recognize the game, let alone beat me at it."

"Maybe I'm better endowed at it than you think." She pats my arm, smiling. "How is Aspen?"

I narrow my eyes, partially forgetting the feel of her disgusting touch. Why would she ask me about Aspen?

No one knows about our relationship, aside from Caroline, and probably Mateo and Nicolo.

And whoever was in the private booth that night to witness the whole alcohol-spilling, jealousy incident.

I don't think Susan is desperate enough to have me followed, but maybe she is.

The fact that she even knows about Aspen makes me clench my teeth. She, of all people, needs to keep her destructive energy far away from her.

Still, I don't take the bait and, instead, stare at her, solemn-faced.

She merely smiles, her red lips appearing grotesque. "You promised to take everything of mine, and I promise to do the same, Kingsley. Especially now that you have more to lose than your billionaire status and that spawn you call a daughter."

With one last revolting touch, she leaves, her steps brisk and measured. And I wish she'd fall on her face and die the most horrible death.

Or maybe I should do it myself, after all, because old dogs like her don't die as easily.

My mood takes a sharp dive to the worst for the rest of the day. Everyone knows to stay the fuck away from me whenever I'm back from a hearing with Susan.

Everyone except Aspen, the main reason behind my sour mood.

I can battle with Susan to infinity and beyond. The reason I'm not finishing her off isn't because I can't but because I need her to suffer and take on more plastic surgeries to fill the hole inside her black soul.

I need her to be on her toes until the day she dies, and when she does, alone and with no beneficiary, she'll go kiss the ground my mother walked on before being shoved into her special place in hell.

But an ominous feeling has been nagging at my chest ever since she asked about Aspen. By name.

So I make my way to her office. The last time I spent time with her was three days ago, when Gwen decided it was a good idea to cock-block me.

As if that's not blasphemous enough, she's proceeded to steal Aspen's time every night since. Sometimes with Nate.

To say my dick is planning mass destruction on those two is the understatement of the century. I might have paid them a visit unannounced last night and cock-blocked Nate until Gwen fell asleep, for which he kicked me in the shin. Naturally, I kicked him back. Then we had a boxing match for old times' sake.

That still didn't relieve the tension, though.

And once again, I refuse to jack off like a thirteen-year-old. So that leaves Aspen with sexual frustration issues to resolve, preferably now.

So imagine my fucking surprise when her assistant, a short

woman with long hair and gold-framed glasses, tells me, "She's taken the afternoon off, sir."

"Are we talking about the same Aspen Leblanc, or have you picked up a side gig and become someone else's assistant?"

She appears stunned for a second, then blurts, "I'm talking about Ms. Leblanc. She usually doesn't work this day of the year."

I check the date on my watch to confirm it's not Gwen's birthday. Aspen mentioned that, since she thought her daughter had died, she got drunk on her grave and mourned her.

Though the getting drunk part is a nasty habit that she has sans mourning.

"Do you know why she doesn't work on this particular day?"

The woman slowly shakes her head. "Ms. Leblanc isn't exactly the sharing type."

Don't I fucking know it.

The dip between my brows could fit the Atlantic Ocean as I leave Aspen's office. There's a fifty percent chance Nate knows what's up, but I'm not willing to risk the other fifty percent and have him smell something.

Besides, considering she's never had a heart-to-heart with him about her dark origins, I might as well lower that percentage to thirty.

I retrieve my phone and pause as I stare at the cockteasing pictures she sent me over the course of the past few days.

Because, apparently, the inability to touch her isn't enough, so she has to taunt me with what I'm missing. Or what I could be doing if Gwen hadn't picked up the habit of hanging around her like a clingy shadow.

I search my surroundings to make sure no one gets a glimpse of her nakedness, then type a text.

Kingsley: You haven't answered my calls all day, so now would be a good time to.

Kingsley: And you better kick Gwen out today at the pretense of having a cold.

No reply.

Not even a *read* sign.

Throughout the day, I send her a thousand texts along the lines of…

In case no one mentioned it, I'm not a patient man, witch. So a push-and-pull game will only get your ass red and your pussy brutalized by my cock.

Can you at least let me know if you're all right?

I swear to fuck, Aspen, I'm going to have Nicolo's dogs search for you and lock you up in some cabin. Then I'll put a tracker on you.

You haven't seen my crazy side for a while, so maybe you missed it, but I promise you, sweetheart, you will regret this stunt when you're unable to walk tomorrow.

Did something happen?

Don't make me file a missing person's report with the incompetent NYPD.

Did you tell your bodyguards not to pick up my calls?

By the time I go home, I'm in a mood that's sourer than vinegar and just as bitter. I called Gwen to snoop around and she said she was having alone time with Nate.

I hung up before she went into disgusting details.

That ruled out Nate as well since the stoic motherfucker actually forgets about the world when he's with my daughter.

Caroline Luciano was of no help either and even proceeded to make my ears bleed with how Aspen is heartless and has only called her once since she finally moved out.

I'm dialing Nicolo's number as I'm stepping out of my car. When I talked to the fucker about the last attack outside of his club, which was undeniably orchestrated by Bruno, he sang the usual tune of "no proof." But he did offer some of his men for protection, whom Aspen refused, choosing Mateo's men instead.

If Bruno is pulling another stunt, I'll severe Nicolo's head from his neck.

My fingers pause when I find Aspen's Range Rover in my circular driveway.

She's…here.

I refuse to honor the feeling in my chest with a name as I stride into the house, hell-bent on spanking her ass until she begs me to stop.

Aspen is crouching in the middle of the grand hall in front of the demon painting, her shoulders slumped and her eyes glued to it.

"Why, and I can't stress this enough, *the fuck* aren't you answering your phone?" I stop in front of her and I'm taken aback by the redness in her cheeks and the bottomless lack of color in the depths of her eyes as she slowly stares up at me.

"I don't know where I threw it," she says, voice low, almost meek.

I grab her by the arm, pulling her to her feet. I'm so used to Aspen being a damn gladiator that it feels off to see her so vulnerable.

The stench of alcohol assaults me when she grabs my face and attempts to kiss me. One of the few times she's gone for it first. Another red flag.

"You're drunk," I state the obvious.

"Don't be the boring alcohol police. And I'm not drunk, just a little tipsy."

"Did you drive while drunk?"

"No. I stole one of your wine bottles once I got here, and I still don't get the hype. Tequila is better."

A muscle tightens in my jaw. "Where's Martha?"

"Don't reproach her about this. She thought I was in Gwen's room." She slides her small hands down my sides and to my cock.

And while the motherfucker would love to get reacquainted with her cunt more than anything, I grab her wrists and pull them free. "What's going on?"

"I want you to fuck me. That's what's going on."

"Believe me, sweetheart, I'll fuck the living daylights out of you, but not before you tell me why you appear as if you've seen a ghost." I comb my fingers through her fiery hair and she shudders, slowly closing her eyes.

"Can't you just fuck me? You'd usually jump all over the opportunity."

"Usually isn't now. So you might as well start talking."

"Goddamn you and your stubbornness and your annoying controlling behavior." She drops her forehead against the center of my torso, but she doesn't hug me, her hands hanging lifeless at either side of her.

"Glad you got all that off your chest."

She shudders, her breathing shattering against my chest and I realize something.

She's hiding.

Fully intent on not letting me see her face.

"Today is the anniversary of Mom's death." She trembles as if the words rattle her. "I have two days a year I allow myself to be emotional. The day I thought my daughter died and the day Mom swallowed all the pills she could get her hands on to finally escape my father. Now that I know Gwen is alive, I think all the stupid emotions are coming back to haunt me. I hate it."

My fingers get lost in her hair, slowly caressing it. She goes still at my touch like a small child who's getting comforted for the first time. "Hate what?"

"The emotions. I'm not good with them, and all I can think about is how useless I was, how I spent as much time as I could outside to keep from going back home and seeing how pathetically weak Mom was. I hated my father for beating her, but I hated her, too, sometimes for not standing up for herself. I hated her when I cleaned her wounds, heated canned food, and bathed her. I hated her for forcing me to become her parent instead of the other way around. So I went out more, stayed at school more, hoping not to witness Dad's violent episodes and her crying sessions that always followed. I also hoped to escape Dad's orbit, because whenever he was mad, really mad, his poison of violence extended to me as well. He didn't hit me as much as he hit Mom, but if I got in his way, I would get a slap in the face or a kick in the stomach. And that life suffocated me. The constant anxiety, fear, and worry crippled me and I had no hopes to change it. Which is why I preferred the impersonal outside world instead. Until one day, I got home and it was too silent. Too...lifeless. She used to always have the radio on, listening to talk shows and focusing on other people's problems instead of her own. That day, it was hauntingly... silent. I think I knew even before I went to her bedroom, I knew something was wrong. Like...like...like..."

"She'd had enough and ended it," I whisper, the words too hoarse for my liking.

"Yeah." Her voice cracks as she digs her fingers into my waist, using me as an anchor. "She was lying in her bed as if she were asleep, but she wasn't breathing, and... For the first time in my life, I saw a smile on her bruised face. She was happy to finally leave and end her misery. To this day, I wonder if I could've saved her if I'd just stayed around more. If I hadn't run off to escape her and Dad's negative orbit. Maybe if I'd been a more reliable daughter, she would've survived."

"No, she wouldn't have. She'd already made up her mind probably months or even years prior to that moment. You were a kid and had no power to stop it, so blaming yourself is not only useless, it's also illogical."

She rests her chin on my chest and stares up at me with an unnatural shine in her eyes. "And yet, you blame yourself for your mother's death."

"I don't blame myself."

"Is that why you're after Susan with the spirit of a vengeful ghost?"

"It's called revenge, sweetheart. My contribution to humanity is ridding it of one gold digger."

"Bullshit," she says softly and reaches a hand out to stroke my cheek, hesitantly at first, as if she has no clue how to do this, then it's more proactive and with pure determination. "You feel as guilty as I do, maybe even more because you chose to stay with your dad to torment your stepmom instead of living with your mom."

"How the hell do you even know that?"

"Nate."

That motherfucker.

"You were young, too, Kingsley. You couldn't have done anything, and it's time to finally let it go."

"You got your revenge against your father by shoving him into prison. I haven't."

"And look where that got me. I've been looking over my shoulder for twenty-five years, counting days and months for his eventual release. Revenge is not the answer, not when more important things are at stake."

My jaw clenches beneath her touch. "I found my mother swimming in her own blood with tears in her eyes and my father's cursed lighter between her fingers when I was damn thirteen. So I will not, under any fucking circumstances, allow the woman who caused that scene to get away with it."

"You're not doing it for her, you're doing it for *you.*" She grabs my tie, shaking me and pulling me close at the same time. "Can't you see how it's stripping away your humanity? How it's torturing you? Even Gwen knows to stay away from you on Susan days because you look more like a stranger than her father. Is that what you want to be for the rest of your life?"

"Are you done?"

"No." She lifts her chin despite the tears gathered there. "You're not going to get rid of me that easily."

This goddamn woman.

I release myself from her hold, or more like force her to let me go and storm to the kitchen and pour myself a glass of water.

My first choice would be whiskey, but bringing that out in front of a closet alcoholic is no different than handing a gun to a fool.

Aspen follows me and unapologetically steps between me and the counter, forcing me to look at her.

At those damn eyes that haunted me for the longest time.

"You can run, but you can't hide from me, King."

My dick jumps in my pants at the way she calls me that. Fuck the asshole and how easily he gets turned on by her.

"You're surprisingly clingy," I say with an unveiled jab.

"And yet, you're still interested."

"Maybe I changed my mind."

"Maybe you're a liar."

Wildfire covers her features as she gingerly gets on her knees with the elegance of an angel.

An angel that I'm transforming into my custom-made devil.

All my plans and thoughts leave the building when she unbuckles my pants and pulls out my cock. The traitor who obviously likes her more than me jumps to his full glory in her hold.

"See?" She gives me a sly smile as she jerks me off slowly. "Your dick thinks you're a liar, too."

"He's physical. His opinion doesn't matter."

Her other hand strokes my balls as her small mouth wraps around the crown, sucking the precum.

"Fuck, sweetheart. Your lips were made for me. Now, be a good girl, open that mouth and suck me like a good little whore."

She takes me—or as much as she can fit of me—all the way inside and sucks with the determination of a succubus.

Jesus fucking Christ.

This woman will make me come like a teenager on his first masturbation session.

My fingers sink into her hair and I wrap it around my fist. Aspen escalates her performance, head bobbing up and down with one need—making me come.

I can see that determination in her bright eyes, the challenge, and even the need to please me.

Not in this life would I have thought that I'd have Aspen in this position. Not only is she prideful, but she hates showing any form of vulnerability.

But she's on her knees for me.

A sense of possessiveness rushes through my bones at the thought.

Aspen might be a wild horse, but she's *my* wild horse.

Using my grip on her hair, I thrust inside, hitting the back of her throat. She stills, her face reddening, and I expect her to fight me, and push me away, even.

But something happens.

She loosens her jaw and hold and lets me fuck her mouth as ruthlessly as I would have fucked her pussy.

I don't hold back and I certainly don't take it easy. Just like we both want. And this wild woman takes every drop of my crazy, even as drool and precum trickle down her chin.

Even as her eyes fill with tears.

Fuck me. This beautiful witch will be the death of me.

I'm about to empty down her pretty throat when the last person I expected to be here calls from down the hall.

"I'm here, Dad!"

TWENTY-FOUR

Aspen

I FREEZE.

And so does Kingsley's hold on my hair.

And so does the world.

For a single second, at least.

Then everything comes crashing back in like a hurricane. Not sure if it's the alcohol or the excessive information I offered Kingsley or the fact that I got on my knees for him, but I feel so out of my element that I wish the earth would swallow me whole.

It doesn't help that having my throat fucked by him has turned me on so much, a few strokes of my clit would be enough to give me an orgasm.

But the sound of Gwen's footsteps down the hall is almost enough to dissipate the haze. *Almost.*

I slowly start to release Kingsley's cock, but he pins me in place with his hold against my hair and thrusts in with a violence that catches me off guard.

What is the crazy asshole doing? If Gwen comes in, she'll see an unflattering scene of both of us. But I don't get a chance to protest or subdue the burning throb between my legs when cum explodes down my throat and floods my mouth. At the same moment, Gwen barges inside. "Dad!"

From my position behind the counter, I can see the tight lines in his face, but it's also his expression when he's angry, so I really hope that's what Gwen sees. Not the pleasure part.

By the time he finally pulls out and tucks himself in, I'm close to hyperventilating. He takes a moment to catch his breath, then says in a tight voice, "What are you doing here, Gwen?"

"It's my house, too, you know. I lived here not too long ago," she says with attitude, and I hear her dropping something, probably her bag, on a stool and climbing onto another. "And don't even think about kicking me out today."

My thoughts of crawling away are completely impossible now that she's so close.

I swallow as much as I can of Kingsley's cum, doing a ninja-level job at not releasing any sound.

He grabs his glass of water and nonchalantly places his other hand on the counter. "We're not really on speaking terms, Gwen."

"How can you ever not be on speaking terms with me, Daddy? Aren't I your little angel?" I can hear the spoiled princess tone in her voice. She really is Daddy's little girl.

"Not when you accuse me of being a woman-beater."

"I'm sorry," she lets out in a huff. "I was just too emotional, because, well, I know you don't like Aspen. Speaking of Aspen, is that her car outside?"

Oh, shit. Shit!

How could I think that I would ever get away with being a regular in Kingsley's house without her finding out?

"No," Kingsley says with his usual cool.

"Then whose is it?"

"One of my acquaintance's," he lies through his teeth with creepy ease.

"Where are they?" Gwen insists.

"In my office."

"And why aren't you in your office?"

"Why aren't you with your husband that you fought me tooth and nail for?" he shoots back.

"I already apologized, so why are you kicking me out?" She huffs. "And Nate had an urgent meeting with a client. He'll also be working late because of a certain partner who's obviously not taking on the manager role."

"So now it's my fault you married a workaholic?"

"Ugh, you never let me win, do you?"

Tell me about it.

I glare up at him and pinch his thigh, to which he remains solemn-faced, so I do it again, harder. This time, he covers his groan with a sip of water and spares me a death glare.

"Not if I can help it," he tells Gwen with a fake smile.

"You're impossible. I'm not surprised no woman wants to settle down with you."

"It's the other way around. I'm the one who's not interested in settling down with anyone."

"Because they wouldn't have you."

"Because *I* wouldn't have them."

There's a pause and I imagine father and daughter glaring at each other, or at least, she is. Kingsley appears to be more entertained than anything.

He's not the one on his knees on the damn floor.

Gwen releases an exasperated sound. "Whatever. At least Aspen is settling down."

Kingsley gives me an amused glance as if saying, "Since when?" then asks Gwen, "Did she tell you that?"

"No, but the other night, when I went to her place, I saw a man's jacket behind a chair. I think he forgot it there." I hear her footsteps around the kitchen and then catch a glimpse of her arm as she reaches into a cupboard. "It was weird because I can't imagine Aspen doing anything sentimental, but maybe she's different with the one she's in a relationship with. Anyway, I'm excited for when she'll introduce me to him."

My heart beats loud in my chest and I'm so focused on her words that the position I'm in doesn't even matter anymore.

Gwen wants me to introduce her to the man I'm in a relationship with. That incidentally happens to be her father, and no introduction will be happening, but still.

"I see." Kingsley sounds so pleased with himself.

"That's all you have to say?" Gwen asks with a note of incredulousness.

"What else should I say?"

"I don't know…you're not jealous?"

Of himself?

"No," he says with the same amusement that's shaking my shoulders.

"Not even a little?" Gwen sounds wounded now. "He'll be taking away Aspen, you know. And maybe you never had a relationship with her in the past, but you've been looking for her all my life."

My lips part as I stare up at him.

He's been looking for me? That's a new piece of information.

Kingsley's playful expression disappears, "I've only been looking for her to give her hell for abandoning you."

"Still…you were never attracted to her?"

"No."

I narrow my eyes and then grab his dick and it slowly jumps to life beneath my hold. *Never been attracted to me, huh?*

He glares down at me, his eyes shining with dark lust before he swiftly switches attention to Gwen who's probably making her favorite tea.

"Your loss," she says. "Aspen is a catch."

"Is that so?" Kingsley asks on my behalf.

"Of course. She's beautiful, smart, and the most accomplished woman I know, so yeah, she's definitely a catch anyone would wish to have but can't. Except for that man, obviously."

A salty taste explodes in my mouth and I realize it's a tear. A happy tear.

I can die an accomplished woman now. I never thought there would be a day where I'd hear my daughter complimenting me.

It makes all the hardships I went through worthwhile. The bad, the scary, and the terribly ugly.

"If only she weren't a bit of an alcoholic." The sadness in Gwen's voice slaps me across the face.

Kingsley eyes me with a gloating *I told you so* expression written all over his face.

"I didn't catch it at first," Gwen continues. "But she always pours alcohol in her coffee when she thinks I'm not looking. The other day, I sat beside her and opened an article about diseases caused by alcohol, but I don't think she noticed it. I don't want to tell her about it directly, because she might hate me for it. Oh, do you think I should ask Caroline?"

"Don't know, don't care. Also, why are you getting all cozy with Aspen when you hated her to death not a few months ago?"

"That was before I got to know her. She just has no clue how to express her feelings, and it's adorable sometimes when she stares blankly while trying to make conversation."

My cheeks heat. Jeez. I've never been ashamed of my character until now. The fact that I'm being discussed in third person while I'm right here is even more embarrassing.

"Besides, you're the one who hates her and I was just following you blindly. Now, I'm my own person."

"Is that so?"

"That's right. So don't interfere or turn her life into hell just to satisfy your ego. I'm watching you, Dad." I can imagine her making a hand gesture.

"Is this the part where I should be scared?"

"Yup. I'm not going to let you hurt my mom after I finally found her."

My heel scratches against the floor in my attempts to stop myself from rising and hugging her. While she's awake this time.

Gwen called me Mom.

Not directly, but it's close.

"What's that noise?" she asks suspiciously.

Damn it.

"The cup," he says without a hint of being flustered. "Now, leave or go to your room so I can work."

"But I want to have dinner with you."

"Not tonight, Gwen."

"Whatever. I'm going to make dinner for Nate instead and you're going to regret not accepting my company."

"I'll live."

"In a boring way." I catch a glimpse of her reaching over the counter to slap a noisy kiss on his cheek, and I shrink farther into my hideout. "Love you, Dad."

His stance and expression soften. "Love you, too, Angel."

I release a breath when her humming and steps disappear, but I remain hidden for a bit longer, just in case.

"Are you campaigning for a second round of sucking my cock?" Kingsley smirks down at me with his otherworldly arrogance.

"As if. I can't believe you came down my throat while our daughter was so close." I pause at how I called her *our* daughter. *Shit.* I need to get it together because I'm starting to believe in *our* things.

Our time.

Our work.

Our relationship.

Jeez. This isn't what I signed up for.

"I wasn't going to let her cock-block me again. Or else I'm going to cock-block her husband worse than I've been doing thus far."

"You're awful." I start to get up and lose balance due to my numb feet.

I fall against Kingsley's chest and he grabs me by the waist and sets me on the counter, then unapologetically gets between my legs, hiking my skirt to my waist.

He unbuttons my shirt and forcibly pulls it down my arms

and throws it on the floor. The bra follows until I'm half-naked and so ready for his ravaging that it's a little scary.

"Pity." He wipes my mouth with his thumb, gathering the cum that remains there, then slides it between my lips. "You looked good on your knees."

"You're the only man I would get on my knees for."

His eyes darken and his grip turns possessive like nothing I've witnessed before. And for some reason, my mouth goes dry.

"And you won't get on your knees for anyone else in the future," he announces out of nowhere.

"What do you mean—" My words are interrupted by a rush of footsteps.

"Dad! It is Aspen's car. It has the same plate—Holy shit!"

Kingsley and I stare at each other with "holy shit" expressions, too.

I bury my face in his torso to hide my nakedness as all hell breaks loose.

TWENTY-FIVE

Kingsley

BEING ACCOUNTABLE TO ANYONE ON THIS WHOLE PLANET IS off the table and not up for negotiation.

But there's one person whose life has been so intertwined with mine that it's impossible not to feel some sort of responsibility toward her. The one person who basically grew up with me and has been there during all the monumental moments of my life.

My moving out of my father's house. My college years. Law school. Passing the bar. Starting Weaver & Shaw. My father's death.

And eventually, finally finding her mother.

And that person is now sitting on the chair facing me and Aspen, who's chosen to cling to the other end of the sofa for dear life.

I was the one in that position two seconds ago—the one she held on to for dear life—but now that she's no longer naked after she hastily put her clothes back on, I apparently have no role to serve.

Aside from being the subject of my daughter's glares, of course.

Gwen has the expression of a haughty princess. Minus the foot tapping and the crossing of her arms.

She and Aspen have been red for the past fifteen minutes, which would've looked comical under different circumstances.

"In case neither of you noticed, I'm waiting for an explanation," she says with unveiled stubbornness, going for the jugular.

She's definitely my and Aspen's daughter.

Her mother shrinks further into her corner of the sofa. She was over the moon after hearing Gwen talk about her earlier, and in order to keep that awe-filled expression longer, I encouraged the conversation.

Now, however, she's clearly out of her element.

Stretching my legs in front of me, I meet Gwen's colorful eyes. "Well, let me inform you that we're under no obligation to explain anything. Last I checked, I'm the parent."

"Last I checked, you said you weren't attracted to her," the little minx shoots back. "Which is obviously incorrect, judging by the nude show I walked in on. I'm going to guess it's not work-related."

"I'm sorry," Aspen whispers, clearing her throat.

"For what?" Gwen's voice softens when she talks to her mother, unlike her bratty attitude with me. I might have spoiled her a bit too much.

Aspen meets her gaze for a brief second. "For you having to witness that."

"Shouldn't you be more sorry that you guys have a thing and didn't tell me?"

"It's not a thing," Aspen blurts, quick to correct Gwen, and I'm so close to choking the shit out of her while fucking her.

"Then what are you?" my daughter asks.

"Good question. Why don't you answer it, witch? What are we?"

She gives me an incredulous stare. *What?* She thought this would be going her way? There's only one way and she just fucked it all up by denying what we are.

"I hope whatever it is, the name is a relationship," Gwen says, still tapping her foot. When neither of us answers, she gasps. "Oh my God, you're friends with benefits?"

"We're not friends," I say with a calm I don't feel.

Aspen's shoulders snap at that, her spine jerking upright, and she adopts that hot bitch persona that only she can pull off. "Yeah, we're not."

"Then it's just benefits?" Gwen throws her hands in the air. "I can't believe this. The last time you guys did this, I came out of the union and lived my whole life without a mother. Thanks for being selfish once again and not considering me in whatever sexual arrangement you have."

Aspen pales.

I glare at Gwen, unblinking. "Watch how you speak to us. We're the parents, not the other way around."

"Then act like it and stop messing with my head." She springs to a standing position and regards Aspen with puppy eyes. "I'm so disappointed in you. I thought we were at a point where you could tell me about these things, but I guess we haven't made any progress at all." She jerks her head in my direction. "And I thought there were no secrets between us, Dad."

"Says the one who married my best friend while I was in a coma."

"Well, I love Nate. I always have. Do you guys love each other?" When neither of us answers, she gives us a dramatic look and throws her bag over her shoulder. "Call me when you decide what your relationship is and where I fit in it."

The door nearly snaps from its hinges when she slams it shut behind her.

Now that's dramatic, unnecessary, and full of Gwen's over-the-top empathetic tendencies.

Aspen, however, seems to have taken it all too seriously, because she gets up, her legs shaking as if attempting to go after Gwen.

I grab her by the waist, then sit her back down. She glares at me over her shoulder. "I thought we weren't friends. Let go of me."

"That's true. We're not friends, sweetheart. You're my fucking woman."

I swear she blushes like a curious case of tomatoes before she lowers her head and clears her throat. "Gwen must hate us."

"No, she was just caught up in the heat of the moment. She'll calm down after she tells Nate all about it and he's the one who will be argumentative on her behalf. The downside is that he's way less emotional than her, which is harder to deal with."

She groans, hiding her face in my chest. "I don't want to lose her."

"You won't. She likes you."

Her eyes explode in a myriad of colors as she stares up at me. "Really?"

"Yeah. And she's the forgiving type. No clue where she got that from."

"Definitely not from you."

"Or you."

She smiles, then it soon drops and she attempts to pull away.

"Where do you think you're going, sweetheart?"

"Home. I think we've caused enough damage for one night."

"Fuck no. The damage has already been done." I grab her chin with two fingers and tilt it up. "Besides, you hate being alone on a night like this, right?"

Her breathing shatters, "How can you even think about sex in a situation like this?"

"I think about sex in every situation when it comes to you, so I fail to see where the surprise is in that."

"Will you ever get enough?"

"Will you?"

She hesitates but doesn't answer, and I don't allow her to when I seal my lips to hers and finish what Gwen interrupted.

Contrary to what I expected, Gwen is putting up a fight.

It's been a week since she walked in on our foreplay, and she's been playing hard to get with the both of us ever since.

As I did expect, however, Nate was the person she spilled her heart to, and he came over with a metaphorical cape and a cardboard knighthood to act as her representative.

Aspen tried to explain, channeling her inner diplomat. I flat out told him I have nothing to explain to him, of all people, when he had sex with my daughter while I was sleeping.

He called me a motherfucking idiot, Aspen glared at me, and then they attempted to leave together to pick up their logical— also spelled *boring*—conversation. Which I didn't allow, of course.

I don't give a fuck that they're just friends. Nate is still the only man she's close to, and at some point, I believed they were fuck buddies.

The only reason I wasn't sure if they were indeed sexual partners is due to the fact that Nate used to discard the women he slept with as if they were used tissues.

Still, a part of me thought maybe Aspen was special enough that he kept a friendship with her.

That thought left a burning fire in my chest. I'm as self-deprecating as a presidential candidate. The only times I would do it is when it's fake.

However, I can't deny the nagging thought that if Aspen had to choose a partner, it would be someone like Nate. Although stoic and detached, he's as level-headed as she is, wouldn't force her hand to do anything, and there's no bickering involved.

Now, don't get me wrong. The chances of me admitting that out loud are nil, but that doesn't mean the thought isn't lurking rent-free in my head.

My solution? Using the Nicolo angle, lying by saying that we have a lunch meeting with him to keep Aspen by my side.

The lunch happened in my house, right after spanking her ass red for refusing to eat, and then ordering her to consume food.

She's currently standing near the window, wearing only my shirt.

And hickeys.

And bite marks.

And my handprint.

Her fair legs are covered in fading bruises. At some point, she stopped complaining about them, except for when she has to use a ton of makeup to cover the ones on her neck.

She did ask me not to bite there anymore, but fuck that.

There's always this animalistic need to mark every inch of her skin so she'll only belong to me.

So I'm the only man who ever gets to own her body and has a mission to conquer her soul.

I never had these feelings about a woman before. There was a hint of wanting more when I first met her, but it wasn't to the extent of this burning obsession.

Not to the extent of being hungry twenty-four seven for a taste of her.

I've never been the type of man who gets attached easily, or at all. Never looked at a woman twice, or came up with one idea after the other to trap her to stay with me.

But the woman standing at the window, checking her phone and massaging her temple, is the exception to all the above.

She's so fucking beautiful, like my tailored fallen angel and the devil's favorite demon.

Unable to resist the urge, I pull on my boxer briefs and walk up to her, then wrap a possessive arm around her waist, cocooning her from behind.

She smells of sex and me.

I always smell myself on her now, and I'm thankful for the sensitive nose that allows me to experience this moment to the fullest.

My other hand massages her head and she sighs. "Mmm. Right there."

"You still have severe headaches?"

"Only when I'm tired. Thanks to someone." She gives me the stink eye and I merely smirk, continuing my task.

Aspen is seven days sober, and I'm going to bet her decision to stop drinking has to do with Gwen calling her an alcoholic. If there's one thing I've learned about Aspen, it's that she despises being weak with a passion. A result of her rough childhood, mobster father, and the lengths she had to go to in order to snatch her position at the top.

And according to her logic, being less than perfect in Gwen's eyes is a sign of weakness.

That's the furthest thing from the truth, but if it makes her stop drinking, then she can believe it all she wants.

She's been an adorably grumpy creature while withdrawing. The first few days were the worst, but she's been gradually adjusting and even started to eat more. And my favorite part? She seeks me out every chance she gets, and when I attempted to ignore her just to get a reaction out of her, she bombarded my phone with her form of invitation—erotic pictures.

Sighing, she relaxes in my hold, and even her movements pause on the phone.

"Still trying to reach Gwen?" I motion at the screen that's opened to her group chat with Caroline and Gwen.

"She's ignoring me but talks to Caroline just fine."

"That's a manifestation of her anger. She'll come around."

"You also said she's the forgiving type, but that personality trait apparently doesn't apply to this." Her voice lowers. "I feel like she's slipping through my fingers after I've finally got her. What if she remains disappointed in me?"

"She's wanted a mother ever since she was a toddler, so the chances of that desire waning is somewhere below zero. Gwen is infuriatingly determined and doesn't give up unless she gets what she wants."

Her face lights up like it does anytime I talk about Gwen and then she wraps an arm around her stomach. "You know, she kicked a lot when she was inside me, sometimes hauling me out of sleep in the middle of the night. I thought she was sick or something and I couldn't do anything about it or I could have triggered my aunt and uncle's abuse."

My jaw clenches and I stop massaging her head to keep from squeezing it or something worse.

Like me, Aspen doesn't like to talk about her past. This is one of the few times she's willingly offered a glimpse.

"Are your aunt and uncle still alive?"

"Thankfully, no. They died in a horrible crash soon after I ran away. My aunt's head was found a mile away from her body."

"Good riddance."

She shudders. "I thought I would feel glad, too, but their death didn't give me back the daughter I lost. Back then, they hit me any chance they got, tried to poison me, too, and locked me up until I thought I was going to die."

"But you didn't. You're here."

"Yeah. I set traps all over the house and made their lives hell. I tried everything under the sun to protect the baby that was growing inside me. I was young but not really a kid, you know, and for the first time in my life, I felt responsible for someone else. I fell in love with her the second I found out about her and I used to read to her a lot, have her listen to all types of music, and tell her happy stories that I was too pragmatic to feel joy from. I...wanted her to be loved and cared for and to have a story different from mine. So when they put that dead baby in my arms, I lost all my purpose and merely survived. Until...well, now. I want to give her everything I have and don't have, despite the fact that she's not a kid and is married. Is that weird?"

"No, it just means you're a parent. And if it's any consolation, I also wanted her to have a story different from mine. Which is probably why I spoiled and sheltered her too much."

She faces me, forcing me to let her go. "You're a great father, Kingsley. The best father I know."

"Either you don't know many fathers, or that was meant to be a compliment."

A blush explodes on her neck and she whispers, "Shut up."

"Don't worry. I'll keep your emotions a secret, sweetheart. Not even our daughter will find out about it."

She pauses, her lips falling open. "You…just… Did you just call her our daughter?"

"Well, isn't she?"

"Yeah, but you've never said that before."

"You called her our daughter first the other day. So I'm just keeping up with the trend."

She flashes me a smile. "Thank you."

"Did the world just end or did you thank me?"

"Just go with it and stop being a smartass."

I pull her against me. "Am I?"

"The worst of all." She sighs, nuzzling her nose against my chest. "But hey, your smell definitely chases away the withdrawal headache."

"I charge with a fuck for every hug."

Her shoulders shake with laughter. "Sex addict."

I stroke her fiery hair. "I plead guilty, Your Honor."

We remain like that for a while, her arms wrapped around my waist, face buried in my chest, and my fingers playing with her hair.

And if time could stop, this would be the perfect moment.

"You should tell Gwen what you just told me," I say after a while. "She'd understand."

"I'd rather not."

"You don't have to be strong all the time, Aspen. There are people, your flesh and blood included, who should see you for who you are. Flaws, weaknesses, and all. Someone as empathetic as Gwen will appreciate it."

"I…will think about it." She releases a breath. "It just feels so weird after all these years. A lot of things do."

"Like what?"

"Like how I found you, Caroline, and Gwen. It's like that sudden surge of life dying patients get before they die."

"That's a depressing analogy."

"I know. I just can't help thinking about it."

"What I can't help thinking about is how your aunt and uncle found me."

She lifts her head, frowning. "Me either. All these years, I thought Caroline helped them, but she swore it wasn't the case."

I don't like this. It's a missing piece in a puzzle and a black hole that disrupts the whole picture. The worst part is that the only links to this theory, Aspen's aunt and uncle, are gone.

As if it was all planned.

My phone beeps on the floor beside us, but I pay it no attention.

Aspen stiffens a little before she subtly pulls away. "I'm going to get back to work."

I clutch her wrist before she's out of view. "Why?"

"What do you mean why? I have a meeting with a client."

"That's not what I'm wondering about. Why did you pull away from me just now?"

"I...did not."

"You're not even meeting my gaze." I tilt her head up to be greeted by her muted eyes.

All light has vanished from them as if she's in battle mode. She has this mode sometimes where she escapes into a deeper part of herself, where it's impossible to find her.

"I have work, Kingsley. Not all of us have billions to fall back on."

"Your social discrimination bitterness is not only pathetic but holds no logic."

"Then I'm pathetic." She forcibly pushes me away, grabs her clothes from the floor, and slams the bathroom door shut.

I'm about to haul her out of there and see what the fuck got her nonexistent panties in a twist, but that would only lead to a fight.

Considering our equally headstrong personalities, it's better to just let things cool off sometimes.

I grab my phone and pause when I see a text on the screen from one of my previous side pieces.

Hey, sexy.

I narrow my eyes on it, then on the bathroom door. Aspen couldn't have seen it.

If she did, she would've raised hell about it.

I delete the text, block the number, and consider changing mine. Too many women know it when they should've taken their NDAs seriously.

They don't matter anymore.

In fact, they never did.

The only woman who does is apparently mad at me.

TWENTY-SIX

Aspen

I'M A LOGICAL PERSON.

In fact, I've felt older than my actual age since I was a child for this reason.

I don't let emotions sway me, not even when I was a hormonal teenager with an unexpected pregnancy and unresolved feelings.

My main goal has always been to survive, escape the hole I was born into, and lead a life that's entirely different from my parents'.

I chose to practice law so no one would be given the chance to walk all over me. So I could beat the statistics about runaways and prove we can be accomplished.

Our origins don't dictate who we are, our actions do.

I wanted to rewrite my history, to start anew and bury my past.

Little did I know that it would catch up to me. Or that I'd find myself the most illogical person I've ever met.

It's been a week since the day I saw another woman's text to Kingsley.

A whole week of struggling with the gloomy emotions that have no business attacking me.

During that week, I've attempted to pull away, but Kingsley is a damn beast who doesn't allow me any alone time.

In the midst of dirty sex, spanking me, marking my flesh with his barbaric bites, I've had no time to catch my breath.

I hate that I've gotten used to his rough hand during sex and how it becomes gentle yet firm when he washes my hair, worshipping every strand. Or the way he feeds me special recipes he's found specifically to help with my withdrawals.

Or how he drags me to his home gym to work on my stamina, and always, without a doubt, ends up fucking me mid-workout because he's an animal who never gets enough.

But what I hate the most is that my vision about this whole thing is starting to blur.

Which is why I needed to gather what's left of my will, summon my logical side, and remind myself that what I saw that day was nothing.

That he didn't actually sleep with her.

Though I wasn't doing a great job at convincing myself of that fact, considering that I had to physically struggle with not checking his phone.

I caved two nights ago and typed in his password while he was sleeping. The only reason I even know his password is because he's so open about typing it in front of me as if he trusts me or something.

Well, he shouldn't have, because I totally broke that trust. However, there was no trace of the text I saw. Her name, Britney, was not in his contacts either.

To other people, that could've been a good sign, but it pushed my suspicious meter up a notch, and I felt so disgusted with myself for snooping in his stuff that I had nausea all night long.

I'm not this person. I don't get jealous, I don't allow anyone to make me feel small, let alone play me.

So why do I feel like crying from frustration?

Releasing a long breath, I try to push the thought of Kingsley out of my head and lift my hand to hit the doorbell of Gwen's house.

Nate invited me over for dinner and I wouldn't miss this chance for the world. My daughter has been actively avoiding me, and that's part of why I've been on edge lately.

Their house is spacious, but not cathedral-level like Kingsley's. It has Gwen's touch with the endless colorful flower beds in the garden. There are also cozy-looking chairs in the front yard that I can imagine her and Nate sitting in on peaceful evenings.

Despite his fortune, Nate always lived in an apartment and only used it to sleep. He's as much of a workaholic as I am, with no personal life to speak of.

Or he used to be, anyway.

Now, he habitually leaves early, has strict boundaries on his personal time, and has taken more vacations in the last few months than in his whole life. And the most endearing part is that all his personal time is dedicated to hiking and traveling with Gwen.

I would've never imagined that Nate would change into this family man, and it feels a bit lonely since I always thought we shared the same mindset.

Not that I'm jealous or anything. I'm not.

The door opens before I push the bell and I swallow as Gwen appears in the entrance.

She's wearing comfy-looking shorts and a matching T-shirt that has "Vanilla is The New Kink" written on it. Her hair is gathered in a messy bun and some flour dusts her cheek.

"Hey," I say, feeling more nervous than I've ever been before.

Apparently, I'm confident in everything, except when it comes to my daughter.

And her father.

No. Stop thinking about him.

"Nate invited me over," I say when she remains silent, then I give her a box of cake. "I made a vanilla cake. The easiest. I burned the first three, but this one survived—although barely. I used to eat these from a stand on the side of our street. There was this middle-aged lady who gave us some for free. Us, as in, me and Caroline. Mostly Callie because she made friends with the food people so they would give her any leftovers, then she shared them with me. I preferred to starve than beg for food…" I wince, realizing I've been talking for too long. "Sorry for blabbering."

"Now I know who I got my love for vanilla from. And some blabbering habits, too." Gwen takes the cake from my hand with a small smile. "Are you going to stand there all night long? Come in."

I follow behind her and she leads me to the dining room, where the table is already set for three people. Nate sits at the head, looking relaxed in his khaki pants and polo shirt. "Aspen."

"Nate," I greet back.

Gwen pulls back my chair and I take the cue to sit down.

"Did you know I was coming?" I ask, staring between her and her husband.

"Of course. Nate already told me."

"Oh." That's much better than taking her off guard, and at least she doesn't oppose the idea of me coming over to her house.

"I'm going to change real quick," she tells us, then disappears around the corner.

Nate's attentive gaze follows her until she's out of view and remains there for a second too long. I'm glad the brute Kingsley isn't here or he would've started a drama. Though I do understand that an overprotective father like him finds it hard not to think of her as a little girl.

I can't imagine what he must've felt like when he first found out that his best friend married his "angel," as he calls her.

But then again, even Kingsley's brutishness could see how much Nate adores the ground Gwen walks on.

Nothing could've stopped Nate from marrying Gwen. Not even her father.

"She spent the whole afternoon cooking, baking, and hiding alcohol because she knows you've stopped drinking," he says, finally looking at me. "I offered to help, but she completely refused it."

My heart squeezes. "Now I feel bad for the cake that's probably not edible."

"Believe me, she'll eat it even if she has to drink a gallon of milkshake with it."

I smile. "Thank you, Nate."

"For what?"

"For letting me come here." I've been wanting a chance to talk to her face to face but have always chickened out, scared of her rejection.

If it were Kingsley, he would've snatched that chance. In fact, I heard him talking to her on the phone the other day as if nothing had happened.

But the truth remains, he's been her father, mother, and best friend all these years. She can't really be mad at him for long. I'm an entirely different equation.

Nate pours a glass of water and takes a sip. "Inviting you was her idea."

"Really?"

"Yes. Besides, she needs you as much as you need her, Aspen. But she has both your and King's stubbornness, so it may take her a little while to admit it out loud."

"It's fine. I can wait. I waited for twenty years to find some balance after losing her, so this is nothing."

"While you're waiting…" He slides his elbows on the table and interlinks his fingers. "Shouldn't you sort out whatever you have with King first?"

My stomach contracts at the mention of his name and I drink a whole glass of water. That's what I've been doing lately whenever I have the urge to drink. "It's nothing."

"I'll be ready to believe your warped sense of nothing if you stop disappearing in each other's offices in plain sight or if he stops suddenly kicking out anyone who's in the room with him when he gets a text. Or when you stop looking at each other with the full intention of tearing one another's clothes off."

My neck heats and I pour more water, the glass almost over-flowing. Are we that obvious?

More like, is Kingsley? He doesn't miss a chance to drag me into a dark corner so he can have his way with me. Ravage me.

Leave me completely spent.

"Honestly, I don't care what two adults do with their sex lives and I'm not even going to think about how you get bruises all over your neck and even your wrists."

I splutter on my water. "You…you saw?"

"Yeah, your makeup game is sloppy sometimes. Not to mention, he puts his mark on places you can't see." He motions at me. "Like your nape."

I slap a hand over it, surprised the glass doesn't splinter into pieces in my other hand. "That fucking asshole."

"I take it there's no forcing involved?"

My cheeks burn further. "I would kill him before he forces me into anything."

"That's what I thought. Just wanted to check, because he's a cold human being who doesn't like to be defied."

"He's not cold…he's just not warm, but he does care. I mean, look at him with Gwen, even when they have their differences, they send each other good morning and good night texts, and he makes sure I eat and he's one of the reasons I stopped drinking and…" I trail off when a slow smile spreads across Nate's lips. "What?"

"Is it me or did you just defend King?"

"I did not." *Shit. I did.*

What the hell is wrong with me?

"Right," he says in a mocking way. "Whatever it is you're doing, can you make sure it's clear? It's confusing Gwyneth, and I'm un-doubtedly on her side, not yours or King's."

The sound of footsteps kills any response I had. My thoughts are scattered when I see what Gwen is wearing.

It's the same dress I had sent to her house right before she came back from her honeymoon.

"You look stunning, wife," Nate says, his voice deepening.

"Thank you, husband." She quickly kisses his lips, then sits down. "Aspen bought it for me."

"It looks perfect," I say, my words strangled by stupid emotions.

"Thanks." She smiles a little. "I made mushrooms, pasta à la bolognese, and steak. I didn't know what your favorite food is, so I didn't know what to cook. If you like something else, I can—"

"It's fine. I don't have a favorite food. I don't like it that much, actually."

Gwen frowns. "Why not?"

"I guess eating was just a tedious chore when I was young, because food was hard to come by. Being hungry hurt and sucked my energy, so I dreaded the sensation. After I grew up, I started eating for necessity only." Until recently.

Until Kingsley sat me on his lap, on the counter, and made me eat. Or when he did filthy things to my body while I ate.

Until I started to associate food with our heated debates and a delicious burn on my ass.

"That's because you did it alone." Gwen scoops some of the pasta on a plate. "Food should be consumed while in someone's company, so if you have no one to eat with, call me...or Dad." She slides the dish in front of me with a shy, "I hope you like it."

I take a forkful of the pasta and chew on it to keep from choking on the lump in my throat. "It's delicious. Thank you."

"You're welcome. Dad taught me how to cook. He taught me everything I know."

I swallow the mouthful of food. "I'm glad you had him."

"Me, too." She fiddles with the napkin on her lap, eyes downcast. "I'm sorry I blamed you for what happened in the past. Truth is, it wasn't your fault and you were only a child when you were pregnant with me. I was illogical and emotional and shouldn't have taken it out on you."

"Gwen, no..."

"Let me finish." Her voice turns brittle. "I missed you so much when I didn't have you and I was hurt thinking you abandoned me, but you didn't. Yesterday, Daddy took me to the grave you visited yearly, thinking it was me, and told me you were severely abused, starved, and beaten to within an inch of your life, but you still tried your best to protect me. He said losing me shaped who you became as a person and if I couldn't understand your circumstances, then I don't deserve you as a mother."

My lips part. Kingsley told her that? He…defended me in front of her?

Like, what is he playing at now? Is this another tactic to make me trust him just so he can pull the world from beneath my feet?

"You'd deserve me anyway, Gwen."

"No, he's right." Her colorful eyes meet mine with a shine in them. "I'm sorry you had to go through all of that. I had no idea your life was that hard."

"I…survived."

"Doesn't mean it wasn't hard. I'm an adult now, you know, so you don't have to protect me anymore. I can do that myself just fine and can even protect you, Dad, and Nate if need be."

My fingers shake on the utensils and I couldn't control them even if I wanted to. God. What have I done to deserve a daughter like her? No wonder Kingsley calls her an angel. She's the purest soul ever.

She makes me eat from every dish, channeling her father's behavior, and I do it, not because I like the food, but because she's there.

The three of us talk about the firm and her law school application. Nate and I give her advice on her options, relying on our experience.

And in the midst of the peaceful, familial atmosphere, I hate that I wish Kingsley were here to join in on the conversation. He makes his larger-than-life presence known by his absence.

At this point, I don't know if I could ever purge him out of my system instead of letting him fester inside.

After dinner, Nate goes to search for some board games while Gwen shows me around the house.

"It's a beautiful place," I tell her when we reach a small living area that overlooks the illuminated pool.

She faces me, a sly smile on her lips. "Not more beautiful than Dad's house."

"They have different attributes, I guess."

She watches me intently, slightly narrowing her eyes.

"What?" I take a sip from the small bottle of water I've been carrying around.

"Do you love my dad?"

I choke on the water for the second time tonight. "W-what? No..."

Her brow furrows as if the answer is disappointing. "I know I said he's evil sometimes, but he's the best father ever. And okay, maybe his legal battles with Susan are over the top, but she provokes him, too, and she was the reason behind Grandma's death and still calls her names. Also, he's a good man deep down, so give him a chance."

"A chance for what?"

"To love him."

"That's not how it works, Gwen."

"But what if Dad loves you?"

"Believe me, that's not the case." He's not capable of loving another person. The only reason he loves Gwen is because she's his flesh and blood.

She's part of him. I most definitely am not.

"How can you be so sure? Did you ask him?"

"No, and I absolutely won't." Unless I want to make a bigger fool out of myself. "If whatever we have makes you uncomfortable, then I can..."

The words *end it* get stuck in my throat and I don't know why the hell I'm on the verge of tears at the thought.

"You can what?" Gwen gauges my expression. "End it?"

"If...you prefer. It's better than you holding out vain hope that this is a reunion or something. Kingsley and I never had a relationship in the first place."

"But you had a connection, right? Auntie Callie told me you never shut up about him back then."

Since when does she call Caroline 'Auntie Callie' and why is that big-mouthed idiot telling my secrets? "I was a clueless teenager. I thankfully got over those hormonal emotions."

"I don't think you can completely get over your first crush. They hold a piece of you forever. Look at me. I had a crush on Nate since I was fifteen, and even though he rejected me years later, I still couldn't get him out of my mind."

"That's different. Nate eventually reciprocated, and honestly, he didn't stand a chance with your determination. Kingsley, however…"

"What?"

"You know full well that your father doesn't love anyone but you."

"Well, true. But hey, he can add you to his shortlist."

Can and will are entirely different, and I'm older and emotionally mature enough not to wish for the impossible.

I direct the conversation back to her and Nate so I don't get caught up in my own thoughts again.

The three of us play a board game and watch a horror movie, per Gwen's request, in the middle of which she falls asleep against my arm.

Nate carries her away too soon. "Let me get her to bed and I'll be back."

"No need. I can find my way out." I lean over and kiss her forehead, my lips lingering there for a bit. "Night, baby."

I put on my shoes and drink a whole bottle of water from the kitchen.

"Aspen, wait."

I turn around with my hand on my car door handle.

Nate steps into the night, carrying a photo album, then offers it to me. "She forgot, but she intended to give you this."

"What is it?"

"A journal of sorts in which she added commentary to every

picture of herself. She wanted you to have this so you can see how she grew up over the years."

I hug the album to my chest and touch his arm. "Thank you, Nate."

He pats my hand. "You would've been a great mother, Aspen. You still are. Don't let King or anyone else tell you otherwise."

I don't know if it's his words, the treasure in my hands, how close Gwen felt throughout this night, or the gloomy feeling inside me, but I can't control the tears that stream down my cheeks.

"Hey." Nate pulls me into a brotherly hug with one hand on my shoulder.

"It hurts. Not being there for her from the beginning really hurts and…I don't know how to show how grateful I am that I'm getting another chance. I wish I could've watched her grow up into who she is."

"You can do it from now on. It's never too late to be a part of her life."

I nod and we start to pull away from each other when Nate jerks backward. I gasp when Kingsley appears like a dark shadow with his fist raised.

TWENTY-SEVEN

Kingsley

WHEN GWEN SENT ME A SIDE ANGLE SHOT OF ASPEN BESIDE her with "Guess who's my date tonight?" I had the decency to ignore it.

Or pretend to, anyway.

Fifteen minutes later, the pretense wasn't holding so well and I might have flipped poker night at Nicolo's the middle finger and flown here.

Partly because Gwen's attempts at playing cupid are embarrassingly obvious and I couldn't just ignore them.

Partly because...fuck it. I wanted to see Aspen's face. She's been claiming every reason under the sun to avoid me lately and that's something neither my dick nor I were going to accept.

Actually, my dick gets his fill of her cunt just fine. It's the disappearing after part that's frowned upon in his limited emotional repertoire.

The worst part is that it isn't always physical disappearance. I got used to her enough to recognize when she's performing a mental slam, witch style. She'd be there in body but not in spirit.

And that shit needed to end.

So imagine my fucking reaction when I find her hugging Nate. Or him hugging her or what-the-fuck-ever.

My vision has been a hazy red ever since, so I'm not keen on the details right now. Except for the need to bash the motherfucker's head in. I raise my fist to dislocate his jaw and send him to the nearest ER when something hard smashes against my head.

The hit takes me so completely off guard that my hold loosens around his collar and I'm ready to murder whoever interrupted me. When I turn around, however, I find a furious Aspen holding on to the weapon of the crime—a thick album.

Only the scattered light posts offer a view of the otherwise dark night, but it's enough to highlight her rigid posture.

My jaw sets into a harsh line. "You stay put. I'll be with you in a minute."

If eyes could catch fire, hers would be a volcano as she gets between us, forcing me to release Nate. Her nostrils flare and her chin is tipped so high, it nearly reaches the sky. "What the hell is wrong with you?"

"Step. Aside." I don't know how I speak in mock calm when lava courses through my veins.

"So you'd be a barbarian and hit your partner and best friend who, oh, I don't know, happens to be your damn daughter's husband? Have you thought about what she'd think if she saw this?"

"Did you when you threw yourself into his arms, thirsty for attention?"

The *slap* comes first, and the sting follows. My face hardens, and in one single motion, I wrap my hand around her throat, squeezing the sides until I nearly lift her off the ground. I have enough control not to choke the living fuck out of her, but my hold is firm enough that she and Nate know she's mine.

"You will regret that, sweetheart."

A big hand grabs me by the shoulder harshly and could normally, under any other circumstances, peel me off her, but not now.

Not when the need to fucking devour this woman and teach her who she belongs to pulses in me like a second being.

"Let her go, King." Nate's voice is calm but firm.

Aspen continues glaring at me even when her face reddens to the darkest shade I've seen. Even when her eyes nearly bulge out of their sockets.

The witch doesn't fight me, probably using some silent warfare tactic to intimidate me.

"You're choking her. Let the fuck go, Kingsley."

I slowly loosen my hold but don't release her. I'm not going to release her, even if she never stops hating me and continues to glare at me every day for the rest of our lives.

"King…" There's a warning in Nate's tone that he won't hesitate to escalate it into action.

"It's okay, Nate," she croaks. "Go back to Gwen."

"Are you sure? He's in his crazy mode right now."

She doesn't break eye contact with me, her chin rising. "I can handle him."

You fucking wish, sweetheart.

Nate leans in to whisper in my ear, "Your jealousy is irrational, nonsensical, and has a margin of error the size of the Pacific Ocean. Question my devotion to my wife again and I'll be the one to fucking kill you."

And then, he leaves us alone with one last shake of his head.

My gaze clashes with Aspen's defiant one. She looks younger, more carefree in a light-colored casual dress and a flowery sweater that she most likely borrowed from Caroline, because her wardrobe is as grim as mine.

She's holding on to a photo album with both hands as if it's her anchor.

"Are you going to let me go, or should Gwen see this scene, too?" she whisper-yells in my face and I'm tempted to bite her lips and tear them in my mouth.

"What were you doing with Nate just now?"

"Last I checked, it's none of your business."

"Don't fucking test me, Aspen. I'm very close to the point of eruption, so unless you want to witness the brand of unhinged I turn into, speak."

"You're acting like a damn brute and I refuse to negotiate with terrorists."

If I weren't on the edge of anger, I would've cracked up, but now, her stubbornness only fuels the volcanic emotions invading my insides.

"I swear to fuck, if you don't talk—"

"What?" She cuts me off. "What are you going to do?"

Still gripping her by the throat, I pull her to the side of her car that's hidden by a tree, camouflaging the view from the house. She yelps, letting the album fall to the side when I push her against the hood.

My body crushes hers from behind and it's a full-on slam of flesh against flesh that leaves her panting.

Before she can gather her bearings, I yank her dress up, hitching it up her thighs. She tries to grab me with uncoordinated movements, but my hand comes down on her ass with a smack that reverberates in the silence and makes her pause.

"Is this the reason you've been pulling away from me lately, huh?" I don't bother with removing her panties and rip them off her pussy with enough force to leave her gasping. "Have you changed your mind from wanting me to wanting our dear son-in-law?"

"You're a sick motherfucker." Her voice is shaky, brittle, but it's clear enough to convey her disregard.

"Then what is it? What's the reason you barely look me in the eye lately?"

Her lips quiver, but she mutters, "Fuck you."

"If you insist." I thrust two fingers in her pussy and her walls clench around me. "Look at how your cunt is dripping and begging to be fucked. You don't even care that we're outside, no?"

She turns her face the other way, hands digging into the Range Rover's metal, but I thrust another finger in her and pull her chin up so that she looks at me. "You want me to fuck this pussy until you're dripping wet all over the place like a dirty little whore, don't you?"

The challenge in her face is an aphrodisiac that I can't get enough of, so I add a fourth finger, to which she whimpers. "I bet you can take my whole fist up this cunt."

Her moan is the only answer I get as I pump my fingers inside her faster, harder. Then, just to fuck with her, I curl two to hit that secret spot that drives her insane.

She physically jolts, but her noises that are usually my favorite symphony are now muffled.

So the witch decides to put up a fight?

Fine. Let's see how far she'll go.

"Your greedy pussy is drenching me, sweetheart. No matter how tight it gets, it still needs my thick cock, doesn't it?"

Her breaths turn shallow and her eyes hardly stay open. When her pussy starts soaking my fingers, I know she's getting close.

"Say you want me to fuck you."

"No," she grits out, teeth sinking in the cushion of her lower lip to stop other sounds from slipping out.

I up my pace until she's flat out panting, her skin turning hot and tingly beneath mine. Then I bite the shell of her ear, throwing her in a loop of pleasure and pain.

Just when she's about to come, I pull out my fingers with a jerk.

Aspen groans, tears gathering in her eyes from frustration or something else, I don't know.

Her face that could be sculpted to match the most ruthless generals fixates me with a glare. "You think I can't do it myself?"

She reaches a hand between her thighs, but before she can relieve herself, I release her chin. Her head falls against the trunk as I slap her pussy and then her ass so hard, she gasps, her body jolting against the car.

"No touching yourself when I'm around." I lather my fingers with her wetness, and the sloppy sound her folds make turn my dick fucking hard. "See how much of a little whore you are for me? You're dripping between your thighs. Do you want me to fuck you that badly?"

"Shut up."

I slide a generous amount of her arousal to her back hole and thrust a finger in. She goes still, and I smile, my lips meeting her ear. "I'm going to fuck you here tonight and you're going to take my dick up the ass like a good girl."

Her flaming hair cocoons her face, nearly hiding her expression from me, so I add another finger, making her groan.

"This is your first, isn't it? Your ass is a virgin like your cunt was a virgin the first time I tore through it." I pound my fingers in, lubing her with her own juices, slapping her thighs and ass for good measure because it gets her so fucking wet and paints the best erotic picture I've ever seen.

"Who's Britney?"

Her question, albeit low and shrouded with gloom, reaches me loud and clear.

"Who?" I slap her ass again and she startles and swallows a few times.

"The Britney who sent you a 'Hey sexy' text, then miraculously disappeared from your phone. Who is she?"

"Are you going through my things, sweetheart?" I thrust another finger in her ass, stretching her wide and to the fullest.

Her whimpers echo in the air, but she repeats, "Who is she? Are you sleeping with her?"

"And if I am? Will your little cunt drip for me any less or will your ass loosen for me less readily?"

She bucks against the car, trying to twist around, and I slap her ass three consecutive times, making her shriek. Then she slams a hand on her mouth to mute it, probably remembering where she is.

"Stay fucking still unless you want me to tear your back hole."

"Let me go," she orders in a broken, hurt tone. "Don't touch me with the same hands that were all over someone else. I'm not anyone's second choice."

"You were never a second fucking choice." I hoist her head up with a savage grip on her hair until her face is eye level with mine. "Other people mean fuck to me as they should mean fuck to you. The only thing that matters is that you're mine, body and fucking soul, Aspen. I was your first and I'll make sure to be your last."

Her lips part and she moans when I ram my fingers inside her ass with savage energy. Her thighs tremble and shake with each in and out.

Once I feel her close, I edge her until her hips are rocking, her walls strangling me like a vise.

And just when she's about to reach the peak, I up my rhythm. She screams and I bite her lips in my mouth as the orgasm shakes her to the core.

Then I release her hair, letting it fall on the hood, and free my hard, ready cock. It points straight at her ass and I remove my fingers, relishing in how her rings of muscle clench around me, attempting to keep me in.

"I'm going to own every last inch of you, Aspen." That way, she'll have no place else to go or turn to.

That way, whatever path she takes will only lead her to me.

I'll trap her, give her no escape, and force her to accept the reality that is us, even if I have to demolish every bit of her walls for it.

Is it wrong? Maybe.

But I don't give a fuck at this point. All I care about is that this woman needs to be mine. There will be no other men and certainly no relationships after me. I might have started this to be a temporary thing, but now, any sorry fucks who attempt to get close to her will have their balls on sticks.

Grabbing her by the hips, I thrust the first few inches of my cock in. The resistance is real and I have to stop.

Aspen's breaths are fractured and her body trembles even as she remains completely still. The view of her back, of her beneath me, submitting to me, will never get old.

"You need to relax, sweetheart, or I won't be able to get all the way in."

Her head whips in my direction, her lips swollen and her hair in disarray from our earlier kiss. "You…you're not all the way in?"

"My cock has been inside your cunt countless times and you forgot the size?" I rock my hips. "Relax your ass and let me in."

She shakes her head frantically. "I…can't. It's…it's too big."

"Your pussy has taken my cock and so will your ass." I release her hip and slap her ass cheek. "Now, be a good girl and stop pushing me out."

She startles and whimpers, but she relaxes enough to do as I say.

I use the chance to thrust all the way in, making her buck off the hood, and nearly fall to the side if it weren't for my hold on her.

"Ah, fuck," I grunt at the feel of being inside her. She's tight and so much like the place I don't want to leave for the rest of my life.

"King…" she moans, her voice shaky. "Do something…"

"Like what?"

"Anything…" She cranes her head sideways, revealing tears that cling to her lashes, probably from pain and frustrated pleasure.

"You'll have to specify, sweetheart."

"Ugh, fuck me, you jerk."

"Fuck you where?"

"In the ass…" she shudders. "Fuck me in the ass."

"Tell me I'm the first to touch this ass. Tell me that you haven't allowed any other motherfucker to claim this part of you and that I'm the only one you trust enough to give it to."

"I'm not…feeding your ego."

"We'll just stay like this all night long then." I lean over and lick her cheek, the tears that have gathered in her eyes, then I bite her neck enough to have her wiggle beneath me, clench around me, and release groans. "Until Gwen comes and sees us in the morning. Maybe Nate, too. Maybe the whole fucking neighborhood."

"Stop it…just fuck me already."

"Say it."

"Screw you."

"Those aren't the exact words I asked for. Try again."

"Kingsley..." she warns, but her voice is more aroused than anything.

"What, sweetheart?"

"You're the first I've done anal with," she lets out in a huff. "But I don't fucking trust you."

I smile, but it probably looks like a smirk as I rock my hips and give a few shallow thrusts.

As soon as she starts to get used to it, I up the pace until her whole body is in tune with mine. I retreat almost all the way until only the tip is inside, then thrust back in so deep that my groin slaps against her ass.

Aspen shrieks and I jam two fingers in her mouth to keep her quiet. "You're going to alert them to what we do in the dark, sweetheart."

I drive into her with a maddening rhythm that leaves both of us breathless. She bites my fingers when she shatters all around me, and I bite her nape, her collarbone, and anywhere I can reach.

My balls tighten and I fuck her harder into the hood until her breath shatters and the car moves with each of my thrusts.

When I come, I pause midway, groaning as I pull out and spray my cum all over her red ass and swollen pussy.

Aspen hisses, shoving my fingers out of her mouth with her tongue. I coat them with my cum, then thrust them back between her lips, making her suck on them as if they're her favorite Popsicles.

"Good girl," I muse, a sense of possessiveness gripping me by the gut.

I always thought I could only get along with a woman who kneeled inside and outside the bedroom. I had a zero-tolerance policy of anything that went against me.

But this witch has made me want to jump into a volcano headfirst just because she's in the middle of it. I'd probably enjoy every burn, too.

Which is why there's no way in fuck she's ever getting away now.

There's something powerful about owning a defiant woman like Aspen. I'm not exactly taming her, but I have her submit to me when my body talks to hers. I have a fireball on my hands and I can't wait for what she comes up with next.

She spits out my fingers again, her eyes filled with tears as she straightens on very wobbly feet that I wouldn't trust to keep me standing if I were her.

Sure enough, she stumbles forward against me and I grab her by the waist. "There, take it easy."

Aspen struggles away from me, planting both her hands on the car to remain upright. She's panting, her lids glittery, and her face red. "What am I to you, Kingsley?"

"What's with the sudden question?"

"Answer me." Her voice cracks and she swallows.

"You're mine, Aspen. That's what you are."

"What does that mean?"

"It means that I'm the only man who gets to touch you." I grab a handful of her ass, making her wince when I press on the red flesh. "No one but me gets to own you."

Her lips tremble and a tear slides down her cheek. "Fuck you."

It's a low tone, broken almost, but I don't get to focus on that as she shoves me away, grabs the album from the ground, and barges to the driver's side of her car.

She speeds off the property, the sound of gravel crunching under the tires echoing in the air.

All I'm left with are questions, confusion, and a fucking twist in my chest.

TWENTY-EIGHT

Aspen

TEARS WON'T STOP STAINING MY FACE LONG AFTER I'M IN MY apartment, curled up in bed and begging for sleep.

My ass burns, my pussy aches, and my whole body hurts. But none of that compares to the shattering pain in my chest.

I told myself I'd cool down after a while, pick up my pieces and move on, but it's been hours and no improvement is in sight.

In fact, I remember Kingsley's words and I'm hit with a fresh wave of loathing directed at myself and him at the same time.

Why did I even have to get emotional after he fucked me like an animal right outside our daughter's house?

What did I expect anyway?

Going into this, I knew full well he wouldn't take it anywhere beyond the physical. I read an article once about how men and women release different brain chemicals after sex. While both release dopamine, women have excessive oxytocin that forcibly bonds them to the person they experience pleasure with. Which isn't the same for men; their oxytocin's mere purpose is the production of semen. Dopamine is the only prominent hormone for them, and it doesn't matter who they get it from.

Considering I never actually formed a bond, or even allowed myself to get close to my previous partners, I thought myself immune to such phenomenon. But then again, they weren't Kingsley.

They weren't the man who flipped my world upside down in more ways than one.

And although I hoped to keep this whole relationship physical, I might have lost the battle way before I even realized it. Kingsley, however, is still firm in his convictions about what this whole thing is. He calls me a whore, after all, and although it's only during sex and I don't deny being turned on by it, maybe that's all he thinks of me as.

But I guess I was blinded enough by his caring side to hope for more.

Now, I need to kill those hopes and whatever we have, because sooner or later, it'll drain me. There will be extra baggage, self-loathing, and a new hope that will blossom at any of his gestures.

Like how he defended me in front of Gwen.

Irony is my least favorite bitch because she's repeating the scenario from twenty-one years ago. I waited for him then, I searched for him, I wanted to preserve the connection we had during that one night. In the midst of the messy sex, drinking, and our sporadic conversations, I had more fun with him than I'd had in fourteen years.

He opened my eyes to a world I had no idea existed, and I was greedy for more. More thought-provoking debates, violent tendencies, and him.

I tried to find him even before I knew I was pregnant. That was out of mere selfishness as I entertained a pipe dream where I could ever belong in his world.

Eventually, I rose to his level. Eventually, I stood toe to toe with him, worked with him, sparred with him, and slept with him.

But that's the furthest extent I'll go to.

A rotten mouse from the ghetto will always, without a doubt, be eaten by the suburban cat.

And I guess I'm in the middle of that process now.

I want to tell myself that it's okay, that I've survived worse, but instead of being relieved, more tears stream down my cheeks.

My phone lights up with a text and I stare at it through my blurry vision in the darkness.

He's been calling nonstop since I left and sent a series of texts urging me to pick up the phone when I refused to answer.

The last one he sent just now is different.

Kingsley: At least drink water and tell me you're all right.

My broken heart squeezes and I wish I could reach inside my chest and kill that jerk. The stupid organ that I thought I neutralized long ago is up and running and not even pretending to be on my side anymore.

One gentle text from the asshole and it's beating like crazy.

The true man wants two things—danger and play. For that reason, he wants women as the most dangerous plaything.

Nietzsche's words slip into my consciousness, translating everything I feel about this situation. I don't want to be a plaything.

Not even Kingsley's.

You know what? I'm not going to keep this bottled up inside. Sitting up in bed, I sniffle and type.

Aspen: Remember that night twenty-one years ago?

His reply is immediate.

Kingsley: Of course. It was the night Gwen was conceived.

Aspen: Aside from that, what did it mean to you?

Kingsley: It was the first time I met you.

Aspen: No, that was the first time you met the old version of me. The bruised, traumatized but still trying to be strong version. The version who still longed to be accepted deep down in her naïve heart. She was the Aspen who lied about her age, got drunk for courage, and wanted you with all her little girl hormones. But she was broken by relatives, an early teen pregnancy, and holding her stillborn baby when she was barely fifteen.

Kingsley: Are you blaming me for not being there?

Aspen: No, I'm blaming myself for wanting you to be there.

For searching for you and yearning for your company when you were nothing more than a stranger. I thought if I'd had you, I could've protected my child and had a healthier pregnancy. I fell into the Cinderella complex that I often chastised Callie about, and it was downright pathetic. Losing my baby gave me the slap in the face and wake-up call I needed badly. I burned everything I had of you, of the old Aspen and her naïve feelings and little dreams. So the real Aspen is the woman you met seven years ago in court, trying to rip you and your client a new one. That's the only Aspen that exists, Kingsley. I refuse to spiral back into the old, pathetic Aspen.

Kingsley: I'm coming over.

Aspen: No, don't.

Kingsley: This isn't a conversation we should be having over texts.

Aspen: This is exactly how I want it, so if you have anything to say, do it this way.

I don't think I could control myself, be strong enough, or have the right assertiveness to push him away if he were here in person.

He rattles me so much that it's impossible to think straight while I'm with him.

Kingsley: First of all, the old Aspen wasn't pathetic. She was a bit naïve, yes, young and lost, also yes. But she was a brave survivor, too, so I forbid you to talk shit about her. Second of all, there is no real Aspen. The woman I met seven years ago was as smart and hot as the devil, but she was empty, too. She's not the woman who drives me fucking insane by merely existing.

A tingle starts in my chest and spreads all over my body, and I hate it. I hate how a few words from him are able to break me and tear me apart in such a short time.

Aspen: You're saying that to get in my pants.

Kingsley: I can get in your pants without saying that, sweetheart.

Aspen: So I'm just your warm hole who's good at spreading my legs?

Kingsley: You have warm holes. Plural. And I love when you spread your legs, but we both know you're way more than that.

My fingers shake as I spill my bitter vulnerability on the keyboard.

Aspen: Maybe I don't know.

Kingsley: You used to jump down my throat for sport and now you're telling me you don't know your worth?

Aspen: I used to and still do, by the way, jump down your throat because you're an antagonistic asshole and I refuse to be stomped upon.

Kingsley: That translates to a strong bitch, I mean witch. You're also more intelligent than anyone I know and so stubborn that I'm often, or more accurately, always, tempted to hate-fuck you.

Aspen: What if I say no?

Kingsley: We both know your cunt and now your ass are in a polyamorous relationship with my dick. So your "no" is out of mere spite.

Aspen: I don't want to have sex anymore.

Kingsley: Why not?

Because I want to see if he only wants me for that. If, aside from that, I mean little to nothing in his grand agenda.

Instead of saying that, I type.

Aspen: I just don't want to. Are you okay with that?

Kingsley: Depends on the duration. An hour? Two? Worse, a day?

Aspen: A month.

Kingsley: What type of celibacy drug are you fucking on? Did you pick up a religion or something? Highly not recommended, by the way. Not only do they shame your precious Nietzsche, but all religions are anti-hedonist and should burn in hell.

Aspen: Is that a no?

Kingsley: No, it's a what the fuck, Aspen? Why the hell would you want us to stop fucking like the best animals that ever roamed the planet for a whole thirty days? Are you physically hurt?

I'm emotionally hurt, bruised, and stomped upon, and I need this to try to pick up my pieces, but I don't tell him that.

Aspen: No, I'm not, but I still want this. What's your reply?

Kingsley: This is fucking blasphemy and you know it. I have never gone a whole month without having sex.

Aspen: So is that a no?

Kingsley: No, it's not a no. I have no fucking clue what game you're playing. But fine, let's do this shit. Only penetrative sex?

Aspen: All sex.

Kingsley: Are you out of your fucking mind? What type of screwed-up torture method is that?

Aspen: Take it or leave it.

I can almost see his narrowed eyes and flared nostrils. Kingsley isn't the type of man who can be pressured into doing anything, let alone be forced out of his comfort zone, and this is a true test of whether he wants me or my body.

Kingsley: And if I refuse?

Aspen: Then we're over. You can go relieve your sexual urges with your side pieces. Namely, Britney. And I'll go find myself a new dick.

My whole body tightens as I hit Send. That's the last scenario I want. The thought of him with damn Britney or any other woman hurts my chest to the point of physical pain coupled with nausea.

Kingsley: Your jealousy is fucking cute and there will be no other dicks in the picture unless you're ready to add first-degree murder to my résumé of fucked up. The only dick you'll have is mine after the damn thirty days, witch.

A smile lifts my lips as I read and reread the text.

He...agreed.

He really agreed.

I hug the phone to my chest, the giddiness inside me so similar to the old version of me.

The Aspen who had one tragedy after another but still held on to the black mask she wore that night.

TWENTY-NINE

Aspen

THE FIRST WEEK OF MY SELF-IMPOSED CELIBACY IS HELL ON earth.

Kingsley became moodier than snobbish royalty and has been asking Nate to box with him almost every day.

A fact that Gwen wasn't happy about, because her father is stealing her husband's time—which is limited already.

The second week, Nate put an end to Kingsley's demands and told him, "I'm sorry, but I prefer my wife's company." To which Kingsley nearly punched him.

He started to work out more than should be healthy, almost picked up smoking again, and everyone at the firm avoids him like the plague.

Five employees nearly lost their job for simply talking to him when he was in a foul mood. Which is more often than not lately.

I try to keep his mind off things with work, simple discussions, or even promising to eat everything he's cooked.

That's what we've finished doing just now—eating. We're sitting at the counter of my kitchen with a chair between us. It's just insurance because he has no qualms whatsoever about forcing me to remove the "illegal ban," as he likes to call it.

For the past couple of weeks, we've developed the habit of dining out. Partly because being indoors is stifling and partly because…I guess we're dating. Or that's what Gwen and Callie called it, gushing and throwing a hundred hearts in the group chat.

Kingsley never called it that, though. I didn't either, so no clue where that leaves us.

Sex was all our relationship was about, and now that it's out of the equation, it feels like we're a couple who've been together for years. We get ready for work together, discuss cases over dinner, and have conversations that leave me breathless. Not only that, but lately, we've been spending more time together than before.

We went on a long ride yesterday in one of Kingsley's convertibles, and even though I lost a scarf and had a horrible hair day, I felt so wild—outside of sex, of course. And yes, apparently Kingsley has a collection of sports cars. No surprise there. He's a fast-paced man and loves the rush of speed, the fire of challenge, and the unpredictability of situations.

But he also thrives on control, so the fact that he has none on this particular turn of events has changed him into a grouchy creature.

I wipe my mouth after actually having finished my entire plate of pasta. Ever since I stopped drinking, my appetite has gradually returned. I still don't really like food, but Kingsley doesn't allow me to have an empty stomach. Gwen, either. I swear both father and daughter are ganging up on me.

"It's delicious," I tell him.

He grumbles as a response and glares at the space separating us. "And what is this chair between us trying to serve?"

"Safe distance."

"More like useless distance. If I decide to pounce on you, no fucking chair will save you from me."

"But you won't," I remind him, half fearful that he'll actually crumble everything to the ground.

"Maybe I will."

"You…have held on fine for two weeks."

"It's not fucking withdrawal from addiction, Aspen. It gets worse, not better with time."

"So? What does that mean?" I sound unusually careful, scared almost.

"It means you're a damn dictator. Maybe I should keep a negative words list like Gwen does and put your name on it."

That rips a smile out of me, and I throw a napkin in his direction that he catches with a grin so charming that I'm the one who starts to rethink the decision behind the stupid ban.

I clear my throat. "She told me about that list and said it was something that helped her cope with her empathetic reaction to negative words, but she thought you didn't know about it."

"Of course I did. She's shit at covering her tracks and even shittier at hiding stuff, which is why I was blindsided by her feelings for Nate."

"She must've put extra effort into fooling you."

"She wouldn't have needed to if it weren't for the daughter-stealer Nate."

I roll my eyes and toss a grape into my mouth. "She would've gotten married eventually."

"Eventually is not at twenty. I thought I had a few more years with her."

"Nate was right. You and Gwen are codependent."

"Nate is an asshole, so his opinion holds the importance of a used tissue. And it's not codependence. My daughter and I are just close because we've been each other's world for two decades…" he trails off when my shoulders drop. "Which is a time frame you'll catch up to by being in her world for future decades."

"Thank you." I slide to the seat between us and place my hand over his. "And not only because you accepted me as her mother, but also because you told her about my past. She looks at me differently now, with more respect and…love. And I know you had something to do with her change of attitude."

"If you really want to thank me, which I highly recommend, you could use a different currency than words."

I hit his shoulder, smiling, and spring to my feet. "I'll do the dishes. Go pick a show that is *not Breaking Bad*."

"That's the only superior show TV has ever produced. And is that a no on the sucking my cock part?"

I lean closer until I breathe his air, and I brush my fingers over his chin, making his nostrils flare, then whisper, "It's a maybe. Try again in fourteen days."

"You little cock-fucking-tease," he mutters when I escape behind the counter, and he motions at his tenting pants. "Look what you've done."

"You're always in that state."

"Around you. So you should solve the problem you caused."

"In fourteen days."

"You better take sick leave in fourteen days, because you're going to lose the ability to walk." His voice darkens and I choose to stare at the wall to keep from getting caught in the otherworldly energy he creates by merely existing.

And he really needs to stop being attractive when he's in casual slacks and a polo shirt. It doesn't make sense for him to be a walking sex god no matter what he wears. Or maybe I'm more affected by the ban than I care to admit.

"By the way." I occupy myself with cleaning the counter to not look at him. "Congrats on your case win today."

We do that now—get involved in each other's cases—and it's brought more harmony than I ever thought possible. I like his advice, and he surprisingly appreciates mine, too, even though we're in different fields.

Kingsley scoops a green apple from the counter and crunches on it. "It was a matter of time before I won. The prosecutor barely had any case."

"Are you being modest? It was a difficult case that had everything stacked up against you. I don't know how you do it."

"Do what?" He leans against the counter, eating his apple, and tracking my movements as I tidy the counter.

"Win all the time."

"Not all the time."

"Ninety-six percent of the time."

"My, sweetheart." A shit-eating grin curves his lips. "Are you keeping track of my percentage? I didn't know you cared about me this much."

My face turns hotter than the room temperature. "I do not. I just know it because it's one percent higher than mine. Which isn't fair by the way. I'm more protocol-abiding than you and should have a higher winning rate."

"And yet you don't."

"That will change."

"You talk as if you're my rival." He pauses chewing when my fingers falter on a cup. "Hold on a second. You do consider me a rival, don't you?"

"And you don't?"

"No. You're senior partner at my firm. We're supposed to be subordinates, not rivals."

"Then why were you trying to sabotage my cases when you first found out I'm Gwen's mother?"

"Pure spite."

"Not rivalry?"

"No."

I sigh. "I can't believe I've been at this rivalry thing on my own all this time."

"It's adorable, though. Thinking about you trying to beat my percentage and getting worked up about it, is kind of a turn on. Want to fuck it out of our systems?"

"No, Kingsley."

He lifts a shoulder and dunks the remains of the apple in the trash can. "Worth a try."

I catch a glimpse of him disappearing into the living room and browsing through Netflix as I load the dishes in the dishwasher.

"Do you have any other pillows that don't advocate Caroline's Barbie personality?" he calls, kicking away the fluffy pillows.

I smile. "In the closet of the room down the hall."

He throws one more fluffy pillow away with no other intention than pure malice before he heads to where I directed him. I grab some snacks and shove some popcorn in the microwave. It isn't until the eerie silence of the apartment stabs me in the chest that I recall what else is in the closet of the room Kingsley just went to.

Damn it.

I practically jog down the hall and all breaths are knocked out of my lungs when I find a scene that's straight out of my most dreaded situations.

The dim yellow light casts a soft glow on Kingsley as he stands in front of the open closet. The pillows he came for are scattered on the floor as his whole attention zeroes in on the box in his hand.

I slowly step to his side, my heart beating in my throat. "It's... not what you think."

His eyes turn into molten lava as they slide from the box to me. "Are you telling me these are not in fact the mask and scarf you had on the night I knocked you up?"

"They are, but..." I trail off, completely distracted by the way he glides his fingers over the flannel scarf as if it's my body.

Damn it, me. This is about the worst time to get horny.

"But what?"

"They don't mean anything."

"Liar. You kept these things for twenty-one years, so they most definitely mean something. You liked me that much, huh?"

"Shut up."

"No. You're not going to hide this time. I thought you burned everything to do with me, but I guess this mask and scarf miraculously escaped the fire."

"Can you pretend you didn't see them?"

"No can do. Admit it, you were infatuated with me."

I groan. "So what if I was? It was a stupid teenage crush."

"Crush, huh?" He grins, and it's so carefree that I'm caught off guard.

"Why have you omitted the 'stupid' and 'teenage' part?"

"I didn't hear anything aside from the word *crush*." He slides the black mask over my eyes, letting the black ribbons dangle on either side of my face.

All air is sucked from my lungs at the raw quality in his eyes. I might have been wrong before, because the storm in him won't stop until it flips the sea in me over.

"What are you doing?" I whisper, scared of my own voice.

"Recalling memories."

"Like...what?"

"Like how I'll fuck you with this mask on when the illegal ban is over and you'll scream my name like a little whore, not a femme fatale."

"Stop it." I push his hand away, mainly to control my reaction to his promises. "Let's go watch something."

"Not so fast." He grabs me by the arm, his finger digging into it. "You never told me why you left that morning."

"We were strangers, and you were kind of threatening. I saved my skin."

"Bullshit. There's something more to it."

"It's mainly because you were threatening and reminded me of my dad, but also...because I was scared of your reaction if you found out my actual age. I had to study for exams anyway, so.... yeah, I thought the safest option was to leave."

"Do I still remind you of your father?"

"No. You have antisocial tendencies, but you care. He's a true psychopath who only values his own gain." I pause. "What were you really planning to do that night?"

"Just some Devil Night's arson."

"Wow. I can't believe a delinquent like you became a lawyer."

"I only did that to use the law to my benefit. I'm innocent of any charges that would accuse me of upholding justice."

I laugh. "You were the definition of a bad boy and a jock, huh?"

"Pretty much. Nate had to stop me from committing an actual crime since we were teens."

"But he wasn't a jock."

"No. He thought it was a needless, self-serving type of violence."

"Well, he isn't wrong. Let me guess, the guy who wore the Joker's costume that night was a jock, too."

"You guessed correctly. He tried to have his parents report me for assault and battery after that night, but my father sewed their mouths shut with a few thousand bucks."

"Fitting."

"Not really. I could've sewn his mouth shut with my fist."

"Brute." I stare at where his thumb presses on my arm, unable to look him in the eye. "Did you keep anything from that night?"

"Aside from Gwen?"

I gaze up at him, my voice too low and vulnerable for my liking. "Aside from Gwen."

"If you're asking about the Anonymous mask, Susan threw it away since she had the habit of ruining my things out of contempt. I only found out about it days later."

"Oh."

"I threw her entire vintage clothes collection in the trash as payback, but that wasn't enough. That bitch needs to go down."

"You really won't let the Susan thing go?"

"Not in this lifetime."

"Do you remember my favorite quote?"

His expression softens and mischievousness lights up his dark eyes. "If you gaze into an abyss for long, the abyss gazes into you."

"The whole version is. He who fights with monsters might take care lest he thereby becomes a monster. And if you gaze into an abyss for long, the abyss gazes into you." I stroke his face. "Don't become a monster, Kingsley."

By day eighteen of the ban, Kingsley has turned into an utter pain who's dripping with toxic, antagonistic masculinity. No one wants to deal with him at work.

No kidding. The other day, an associate lawyer saw him coming down the hall and immediately changed direction.

"Whatever you did, undo it," Nate tells me, subtly pushing me in the direction of Kingsley's office.

"And what makes you think I have something to do with any of this?"

"The fact that he looks at you like he wants to fuck you, then kill you. Or kill you, then fuck you. I'm not entirely sure about his hard limits and if they include necrophilia."

"You're being dramatic."

"And he's being a major dick with a loose screw. Deny it all you want, but we both know it's all because of you. Go inside before he kills Susan for real this time."

I pause. "Susan's here?"

"Yes. She's performing her annoying show for the month."

"I thought she was banned from Weaver & Shaw."

"She got a court order that says since she's suing for shares, she has the right to enter the building."

"Shit."

"Shit, indeed. With his current mood, even a damn ant isn't safe from his wrath. Let alone a hyena."

"I'll see what I can do." I head toward his office, questioning my decision for the first time.

Actually, no. I started questioning it about two days in when I went through a stupid case of sex withdrawal. I like to think I'm surviving and that this is for the greater good.

Kingsley has been tempting me to have sex since day one. The fact that he doesn't know why exactly I'm doing this is frustrating him more than the ban itself.

In contrast, we've been doing a lot of outdoorsy activities together, such as running and even hiking with Nate and Gwen last weekend.

Oftentimes, I wake up with his huge erection nuzzled against

my ass or stomach. He'll groan, call me a sex terrorist, and go take
care of business in the bathroom.

"Thanks for the trip back in time. Now, I'm a pubescent loser
who jerks off in the shower again," is what he told me the first time
he caved and masturbated. A week after the ban.

His toxic sarcasm has gone up a notch and he's always saying
things that made me chuckle like...

*My dick is suing you for bodily harm, so you better be ready for
compensation.*

*You realize I'm going to break the fuck out of your pussy and ass
the moment the ban is lifted, right? Are you sure you don't want to
lessen the blow?*

*The religions called, and they said that even this is blasphemy in
their holy scripts.*

*Maybe I should become a monk or something. At least the ban
will make sense then.*

To say I'm completely immune would be a lie. Not only do
I crave his touch, but it's also becoming harder and harder to ignore it or brush it off.

Which is why I try to plan our week so that it's mostly spent
outside, with Gwen and Nate or even with Callie and Mateo.

It's a fruitless attempt to keep our minds off the frustration
that's building in the background. Or in the forefront for Kingsley.

The fact that he has to deal with Susan on top of everything
else isn't something I'll allow, though.

I knock on the door and step inside before he can even say
anything.

Kingsley leans against a chair by the large window that overlooks a gloomy version of New York. He appears relaxed with
his arms and legs crossed. Not to mention confident and sexy as
the devil in his tailored black suit and tie that I put on him this
morning.

I barely go back to my apartment lately and half his closet is
full of my clothes.

Which is why we kind of smell like each other now. The

domestication is a bit weird, but in moments like these, I feel as if I'm facing a partner. The man who I want with me every step of the way.

The man, who, when I think about his disappearance, drives me down a depressive path.

Susan's head flips in my direction. She's sitting on the sofa, her loud pink dress standing out like a sore thumb.

Her lips twist in a smile. "Aspen Leblanc, nice to finally meet Gwyneth's mother."

Kingsley, who appeared bored not two seconds ago, raises to his full height and marches to my side. He doesn't say anything, but he doesn't have to. Even without words, he's letting Susan know that we're together and she shouldn't mess with me.

Not that she'll be able to.

I dealt with my aunt, who was a worse, more violent version of Susan. I can deal with a snobbish, gold-digging stepmother.

"Though this isn't the first time." She taps her pointy chin. "There was that time in the hospital, right?"

I stiffen, and Kingsley asks slowly, "What are you talking about?"

"Twenty-one years ago, I was visited by a married couple who claimed you impregnated their foster daughter. They wanted money, as all poor folks did. I gave it to them, but only if things went according to my plan. I'm the one who suggested the still-born idea and was there to make sure it was well executed. I'm the one who brought back Gwyneth with me and typed that note before abandoning her in front of the house. You thought you could make my life hell, but you're decades overdue, Kingsley. I already made you a single father at seventeen and had a front-row seat of watching you lose your mind searching for the mother of your child when I knew exactly who she was. You thought you were tormenting me, but guess who had the upper hand all along?"

One moment, Susan is sitting, and the next, Kingsley lifts her up by the extravagant lapels of her dress until her feet leave the ground.

I snap out of my haze at the load of information she just admitted to.

I run to his side and slowly touch his arm, forcing calm into my voice. "Let her go, King."

"She killed my mother, separated you from Gwen, made my daughter live without a mother, and took you away from me. This is the final nail in her coffin." He's speaking in a clipped tone that's filled with enough tension to crumble a mountain.

I have no doubt that he'll snap her neck in the next minute if I don't stop him.

"There's no one in this room who wants her dead as much as I do." I pull his arm. "But she'll get what she's wanted all along, King. She'll break you, separate you from Gwen, and take you away from me. Don't let her get into your head. The bitch doesn't deserve that."

"Do it, you devil. Kill me." She smiles. "Everyone you know dies anyway. Your own mother didn't stay around for your sake. She saw the monster in you early on and decided to leave. Your father also knew how much of an ugly monster you are."

"You're not a monster." I stroke his harsh face. "You're the best father to ever exist and you care about those who deserve it." *You're the love of my life*, I want to say, then stop at the last second.

"Let her go." I soften my voice. "Please, King. Let yourself go."

Because it's not Susan he's been holding in a chokehold since his mother committed suicide. It's himself.

My younger version was naïve.

His was soulless because he never forgave himself.

He slowly starts to release her, then shoves her against the nearest wall.

She straightens with a crackle that fills the whole office. "You're done for, Kingsley. I'm going to sue you for assault."

I stand in front of him, partly shielding his view from her. His nostrils are flaring and the last thing I want is for him to actually kill her this time.

"He's going to sue you for every dime to your name," I say

with a calm I don't feel. "You just admitted to breaching the pre-nup you signed with Benjamin Shaw that states you're to lose ev-erything you owned after marriage if you harm the Shaw family or its members physically, emotionally, or mentally. Separating Gwyneth from me is the personification of emotional and men-tal harm. By doing this, you relinquished any rights to the com-munity property, so you no longer have any claim to any of your late husband's money. Prepare to live in the streets for the rest of your miserable life."

Her laughter disappears and she pales, realizing that she's dug her own grave. She could've kept that information to herself, but her need for grandiose narcissism pushed her over the edge.

"You also breached the restraining order. Being allowed in the building doesn't give you the right to approach Kingsley. Now, get out and be afraid, Susan. Be very afraid, because I will make you pay for the helplessness and loss I felt in that hospital. We will make you pay for all the damage you've done to the three of us until you wish you never existed."

She stumbles, her beady eyes watching Kingsley's raging ones as she steps out the door.

As soon as she's gone, I turn around and look at him. His shoulders are tense, his face so tight, I'm scared he'll have a stroke.

I palm his cheek, caressing it slowly, as if he's an injured ani-mal. "It's okay. She's not important."

"She knew." His tone is clipped. "She fucking knew about you and kept it from me."

"We still found each other anyway."

"After twenty-one years, during which Gwen suffered being motherless."

"I know, but that's okay, I'm here now and I'm not going anywhere."

His head drops onto my shoulder and I breathe heavily, slid-ing my fingers through his hair, listening to his harsh breaths.

I can tell he's holding it in, and that under different circum-stances, Susan's body would be on the floor of his office.

We remain like that for a long time, until his breathing is a bit more controlled, and he pulls back. "I'm sorry."

"For what?"

"For not looking hard enough."

"Me, too." I sniffle, fighting the tears that have gathered in my eyes. "Now, we just need to prove she breached that prenup."

"I recorded her just now."

I step back to stare at him. "You did?"

"I always record her in case I can use her words against her."

I release a breath, refusing to think about what that woman has cost us. Years of separation. Decades of missing my daughter. Time when I could've been with both Gwen and Kingsley. I should've been with my baby all along, and there's no justifying the time that I've missed with her.

But maybe neither Kingsley nor I were ready for one another then. Maybe we needed the time to reach this version of ourselves. A version that's a little bit broken, a little bit dark, but still fits the other anyway.

A version in which we're each other's worlds. Or at least, he's mine. I'm not sure where I fit in his equation.

I know he cares about me, I do, but Kingsley is a closed-off man in the feelings department. And the thought of being emotionally vulnerable in front of him just to be rejected scares the shit out of me.

"Let's have lunch together," he says.

"Gwen beat you to it."

"The three of us can eat together."

"No, I promised to go shopping with her afterward, then we'll make dinner together. You and Nate can meet us then. Can you promise not to fire or kill anyone in the meantime?"

He grunts, obviously remembering the ban. "And what do I get in return?"

I go up on my tiptoes and brush my lips against his. "Let's leave that as a surprise."

His hand shoots for my waist, but I escape before he can trap me, laughing even after I step out the door.

I force myself to stop before I traumatize a poor employee for seeing me laugh for the first time.

Gwen agreed to pick me up from the firm and I have a wild guess that it's because she wants to see Nate during work hours.

It always makes me smile whenever Kingsley acts butthurt because she didn't come for him first.

I call her on my way to the parking garage and frown when she doesn't pick up two times in a row.

So I dial Nate. "Hey, is Gwen with you?"

"No, she didn't come to see me."

My phone beeps with an incoming call and I unlock my car. "It's her. I'll call you back."

I hit End and accept her call. "I'm in the parking garage. Where are you?"

There's a rustle from the other end before a muffled scream comes. I go still, my heart nearly beating out of my chest. "Gwen?"

"Hello there, my red dahlia."

THIRTY

Kingsley

WHOEVER SAID DRUGS ARE THE NEW KILLING MACHINE didn't try fucking celibacy.

The thing should be banned from existence.

Or else the cemeteries would be overcrowded in the span of a few days. That's all I've been thinking about since Aspen came up with this fucked-up kink—or lack thereof.

Murder.

Specifically, the part of her that thought this was such an excellent idea.

Incidentally, the little minx was the one who stopped definite murder just now and saved Susan from meeting her maker a bit sooner.

But now that my mind is slowly snapping back into focus, I realize that taking away the bitch's favorite toy—money—is the best way to make her suffer for what she's done.

I should've suspected she had something to do with it ever since Gwen showed up at our door. Susan had a mild reaction and suggested we put her up for adoption, but didn't push for that option as I would've expected. An option both my father and I refused. She was a Shaw and had to be brought up as one.

The only time my old man and I were actually on the same page.

I flop back behind my desk in a hopeless attempt to focus on work. Problem is, sexual frustration is a fucking bitch with moody issues. Not to mention that my dick hates me and is now crossing days off his calendar with the diligence of a creep until the end of the illegal ban.

That damn witch will regret this once she's unable to move for days at a time.

I'm not stupid, I know this is some sort of a test. *For what?* is the real fucking question. It can't be some new torture device to figure out how long we can keep our hands off each other, because she touched herself last night when she walked in on me jerking off.

Then she ran away because she was well aware she'd be fucked the moment I caught her.

That woman is tilting my world off its axis and I'm relishing in every second of the act.

Aspen is the one person who's not scared of my darker tendencies and even seeks them out. She's always up for going against me, whether it's for something big or small.

The other day, in her quest to keep us from spending so much time cooped in the house, she planned a thorough cleanup of the old cottage where I fucked her that first time.

She didn't let me hire help either.

"You have too much excess energy, so use it here instead of harassing Nate for boxing matches."

Then she had us clean the whole goddamned thing, and paint some of it. Then we ordered food, lay on the grass, and watched the sun go down like some middle-class idiots.

It was the most peaceful day in recent memory.

My phone dings and I check it, hoping she's changed her mind about the abrasive ban and is sending me a picture of her in lingerie.

Instead, an annoying name pops up on my screen. She shouldn't even have my number but does, despite my and her husband's objections.

Her text, however, piques my interest.

Caroline: Hey, asshole! I went through some of my old stuff and guess what I found?

Kingsley: Wrong number.

Caroline: Are you sure? Because I have some pages from Aspen's diaries. You know, the ones she wrote in when we were teens. Want to see them?

Kingsley: Save the hard-to-get nonsense for Mateo and send me pictures.

Caroline: Do you promise to treat her right and make all her dreams come true?

Kingsley: You're cheesier than a Disney princess.

Caroline: Guess you don't need the pictures, huh?

Kingsley: Fine, I promise. Now, send them over.

Caroline: That wasn't so hard, was it?

She sends another series of texts about how Aspen will kill her, but she's doing this for her sake because she wouldn't admit it otherwise, but I ignore her and open the attachments.

The words on the plain paper force me to stop and stare for a moment. Aspen's handwriting is small, neat, and so elegant, it belongs in some calligraphy class.

That hasn't changed over all these decades.

I start reading the lines the teenage version of her—the old Aspen, as she called it—wrote.

Mom,

I wish you were here so I could tell you this in person. Last night, I experienced something that I will remember for the rest of my life.

Callie dragged me to one of her parties, as usual, or I kind of tagged along because Aunt Sharon and Uncle Bob were being their usual asshole selves. I'd planned to leave after a while, I swear, but I ended up drinking, lying about my age, and staying almost all night.

I also lost my virginity. There was a lot of blood on my thighs this morning, but I washed it off, so I think it's fine now. It hurts a little when I walk and I can almost feel his penis inside me with every move.

He called me beautiful when he tore into me, even though I hadn't removed my mask. I think I cried—not because of the pain, but because he made me feel beautiful, too.

I wish I'd taken off his mask before I left, but I freaked out when I woke up in his arms. He had violent tendencies like Dad and I thought maybe he'd be angry because I lied about my age and where I come from.

I thought maybe Dad called you beautiful, too, when he first had sex with you but ended up driving you to your death.

Maybe Dad stole your girlhood dreams, too, and when you finally found out, it was too late.

But I don't want to be you, Mom. I read and watch people a lot so I can see red flags early on. I hang out on the outskirts of every situation so I'll always have a way out and not be trapped like you.

I couldn't be trapped with that stranger.

So I ran away and didn't look back.

But now, I'm not sure if I did the right thing. Maybe I let my paranoia get the better of me and should've thought about it more.

After all, the masked stranger is the only person who's ever listened to me blabber about Nietzsche and philosophy and the world for hours. He didn't call me pretentious or a know-it-all. He didn't tell me I was too smart for my own good and that I shouldn't concern my brain with stuff like that.

He even debated with me and taught me philosophies and theories I didn't know. I wrote them all down in my notebook to search through later.

Why does a stranger understand me better than people who've known me all my life? He even understands me better than you ever did, Mom.

I didn't think about stopping him when he lifted his mask just enough to kiss me. Or when he carried me inside a cabin, removed my clothes, and took my virginity.

Callie says to bless my naïve heart because he seduced me so easily by playing on my nerd tendencies. She could be right, but her opinion doesn't really matter, because she also said that he better be loaded.

Is it wrong that I want to find him, Mom? Talk to him again? Ask for his name and tell him mine?

Or was the whole connection a fantasy of my own making and I should finally wake up?

Two days later.

Mom,

I decided to find him, after all. If only to satisfy my curiosity.

Callie and I went back to the house in which the party was held, but the staff was of no help. Apparently, a few guests wore an Anonymous mask that night and they didn't keep track of them.

So we went to that cabin he took me to, but it appeared abandoned and no people were in sight. Callie was scared shitless of the place and said we should go before we were abducted by some serial killer.

We walked into the nice part of town and I felt like a weight was sitting on my chest. Callie tried to cheer me up by buying us ice cream and singing off-key. She can't hit a note to save her life, but her attempts offered much-needed comfort. She also pointed at two rich girls getting in their luxurious car and said one day, that would be us.

But I haven't paid much attention, because my chest hurts.

Why does my chest hurt, Mom? It's similar to when I found you sleeping and not breathing.

I hate it.

Five days later.

Mom,

    I can't stop thinking about the masked stranger and the conversations and the sex.

    Whether it's during class or in the house or when Aunt Sharon is making my life hell.

    And my chest still hurts.

    Callie says I'm experiencing a broken heart and stuffed me with ice cream and vanilla cake—that she probably stole. Even though I don't really like sweets, I ate them all and even snatched her share.

    Because Callie is a liar and a bad friend. How can I have a broken heart when I don't even know him?

    But that doesn't stop me from going back to the nice side of town, walking aimlessly through it, and having no clue where to go. I even took Callie to that cabin again, but she started shaking, and since there was no one there anyway, we called it a day.

    You once told me that those who love too hard get hurt badly, which I think is what happened to you.

    I don't want that, Mom. I want to be everything you weren't.

    I want to be emotionless and without pain in my chest.

Three weeks later.

Mom,

    I got over him. I don't go back to the nice part of town and I don't let Callie play a clown's role to cheer me up.

    It's fine.

    I was in a temporary phase where I pretended I wasn't Aspen from the ghetto, but I've woken up now.

    Aunt Sharon helped in bringing me back to reality with a slap that turned my cheek red, but yeah, it's all fine now.

    I just need to throw away the scarf he gave me and the black *mask I wore that night. Callie asked me to give it back, but I lied and said that I lost it.*

I'll make it up to her one day.

Twenty weeks later.
Mom,

I'm pregnant.

I've been feeling funny lately, more hungry than before and Callie had to steal from her dad so she could buy me junk food.

The other day, I fainted while Aunt Sharon was kicking me. They took me to a doctor, probably so I wouldn't die on their watch. He told us I was twenty-six weeks pregnant. When Aunt Sharon asked about abortion, he said it's illegal in New York after twenty-four weeks. She slapped me as soon as we got home and Uncle Bob punched me in my stomach.

And now they've locked me up in the attic and took away my phone so I can't even see or call Callie.

It hurts, Mom. My belly hurts.

What if the baby is in pain, too? It's so tiny and can't defend itself in front of my aunt and uncle. What if it dies like you did?

What should I do, Mom?

I'm scared.

I swipe for the next picture, but nothing comes.

My fist clenches as I read the last words Aspen has written.

I'm scared.

Due to how mature she seemed, sometimes I forget how young she actually was at the time. She must've been utterly confused and terrified about bearing a child when she was a kid herself.

I know because even though I wasn't as young as she was, the moment I found Gwen at my doorstep, I had a chaotic confusion of epic proportions. It took me months to come to terms with the fact that I was a teen father. That if I didn't protect my flesh and blood, she wouldn't survive. Or worse, she'd be deliberately hurt by Susan. It's why I moved out of my father's house even before I graduated from high school.

No amount of a grudge against Susan was worth putting my daughter's life in jeopardy.

Gwen has always been my miracle. The blessing who saved me from my destructive thoughts, but knowing she came with such sacrifice sheds a different light on how much Aspen suffered.

I might have raised her for twenty years, but it was Aspen who protected her when she was the most vulnerable.

My phone vibrates and I expect more photos from Caroline. Instead, it's a text from Aspen.

Nietzsche.

The air in the room tightens around me and I spring up, calling her.

She doesn't pick up. *Fuck, fuck, fuck!*

I hang up and dial her bodyguard. One of them picks up with a bored, "Hello."

"Where's Aspen?"

"She left fifteen minutes ago and asked us not to follow her."

"And you fucking incompetent fools listened?" I hang up on him before he can respond and call Nicolo.

He answers after one ring. "I was going to call. We have a situation."

"You think?"

"Bruno escaped from Attica in the midst of a carefully planned prison uproar. He disappeared off the face of the earth so that not even his own soldiers know where he is."

"Fuck." I storm out of the office. "Do you have any idea where he would go?"

"I can only guess, and judging by your voice, that would take more time than we have to spare."

"Can your people track a phone?"

"Can do. Whose phone?"

"Aspen's. He must've lured her somewhere, because she asked her bodyguards not to follow."

"On it."

"Don't even think about protecting him this time, Nicolo."

"I won't. He disobeyed clear orders. I have no use for insubordinate soldiers. But, King?"

I punch the elevator's call button and step inside. "Yes?"

"I have to say this for your own sake. Prepare for the worst."

THIRTY-ONE

Aspen

I STAND IN FRONT OF AN ABANDONED TWENTY-STORY BUILDING.
Under the afternoon light, the construction debris that surrounds it looks like apocalyptic crops.

But this isn't just any building.

This is the same hideous, half-naked building in which my father killed someone in cold blood while the FBI witnessed it. They were late and couldn't save my father's victim, but they arrested him.

Back then, I stood by the corner, shielded by two agents, and watched as they led him out of the building, handcuffed and with a sneer on his lips.

A few hours before that, I'd heard him talking on the phone with one of his underlings about a guy he was personally going to kill to send a message to some rival family. It wasn't the first time I'd heard such a conversation. My father was arrogant enough to overlook me and my morals that developed completely independent from his.

Before that, I had been too scared to go against him, and I still was, but the image of my dead mother is what pushed me to follow him and make that call to 911. They forwarded me to the FBI because he was already under close scrutiny by them, so any information was welcome.

Honestly, I was half expecting the operation to fail and for my father to kill me, but when I saw him being led out by the officers, a huge weight lifted off my chest.

It was also one of the few times I allowed myself to cry until no tears could come out.

That's when I realized I was truly on my own.

I thought I would feel relieved for avenging my mother's death and sending him where he belonged, but those emotions were short-lived after I realized how dangerous of a man he actually is.

The fact that he chose this place twenty-five years later is a reminder that he always had a hold on me, even from behind bars.

I can't be weak, though. Not now when he has my daughter.

Straightening my spine, I enter through the half-built door. The stench of piss, alcohol, and something rotten hits me in the face. An indication that this place was used by all the lowlifes that roam the city.

I take the stairs as fast as I can, hoping, no, praying for the first time in my life that Kingsley will be able to find us.

With Nicolo's help, he might.

As per my father's instructions, I had to leave my bag, phone, and everything else behind. I parked the car a few blocks away as he told me, but I hope it's close enough for Kingsley to guess where we are.

Naturally, I couldn't call the police or let my bodyguards follow me.

This is family business.

Also, I couldn't risk having Gwen hurt in the process.

By the time I arrive at the top level, I'm panting like a dog. My jacket and hair stick to my neck with sweat and my feet scream in pain.

However, all discomfort disappears when I catch a glimpse of Gwen strapped to a rolling chair that's a few inches away from the edge. As in, the edge of a dilapidated balcony with no railings, from which she can be pushed to her unavoidable demise.

Duct tape is strapped around her mouth, nearly reaching her ears. The afternoon light casts a haunting halo on her silhouette in a shock of yellow and orange. Her hair is disheveled, and her eyes almost bulge out as she observes the dark corners of the piece and the construction debris lying on the ground.

When she sees me, moisture gathers along her lids, and relief like I've never witnessed on her face rushes in.

"Gwen...don't worry. I'm here." I jog toward her.

My feet come to an abrupt halt when a shadow strolls from around the corner and stops beside Gwen's chair.

It's been twenty-five years since I last saw him and those years didn't treat him well.

Bruno Locatelli has mean looks, narrowed brown eyes, and a pointy nose. A slash that's the result of an assassination attempt runs down his left cheek to his thin lips.

His hair that was once black is now almost completely white. He's always been a big man, but now he's plumped up in an extravagance of muscles and fat.

The only thing he passed down to me is his height and a strong bone structure. Otherwise, I always looked like a non-docile version of my mom.

"Hello, my red dahlia."

There's no sneer in his slightly accented words, no mocking, and almost no infliction whatsoever.

I suspected my father was abnormal after I saw him kill the neighbor's dog for making too much noise and then threatening to kill said neighbor's son when he came asking about his dog. Later on, I realized he was definitely on the antisocial spectrum and used the mob life to quench his thirst for control, blood, and manipulation. So the fact that I put a damper on his plans sits wrong with him.

Very wrong.

"What do you want?" I ask in a neutral voice that doesn't

betray my shaking insides or how my heart nearly spills out onto the ground.

I always thought I'd clash with my father. That sooner or later he'd find me. And I've been ready for it all my life—and that includes the times when I was trying to rise above it.

The only difference is that before now, I didn't have Gwen or Kingsley. I didn't have a life that I wanted to protect with everything I have.

"Is that any way to greet me after all these years? Shouldn't you at least come hug me?"

"You never hugged me before. Why should I do so now?"

A distorted smirk lifts his lips, revealing a golden tooth. "You were always a resilient one, my red dahlia. I should've named you that. It fits you better than the name your mother chose for you. She said Aspen is a tree with delicate heart-shaped leaves that quake with the gentlest breeze. We both know your mother was a hopeless cause and you're anything but what she envisioned for you. Despite being a woman, you grew up to be tougher than all of my men combined and even willingly chose the mob life. That was an audacious move that you'll pay for. Not only did you pick up the life you locked me up for, but you also turned my boss against me. But if Nicolo thinks I'll let you go just because he told me to, he must not understand the extent of my need for revenge. This is personal and he had no room to fucking interfere, which is why I escaped."

"You...escaped?" *But why didn't the guard call me?*

"He's dead." My father circles Gwen like a deadly animal, and she watches his every move, shrinking into her seat.

"Who's dead?"

"The guard you bribed to watch me. I stabbed him ten times in the fucking heart. One for every year he spied on me for you. Oh, and by the way, he had two beautiful children that he often talked to the other guards about, so congratulations for orphaning them."

My fingers tremble, but I clasp them together, refusing to give him the reaction he's trying to get out of me. "Nicolo won't let your disobedience slide. I work for the family now."

"Nicolo can go fuck himself. I'll just go solo after I take care of you. Though I must say, I like how smart you've become. You take that after me. Shouldn't you thank me for it?"

"Thank you for what, exactly?" My blood boils and I march toward him until I'm only a few steps away from him and Gwen. "For supplying me with a shitty childhood, or abusing my mother until she took her own life? Which part should I be grateful for?"

His expression doesn't change, appearing completely unaffected by my outburst. "The part where you're still alive and have come this far. If I hadn't asked my subordinates to raise you after I was arrested, thanks to your betrayal, you wouldn't have had enough misfortunes to harden your soul and expel the naïvety your mother implanted in your heart. You can never be strong if you aren't broken."

"You…you were behind Aunt Sharon and Uncle Bob?"

"Of course. They were all a pawn in my game. I told them to roughen you up a little and give you colorful memories to carry. You might have put a guard to watch me ten years ago when you became a lawyer, but I've been observing you every step of your life. I had my men follow you around and two live-ins. That was Bob and his wife, Sharon. But the two idiots screwed it up when you got pregnant. I planned to make you a single mother, but Bob and Sharon overhead my other men who followed you around talking about the potential father and acted out of pure greed. When they took that rich woman's money and let you run away, I got rid of them."

"But why?"

"I had no use for them anymore. But seeing how broken you were from losing the baby, I let it slide. It was better torture than having you become a teen mom."

I shake my head, fighting the tears that are trying to escape.

"No. Why did you do all of that? Was it your god complex? Revenge?"

"Nothing that immature, no. It was just so you'd be aware that your life was in the palm of my hand, my red dahlia. The moment I decide to crush you, I will. That moment happens to be now."

He pushes Gwen's chair and it slides to the edge. Her muffled shriek sounds haunted in the silence when she's about to tumble down. I jerk forward, but he slams his leather shoe against the foot of the chair, catching her at the last second.

I swear my lifespan has shortened by a few years as I stare into her huge, bugging-out eyes. But I force myself to go still even as my heart beats so loudly, I can hear the thumps in my ears.

"Why now?" I ask with a calm I don't feel. I need to keep him talking, to distract him enough until help comes.

"See, ever since you sent me to prison, I've been waiting for the moment when you had everything you wanted. A career, a family, a man. The reason I didn't get out isn't because I couldn't, it's because the right moment hadn't come yet. As you can see, I could've escaped at any time, yet I didn't for the Lucianos' sake. But I have no loyalty to whoever takes away my revenge. I will make you feel what it means to lose everything."

He pushes the chair and she tips to the edge so that she's half dangling and only my father's hold on her collar keeps her upright.

Gwen screams again, her whole body going into shock. I swallow any sounds bubbling in my throat so as not to freak her out. So even though I'm being ripped apart from the inside, I give my daughter a reassuring glance and tell her what I used to say to her while patting my belly. "It's okay, baby. It's going to be okay. I'll protect you."

"That's a bold promise." My father's grating voice cuts through my head as he nonchalantly retrieves his phone while still holding Gwen by a handful of her dress. "My sniper on the other end of this line will take out your baby's father in the blink of an eye."

Both Gwen and I freeze.

"What?" He smiles in that manic way. "You thought I'd make it easy for you and only capture your daughter? Where's the fun in that?"

My lips tremble, but I set them in a line. If I get lost in the emotional loop he's trying to lure me into, I'll definitely lose both Gwen and Kingsley.

"Tell me what you want." I lift my chin, refusing to cower.

"To make you pick. Will you watch your daughter's brains explode on the concrete below or receive your lover's head on a platter? I'm curious which poison you will choose to swallow, my red dahlia. Your child or the man who gave you that child? If you choose her, she'll hate you for the rest of her life for being the cause of her father's death. If you choose him, you'll hate each other for losing her. Isn't this a beautiful conundrum?"

A tear falls down my cheek as the scenarios he just painted repeat in my head like a distorted film.

I wouldn't be able to live with myself either way. No matter which choice I make.

A pained, muffled sound comes from Gwen as she shakes her head frantically and struggles against her bindings.

"It's okay," I say with fake strength.

"What's it going to be?" my father asks, jamming the gun against her head.

"Let me hug her first."

He pushes the whole chair and I run forward, but he pulls her back again right before she falls off. "Why do you look like the dead? Have you no sense of humor? I was only testing her resolve, which is extremely weak, by the way."

My body feels foreign as I gulp in large intakes of air, closing the small distance between me and Gwen.

My father steps aside. "So it's going to be her father? You re- alize he sacrificed his youth for her, right? Do you think you'll be alive for long if he knows you killed his daughter? With his character, he might become your new worst enemy, even more than me. Your desperate attempts to escape his wrath will be fun to watch, though."

I ignore him and kneel in front of Gwen, then remove her duct tape as gently as possible.

"Don't…" she sobs as soon as the duct tape is off, gasping and panting and barely able to get the words out. "Don't choose me, please. I can't live without Dad."

I pull her head against my chest, holding her with a hand in her hair. I don't know if the shaking is her or me. Or both of us. My voice is brittle when I attempt to soothe her, "Shhh. It's okay, Gwen. It's going to be fine. I promise."

"Please…please…not Daddy…please…"

I step back and stroke her hair away from her face. "You're the most beautiful thing that has happened in my life, Gwen. I would have you all over again if I got the choice. I love you more than I love myself."

Two tears stream down her cheeks. "I love you, too. I always wanted you in my life, but not like this. Please don't choose me…please…"

I squeeze her in another hug and whisper in her ear, "Tell King that I love him."

And with that, I release her.

The shocked expression on her face slowly morphs into realization, but I don't focus on her as I turn to my father.

"So touching. I almost shed a tear," he says with an expressionless face. "Who's it going to be, my red dahlia?"

"Can I hug you first?"

The request takes him aback and he narrows his eyes on me. "What kind of game are you playing?"

"You wanted a hug earlier. Forget it if you don't want it."

"You think I'll fall for that?"

"Gwen, roll away!" I shriek, pushing her from the edge as hard as I can.

When my father sees, he curses and starts toward her, but I use the small distraction to push my body against his. He's way bigger than me, so the element of surprise plays in my favor.

I share one last look with Gwen and mouth, "I love you."

"Mom, no!"

The sound of "Mom" from her mouth puts a smile on my lips, and a tear slides down my cheek as I hug my father and push us both off the edge.

"I choose you, asshole," I say as we both tumble down.

In the last moments, I think I hear Kingsley's voice calling my name.

THIRTY-TWO

Kingsley

T HE FIRST TIME I MET ASPEN WAS DURING A NIGHT THAT I was fully prepared to turn to debauchery, arson, and an adrenaline fix.

Little did I know that the femme fatale who spoke nerdy as a favorite sparring method would offer all of those and more.

I never took anyone to my mother's cabin, not even Nate. Even my father had forgotten about the property a few years before he divorced my mother. I was the only one who paid the place a visit, whenever my mind got too loud.

And because it was my safe place, my *secret* place, I had no business taking a stranger there. But maybe the fact that she was a stranger was what allowed me to let go, even temporarily.

But what I didn't count on was how much she'd get under my skin. I'd intended to only be physical that night, but those thoughts soon turned into more. She was a free spirit in my stifling world. A breeze of fresh yet bold innocence that was rare to find in a time when everything was a copy of a copy.

And even though I was drunk, I couldn't let go. I remember

planning to not let her go. I remember my decision to keep her so well.

So imagine my fucking surprise when I woke up the next morning and found out she'd disappeared from my life as suddenly as she'd appeared. For a moment, I thought maybe it was all a figment of my imagination and my demons had seriously lost their minds. But that thought disappeared when I found blood coating my dick.

My first reaction was anger. How dare she leave without telling me? I was almost sure we'd shared a connection, but that was only me, because she'd had no qualms about disappearing.

So I decided to forget about the whole fucking experience, even if that didn't stop me from asking around about a certain femme fatale in a black mask. No one seemed to remember her, and the night remained in the background.

That is, until Gwen showed up at my door.

I knew without a sliver of a doubt that the femme fatale from that night was the mother. She was the only one I'd ever forgotten to use a condom with.

And the obsession to find her started all over again.

Twenty-one years.

It took twenty-one fucking years to put a name and a face to the girl from that night.

And while I'd intended to exact revenge, to punish her for abandoning Gwen, it became so much more.

It became an uncontrollable lust, an unhinged obsession, and the darkest feelings.

What started as a hate-fuck, as a need to get her out of my system, gradually turned into the most peaceful, balanced time of my life.

She matches my fire, but she also tames it. Douses it. Sings soul-soothing lullabies only she knows the lyrics to. And for the first time in my life, I want someone to be there for me.

Someone who doesn't shy away from my destructive energy

and, instead, stands tall in front of it and me. A woman who can be my partner, my lover, and my submissive all at the same time.

And I'm only getting started with her, so there's no way in fuck her father or the damn universe will be able to take her away from me.

Nicolo himself joins me with a dozen of his guards. I knew he'd taken Bruno's betrayal personally the moment he didn't let his underlings handle the job and summoned his best men. The men he usually doesn't allow to peek from the shadows.

He's also the one who guided us straight to the old building that should see its maker sooner rather than later.

"Are you sure she's here?" I ask as his men disperse all over the property with a mere nod from him.

"He is." He slides a cigar to the corner of his lips, but doesn't light it. "He's a poetic one, Bruno. He might not have chosen her birthday as I thought he would, but he'd definitely bring her to the place she betrayed him in."

I march to the stairs, my spine crowding with tension and each step echoing with the buzz in my ears.

A hand drops on my shoulder, but Nicolo doesn't stop me. He merely walks alongside me. "Where do you think you're going, rich boy? Let me take care of this."

"Like fuck I'll trust you to."

"Bruno will be taken care of. I give you my word."

"I will be there."

"Don't blame me if you accidentally get shot." He releases me with a mere shrug but strides alongside me. Or half jogs, because I eat the stairs in no time.

But the scene that greets me nearly sends me tumbling back down. Gwen is tied to a chair, trying to roll to the edge, where Aspen and Bruno are.

My chest explodes with a myriad of fucked-up emotions that start and end with fear.

The all-encompassing type.

The type I've never felt in my goddamn existence.

"Mom, no!" Gwen's loud shriek rattles the walls and I don't even think about it as I sprint to where Aspen is trying to shove Bruno off the edge.

And succeeds.

The world pauses for a second as they both tumble down and I dive, grabbing anything I can touch.

Her arm.

My fingers dig into her skin and I flatten myself on my stomach to grab her with both hands.

She's fucking heavy.

I find the reason behind the unusual weight that's definitely not Aspen's when I stare down to find Bruno holding on to her waist, with both his arms and looking up with a maniacal expression.

Aspen, however, isn't. Her eyes are closed and there's a gash on the side of her head that's streaming with blood.

Fuck, fuck, fuck.

My shoulders nearly snap from their sockets, but I still try to lift her up. It'd be better to throw a rock at the parasite's head and get rid of him, but if I release Aspen, she's sure to follow him.

A shot pierces the air and I freeze, thinking something has happened to Gwen, but then the weight becomes lighter as Bruno releases Aspen. A hole is lodged between his vacant eyes as he falls, and his head smashes against the ground.

"No one fucks with me and lives to talk about it," Nicolo says nonchalantly from his standing position, slowly hiding his gun away.

Then he gets on his knees to help me pull Aspen up, but I already have her halfway on the edge. Once she's completely on solid ground, I make sure she's breathing, then tap her cheek. "Aspen, sweetheart, open your eyes."

"Mom!" Gwen falls to her knees beside us, probably having been untied by one of Nicolo's men. "Daddy, is she going to be okay?"

I cradle Aspen's head against my chest. "She will be."

She fucking has to be.

I've been pacing the length of the hospital hall, back and forth like a caged animal.

The shuffling of nurses buzzing around, coupled with the rancid antiseptic smell closes my throat. Now, I understand why the fuck Aspen hates this place. It smells of death, blood, and the worst nightmares.

No.

I'm not going to think about death under such situations. I simply will not.

The doctors have been with Aspen for what seems like an eternity, and the nurse who came out earlier didn't say anything, even when I threatened to sue this place and have her fired.

"Dad…"

I come to a halt and stare at Gwen, who's sitting on a chair, rocking back and forth like when she was distressed as a child. Her shirt is torn at the collar, but her shoulders are covered with my jacket that I draped on her earlier. Her face is dirtied, streaks of dry and fresh tears mapping out her cheeks.

"What if…what if she doesn't make it? What if…she goes into a coma like you did?"

"Hey." I sit beside her, wrap an arm around her and adopt my soothing parental tone, even though her thoughts mirror mine. "She's strong as hell and won't let this bring her down."

"But she's not immortal." She cries into my chest. "And she seemed resolved about dying, too. Her father…made her choose between you and me, but she chose to sacrifice herself, Dad. She chose to throw herself off the edge instead of seeing any of us die. But what if we're the ones who lose her? I just found her…"

My chest quakes from the haunting force of Gwen's sadness, and I continue stroking her shoulder to try and stay calm.

To try to delude my brain into thinking that Aspen will be fine.

"I just found her, too, and I won't let her go that easily. She'll come out of this."

"Promise?" Gwen stares up at me with eyes that flood with tears.

"Promise, Angel."

The door slides open and both of us spring to our feet as the doctor steps out, removing his cap.

"How is my mom?" Gwen asks in a quivering voice.

"She's stable now, but we won't know until she wakes up and we run more tests."

My daughter staggers against my side as the doctor tells us about her head injury that's not critical and the tests they'll be running.

By the time he leaves, Nate arrives. I called him so he could take Gwen home. She's had too much stress for one day and can barely stay on her feet.

"Nate." She throws herself in his arms. "Mom is hurt and she's not waking up."

He wraps a protective arm around her and looks at me over her head. Probably thinking the same as me.

Since when does she call Aspen Mom?

Now, apparently, because she's only ever addressed her as such today.

"Take her home. She's exhausted," I tell him, not sure how the fuck I even sound normal.

"I want to stay," she protests, staring at me.

"Go change and get some rest, then come back, Angel. You don't want her to see you looking like a survivor from a horror movie, do you?"

"No," she grumbles.

"Will you be okay?" It's Nate who asks.

I release a vague sound and wave him away.

Three minutes later, they're gone and I'm breathing heavily, bracing a hand on the wall. I just need to get it together for when she wakes up.

And she will fucking wake up.

"The cleanup is done. No police business will be happening."

I stagger from the wall to find the source of the voice. Nicolo stands in his usual nonchalant stance, a hand in his pocket. His three-piece suit he wore earlier is still pressed and clean with no dirt or blood on it.

"What are you doing here?" I stand to my full height, facing him.

"Thought I would deliver the good news myself. You won't have to deal with Bruno's body, blood, or the questions the police could ask. As for the redhead, I'm sure she'll survive."

"Yes, she will, and when she does, you'll release her from your dirty business."

"We had a deal, King. My protection for her services."

"A sloppy protection that put her in fucking danger. Either you release her or you can kiss my billions goodbye."

He raises a brow. "You would put that much money on the table for her?"

I'd give my whole fucking fortune up for her, but instead of admitting that, I say, "You'll release her."

"And you'll keep your investments."

"Yes, but I will not be your acting defense council anymore. Go find someone else to clean your messes."

"Deal." He turns to go, placing a cigar between his lips and lighting it, then stops and faces me again. "Are you sure she's still not your woman?"

"She is my fucking woman." *The only woman I've ever wanted to be mine.*

He gives a slight nod, a smirk, and leaves. A nurse stops him, probably to tell him he shouldn't be smoking in the hospital, but he blows a cloud of smoke in her face and continues on his way.

Me, on the other hand? I pray for the first fucking time in my life. Not to a god, but to the woman sleeping inside.

Don't even think about leaving me, witch.

THIRTY-THREE

Aspen

PAIN SPREADS IN MY HEAD AND I GROAN, MY EYES SLOWLY
opening.

Please tell me I wasn't assigned to the same section of hell
as my father. Yes, I killed him and myself, but he definitely has
more blood on his hands.

The least the managers of this place could do is separate us.

Or maybe my custom-made hell is to be with him so he'll
have a hold on me even after death.

"Mom…!"

I jolt, then I remain completely still as a shock of white, antiseptic, and vanilla scent surrounds me.

Is this a heartless play of my imagination?

Otherwise, how could Gwen be here and even call me Mom?

A shadow perches over me and I squint when her soft, beautiful face comes into focus.

A wide smile pulls at her lips. "You're finally awake."

I cough, my throat scratching, and with it comes that faint
pain again.

"Oh, here, drink some water." She helps me to sit up and places a glass of water with a straw to my lips.

I take greedy gulps, letting the liquid soothe my dry throat, but I can't stop staring at her. At her wild ginger hair and red puffy eyes.

It's starting to look so freakishly real and I can't afford to have such hope now.

I reach a finger to her face and wipe at the dry tear streaks on her cheek. But no matter how much I touch her, she doesn't disappear. "You were crying."

"Of course I was crying." She nestles the glass of water between her elegant fingers. "I thought you were going to die with that crazy jerk, and then when you were sleeping for two days, I was so scared that it'd be Dad's coma all over again."

My lips part as stabs of my memory start rolling through my head. I think I heard Kingsley's voice in those last moments.

Is the reason I'm alive because he's…

"K-King…" My voice trembles. "Is he…"

"Right outside, kind of threatening your doctor with a lawsuit because you wouldn't wake up. He can be extra like that, my dad." She grins. "But you should've seen him when he came running the moment you were falling. He singlehandedly pulled you from the edge, even when your father was trying to drag you with him. Daddy looked like a superhero."

I release a long, shattered breath that seems to have left my soul. I think I hit something in the middle of the fall, which is why I started to lose consciousness, but I held on to my father with all of my might. I couldn't have let him survive.

"How about…my father?" I ask Gwen.

"He's dead," she says softly. "Dad's scary-looking friend took his body with him."

It must've been Nicolo.

The reality hits me then. I'm finally free.

Free of fearing him.

Of trying to escape the shadow he cast on my life.

Free.

It's too surreal to wrap my head around that knowledge, so I stroke Gwen's hair. "Are you okay?"

"Yeah. Totally fine."

"I'm sorry you had to go through that because of me."

She frantically shakes her head. "You don't have to apologize. Dad told me all about you and your father, and I know you did everything to protect me. But don't sacrifice yourself again, or I won't talk to you. I was so scared you'd die now after I finally have you, Mom."

My chest squeezes so hard, I'm surprised it doesn't burst. "What…what did you just call me?"

"Mom," she repeats, more determined this time. "You were always my mom, even when you weren't there."

I wrap my arms around her and hide my face in her neck, partially so the tears aren't visible. "Thank you, Gwen."

She squeezes me back, her voice trembling. "No, thank you for being my mom."

I think I just upgraded to a different level of existence. No one told me that being someone's mom felt so revering. It doesn't even matter that I'm in one of the hospitals I loathed so much, and it has everything to do with the girl in my arms.

She's not a stillborn baby. She's alive, hugging me, and has called me "Mom."

We remain like that for a moment too long, until our breathing is in sync. The door opens and we reluctantly break apart.

Kingsley appears in the doorway, larger than life, even when his hair is disheveled and his shoulders nearly rip out from his shirt due to how tense they are.

My chest expands and my stomach contracts so hard, it's a miracle no one hears the sound.

Being in the same room with Kingsley has always been an experience. Like sinking in dark waters and knowing he'll be the one to provide me with oxygen.

He drips with power and authority that speaks to the secret submissive part of me without words.

But right now, he's channeling the devil himself, looking dark, broody, and like he has a taste for violence.

"Um…I'll be right outside." Gwen grins, then whispers so only I can hear her. "I didn't tell him you love him, so you can do that yourself."

Then she dashes out, shouldering past her father.

He kicks the door shut, then stalks toward me. "What, and I can't stress this enough, *the fuck* were you thinking, Aspen? Do you have a death wish at thirty-fucking-five? Or do you like playing Russian roulette with your life? Why would you do that—"

I pull him by a handful of his shirt and slam my lips to his. Kingsley growls in my mouth, then wraps a big hand around my neck and kisses me with a hunger that steals my breath.

Our teeth, tongues, and even our souls collide in a shattering kiss that turns my limbs into Jell-O. I kiss him with the desperation of a reborn woman while he breathes life into me.

"Fuck," he whispers against my lips when we break apart and he drops his forehead against mine. "This doesn't let you off the hook."

"I know. It was a thank-you, not only for saving me but also for being there for both me and Gwen. Thank you, King."

He grunts as the tension he carried on his shoulders as a badge slowly withers away and he sits on the bed, unapologetically pulling me onto his lap.

I sit, facing him as he wraps both arms around my waist with a tightness that suggests he'll never let go.

"You'll have to do a lot more than kissing me in thanks, sweetheart."

"Like what?"

"Lifting the illegal ban, for one. As soon as you're healthy, I'm going to sink my teeth into your neck while I fuck your pussy, then your ass."

I hesitate, directing my gaze sideways.

He uses two of his fingers to grab my chin and bring my attention back to him. "What is it?"

"Nothing."

"Fuck that, Aspen. You started that ban for a reason, and if you don't tell me about it, I won't be able to figure it out. I'm smart, but I'm not a mind reader."

"I just…don't want sex to be our only connection. If that's why you want me, one day you'll get me out of your system or maybe you'll get bored of my fight and find someone who kneels to your will, and it'll be all over."

"Are you fucking serious?" He plasters me to his chest, his fingers digging into my nape, and speaks so close to my mouth, I feel every word instead of hearing it. "I had a connection with you before sex was even involved. Yes, I love your submission to my dominance and how you secretly enjoy the way I mark your skin, and sex plays a role in what we have, but it's not all we are. You chase away my darkness and understand me on a level no one else does. You never shied away from my callous side. If anything, you stood right in the path of its destruction, challenging me for more. Not only are you my match and the woman who gave me Gwen, but you also make me a better man, sweetheart."

"You make me a better woman, too, King," I whisper in an emotional voice I usually wouldn't allow myself to speak in. "I've wanted you since I was fourteen and I think I never stopped wanting you since. You're the one man who sees inside both the old and new Aspen. You make me want to embrace my weaknesses and my scars because they're a form of strength, too."

"As you should. They're as beautiful as you."

"So you don't hate me anymore?" I ask with pathetic hopefulness.

"I don't think I ever did."

"Then why were you a jerk all that time? Especially after you found out I was Gwen's mother?"

"Truth is, I searched for you more than you searched for me. In the beginning, I thought it was to teach you a lesson for abandoning Gwen, but in reality, I wanted you all for myself. You were the only woman who made me feel at a time I thought I was incapable of it. You looked at me as if I were the only person in the world."

"And you looked at me as if I were important. I never felt important until that moment." I reach a hand out and stroke his cheek. "I love you, King. I think I've loved you since that first time."

He briefly closes his eyes, nostrils flaring with each harsh intake of air. When he opens them again, they look like my custom-made storm that will drag me into its depths and never allow me to surface.

And the worst part? I don't want to surface. If he's dark, then I'm willing to embrace that darkness.

His pulse thumps loud against my chest as if his heart wants to fuse with mine. "What I felt for you was obsession at its finest, but over time, I realized, this type of obsession ran deeper and wilder than I ever anticipated. This type obsession is a twisted translation of love. You had me long before either of us knew, but now you own my heart, body, and soul, sweetheart. Just like I plan to own yours."

I smile, murmuring. "You already have them."

"I do?"

"Yeah. You're my king and I want to be your queen."

"You already are."

He kills the small distance between us, devouring my lips in a kiss that I'll remember for the rest of our lives.

I'm his.

He's mine.

This time, permanently.

EPILOGUE 1

Aspen

Three months later

"**R**EDUCING THE BUDGET OF THE IMMIGRATION department means we'll take on fewer pro bono cases, and that doesn't play into the firm's future vision, not to mention it's a downright capitalist approach," I tell Kingsley, getting in his face.

At some point, I left my seat at the conference table and we're both standing toe to toe.

"Capitalism plays little to no role in my attempts to eliminate frauds and wasting time our associate attorneys can use to tackle other important cases."

"Such as what? Let me guess, corporate? Aka the arm of your beloved capitalism."

"Criminal, Ms. Leblanc. The prisons are full and we need more lawyers there instead of fighting useless battles with ICE."

"They're not useless if we save someone from being deported from US soil to a country that discriminates against them."

"I will not dedicate a budget that can get five-plus wrongfully convicted people out of jail with mere hope to save one person."

"We'll not see eye to eye on this matter, so I guess we'll have to vote."

"Who will vote? You and your alter ego?"

"The board, of course. If you're against lowering the immigration department's budget, raise your hand." I do so first, then cast a glance to see who's on my side.

Only empty chairs are in sight. "Where is…everyone?"

"They obviously left in the middle of our heated argument."

I face Kingsley, who looks dashing in his dark suit, like a devil lord fresh out of hell. A small smile tilts his lips as he watches me with that gleam that I recognize so well.

My hand drops to my side. "I can't believe Nate left, too."

"He led the crowd out, pointing at his watch because, apparently, the meeting ran longer than it should."

"Whatever." I flip my hair. "We're going to have a vote about this during the next board meeting, and I will win, asshole."

"Don't act butthurt when you lose, sweetheart."

"Screw you."

His hand shoots for me before I can consider escaping and wraps possessively around my waist. He effortlessly lifts me up and sits me on the conference table, then barges between my legs, parting them as wide as possible.

"Don't tempt me."

A shock of excitement rushes through me, then pools between my thighs. No clue if it's because we finally got together or because we missed so many years in the process, but we're always desperate for each other.

Sometimes even the moment we stop touching.

It's the best type of addiction I've ever had. Better than alcohol, better than success.

He's my favorite drug.

I honestly don't know how the hell I survived during the "illegal ban" that Kingsley doesn't want to be reminded of ever again.

He said he'll tell stories about it to his Grim Reaper.

It doesn't help that we're still at each other's throats at the firm. We're definitely not the lovey-dovey couple, and won't sugarcoat shit for each other.

One thing's for sure, we have each other's backs and obviously want each other to the point of madness.

Nietzsche said that there's always some madness in love, but there's also always some reason in madness.

And this infuriating man is my reason and my madness.

These past few months have been closer to a dream than reality. Not only is my father finally out of the picture, but Gwen calls me "Mom" and has accepted me as her mother.

Callie and I are as close as ever. The other day, we celebrated her long-awaited pregnancy with lots of juice and not a drop of alcohol, naturally.

I'm one hundred twenty-one days clean.

I broke away from the mafia, and I know it's because Kingsley took care of it, and not due to Nicolo letting me go out of the goodness of his stone heart.

And to make our lives even more peaceful, Kingsley sued Susan, making her lose every dime she owned as I promised, and she escaped from the state soon after.

The most important thing is that I have this man as my love, my partner, and the father of my little girl.

I know that he'll probably never be Prince Charming or waive some knighthood, but I never needed those things anyway. His edge of intensity is what attracted me to him in the first place. And even though we still bicker all the time, his arms are my safest home.

I focus on his lips and speak in a sultry tone. "What if I do tempt you?"

"Then you won't be able to walk out of here. At least, not properly."

I lean close until my lips nearly graze his. I'm only a hair's breadth away, getting more intoxicated by his cedarwood scent.

EMPIRE OF LUST | 349

His nostrils flare, expecting the kiss, but I pull back. "Maybe another time."

The words are barely out of my mouth when he dives in, his eyes a penetrating storm as he captures my lips.

It's a soul-shattering kiss that steals my breath, my sanity, and leaves me like putty in his hands.

Hands that are everywhere—on my back, my waist, my nape. He has the type of command that leaves me no choice but to bend to him.

Yes, I fight him. Yes, we rarely agree on anything, but when his body speaks to mine, all I can do is listen.

He makes quick work of pulling off my clothes and releasing his cock, and then he thrusts inside me in one delicious go.

His rhythm is slow at first, maddening even, as he hits every deep, pleasurable place inside me over and over until I'm moaning in his mouth. Until I'm dripping on the table and unable to stop myself.

It's crazy how he knows my body better than I do and hits the right places that nearly push me over the edge.

"More," I murmur against his lips.

"More what?" he asks with dripping seductiveness.

"Fuck me harder," I beg, rotating my hips, and then I bare my shoulder, where there's a hickey he left yesterday. "Like when you gave me this."

"You little conniving witch." His teeth sink into the red mark and he drives into me faster, longer, and with so much intensity, I can't breathe.

My arms wrap around his neck and my heels dig into the firmness of his ass as I come undone around him.

His breathing becomes unhinged and I know he's also close when his dick twitches inside me.

"Say it," he grunts against my neck, leaving another bite mark.

"W-what?"

"That you love me."

"I do." I shudder, surprisingly more turned on like whenever he makes me admit my feelings during sex. "I love you, King."

He comes so long and deep inside me that it triggers another orgasm.

I slump against him, my head falling in the nook of his shoulder as the smell of sex surrounds us.

He's right. It's going to take me some time to walk out of here.

I sigh, then wince when the bite on my neck burns. My fingers touch it and I scowl at him. "Seriously, stop the animal behavior."

His face lights up with pure mischief. "How else will people know you're mine?"

"The fact that you've been announcing it at every event we attend together maybe? With your hand around my waist."

The attention was suffocating at first, but taking a public family picture with him, Gwen, and Nate is so worth it.

Besides, I know that a man like Kingsley comes with a lot of baggage, and I love that, just like every other part of him.

In fact, I'm a bit twisted and love his dark side a tad too much. It's the part that's exclusive to me.

I'm the only one who knows about his past, his relationship with his parents, and how he's finally coming to terms with no longer blaming himself for his mother's suicide.

I'm the one who saw the devil in his eyes and fell head over heels for it.

We're a match made in hell like that.

"Showing you off at events and in front of the press is still not enough," he says, referring to my earlier words.

"You can't possibly be thinking about biting me forever. Are you?"

"I don't see why I wouldn't."

"I can't believe this. Next time, you'll put a collar on me."

His eyes glint like when he's thinking something mischievous.

"Don't tell me you're thinking about that?"

"Not a collar, no." His voice drops. "A ring."

"What type of ring?"

"A wedding ring."

I choke on my own spit, my heart nearly spilling free from behind my rib cage. "You…are you kidding?"

"Do I look like I'm kidding?"

"You want to marry me?"

"Of course I do. Where did you think this was going?"

"I…don't know."

"Well, now, you do." He grips me by the throat, his fingers digging into the flesh. "You're the only woman I want with me every step of the way for the rest of my life, Aspen. When anyone looks at you, I want them to know you're fucking mine."

"Is that a proposal?"

"Depends. Are you going to say yes?"

"You're such a dick, even when you're proposing."

"But I'm your dick. Literally and figuratively."

I smile. "I never thought about getting married, you know. But I want that with you."

His mirrored smile is blinding as he pulls me close. "That's because you're smart as fuck, sweetheart."

And then he seals the proposal with a tingle-inducing kiss.

EPILOGUE 2

Kingsley

One year later

DURING ALL MY TIME AS A CRIMINAL DEFENSE ATTORNEY, the media's "Savage Devil," and the law circuit's untouchable god, I've never failed to read anyone's motives.

And yet, the current situation is making me draw a blank that I've never experienced before.

Worst part, I don't think my usual solution of punching or intimidating it until it resolves itself is going to work this time.

"Maybe we should get a psychic," I announce to Nate and Gwen while we sit in my living room.

Or they're sitting. I'm pacing like a caged big fucking animal and flipping my Zippo manically.

Martha, who brought fresh drinks, gives me an "Are you out of your mind?" look, then leaves.

Nate rolls his eyes, stroking Gwen's hand that's on his lap and I can't even put myself in an "I'm going to kill the daughter-stealer" mood. "For your crazy?"

"For your upcoming murder," I shoot back.

"Just go talk to her, Dad," Gwen says, obviously the voice of reason in this whole situation. "Mom locked herself up in your room and has refused to speak to anyone for two hours now. Surely you know how to get her to talk."

That's the problem. I don't think I fucking can—not in this situation, at least.

It's the first time Aspen has pulled away from all of us, Gwen included. The same Gwen that she treats like the apple of her eye and always dedicates time for.

Not that I'm jealous of my own daughter or anything.

Fine. A little.

But I digress.

In the time Aspen and I have been married, she's never been like this. It's been exactly a year, because I sure as fuck married her the week after she accepted the proposal. What? I couldn't have her change her mind the next time we got into an argument.

And we have those a lot, so I wasn't going to take the risk. Therefore, I made her a custom ring with a rare rock that matches the color of her eyes and changes under the sun.

We had a small ceremony and she wore this simple white dress that still makes my dick hard whenever I think about it.

Needless to say, I fucked her while she was in it, then outside of it more times than either of us could count.

Our professional life has been smooth sailing, aside from our special flavor of debates that Nate doesn't care for and Gwen has the audacity to call "cute."

Nothing is cute about this situation, though, because for the first time in ever, Aspen refuses to talk to me.

"Just go, Dad. You've got this."

At least one of us believes that.

Gwen gives me an encouraging smile and crosses her fingers as if that will magically solve this.

Whatever the case, I slip my Zippo back into my pocket and ascend the stairs to Aspen's chosen tower.

It's just our room, but the fact that she's made it a point to not allow anyone near her today after kicking me out this morning makes it seem like a witch's coven.

I slowly open the door, half expecting her band of vigilantes—mainly Caroline, Martha, and Gwen when in the mood—to jump me, half expecting Aspen to finish the job.

Surprisingly, she's not in the room. The bathroom door is closed, though, so I assume she changed locations.

I try the handle first, but the door is locked, so I tap on it, channeling the nonexistent gentleman inside me. "Aspen...open up, sweetheart."

"Go away," her muffled voice comes from inside.

"Not until I know what's wrong with you."

"Leave me alone, Kingsley!"

"Aspen," I grit out, then force my voice to calm down. "I'm being nice here, so come out and talk to me. Don't force me to bring this door down."

She doesn't reply.

"You asked for this." I step back to break the thing off its hinges.

The sound of the lock tripping comes first, followed by the small creak of the door.

Aspen comes out, still wearing the blue satin gown from last night that molds against her gorgeous curves.

Her hair spills like red lava over her bare shoulders that are filled with red bite marks.

So I lied. Just because I married her doesn't mean I'll stop marking her whenever I fuck her.

There's this constant need to put my hands on her, to chain her to me for eternity, so there's no way out, no matter how much she tries.

She's a witch, after all. Not only did she cast a spell on my soul, but she also imprisoned my heart and enchanted my brain.

I study her worn-out face that's so pale, it could compete

with the white tiles and force myself to ask with a calm tone, "What's the problem?"

She releases a shaky breath that stabs straight through my chest.

"Whatever it is, you can tell me, Aspen."

She remains silent, but her lips tremble. And Aspen doesn't fucking tremble—at least, not outside of when I'm fucking her brains out.

Jesus Christ.

"Is it cancer or some medical shit?"

She shakes her head.

"Did you lose a case and you're blaming yourself for it?"

"No."

"Did your father possibly rise from the dead? Or is it your mother? Maybe *my* mother? Did Susan show up from whatever hole she's begging from and bother you?"

"No," she says with slight exasperation.

"Now that the most unlikely is out of the way, let's move to the more likely. Did you find out about the thugs I had Nicolo kill?"

Her eyes widen. "What thugs?"

"It's a no then."

"What thugs did you have killed, King?" she asks in that determined tone that gets my dick fucking hard.

"The ones who beat you up per your father's orders, of course. I couldn't have them roam free after they hurt you."

"Are you a brute?"

"I'm way fucking worse when it comes to you, sweetheart. You know that, I know that, and whatever is bothering you will know that when I destroy it. Now, spill. Is it Gwen? She's right downstairs worried as shit about you, by the way. Did you by any chance find out your family has a genetic disease that will kill you when you're a hundred years old?"

"No, you asshole. I'm pregnant."

I'm about to tell her another batch of crazy theories

running through my head when I finally circle back to the words that came out of her mouth.

"Did you just say you're pregnant?"

"Yeah." Her shoulders drop. "And I shouldn't be. I'm on the pill, for God's sake. But I felt weird yesterday and went for a checkup, and the doctor said I'm six weeks pregnant."

I rake my eyes over her again. No wonder she's been glowing lately. My dick liked to think it was because of how much cum he's filling her with.

"Are you healthy?"

"Is that all you have to say?" She lifts her chin. "This is all your damn fault, you bastard. Once again, you had a fast swimmer that couldn't even be stopped by birth control."

"My dick is pleased to be up for the challenge."

"That's not a compliment." She touches her hair, then her neck. "I shouldn't be pregnant. I don't know what to do about this. What will Gwen say?"

"Considering she married my best friend while I was in a coma, Gwen's say in this should hold no importance. Besides, this is between you and me, sweetheart."

"Do you…want this?"

"Do I want my baby inside you? Of course I fucking do. But not at the expense of your mental and physical state."

She steps toward me. "Aren't we too old for kids?"

"No one is ever too old for kids. Thirty-six is not old, sweetheart. It's mature."

"What if…what if I want this? I want to do it properly this time."

"Then we'll do it properly. This time, I'll be with you every step of the way."

She throws herself against my chest and I wrap my arms around her, kissing the top of her head. "I bet you'll look sexy as fuck while you're pregnant with my baby."

"Stop it," she chastises with a smile in her voice, then looks up. "Thank you."

"For what?"

"For being the father of my children."

"I would have no other mother for them. You're mine, Mrs. Shaw."

She pulls me down with a fistful of my shirt. "And you're mine, Mr. Shaw."

THE END

Next up is a dark new adult series called Legacy of Gods, and the first book is titled *God of Malice*.

Curious about Nathaniel and Gwyneth who were mentioned in this book? You can read their story in *Empire of Desire*.

WHAT'S NEXT?

Thank you so much for reading *Empire of Lust*! If you liked it, please leave a review.
Your support means the world to me.

If you're thirsty for more discussions with other readers of the series, you can join the Facebook group, *Rina Kent's Spoilers Room*.

Next up is a brand-new series called *Legacy of Gods*. It'll feature the second generation of *Royal Elite Series* couples, but you don't need to read that series to understand this one. You can now pre-order the first book, *God of Malice*!

ALSO BY RINA KENT

For more books by the author and a reading order, please visit:
www.rinakent.com/books

ABOUT THE AUTHOR

Rina Kent is a *USA Today*, international, and #1 Amazon bestselling author of everything enemies to lovers romance.

She's known to write unapologetic anti-heroes and villains because she often fell in love with men no one roots for. Her books are sprinkled with a touch of darkness, a pinch of angst, and an unhealthy dose of intensity.

She spends her private days in London laughing like an evil mastermind about adding mayhem to her expanding universe. When she's not writing, Rina travels, hikes, and spoils cats in a pure Cat Lady fashion.

Find Rina Below:

Website: www.rinakent.com
Neswsletter: www.subscribepage.com/rinakent
BookBub: www.bookbub.com/profile/rina-kent
Amazon: www.amazon.com/Rina-Kent/e/B07MM54G22
Goodreads: www.goodreads.com/author/show/18697906.Rina_Kent
Instagram: www.instagram.com/author_rina
Facebook: www.facebook.com/rinaakent
Reader Group: www.facebook.com/groups/rinakent.club
Pinterest: www.pinterest.co.uk/AuthorRina/boards
Tiktok: www.tiktok.com/@rina.kent
Twitter: twitter.com/AuthorRina

Made in the USA
Monee, IL
17 September 2024

65934127R00218